What others are say

"Emma's Quest is a delight to read! Using descriptive word pictures, Ms. Ayers ushers us into the center of Emma's world. Once there, she leads steadily, unpredictably, and delivers heartily."

~Janet Paschal, Gospel Music Hall of Fame 2019

"What a thoroughly enchanting story! *Emma's Quest* is a dual-time novel that moves effortlessly between past and present, weaving together the characters' lives as they seek to unlock secrets of the past and to navigate their way through love and war, doubt and faith. The characters gripped me from the very beginning, and I couldn't wait to see how their lives unfolded. This is at once a suspenseful and a heart-satisfying read."

~Ann Tatlock, novelist, editor, and children's book author

"Starr Ayers has done it again with her sequel **Emma's Quest.** Just like *For the Love of Emma,* you will be captivated by Starr's masterful storytelling from the first page. Curl up with this beautiful book and treat yourself to the magic and inspiration of this wonderful tale."

~Erica Wiggenhorn, author of Letting God Be Enough: Why Striving Keeps You Stuck and How Surrender Sets You Free

"*Emma's Quest* is a beautiful sequel to *For the Love of Emma.* Starr Ayers seamlessly blends present and past to create a delightful story set during WWII. Across three continents and with a delightful and believable cast of characters, the reader is caught up in the romance and heartbreak as the devastating circumstances of war separate loved ones. Ms. Ayers is a talented writer who holds her audience in her hands as she moves them through time with just the right amount of suspense. *Emma's Quest* is truly a touching story you don't want to miss!"

~Norma Gail, author of Land of My Dreams and Within Golden Bands.

"A poignant depiction of love and loss, hope and faith amidst the backdrop of the Second World War. I adore split-time novels. Starr Ayers does not disappoint. A heart-warming and life-affirming sequel to *For the Love of Emma*.

~Lisa Carter, Carol Award winning author of Under a Turquoise Sky and The Christmas Bargain

"Still grieving over the loss of her first love, Emma exchanges the simple pleasures of a small town in North Carolina for the excitement and dazzling lights of Chicago—on a whim! The overseas battles of World War II are brought home as nearly every relationship in Emma's life suffers casualties. Emma draws on her faith to sustain her as she is torn between big city excitement and small-town stability. Starr Ayers set the bar high with her first book *For the Love of Emma*. This second book will bring suspense and delight for all who read it."

~Mark "Coach" Prasek, Founder and Host, PJNET.tv

Emma's Quest

Dream Beyond Tomorrow Series

Book One: For the Love of Emma
Book Two: Emma's Quest

Emma's Quest

By
Starr Ayers

MBI

Emma's Quest
Published by Mountain Brook Ink
White Salmon, WA U.S.A.

Scripture quotations are taken from the King James Version of the Bible. Public domain.
ISBN 978-1-953957-16-0
© 2022 Starr Ayers

The Team: Miralee Ferrell, Alyssa Roat, Kristen Johnson, Tim Pietz, and Cindy Jackson
Cover Design: Indie Cover Design, Lynnette Bonner Designer
Cover Photo: Collaborative artists, Donna Allen of Donna Allen Photography and Starr Ayers
Cover Model: Gina Allen McKee
"Another Soldier's Coming Home" Words and Music: Janet Paschal, Copyright 1997 Maplesong Music, BMM Music (ASCAP) All rights reserved.

Mountain Brook Ink is an inspirational publisher offering fiction you can believe in.
Printed in the United States of America

Dedication

To my sister, April
(aka Caroline's *older* sister Kate)

I've known you longer than anyone on earth.
You were my first and dearest friend.
We've shared mountains of laughter,
and valleys of a thousand tears.

You've encouraged me, admonished me,
picked me up when I thought I couldn't make it,
and applauded me when I did.

When I've needed truth, you've spoken it in love.
You've never been self-seeking,
always thoughtful and giving.

God gave us a multitude of yesterdays,
has graced us with the gift of today,
and grants us dreams for our tomorrows.

As long as we're together,
a measure of our childhood will never be lost,
and our dreams beyond tomorrow
will prove greater than we can ask, hope, or imagine.

You're a gift—
the best one Mom and Dad ever gave me.

I LOVE YOU! Starr

Acknowledgments

"A book is a dream that you hold in your hands." –Neil Gaiman

Today, I hold mine with tremendous gratitude because of the following people. A special thanks to …

My husband, Michael – How do I thank you for giving me the space to chase my dreams and be who God has called me to be. Without your understanding, encouragement, and support, Emma's story would still be in the box. When I'm down, you never fail to lift my spirits. When I no longer believe in myself, you do. Yes, God knew what He was doing when He gave me you!

Cyle Young, my agent from Hartline Literary Agency who found Emma's story a forever home.

Miralee Ferrell of Mountain Brook Ink, my publisher and editor who contracted this fledgling author for not one but two books. I believed I had a story. You knew I had two. Your wisdom and editing expertise have proven invaluable to me. Thank you for being open to my requests and for stretching me so *Emma's Quest* could shine.

Alyssa Roat, Kristen Johnson, and **Cindy Jackson,** MBI's team members who've overseen every aspect of this complex process. To MBI's talented cover designer, **Lynnette Bonner**, thank you for your outstanding covers. I appreciate your eye for design, attention to detail, and willingness to listen and include elements important to me.

Donna Allen of Donna Allen Photography – I appreciate your enthusiasm and willingness to participate on such short notice. The staging and dress you chose for your lovely daughter, **Gina Allen McKee**, couldn't have been more ideal—nor could she. She made the perfect Emma. Thank you both.

Bonnie Beardsley, Linda Dindzans, Sandra Hart, Denise Holmberg, and Deborah Sprinkle, we are more than critique partners—we are family. I cherish our monthly online Word Weaver sessions. You provide skilled instruction, wise counsel, timely encouragement, and a safe place to fall. You pick me up when I stumble and show up at conferences to cheer me on. **Word Weavers Page 3**, you're the best!

WOW! Bible Study – You've prayed for me, encouraged me, rejoiced with me, and purchased my novels. You're more precious to me than you will ever know. It's an honor and blessing to pray and study God's Word with you each week.

Lisa Carter, Norma Gail Holtman, Janet Paschal, Mark Prasek, Anne Tatlock, and Erica Wiggenhorn, endorsers of *Emma's Quest*. I appreciate your willingness to read my manuscript and give my story a supportive thumbs up. I'm humbled by your kind words. You are all creatives whose works I admire. I pray God will continue to establish the work of your hands.

Emma's Quest **Launch Team** – Although there is not enough space here to list your names, know I hold you close to my heart. I've appreciated your encouragement, your input, your prayers, and all you do to see that *Emma's Quest* gets into the hands of readers everywhere. I pray God blesses you for blessing me.

My Heavenly Father – I stand in awe of how You use imperfect vessels to accomplish Your work on earth. All glory belongs to You! Thank You for the gift of writing. I lift these pages to You and pray You'll reveal Your heart to all who read them.

Chapter One

I followed Kate up the concrete steps of the modest frame house, which sat within a stone's throw of Camden Road. Looping one arm through my sister's, I inhaled deeply, then released it. "Are you ready for what we might hear today?"

She shrugged. "Ready as ever, Caroline."

Spotting the doorbell coated with multiple layers of cracked and peeling paint, I noted above it the black and yellow caution sign—OXYGEN. NO SMOKING—and pressed the button. Gusts of warm air peppered our backs as traffic on the extensively traveled Hope Mills thoroughfare whizzed past.

"I didn't hear it ring, did you?" Kate said above the roar.

I tried once more before knocking on the faded, olive-green door. This time, we heard the slow shuffle of feet approaching. As someone fumbled with the latch, I nervously scrubbed at the powdery white residue left from the bell on my fingertip. *What else would we learn about Mother?* The door cracked open, its security chain still in place.

"Who is it?"

"It's Caroline Myers and Kate Gordon, Mr. Baldwin."

"Who?"

I raised my voice. "Caroline Myers and Kate Gordon—Emma Walsh's daughters. You said we could stop by this afternoon and chat."

"Well, whaddya know." The chain fell away from the latch and bounced against the door frame. "Yes. Yes. Of course.

Emma's girls." He swung the door open and motioned with his cane. "Come in. Come in. You'll have to forgive me, ladies. A fella's brain doesn't recollect as fast this side of ninety."

I laughed and stepped inside. "Don't worry. We can totally relate. One doesn't on this side of sixty, either."

Kate pushed my shoulder. "Ahem. A little less *we* there, please."

I blinked as my eyes struggled to adjust to the darkened hallway. "It was kind of you to invite us, Mr. Baldwin."

"Of course." He peered over his wire-rimmed glasses. "But, we're gonna settle something right here and now."

My breath caught in my throat as I attempted to read his stern expression. "What's that?"

"I do remember *some* things, ya know."

Kate shot me a baffled look.

A smile crept across his weathered face. "Gotcha," he said as he threw back his head and laughed. "We decided at your mama's grave that y'all would call me Tucker. Remember?"

Kate and I both sighed with relief. "Ah, yes. We sure did—Tucker."

He raised his cane and gestured toward the end of the hall. "Let's go to the den, where my nurse has me set up."

We walked down the pine-paneled hallway toward a sparsely furnished room adjacent to the kitchen. Separating the two spaces was a small dining area with sliding glass doors opening onto a concrete patio surrounded by overgrown shrubs. The soft tinkling of glass wind chimes caught by the warm afternoon breeze filtered through the screen door and into the cozy sitting room.

"Please have a seat ... over there." Tucker labored to catch his breath as he pointed to an Early American patterned sofa against the wall. "Claire stepped out to run a few errands." His chest rose and fell with each breath. "You remember Claire from the cemetery, don't you?"

Kate nodded.

"Yes, of course. Very pleasant," I said.

Tucker steadied himself in front of an over-stuffed, burgundy recliner and dropped down. "Whew. Pardon me a moment."

"That's quite all right. Take your time," Kate said.

He propped his cane against a small pine drop-leaf table stacked with newspapers and magazines. A thick, large-print Bible lay open on top of them. Beside the table, on top of a chrome stool with a red vinyl top, sat an oscillating fan. On the opposite side of his chair was a black metal TV tray with several crossword puzzle books, a few pens, and a large plastic *Cumberland County Hospice* cup. He picked it up and took a couple of long sips through the straw. Then with the hand holding his cup, he motioned toward the kitchen. "You ladies help yourself. There should be soda and bottled water in the fridge."

We both politely declined his kind offer.

Directly across the room was a red-brick fireplace, its hearth and mantle crowded with framed photographs. On the wall between it and the sliding glass doors hung a large sunburst clock and several framed certificates and medals.

Tucker coughed and cleared his throat. "Let's see now. Refresh my memory. You're both from Asheville, aren't you?"

"No, sir. We're from Asheboro—the geographic center of the state, home of the North Carolina State Zoo."

He nodded his head. "Oh, yes. That's right. Great zoo, I hear. If I were younger, I'd make a trip over there. Guess my traveling days are behind me. It's all I can do to walk from one room to the other now."

"We're sorry. It's nice you have Claire to help you."

"Yes. Don't know what I'd do without her. Been widowed twenty-two years. My son is an accountant in San Diego, and my daughter and her family live in Charleston. She's an RN and works part-time in a doctor's office. She's coming in August to spend a couple of weeks with me while Claire is on vacation. My grandson may come with her."

"Wonderful. Maybe we'll get to meet them."

"Hope so." Tucker shifted in his chair and dug into his

pocket. "Caroline, I've noticed you're still wearing Emma's cross."

I fingered the delicate silver necklace. "Yes. You told us it was a gift from you."

"You heard right. Gave it to Emma the same day she gave me this." He held out his hand.

I stood and lifted the silver cross from his palm, then returned to the couch so Kate could see it too. Flipping it over, I read, "A friend loveth at all times—Proverbs 17:17. It matches the Scripture reference on my necklace." I stepped across the room and handed the cross back to him.

"Yep. Funny how it happened." He stared at the shiny object in his hand and rubbed it with his thumb. "I think of that night often. Your mother and I sat in the car at the depot while waiting for her train. She gave me the pocket cross first. I was surprised when I saw the Scripture. She had no clue I was about to give her the necklace." He looked up at us, tears threatening to spill from his eyes. "I guess it shows we were true soul mates. It was hard to let her go." He chuckled. "Not that I had much say in it. Emma Rose did what she set her mind to do."

I rolled my eyes and laughed along with Kate.

He sat in deep thought before speaking again. "Foremost, I wanted her to be happy. Sometimes I wonder if things would've been different if I'd told her that night how I really felt. For a moment there in the car, I thought I would, but she was so giddy about meeting Drew and seeing the big city of Chicago, I couldn't bring myself to stand in her way. I learned a long time ago you can't live with regret. I guess we all ask *what if* at times, but *if onlys*—they're deal-breakers. Can't live there. Gotta learn to let go."

He laid his head back on the chair and locked his eyes on the ceiling fan's slow rotation. "When I put your mama on the train that evening, I didn't know things would take the turn they did, but I can't say I was disappointed."

Chapter Two

Saturday, September 2, 1939
Emma

Emma combed the colorful skeins of embroidery thread with her fingers while rolling hills, neatly cultivated farms, and picturesque towns streaked past the train's window. The speed with which each scene appeared and then swiftly slid from view couldn't rival the rush of images that flashed through her mind or the flood of tears that threatened to spill from her eyes.

It wasn't that Mama T, her elderly landlady, disliked Andrew Brown, fittingly called Drew. He was charming. A modest soul, unlike so many blessed with similar artistic abilities. In fact, his distinguished good looks, Scottish brogue, and quick wit won over everyone who met him.

Although Mama T had tried her best to conceal her apprehension, the angst that cloaked her face was easy for Emma to read. Her plans to move to Chicago to be closer to a man twelve years her senior and one she'd only known for a little more than six months had shaken Mama T to her core. Nevertheless, the kind woman respected her wishes. "It's your footpath to tread, baby doll. Just make sure you're followin' the good Lord's leadin'."

Leaving Fayetteville had been gut-wrenching. Although Emma had resided less than two years in the two-story, yellow clapboard house on Maiden Lane, she'd developed a deep affection for her landlady. From the minute she'd spotted the floor-to-ceiling bookshelves lining the parlor's walls, she knew she'd found a kindred spirit in Florence Turner. A gentle

Southern woman, widowed after sixty-three years of marriage with no children of her own, she'd all but adopted Emma and insisted from the outset she call her Mama T.

Although Emma lamented the fact that she'd broken her dear Mama T's heart, she believed it imperative to follow her own.

"Ticket, miss?"

Startled by the conductor's sudden appearance, Emma dropped her embroidery hoop and scrambled to catch it as it tumbled to the floor. The portly gentleman, a sixtyish man with a monocle perched on his cheek that made one eye appear larger than the other, handed it to her. "Sorry I frightened you, young lady."

"It's okay," she said with a dismissive wave. "Think nothing of it."

Reaching over to the seat beside her, she slipped her ticket from between the pages of Somerset Maugham's *The Moon and Sixpence* and handed it to him.

He punched it, then returned the stub. "Got someone meeting you at the station this evening?"

"I do."

"That's good. The sun will be pretty much set by the time we pull in. Good idea for a lovely young lady like you to have someone to accompany you." He moved along, restlessly clicking his punch.

Emma double-checked her arrival time, slipped the stub into the buttoned compartment of her purse, and returned to her needlework. Piercing the cream-colored linen with her needle, she meticulously followed the faint pattern of a flower with a periwinkle blue chain stitch. Her down-and-up, in-and-out rhythm quickly kept tempo with the clickety-clack of the train's wheels rolling over the iron rails.

Mama T had been impressed with how fast Emma had

caught on to the craft, but she'd learned by watching Mama T during their frequent late-night chats. She pictured her bent in her chair, peering through wire-rimmed spectacles, stitching handkerchiefs for First Baptist's bereavement ministry. Of course, the secret to her hour-upon-hour tenacity was her attempt to not disturb Chummy. He'd often lie sprawled across her feet, his paws and whiskers twitching as he undoubtedly dreamed of field mice scampering toward the barn.

"Sir." Emma waved her hand in the air as the conductor edged his way back through the aisle. "Do you think the train will arrive on time this evening?"

He pulled a gold timepiece from his vest pocket, then squinted and tipped his head. "Shouldn't be a problem. Appears we're right on schedule." He lifted his hat and brushed his hand over what was left of his silvery-white hair. "Ready to get there, are you?"

"I am. It's been a long trip."

"Yup." He plopped his cap back on his head. "I've been riding these rails so long now I forget how tiring the distance can be for someone who's not used to it." He nodded toward a neatly arranged stack of books and magazines by her side, topped with a pile of brightly colored skeins of embroidery thread. "I see you came prepared with plenty to keep you busy. Smart."

Emma chuckled to herself. She'd never been one to sit idle.

"You coming back this way soon?"

Her thoughts raced to Lily, Mama T, the Rainbow Girls, and—her hand went to the silver cross around her neck. "Yes. I hope to make it back before too long."

He clicked his hole puncher several times. "I'd better be movin' on. Enjoy the rest of your trip. At least you'll have these two seats to yourself. Stretch out if you need to."

She smiled. "Thank you. I might do that."

Emma picked up a dog-eared envelope from the stack of books and examined its surface. The pen-and-ink drawing of the Hotel Monterey in the upper left-hand corner looked like something Drew would sketch. She squinted to make out the faint postmark—Janesville, Wis., July 29, 1939, 3:30 p.m.

Studying the image of the six-story art deco building with its impressive corner tower and parapets, she imagined a warm summer breeze catching the American flag at its peak. Counting the windows, she wondered which one Drew had sat in front of while penning her cherished letter.

> Hello, Peaches,
>
> This is the first time I've ever written anything like this, so you'll have to excuse me if it's not perfect. What I'm trying to say is—will you marry me? I love you and need you. I know you won't be getting much of a bargain, but I'll try very hard to make you happy. So, sweet, write and tell me your answer, then we'll go on from there. It can't be soon enough for me. I'm sure we could be very happy together—so dear, don't keep me in suspense.
>
> I hope you love me enough to say yes. I know I'm not much good at this sort of thing, but I'm trying my best.
>
> Waiting for your answer with my fingers crossed.
> All my love,
> Drew

Emma sighed, propped her elbow on the armrest, and dropped her chin in her hand. She sat mesmerized by the late-summer sun making its descent. As it dipped behind the trees lining the horizon, the fleeting colors of dusk melted into vibrant streaks of pink and orange against the deepening indigo sky.

Emma could still sense the warmth of Drew's parting embrace—the lingering scent of his favored Old Spice—and feel the remaining moistness of his soft kiss. She'd thought her heart would snap when tears welled in his crystal-blue eyes, and he whispered, "See you soon, Peaches." It had taken every ounce of resolve she could muster to suppress her tears—but only until the train exited the station. Only until she could no longer see his impassioned over-the-head wave.

Why must love hurt so?

"Chicago!"

The conductor stopped at Emma's seat. "Almost there, miss. Be sure you have all of your belongings. I'd hate for you to leave something behind." He tipped his hat and bellowed again as he hurried toward the front of the train.

Not a chance. She'd left a huge part of her heart behind once—never again. This time, she would follow it. Things would be different. She'd make certain—she'd cling tighter, pray harder, and fight longer for the man she loved.

As the train pulled into the depot, Emma gathered her things and tucked them into the souvenir tote bag Drew had sent her from Chicago's Grand Central Station. The forlorn blast of the train's whistle accompanied by the hissing of brakes brought the rusty wheels of the B&O *Capitol Limited* to a screeching halt. While well-dressed businessmen, excited children, and women with fretting babies jockeyed for positions in the aisle, Emma flipped open her leather train case and glanced in the mirror. She grimaced, then fluffed her long, dark tresses and gave each cheek a pinch before snapping the lid shut.

Straightening in her seat, she searched the congested platform. It wasn't easy to differentiate one gentleman from the other. Most wore business suits topped with seasonable overcoats and fashionable fedoras. While studying their faces with no sign of Drew, a horde of "what ifs" descended like a suffocating cloud. What if he never came? What if she'd made a mistake? What if the small amount of money she'd saved wouldn't cover a ticket home? But as quickly as the notion flooded in, she evicted it from her mind. It was nonsense. She was here—Drew would be too.

She stood and claimed her place in the aisle behind twin boys who jabbed and shoved one another toward the exit while their mother struggled with a distraught baby. Stepping into the vestibule, a blast of Chicago's brisk fall air sent a chill up her spine. The conductor reached for her hand. "Watch your step, miss."

"Thank you, sir," she said as her feet touched the wooden platform. Releasing his hand, she stepped to one side and scanned the crowd. Terror nipped at her heart. *Where was Drew?* Zigzagging her way through outbound passengers, her eyes darted from one face to another. Then, pausing to allow a baggage handler to cross in front of her, she spotted him.

"Drew!" Signaling with a spirited wave, she ran. "I'm over—"

As the distinguished-looking gentleman took off his fedora and turned to face her, her legs grew weak, and her heart fell. How could she have been so mistaken?

The man lifted a young lady from the platform, spun her around, and kissed her before escorting her into the terminal.

Emma followed them inside and walked to the Western Union desk. After sending Penny a telegram, she motioned for a porter who carried her suitcases outside. She tipped him and sat on a wooden bench beneath a gaslight. The B&O had pulled away and was nearly out of sight. All was quiet but for the pounding of her heart.

Lily, Mama T, her friends, they'd all cautioned her to take her time, to follow her head and "the good Lord's leadin'" above her impetuous heart. Tucker, especially, had warned her of traveling men. Perhaps he was right. Maybe she'd misread Drew. Had her quest to heal her heartbreak and desire to see places beyond North Carolina's Sandhills caused her to dismiss warning bells and ignore common sense? Hundreds of miles now separated her from all that was familiar and the people she loved.

She was here, but where—where was Drew?

Chapter Three

Tucker checked the clock above the nurses' desk at Fort Bragg's Station Hospital, picked up Private Ben Simmons's chart, and grinned. Louisville, huh? Reading further, he shook his head. "Hmm ... whaddya know."

Pulling a chair from the alcove, he wheeled it down the hall to Room 204 and slid back the curtain on bed B. A fair-haired, baby-faced new recruit lay gazing out the window.

"Hiya, sport. How are you feeling this afternoon? You must have slipped in yesterday on my day off."

He grimaced. "Afraid so. Was rushed in for an emergency appendectomy. I'm a bit sore today, but it beats yesterday's pain."

"I bet so." He extended his hand and grinned. I'm Sergeant Baldwin ... reporting for duty. Seems I'm to take you down the hall for some follow-up. You think you're up for the ride?"

"I can try." Wincing, he inched up in the bed and threw back the sheet. "Might need a little help getting into that chair, though."

"Not a problem." Tucker took hold of his arm. "That's how I earn my keep around here. It seems Uncle Sam prefers I stay busy." He eased him into the chair, slid army-issued slippers on his feet, and rolled him out the door and down the hall. "I saw on your chart that you're from Louisville. Lived there long?"

"All my life. You been there?"

"I have." He stopped to allow a medic pushing a gurney toward the surgery wing to pass and then moved on.

"Are you familiar with Brooks Street, not far from St. Joseph's Infirmary?"

"I am, my man. As a matter of fact, it appears we're neighbors."

Ben's eyes widened as he looked back at Tucker. "No joke?"

"My family owns a rooming house west of there on Fourth called the Captain's Inn."

He shook his head. "Now, isn't that a coincidence. I know exactly where it is. Driven by there many times. What a small world."

"Yep. Lived there all my life. Born at St. Joseph's. Pop is a tugboat captain on the Ohio River."

"You don't say. Sounds like an interesting life. How long you been at Bragg?"

"A little over three years."

"Wow. I've been here six weeks and already miss my family like crazy … not to mention my girl. You married? Gotta lady?"

Tucker shook his head. "Nope, on both counts. Almost took the leap earlier this year, but we broke up."

"Oh, man, sorry to hear that. Was your girl from the city too?"

"She was. Still is. She's in nursing school over at St. Joseph's. You know any Warrens in the area?"

"I know Mike Warren, a floor clerk over at Levy Bros. on Third and Market."

He raised his eyebrows. "Oh, you do? Suck in then. Your small world is about to get a bit tighter. I dated his daughter, Collette, for two years."

"No, kidding? I bumped into her once in the store. She's quite a looker." He glanced up at Tucker. "I'm sorry. I hope I didn't offend you."

"No problem. Seems like most guys notice. She's someone else's girl to lose now. Losing one's sweetheart is a common occurrence for us soldiers. It's hard to overcome the distance."

"Sheesh. That's what I'm afraid of. I write my Margie every day."

"You're a smart guy. Keep that ink flowing. It's gonna be your lifeblood." Tucker pushed Ben into the radiology department, passed his chart to the medic behind the desk, then extended his hand to the young soldier. "It's been nice chatting with you, neighbor, but this is where my tour ends. Take it easy, you hear. Perhaps, we'll meet up again later."

"Sounds like a plan, but not in here, I hope. I've enjoyed our talk and feel closer to home already. You have a good evening, sir."

Tucker nodded and lifted his hand as he walked away. "I'm counting on it." Glancing at his watch, he sighed and headed back to his wing. Almost quitting time … and nearly time for Emma to arrive in Chicago.

Yep, he was batting a thousand when it came to striking out with the ladies, and reenlistment looked more probable by the day. As for his future, he had two choices—or so he thought. He could return to Louisville and push coal up and down the river at five miles per hour for twenty-eight-day stints, or he could remain enlisted and continue to do what he loved. Knowing first-hand the toll river life takes on a family, and in light of yesterday's news of Germany's invasion of Poland, he believed life as an Army medic would render the greater good.

"Hey, Tuck! It's about time for you to call it a day, isn't it?"

Tucker turned to see his friend, Henry "Hank" Morrison, strolling through the corridor with his jacket slung over his shoulder.

"Sure is. Looks like you're headed out too. Wanna grab a bite at the Rainbow in a bit?"

Never breaking his stride, Hank flashed a toothy grin. "Now, you're talkin'. I'll wait for you out back."

"Perfect. Look for me in ten minutes."

Lumbering on, Hank nodded and pulled a pack of Lucky

Strikes from his shirt pocket.

Tucker threw open the door to the Rainbow. "You first, my man."

Hank pitched his cigarette into the gutter and stepped inside the popular Hay Street restaurant. The after-dinner crowd was sparse, and Penny sat at a table filling shakers for Monday's early morning diners. Sliding into the corner booth in her station, Tucker said, "Have you got time to serve a couple of famished GIs, ma'am?"

A broad smile spread across her face. "You bet I do." She stood and pulled her order pad from her pocket and slipped the pencil from behind her ear. She nodded at Hank, then leaned over and hugged Tucker. "I've had you on my mind all day. You doing all right?"

"I'm okay." He glanced at the daily specials on a board behind the counter. "You can believe I've had my eyes on the clock, though. Any news from Emma?"

"No. Not yet. But surely, we'll hear something soon. What can I get for you both?"

Hank turned in his seat and ordered from the board. "A BLT with fries and a glass of milk for me. And would you tell the guys in the kitchen to fry up that bacon extra crispy?"

"Of course. How about you, Tucker?"

He placed his back against the wall, stretched out his legs on the seat, and crossed them at the ankles. "Two hotdogs all the way, fries, and a Coke."

"Sounds easy enough. I'll bring your water and drinks right out."

Hank pulled a few napkins from the container and tossed Tucker a straw. "So Emma's gone to meet her man in Chicago, huh? That was a pretty gutsy move. Must be love."

Tucker fixed his eyes on lights snaking their way around the jukebox in the corner and drummed his straw on the table. "For her sake, I hope so. Drew's a fine gentleman, but I would never have guessed Emma would pick up and leave like she did. She seems to think this Scotsman is the one, so who am I to tell her any different?"

"Who's to tell *any* woman different for that matter?" Hank shook his head and laughed. "Maybe we should shift to a topic we can relate to."

"Yeah. You're probably right. Got one?"

"How about last night's news? You think Britain will live up to their promise to come to Poland's defense?"

"I believe they will." Tucker swiveled in his seat, crossed his arms on the table in front of him, and leaned forward. "We're probably sitting on the brink of another world war."

Hank furrowed his brow. "I hope you're wrong, but as much as I don't want to admit it, you're probably not."

As Penny placed their drinks on the table, the bell over the entrance jingled. "Is there a Penny Watson here?"

She turned and held up her hand. "That's me, sir." She sat her tray on the next table and walked toward him, wiping her hands on her apron.

"Telegram, ma'am." The Western Union courier handed her a bright yellow envelope.

Pulling change from her pocket, she passed it to him.

He flashed her a lopsided grin, tipped his hat, and shuffled out the door as quickly as he'd entered.

Penny flapped the envelope in the air, whirled around, and walked back to the table, hips swaying. "Looks like this may be the news we've waited for, fellas," she said in a sing-song voice.

Coke splashed from Tucker's glass as he plunked it on the table, slid back in his seat, and crossed his arms. "So open it. What's she say?"

Carefully tearing the top of the envelope, she unfolded the thin yellow paper. *"Good trip. Arrived on time. So tired. Will write soon. Love, Em XOXO."* She lifted her head. "I guess that answers our questions." She passed the telegram to Tucker. "You want to keep this?"

He stared at the paper in her hand. "Sure. Why not." Pulling out his wallet, he folded the telegram and tucked it inside. "I'm glad to know she's safe." Then he uttered words he'd yet to come to terms with. "I hope—I hope she'll be happy."

Tears welled in Penny's eyes. "Yeah. Me too." She snatched her tray from the table and dashed toward the kitchen. "I'll be right back with your food."

Hank stretched his long, muscular arms and settled back in his seat. "I'm worn out. I tacked quite a few miles onto that ambulance today. It'll be nice to have tomorrow off. How about you? You working?"

He chuckled. "Working at taking it easy. I plan to sleep in."

"Ah. Good deal." He noted a couple of young ladies as they entered the restaurant. "Hey, how about joining me tomorrow afternoon? I'm taking a girl I met a couple of weeks ago to the cinema to see *The Wizard of Oz*. Musicals aren't my preference, but Susie wants to see it. She's asked her friend to come along. We should make it a double.

Tucker sipped his drink, then wiped a wet ring from the table with his napkin. "I don't think so, pal. Appreciate the thought, though. Maybe another time."

"Come on. Sweep in and rescue me, Sergeant." He guffawed. "Two dames and a musical. I need someone who'll have my back and speak my language."

"I'd like to help you out, but I've sworn off women for a while. Haven't done too well in that department lately."

"For Pete's sake, Tuck. I'm not asking you to marry the girl. It's a movie. Lighten up, pal. Have a little fun."

Penny brought their orders and refilled their glasses.

Tucker reached for the catsup and doused his burger and fries. "What's this girl's name? Know much about her?"

"Beth—the last name is Mitchell, I believe. Only met her once, but she's cute and a lifelong friend of Susie." He clicked his tongue and winked. "They come from good stock. Both families live over in the Haymount area." He rubbed his thumb and two fingers together. "Their fathers are loaded."

Tucker rolled his eyes. "Sounds like trouble to me. I believe I'll pass. Try me another time." He rearranged the shakers and condiments on the table. "I believe I'll stroll over to the PX tomorrow, pick up a good book, a copy of this month's Baseball Magazine, and lay low."

Hank stuffed a few fries in his mouth. "Okay, but I think you're missing out."

"Could be, but I'm not ready to wade into those murky waters anytime soon.

Hank shrugged and popped another fry. "Suit yourself."

Chapter Four

Drew? Jolted from her slumber, Emma's eyes sprang open. *Did she really hear Drew calling her name, or was it a dream?* Frantic and trying to focus her eyes, she blinked several times, then scanned Grand Central's platform.

"I'm here, Em. I'm here."

Gasping, she slapped both hands to her chest and leaped from the bench as Drew ran toward her, his fedora in hand.

Sweeping her off her feet, he whirled her around. "Oh, Peaches, I'm so sorry."

Her surroundings swirling about her, she stared with relief into his frightened eyes, then welcomed his quick but impassioned kiss. As he lowered her to the ground, she slipped her arms around his waist and dropped her head to his chest. She could hear the erratic pumping of his heart as her own blood swished in her ears. "I thought you weren't coming, and I didn't have enough money for a train ticket home. I didn't know what to do."

Gently clasping her shoulders, he stepped back and looked deep into her eyes. "Darling, I hope you know I would never intentionally leave you stranded." He pulled her to his chest and rubbed her back. "The cab driver was a new young pup who took me to Union Station instead. I should have kept my eyes on the road, but I was caught up in what the *Daily Tribune* had to say about Germany's invasion of Poland. I didn't notice until he stopped. By the time we cut back through the traffic, I was panic-stricken. Didn't even pay the boy, just threw open the door and darted for the terminal. I was afraid you wouldn't be here. You wouldn't wait." He squeezed her hard. "Thank God you did. Please. Please, forgive me."

She looked into his pained expression and stroked his face. "It's okay, Drew, it's okay. You're forgiven. It wasn't your fault."

He snatched up her two large suitcases. "Grab the rest of your things, and let's get out of here. We'll drop these bags in your hotel room where you can freshen up, and then we'll go for a stroll in the park. How's that sound?"

"Wonderful. Now that you're here with me, I'm ready for anything." She gathered her small belongings and followed him to the front of the terminal, where he hailed a taxi. While the driver loaded the trunk, Drew slid into the backseat beside her and pulled her close. Her anxiety melted in the warmth of his embrace.

The doorman greeted Drew and Emma as they exited the doors of the Union Park Hotel apartments. They paused at the curb to wait for a break in traffic, then darted across the busy street to the freshly manicured thirteen-acre park. As a cool, crisp breeze rustled the leaves overhead, Emma shivered and tugged on her sweater, wrapping it around her as tightly as she could.

"Cold?" Drew said, pulling her closer.

"A little." She smiled. "It's not this chilly yet in Fayetteville."

"I suppose not." He slipped off his sport coat and draped it over her shoulders. "There now, lassie. Is that better?"

"Much. Thank you."

Walking along the well-lit path that wound through the park, Emma looked eastward toward Lake Michigan and took a deep breath. The lights of Chicago's skyline rivaled the stars. "What a beautiful night. This city is magical."

"I knew you'd appreciate this view. I know you're worn out, but I thought perhaps you'd like a glimpse of your new neighborhood before calling it a day." He chuckled. "I promise to have you back in your room before the stroke of midnight."

She met his adoring gaze and laughed, "I feel like a princess every time I'm with you. Thanks for making me feel so special."

"It's not hard." He ran his finger down her slender nose. "You *are* special." Turning, he pulled a pipe from his pocket, lit it, and placed her arm over his before walking on. "How's your room?" He blew a puff of cherry-scented smoke into the air. "Do you have a nice view of the city?"

"I do. I'll sleep with the drapes open tonight for sure—if I can sleep at all, that is." She looked up at his strong profile. "How about you?"

"The view's not as good from the second floor. But I'm at the paper most of the time, so it's not as important to me. A lot more economical too." He motioned to a bench beneath a gas street lamp and sat beside her. "For you, I requested an apartment toward the top. The sixth floor was the highest one they had available."

"It's perfect—more than enough. I never expected a place so lovely." She sighed. "I hope I can find a job soon so that I can make my own way."

He cupped her chin in his hand and turned her face toward his pleading eyes. "Or say yes to my proposal and marry me."

She lowered her head. "I'm not ready yet, Drew." She returned his gaze. "It has nothing to do with you. I simply need more time to adjust to the move before making lifelong decisions. I hope you understand."

He laid his fedora beside him, wrapped his arm around her shoulders, and leaned back against the bench. "I do. Impatient, that's all." A breeze sent a puff of smoke swirling into the cool night air. "I've got someone I want you to meet on Monday."

She inched closer to the warmth of Drew's body and looked into his face. "You do?"

"Yes, my friend, Clement Berghoff. He owns a German restaurant over on West Adams Street—The Berghoff. It's a short walk from work, so I eat dinner there often. Clem and I meshed from the start. When I told him last week you were moving from North Carolina, I bragged about your excellent service at the Rainbow, and he told me to bring you by. They've opened a more casual downstairs café, the Annex, and he needs more help. Think you'd be interested?"

"Interested?" She grabbed his cheeks and kissed him abruptly on the lips. "It sounds perfect. I can't wait to meet him."

"And I can't wait to show you off." He leaned in and kissed her, then briskly rubbed her arms. "You're shivering. We should go back to the hotel."

"You're right. I am cold." She rose from the bench and wrapped his sport coat tighter around her shoulders. "I wouldn't want to be sick in the morning." Jumping in front of him on the path, she walked backward. "So what are our plans for tomorrow. How should I dress?"

Drew took his pipe from his mouth. "The dress is casual, but the place—now that's a surprise."

"You mean you're not going to tell me, Mr. Brown?" She looped her arm through his, looked into his eyes, and batted her lashes. "Not even one little hint?"

Staring straight ahead, he blew a smoke ring in the air and shook his head. "Nope."

"Aw, come on. One teensy-weensy one?"

He moved in silence, nodded at a passerby walking her dog, then took his pipe from his mouth. "Okay. You're pretty hard to resist." He stopped to face her. "Only one, though, you hear?"

She nodded.

"One small hint for you to solve while you're lying awake tonight. Ready?"

She leaned in. "I am."

"In 1916, it broke a world record."

"The world record?"

He nodded and placed his index finger over her lips. "Shush. *One* hint now, remember? That's it. We should call it a night." Taking her by the arm, he ushered her across the street, then wished the doorman a pleasant evening as they entered the building.

"Good night, Mr. Brown, Miss Walsh."

As the doors closed behind them, Emma looked up at the soft-spoken Scotsman and clung to her dreams for tomorrow.

Chapter Five

Sunday, September 3, 1939
Chicago, Illinois
Emma

As the taxi approached Navy Pier, Emma's eyes bulged. Pressing her forehead against the window, she craned her neck, striving to take in the massive neo-classical building which loomed before her. Its two red-brick towers stood like proud sentinels guarding Lake Michigan's waterfront, and rightly so. The magnificent structure had served its country well during the war.

"It's pretty impressive, isn't it?" said Drew.

"Breathtaking."

"There's a lot of history on this waterfront. When the Pier opened in 1916, it was a Great Lakes cargo facility that served as a public gathering place for Chicagoans. Then, less than a year later, it became a barracks for America's soldiers, housed the Red Cross and Home Defense, and functioned as a detention center for draft dodgers."

When the taxi pulled to the curb, Drew opened the door and assisted Emma onto the sidewalk. Then, reaching for his wallet, he pulled out several bills while Emma walked toward the entrance, scanning the building's size.

"Hey, Emma! Smile for me."

She turned and flashed a broad grin for the handsome Scotsman who'd stolen her heart a few months prior. Generally seen with a camera flung over his shoulder to not miss the genesis of a fine painting, Drew enjoyed razzing Emma with his constant clicking of the shutter. Not that she minded the attention. She was more than happy to get a photo or two to tuck in her first letters to Penny and Tucker back home. Like her, Penny had never seen the likes of a big city, and she wanted to share every moment with her friend.

"That was a great one," he said, walking toward her, pulling her close, and kissing her hair. "How can I fail with you as my subject?"

Emma felt the heat rise in her cheeks. "You mean this is the place that broke a world record?"

He nodded. "All 3300 feet of it. When its construction was completed in 1916, it was the largest Pier in the world. You ready to walk the length of it?"

"You know I am. I'm so excited." She wrapped her sweater tightly around her, inhaled the crisp morning air, and fought to keep her hair from her eyes as a stiff lakefront breeze blew in.

Stopping first to purchase a *Chicago Sunday Tribune* from a young boy, Drew placed it under his arm, then grabbed her hand as they trekked to the end of the Pier. "I'll let you take in the magnificent view, and then we'll go for a ride on the carousel."

Emma quickened her pace beside him and bounced on her toes like a child at Christmas. "Seriously? A carousel?"

"Yes." He stopped. "Listen. Hear that music? That's it, and it's the first of many surprises big-city life holds for you, lassie."

Emma linked her arm through Drew's and tried to keep up with his long strides as they passed by open-air shops, eateries, street performers, and souvenir vendors. On the far end of the Pier stood the carousel and a huge domed concert hall and ballroom with panoramic windows overlooking Lake Michigan.

Drew gestured to a bench at the end of the historic landmark and seated himself beside Emma. "Magnificent, isn't it?"

"More beautiful than I could ever dream. I've had to pinch myself several times since I stepped off the train to make sure this is all real." She scooted in closer and laid her head on his shoulder as she watched a sailboat cut across the lake's choppy surface. "Whenever I'm with you, all seems right with the world." At Drew's failure to reply, she lifted her head from his shoulder and looked into his troubled eyes. "Your silence is deafening. Why are you so quiet?"

"Nothing that won't save until later," he said, folding the *Tribune* lying on the bench beside him.

"Drew, stop it." She reached across his lap and grabbed the paper from the bench. Her breath caught in her throat. "'*Britain Declares War on Germany.*' What?"

Snatching the newspaper from her hands, he clutched it to his chest. "We're here to enjoy our day. Let's ride the carousel."

"Drew, read it. I'll worry, either way, so you may as well. I promise I'll put it in the back of my mind. I won't allow anything to steal the joy of our time together."

With a flick of his wrist, Drew snapped the paper open and reluctantly read aloud as Emma gazed across Lake Michigan's deep blue waters.

> *Prime Minister Chamberlain today proclaimed Great Britain is at war with Germany after expiration of a British ultimatum for Germany to withdraw her troops from Poland. The declaration was broadcast to the world fifteen minutes after the deadline given Hitler expired at 10 a.m. (5 a.m. Chicago time). In opening the broadcast, Chamberlain said: "I have to tell you now that this country is at war with Germany."*

As Emma's eyes followed the billowing sails of boats cutting through white-capped waters, Drew's words ricocheted through her head. Her thoughts raced to Tucker. What must he be thinking? Feeling? Although America had not yet been pulled into the war, the involvement of America's greatest ally, Great Britain, brought them one step closer.

Drew folded the paper and leaped from the bench. "It's sobering news. I hate it's come to this, but let's set this aside and talk about it later." Tossing the paper in a nearby trash bin, he held out his hand. "For now, your stallion awaits, my lady."

She smiled and slipped her hand in his. "Now that my prince has come. I'm ready."

Mellow strains of "Onward Christian Soldiers," combined with the delighted squeals of children, greeted them as they approached the carousel. Drew handed the attendant his change and pulled Emma to his side. "That's some merry-go-round, isn't it?"

She shook her head. "I've never seen anything like it. I'm not sure who's more thrilled, the children or their parents. Have you noticed them wave to their little ones every time they come around? So precious."

Drew pulled her closer, kissed her hair, and whispered, "That will be us one day, Peaches."

As the carousel slowed and the children leaped into their parent's arms, begging to 'go again,' Drew helped Emma onto the platform. "Pick your steed, my lady."

Emma walked past one horse and then another before choosing a white one with a carved garland of red roses draped around its neck. After cupping his hands for her to step up and settle into the saddle, Drew mounted the black stallion beside hers, its head tilted, nostrils flared.

Giggling like a schoolgirl, Emma grasped the brass pole and looked at the man at her side. She couldn't have imagined this moment, and the joy Drew would bring to her life on the heels of such grief. As the music played and the galloping menagerie picked up speed, the cheerful calliope tune drowned any doubts she'd had surrounding her decision to come to Chicago.

Once the merry-go-round came to a stop, Drew helped Emma from her horse and lifted her from the platform. "Whoa," she said wide-eyed, stumbling into Drew's arms.

"Aha. A wee bit dizzy, are you?"

She chuckled. "Uh-huh. That was so much fun, but I must find my land legs again."

Drew took her by the hand and pulled her through the crowd. "Come on. I've got you. Do you like cotton candy?"

"Oh, yes. Can we get some?"

As they approached the food kiosk, a vendor stepped in front of Emma and held out a single red rose. His gaze was eerily familiar, and her breath caught in her throat. Darting her eyes to Drew's, she relaxed as he nodded and pulled change from his pocket. She took the rose and thanked the young man who appeared to look deep into her soul. Lifting the flower to her nose, she inhaled its sweet fragrance and with a hint of melancholy whispered, "My favorite."

After purchasing a cone of cotton candy, Drew led Emma to a bench at the pier's edge.

Laying the rose in her lap, she pulled a tuft of the fluffy pink confection from the paper cone in Drew's hand and popped it into her mouth. She sighed as it melted on her tongue. "Yum. It's been forever since I've had cotton candy." Losing herself in Drew's gaze, she said, "It's heavenly ... as is this day. Thank you for bringing me."

"My pleasure," he said as he wiped his mouth with the back of his hand. "I'm the grateful one. You gave up a lot to be with me here in Chicago. I promise I'll try not to disappoint you."

"Disappoint me? You?" Her eyes widened as she shook her head. "I can't imagine ever being disappointed by you."

The warmth of the morning sun enveloped them and insulated them from the cool, crisp breeze. Observing the flurry of activity on the sparkling blue water, Emma scooted closer to Drew and wrapped her arm through his. Smelling the rose, her thoughts melted into cherished moments spent with Noah by the river and the brevity of their days together. Life was so uncertain. She fought to push away the fears that threatened to steal the beauty of the moment. Was her sister Lily right? Were happy endings only found in fairy tales?

"A penny for your thoughts, Miss Walsh."

Emma jolted. "I'm sorry. I suppose I lost myself in the

beauty of this moment. I still can't believe I'm here. And I want to thank you again for lining up a meeting for me with Mr. Berghoff tomorrow. I'm anxious to meet him." She brushed the windswept hair from her eyes. "I hope he likes me."

Drew laughed. "Like you? He'll love you … as will everyone else. You forget, I witnessed your loyal customers in Fayetteville, not to mention the GIs who clamored for your attention. No, lassie. People liking you will not be an issue. I expect Clem's business will triple."

Emma swatted Drew's arm and laughed. "Aren't you the flatterer, Mr. Brown."

"I don't see it as flattery. To me, it's the truth. You'll win him and everyone who meets you with your charm. I'm convinced of it." He held the paper cone of candy toward Emma. "Go ahead. Finish it off, and we'll see what other wonders this day has in store."

Following Drew from the bench, Emma popped the last tuft of pink in her mouth, then stopped at the water fountain to rinse her fingers.

Drew motioned to a man passing by. "Sir. Can I trouble you for a moment of your time?"

He glanced at his wife. "Of course, what can I do for you?"

Drew slipped his camera from around his neck. "Ever used one of these?"

He shook his head. "Not one this elaborate, but if you set it up, I'll snap it."

Drew motioned for Emma to stand at the pier's railing in front of the Chicago skyline, then handed the camera to the man before taking his place beside Emma. Pulling her close, he flashed a broad smile. "Ready, beautiful?"

She tucked strands of her tousled hair behind her ears and nodded.

"Smile big, lovebirds." Snapping the picture, the man shouted above the wind. "Want me to take another?"

"That would be swell," Drew said. He turned Emma toward

him and kissed her.

As she relaxed in his arms, her fingers loosened from the rose, and a stiff breeze stole it from her grasp. Opening her eyes, she gasped as it dropped to the surface of the water and surrendered to the ebb and flow of the waves.

Chapter Six

Monday, September 4, 1939
Drew

Drew held open the door for Emma to step into the lobby of Chicago's 470-foot, neo-Gothic skyscraper, the Tribune Tower. Bringing her to this magnificent North Michigan Avenue 1925 structure, one in which he spent the majority of his waking hours, was exhilarating. He looked forward to giving her a bird's-eye view of the city and introducing her to his friends, namely Joe. He'd met Joe and Helen Roth when he arrived in Toronto from Dundee. They'd been significant factors in his decision to come to the states after working several years with newspapers in Canada.

Joe believed in Drew's talent, took him under his wing, and became his scout—an agent of sorts. He and Helen treated him like a son, and Drew had welcomed their company on the road as he traveled from job to job.

Entering the Hall of Inscriptions, Drew pointed out the giant relief map of North America that hung above the front desk. "It's made of plaster mixed with retired U. S. currency. Pretty extraordinary, isn't it?"

Nodding, Emma stood speechless as her eyes wandered upward to the massive old English Oak beams. The historic building's ornate arches and leaded glass gave the solemn space the feel of a grand cathedral more than it did the headquarters of a big-city newspaper. Its design was meant to reflect the sacred responsibility and aspirations of journalism. Quotations carved in the walls and the floor referenced free speech, freedom of the press, and cited how the truth would set people free.

Drew leaned against the desk, content to stand back and witness Emma's awe as she slowly turned to read aloud the inscribed words of famous world leaders. He slipped his lens cap into the breast pocket of his safari jacket and followed her with his camera. As she walked the perimeter of the room, her footsteps on the marble floor rivaled the clicks of his shutter and echoed throughout the cavernous tower.

Sliding her hand along the polished limestone walls, she paused beneath the carved words of Voltaire, "*I do not agree with a word that you say, but I will defend to the death your right to say it.*" Shaking her head, she turned toward Drew. "How amazing. I never knew a place like this existed. Our nation's history resonates throughout this hall. You are so fortunate to work here."

"I agree. I've never regretted my decision to come to America. How could I? I met you." He walked over and took her hand. "Come on. We've lots more to see today before your interview."

Stepping into an alcove, they waited with several tourists for elevators that accessed the tower's thirty-six floors. Drew hit the call button and pulled Emma closer while waiting for the car to rumble down the shaft. "It's hard to believe you're here with me. I've wanted to show you this ever since I arrived in Chicago."

She slipped her arm around his waist. "I'm so excited my insides are quivering. I've never been in a building this tall."

As Simon, the elevator attendant slid open the brass doors, they crowded in behind eager sightseers, sporting souvenir hats, shouldering cameras, and reading their tower brochures.

"Good morning, Mr. Brown. You're a little late for work this morning, aren't you?"

"Hardly. I'm playing tourist today. Showing my lady the sights." He turned. "Emma, I'd like you to meet my friend, Simon."

He tipped his cap. "My pleasure, ma'am. Welcome to the

Tribune Tower."

"Thank you. I'm thrilled to be here."

A broad grin appeared beneath his graying mustache. "There's no mistaking it, sir, you have a real Southern belle by your side."

Emma laughed. "Indeed, he does. I'm a North Carolina girl."

Simon nodded his approval. "Fine state. Visited a cousin there many years ago." He turned to Drew. "You taking her to the promenade?"

"You guessed it," he said, slipping him some change.

Simon pulled the gate shut and started the car's ascent. As it soared upward, Emma grabbed Drew's arm. "Oh, my ears popped."

"Mine too," said the lady behind her as her toddler crammed his fingers in his ears.

Simon chuckled. "The Tower boasts the fastest elevators in the city—800 feet a minute."

He eased the car to a stop on the twenty-fourth floor. "Observatory. Follow the steps up one floor to the promenade and brace yourself for a jaw-dropping view of the city's bustling business district, known as the Loop."

Drew squeezed Emma's hand as they ascended the steps. "Here we go. I hope you're not afraid of heights."

"Not with you by my side. You will catch me if I teeter, won't you?"

He leaned over and kissed her nose. "I dare anyone to try and stop me."

As the people in front of them raced for places along the Indiana limestone walls, Emma slowly took in her surroundings and gasped. "My heart is about to pound from my chest. I've never seen anything so magnificent, and to think mere men built all of these buildings. I can't even comprehend it."

Drew led her to a telescope and dropped in a coin. "Here, look through this. You can almost read the menus of the patrons at the restaurant across the street."

As Emma scanned and marveled at the view, Drew couldn't take his eyes off of her. Her excitement was like a child at Christmas, and he loved spoiling her.

"If you look to the North, you'll see Wrigley Field. We'll have to take in a game next summer. The Cubs traded for All-Star player Hank Leiber last year, and they finished fourth this season. Leiber ended with a .300 batting average. Hate I missed it all."

Emma straightened, stepped away from the telescope, and looked up at the massive buttresses towering above her. "I have no idea what all that means, but it sounds exciting. I'm willing to learn and would love to go to a game with you sometime."

Drew snapped several shots of Emma before a man with a distinct Irish brogue offered to take their picture together. Afterward, Drew chatted with him about their homelands then ushered Emma down to the twenty-fourth floor, where most of the newspaper's editing was done. Later, he showed her his drawing space and introduced her to several of his pals before exiting the building.

"Where are we headed now?" Emma dodged a lady pushing a stroller.

"Not telling."

"Drew Brown, you're just full of surprises, aren't you? It looks like we're heading toward Navy Pier. Is that where we're going?"

He squeezed her hand and chuckled. "Emma Walsh, you're just full of questions, aren't you? Hold on, you'll see."

After walking several blocks, Drew stopped at a kiosk on the corner near the pier and spoke with the aging attendant. "Brown. Drew. I have a reservation."

"Yes, Mr. Brown," he said with a gravelly voice. "I've got you all fixed up."

Drew reached in his pocket and passed him a couple of bills. "Keep the change."

Smiling, he thanked him and placed them into the leather

money belt, barely visible beneath his bulging stomach. He limped to a small shed, then pulled out a brilliant blue Sun Wasp tandem bicycle and rolled it toward them.

Emma squealed.

Drew grinned. He loved how, when introduced to something new, Emma's hazel eyes grew larger. Her enthusiasm for life and candid responses always made him feel younger and refreshed his spirit. "Have you ever ridden one of these?"

"Ridden? I've not even seen one, except in magazines. I rode a friend's cycle a time or two when I was younger, but never one built for two."

"I thought it would be a great way for you to become familiar with the city. We'll head south first and stop at The Berghoff. Joe and Helen will meet us there for lunch. As soon as you've had your interview with Clem, the four of us will pedal over to Grant Park."

She stood on her toes and kissed his cheek. "You're so thoughtful and have put so much planning into our time together. Thank you. The past couple of days couldn't have been any nicer."

"All right then, my lass. Time's a-wastin'. Place your purse in the basket and climb aboard."

Drew straddled the bike and steadied it while Emma gathered the folds of her plaid skirt and positioned herself on the seat behind him. "Now, all you've got to do is pedal. I'll get us where we need to go."

Emma pulled her mustard-colored knit cap over her ears and took hold of the handlebars. "Sounds wonderful."

Drew pedaled down Michigan Avenue, pointing out the sights along the way, while Emma oohed and ahhed at the latest fall fashions in department store windows. He turned onto West Adams, stopped in front of The Berghoff, and helped Emma onto the sidewalk. Noting another tandem cycle against the wall, he propped theirs beside it. "Looks like Joe and Helen might have beaten us here." Crooking his arm for Emma, he puffed out his chest and escorted her into the restaurant.

Emma

Exiting The Berghoff, Emma and Helen chattered like schoolgirls while Drew and Joe followed close on their heels. Blowing a puff of smoke in the air, Drew reached for Emma's arm and motioned toward a bench under a nearby tree.

"Have a seat, ladies. Joe and I want to enjoy our pipes before chauffeuring you to Grant Park."

Helen, a smartly dressed, petite lady with delicate features and twice Emma's age, sat and patted the place on the bench beside her. "I thought I'd never get to meet you, and now it looks like we'll have plenty of time to get acquainted. I can't remember ever seeing Drew this relaxed and happy. All he does is work and take in an occasional movie. We've waited a long time for him to find the right girl." She placed her hand on Emma's. "He's talked our ears off about you, and everything he's told us is true. Welcome to the 'Windy City.' I hope you'll like it here as much as we do."

Emma's heart leaped at her words concerning Drew. "Thank you. I think I *will* be happy here. I've missed my friends back home and am pleased to find a new friend in you. I'm excited we have so many of the same interests. Mr. Berghoff was delightful today and kind enough to show me around. Although the waitresses were bustling, they all took a moment to greet me." As the wind picked up, she tugged her cap over her ears. "I look forward to shadowing Elise on Thursday."

Helen nodded. "She'll be a great one to learn from. I've always been impressed with her friendly and efficient service."

Drew tapped his pipe several times against his palm and stuffed it into the inside breast pocket of his jacket. "Okay. It's time to hit the road."

As they rose from the bench, Helen took hold of Emma's

arm and patted the back of her hand. "I can't wait to introduce you to my friends. We'll have to meet them one day soon for lunch and shopping." She motioned. "The cutest new boutique shop has opened up a couple of blocks over on State Street. You'll love it and will look stunning in their clothes."

"Lunch sounds wonderful … and I'll enjoy browsing, but it will be a while before I can treat myself to something new."

Helen's brown eyes widened. "Don't fret, dear. I hear they have a sixty-day layaway plan. No interest."

Emma and Helen seated themselves on the cycles behind the men and pedaled East toward Lake Michigan. Helen's words carried by the wind filtered back toward Emma. "Oh—and I know where there is a quaint little book store and a darling stitchery shop too."

Emma inhaled her new surroundings. As colorful storefronts and blurred images of people sped past, it seemed her heart would burst. Shadowed by the frame of the kind Scotsman seated in front of her, she knew her decision to follow him had been a good one. She could hardly wait to write and share her adventures with Penny. Perhaps her sister Lily had been wrong. Maybe happy endings *were* possible in the lives of those who live outside of fairytales.

Chapter Seven

Saturday, June 30, 2012
Hope Mills, North Carolina
Caroline

Tucker took a couple of long sips from the large Hospice cup, returned it to the metal tray beside his chair, and cleared his throat. "Ladies, excuse me. Please make yourselves at home. I'll be right back." Slowly rising, he grabbed his cane and ambled down the hall.

Kate picked up a *National Geographic* magazine from the coffee table and thumbed through it while I walked over to the fireplace. Scanning the pictures lining the mantle and the hearth, I lifted one of the frames and studied the faces of two soldiers leaning against a jeep marked with a large red cross. Walking back to the couch, I handed the picture to Kate. "Look. I wonder if one of these men is Tucker."

She squinted her eyes. "Considering he was a medic in the army, probably so. The mountain range in the background reminds me of Italy."

I returned the frame to the hearth and studied the pictures on the wall. Among them was a medal—a purple heart rimmed in gold, hanging from a purple ribbon. Mounted on the frame was a small engraved plate. "I guess you were right about the mountains of Italy. It appears Tucker received this heart for his service during the Invasion of Sicily in 1943." Hearing Tucker shuffling down the hall, I returned to the couch.

He walked toward us holding a thick black album. "If you don't mind sharing the sofa, ladies, I've got some things in here you might like to see."

"Of course. We'd love that," Kate said.

Kate and I moved to opposite ends of the couch while Tucker lowered himself between us and rested his cane on the coffee table. He took a few moments to catch his breath, then dropped back against the cushions and opened the album.

"This, ladies, contains my exploits as a young man while stationed as a medic at Fort Bragg. Celie, my precious wife, put this together for me before she died. It gave her something to do during her illness." His voice cracked. "We spent many hours recalling my enlistment and our first years together. It was a special time for us in her final months."

"I'm sure it had to be."

He opened the album and brushed his gnarled fingers over the surface of the black and white photographs. "Of course, the pictures on these first pages were all taken before I met my wife. I thought you'd be interested in seeing the ones of Noah. There are several in here of your mother and him together and even a few of her with me."

"How exciting. Thank you for sharing this with us."

As he turned the pages, each photo prompted a story. At times, he'd struggle to keep his composure. "I thought my heart would break when your mother left for Chicago, but whenever she'd write, I'd feel her excitement. She loved being with Drew in the Windy City, and I couldn't bring myself to ask her to come home. I suppose that's the way it is when you truly love someone. You want them to be happy, even if their happiness means you're not part of it. I figured if it were God's will for us to be together, He'd bring her home in His time. Eventually, your mother—"

"Mr. B. I'm back." Claire entered the kitchen door and placed several shopping bags on the counter. "Look at you sitting there on the couch with a pretty lady on each arm. Always the charmer. I can't leave you unattended for one moment, can I?"

Tucker quipped. "I suppose it's hard to tamp down twisted steel and walking romance."

We laughed at his quirky sense of humor. A glimpse into why Mother would have found this man so appealing.

Claire greeted us as she walked into the den, then turned toward Tucker. "I meant to remind you earlier of Caroline and Kate's visit today. I'm sorry I forgot. Did you happen to remember?"

He shook his head. "No, but that's okay. It's not like I was going anywhere." He chuckled. "I'm a bit of a captive audience, you know. I'm not sure how Emma's daughters feel, but I've had a wonderful time reminiscing. I've been surprised at how much I *do* remember."

Claire offered and then brought each of us a glass of iced tea before stepping back into the kitchen to put away the groceries.

As Tucker reached for his cane, Kate and I helped him to his feet. He stretched his legs, then took a few moments to steady himself before shuffling to the comfort of his chair. Settling back, his eyes sparkled as he shared the memories of his years as a medic and all he'd learned of Mother's days in Chicago. What a precious man this Tucker was—a breath of fresh air and a rare example of selflessness amid our entitled, me-first society.

I checked my watch. "Whew. I'm starved. Let's stop by the Rainbow for a late lunch before we head home."

"You've got no argument from me."

I turned the key in the ignition and backed out onto Camden Road. "What a delightful afternoon. The time flew by. I can hardly wait to visit again next Saturday."

"Me either." Kate dug in her purse. "I'm concerned, though. Tucker is so frail."

"I know. He worries me too."

"Being able to share his story of Mother with us seems important to him. You can tell it brings him joy—probably something he finds little of right now."

"I sensed that too. Did you see how his eyes came to life when he spoke of her? It was all I could do to hold it together."

Kate nodded. "Those two had something special. Tucker's such a kind soul. I can see why Mother was attracted to him."

"It was fun to see his pictures, wasn't it? He was one handsome man."

"So was Daddy."

"I agree. I want to hear more about Tucker's life after Mother. It appears he did well for himself. Celie was beautiful. The soft expression in her large dark eyes drew me right in."

"Me too. I believe they were happy together. You could hear it in his voice."

"I hope so. He's the type of person you want the best for."

Kate huffed and continued to shuffle through her purse.

"What in heaven's name are you looking for?" Her voice slid up an octave. "My phone. I can't find my phone. I probably left it on the couch."

"Oh, no. Are you sure?" I pulled the car over on the side of the road.

She tossed several items back into her purse. "I am. It's not in here. I remember laying it on the couch when Tucker walked over to share the photo album with us." She rubbed her forehead. "I'm sorry. We'll have to go back."

"That's okay. At least you discovered it before we got too far down the road." I pulled to the next intersection and made a U-turn.

"Thanks." She put her head back on the seat and closed her eyes. "Sometimes I think these phones are more trouble than they're worth. We certainly got along without them for a lot of years."

"I hear you." Five minutes later, I rounded the curve on Camden road and gasped.

Kate's eyes flew open. "What?"

I couldn't speak. All I could do was shake my head and point to the flashing lights ahead.

Straightening in her seat, Kate slapped her hands to her chest. "Oh, no, Caroline. No way." She slid forward. "Please, Lord. No"

Feeling nauseous, I pulled the car to the side of the road and cut the engine. Kate and I sat speechless as the EMTs rolled Tucker out on a stretcher and slid him into the back of the ambulance.

Claire locked the front door, then stumbled over one of the stepping stones as she hurried to her Hospice car.

As I followed the ambulance to Highsmith Hospital, Kate and I didn't say a word to one another. We only talked to God.

Chapter Eight

Saturday, September 9, 1939
Chicago, Illinois
Emma

Emma glanced at the clock and struggled to keep up with the tables assigned to her at The Berghoff's new basement café, The Annex. The hours she'd spent at night memorizing the menu had infringed on her sleep, and her energy waned. Today, she'd flown solo after shadowing Elise for two days. An hour more, and she'd escape to the comfort of her room at the Union Park Hotel Apartments.

Clearing the dishes from one of the tables, she walked into the kitchen, where Elise assembled an order.

"How are you holding up, Emma? Are you comfortable with the routine yet?"

"I'm okay. Tired though. The stress of learning everything has taken its toll, but I'll be fine. Drew's on an assignment in Wisconsin and won't be back until Monday, so I'll have tomorrow to rest. Church, catching up on my letter writing, and a nap are my only plans for the day."

"Sounds spectacular. I can't remember when I last had an entire day to myself."

Emma straightened the stack of menus in the rack. "I want to thank you for training me this week and for your patience. You've been an excellent mentor."

"Don't mention it. You're a quick learner. I remember the pressure of my first week. I'm willing to help in any way I can." She slid the last of the order onto her tray, lifted it over her head, then bustled past Emma. "Hold on, girl. It's almost quitting time."

Elise reminded her of Penny—minus the Southern drawl, of course. Like her North Carolina friend, she was a hard worker who befriended everyone she met. She, too, carried a heavy responsibility at home as the single mother of a young, mentally-disabled daughter.

Emma returned to the dining room, topped off her customer's cups, and let out a long sigh as she set the carafe on the hot plate at the workstation in the corner. Turning around, she watched as a man entered the restaurant and seated himself at the table she'd just cleared. Her heart sank. *Put your smile on, Emma. Your finish line is in sight.*

Taking a deep breath, she poured a glass of water, straightened her shoulders, and walked to the table. Placing the glass in front of the young man, she greeted him with the most cheerful voice she could muster. "Good evening. Welcome to The Annex. My name is Emma, and I'm happy to serve you."

Slipping a menu from behind the napkin holder, he glanced up, then hesitated before he spoke. "Thank you, but not as happy as I am to be your customer."

Emma smiled and dismissed his comment. "Would you like to hear our specials?"

He shook his head and winked. "No, thanks. I think I'm looking at her."

Emma averted her eyes as heat rose in her cheeks.

"Sorry. That crossed the line."

She nodded.

He looked down at his menu. "I'm only in for coffee and dessert. I'll need a few minutes to make up my mind."

"Certainly. I'll grab your coffee while you decide."

Turning away, she rolled her eyes at the waitress clearing the next table. The man's presence unsettled her, and yet there was something vaguely familiar about this stranger.

At nine o'clock, she took off her apron and approached Elise.

"My shift is over, and I wondered if you'd finish up with my customer at table eighteen. He seems pretty content drinking his coffee and reading the paper, so I hate to rush him."

"Sure, I will. Run along and get some rest. You've worked hard this week. Hopefully, I'll see you at church tomorrow."

"Thank you. And, yes, I'm looking forward to it."

Emma slid the chain in the security latch and tossed her mail onto the kitchen counter. After washing up, she slipped into the flannel pajamas Penny had given her for cold Chicago evenings and brewed a warm cup of chamomile tea. Retiring to the balcony with her mail, she opened several cards and notes from friends back home. She savored every word and saved the thickest envelope for last.

Sunday, September 3, 1939

Hi Emma,

I hope this letter finds you doing well and enjoying the Windy City. I know you're busy settling in, but I hope to hear from you soon. I was at the Rainbow when your telegram arrived the other night. Everyone was happy to know you'd arrived safely in Chicago.

My friend, Hank, invited me to join him and a couple of girls from the Haymount area to see *The Wizard of Oz* this afternoon at the Princess Theater. I told him musicals were not for me and that I'd sworn off the ladies for a while. One man can only take so much rejection.

There is quite a bit of stirring on the base this morning about Prime Minister Chamberlain's announcement of Great Britain's declaration of war on Germany. Not sure what that means for all of us here at the base, but I pray the U.S. takes it slow and easy.

If you haven't already, hopefully, you'll find a job soon. Whoever gets Rainbow Girl #9 will have a gem. I haven't been back to the restaurant since your telegram arrived. Things won't be the same there without you. I know Penny misses you a lot, and I hear Cee is struggling too. Oh, and yes, I can't forget Mama T. I dropped by Maiden Lane for a visit yesterday and found her out on the porch swing with Chummy. She said even Chummy had been moping around since you left. She often finds him upstairs, curled up in the middle of your bed pillows.

How's Drew? I know he's thrilled to have you there with him. Tell him, if he doesn't treat you right, you know a soldier back home who will. Please don't forget us down here in the South. I sure hope you and Drew can come this way for Christmas, if not before.

That's all the news I have for now. I'm not much of a letter writer, but I'll do my best to keep you filled in with what's happening here in Fayetteville. I'm sure Penny will too.

Take care, sweet friend. I treasure my pocket cross and will always keep it with me. Sometimes I pull it out to remind myself that our friendship wasn't a dream and is as alive today as it was the day you gave me the cross. Miles may separate us, but they will never divide our hearts.

"A friend loveth at all times"—and *this* is one of those times.

Tucker

Emma blotted her cheeks with her napkin and laid the letter in her lap. It seemed longer than one week since she'd left her hometown and her friends. Through her tears, Chicago's skyline resembled a glittering impressionist painting. Though exciting and lovely, her new life was foreign to her, and Tucker's familiar words were precisely what she needed—but hadn't they always been?

She thanked God for their friendship, then prayed for his safety and that of the military families she'd served at the Rainbow. Ultimately, she prayed that not one drop of blood would be spilled on American soil and that God would bring a swift end to the horrific war in Europe.

Sunday, September 10, 1939

Emma tucked her scarf into the neck of her green wool sweater jacket, her last purchase from Mae's Boutique in Fayetteville, and pulled her knit cap over her ears. Greeting Carl, the doorman, she slipped on her matching gloves and trotted across Warren Street to Union Park. Except for a few morning dog-walkers and a couple of bleary-eyed mothers strolling their babies, the green inner-city oasis was quiet. Most Chicagoans were still snuggly tucked in their beds where she had wanted to be. But after tossing and turning for the better part of the predawn hours, she'd surrendered the comfort of her warm bed and braved the Windy City's autumn chill.

Since arriving in Chicago, she'd eagerly anticipated her first streetcar ride and welcomed the morning's opportunity to attend Elise's church on the city's south side. She cut through the park to the trolley stop on Ashland Street and took a seat on the bench where a young mother and her child fed the pigeons. "Lovely birds, aren't they. I love their soft cooing."

"Me too," said the bright-eyed petite woman. "Lola comes prepared every Sunday morning with a bag of bread crumbs for her friends. She's named several of them and begs to take them home."

Emma reached out and smoothed the hair of the small towheaded child who intently studied her face. "So sweet."

Their pleasant conversation was interrupted by a Chicago Surface Lines' green and white trolley humming down the steel tracks. At the clanging of its bell, the streetcar's overhead electric wire sparked, and #3231 slowed to a stop in front of them.

She motioned for Lola and her mother to board first, then handed the lanky conductor her ticket and took the seat behind them. As the conductor pulled the cord, the bell clanged to signal the driver that all passengers were safely on board. Lola squealed, and Emma's insides echoed her joy.

As the streetcar passed through the city, she couldn't believe this was her new home and wished Penny could share her adventure. Wiping a tear from her eye, she dug in her purse for a tissue while passengers boarded at the South Halsted Street pickup point. When the streetcar resumed its course, she glanced up to meet the eyes of a man sitting across the aisle, then quickly looked away. His gaze unsettled her.

"Emma?"

She turned to face the nice-looking young man wearing a deep blue shirt with a white Navy Pier emblem on the pocket.

"I thought that was you?"

Her breath caught in her throat as he moved to the seat directly across from hers.

"Remember me? You waited on me last night at The Annex?"

"Yes. I do."

"I'd hoped to see you again before I left."

"I'm sorry." She squirmed. "My shift was over, and I was exhausted—but I left you in good hands."

"That's okay. I was well taken care of." He glanced at his watch. "I don't mean to make you uncomfortable, but I have something I must tell you."

She questioned his advance.

"I'm Tank."

"Tank?"

"Yes. You probably don't remember me. I've lost quite a

few pounds since returning from Bragg."

"Bragg? You were at Fort Bragg?"

"Yes. I often ate at the Rainbow with the guys from my platoon." He grinned. "I had a huge crush on you, but Noah let me know in no uncertain terms that you were his girl."

She giggled as her heart raced. "Oh, yes. I *do* remember you, Tank. It's so nice to see you again."

"Please, call me Paul. I dropped the nickname Tank when I shed the pounds and left Fort Bragg behind." He extended his hand. "Paul Porter is my name. When I saw you at Navy Pier the other morning, I thought it was you but then figured I was mistaken."

"Oh, yes. You … you were the one who handed me the rose."

"I did. I work part-time at the Pier. On weekdays, I attend Woodrow Wilson Junior College, where I'm working toward an accounting degree."

"Wonderful."

"I never would have guessed I'd see you here. What brings you to our glorious city?"

"I came to be closer to the man I plan to marry. You probably never met him—Drew Brown. He's an artist from Scotland and is here on assignment with *The Chicago Tribune*. I met him at the Rainbow when he drew ads for *The Fayetteville Observer*."

"No, don't think I ever met him. He sounds like an interesting fella." He furrowed his brow. "I figured you'd still be with Noah, though. He was head-over-heels in love with you."

She looked down. "I'm certain you haven't heard. Noah was killed in a car crash this past spring. Our relationship had already begun to unravel, but I loved him dearly. It's been hard to move on, but I try."

The light dimmed in his eyes. "I'm sorry. He was one great fellow. I never questioned where I stood with Noah. His honesty was refreshing, and he always spoke highly of you." He shifted in his seat and stared out the window. "So when's the big day with Drew?"

"We've not set one, but we're hoping for next spring."

"We should get together sometime as couples. I'd like to introduce you to my girl, Camille. You two should have a lot in common. She works at one of the eateries on the Pier. We could grab a bite to eat and then give you both a behind-the-scenes tour. I can get us complimentary seats for a river cruise."

She smiled. "Oh, that sounds like fun. I can't wait to tell Drew."

He stood. "This is my stop. I'm headed into work this morning. On Sundays, I help with maintenance." He gave her a nod. "I'm happy I bumped into you. I'll stop by The Annex again soon so we can talk further."

"Wonderful. I'm excited to have another friend in the city. Thank you for speaking."

Emma relaxed in her seat and watched as he exited the car and crossed the street. *Yes, it looks like today is shaping up to be a mighty fine Lord's Day.*

Chapter Nine

Drew held Emma close and inhaled the sweet, herbal scent of her hair. "Did you miss me?"

"Always."

He led her to the couch and pulled her close. "I missed you too. Thought of you every minute."

"Every minute? I'd like to believe that, but I do think you exaggerate, Mr. Brown."

He grinned. "Oh, maybe a wee bit, but you were never far from my thoughts." He cupped her chin in his hand and turned her face toward his. "How's work? Are you settling in okay?"

"I am. Elise has been a huge blessing, and thank you for introducing me to Clem. He's very kind. I think I'll be happy there."

A wave of relief washed over him. "That's good to hear. I'm glad I could oblige." He brushed her lips with his and tapped her nose with his finger. "Got to keep milady happy. Can't have you running home without me."

She grabbed his hands and straightened. "Oh, Drew. Speaking of home, you'll never guess who I ran into."

"Who?"

"Tank."

"Tank?

"I mean, Paul. Paul Porter."

"Who's Paul Porter?"

"Well, I didn't really know him, but I did see him a time or two in the Rainbow."

"In Fayetteville?"

"Yes, I'm so excited. Paul Porter served at Fort Bragg with Noah. He was the man you bought the rose from at Navy Pier."

"You don't say? So where did you bump into him?"

"Actually, I've seen him twice."

He questioned her with his eyes.

"No, it's not what you think. Our meetings were purely coincidental. Paul came into The Annex on Saturday night, and then I saw him again Sunday on the streetcar."

"Hmm ... so the lady says."

She slapped his arm. "Drew, stop it. I'm serious."

"I'm sorry. Carry on."

She leaned back on the sofa. "I was on my way to meet Elise at church when Paul boarded the streetcar. He was headed to work. On Sundays, he helps with maintenance at the pier. He wants to meet you and introduce us to his girlfriend who works there too." She moved forward and locked eyes with Drew. "And listen ... he says he can get us complimentary seats on the *Wendella*. He knows Captain Bo Borgstrom, who's taken people for lake and river tours in his ninety-six-passenger boat for four years. Doesn't that sound exciting?"

"It does. I've not been out on the water since I've been here. I'll welcome the chance to get some shots of Chicago's skyline. It should make a nice painting. Joe took a few of my watercolors into one of the galleries on Michigan Avenue. They asked him if I'd painted any Chicago scenes. The owner said if I'd bring a few in, he'd hang them. Joe says he's very impressed with my work."

She leaned over and kissed his cheek. "Oh, honey. That's wonderful. Who wouldn't want one of your paintings on their wall? I'm so proud of you."

Drew tucked her hair behind her ear. "So getting back to Paul. When is this excursion?"

"I'm not sure. We didn't have a chance to finish our

conversation. The trolley arrived at his stop, and he got off. He told me he'd come by The Annex soon to talk more about it.

"Terrific. I'll look forward to it. Should give me lots of inspiration for my new venture."

She pulled away and rose from the couch. "How about some tea?"

"What? You mean you've already forgotten I'm a teetotaler?" He laughed. "Rainbow Girl #9 *never* forgot."

Placing her hands on her hips, she smirked. "Okay. I know. Coffee with cream and two cubes of sugar coming right up. How's that, Mr. Brown?"

"Sounds like my cup of tea."

Emma rolled her eyes and shook her head. "Oh, my goodness, you're hopeless," she said, walking into the kitchen.

Drew picked up a magazine from the end table and flipped through it. "Something warm will feel good. I can't shake this chill. The wind is brutal tonight."

She pulled two mugs from the cabinet and shouted from the kitchen. "I know what you mean. I'm having a difficult time adjusting to Chicago's temperatures myself. My nose has run all day. It seems like I moved from summer to winter and skipped fall." She carried a tray to the living room and placed it on the coffee table.

Drew moved to the edge of the sofa. "Look at that. English shortbread biscuits." He reached for one and rolled his eyes as he bit in. "Yum. Where did you find these?"

"I stopped in for a pretzel at Dinkel's Bakery on Saturday and couldn't resist. I knew you'd like them." She handed him a napkin. "I should never have gone in there on an empty stomach. Mr. Dinkel's son had just taken them out of the oven and was sliding them into the case. Of course, he offered me one. I walked out with a dozen." She shrugged. "I bit, didn't I?"

Drew laughed. "I'll say, and it was a pretty big bite, but I'm glad you did. Next time, you'll have to try Mr. Dinkel's sour cream donuts." He wiped his mouth with his napkin and reached for his second biscuit. "You'll never again look at donuts the same."

Emma lifted the pot of steeping tea from the tray, filled her mug, and dropped in two sugar cubes before settling back on the couch and sipping its warmth. "Joseph's such a nice man. He told me their family is from Bavaria, and they're worried about their relatives in Germany. His cousin owned a bakery in Berlin. Last November, it was destroyed during Kristallnacht—the night of broken glass. SA Storm Troopers and civilians terrorized the streets, smashing Jewish storefronts with sledgehammers. Ninety-one Jews were killed. Even more, if you count the massive suicides which followed. His nephew and thousands of other Jewish men were beaten and hauled off to concentration camps. His wife hears nothing from him. She's afraid and fears for the life of their one-year-old son. Joseph is trying to help them get to America."

"Gads, I hope he can get them here." Drew shook his head with disgust as anger rose from his toes and coursed through his veins. "Hitler's Germany. Someone needs to assassinate that madman. Too many people turning blind eyes to the evil rising in the streets of their beautiful homeland. Hitler rules by intimidation. Horrible. Sheer evil."

"It *is* unimaginable. I'm sorry I brought it up. Who would have thought tea and shortbread would have sparked this conversation, but we mustn't turn blind eyes either. Our world is in terrible shape. Every night, I pray that the Lord will bring this horrible war in Europe to a swift end and that He'll keep it away from America's shores."

"Anything else exciting happen while I was gone?"

She sipped her tea. "Mmm. Yes. I visited Elise's church—First Baptist, over on 50th Street. It was a very nice service, and I met her daughter, Abigail. Have you met her?"

"I have. Abby is delightful. Disability or not, she lifts the spirits of everyone she meets. Her laughter is infectious."

"It is. One would have thought she'd known me her whole

life. She scooted right in beside me on the pew and studied my every move. When the congregation stood to sing, she sang at the top of her lungs and moved with the music. That child's got rhythm. I'm sure she brought a smile to her heavenly Father's face."

He chuckled. "A big one for sure."

"I told Elise I'd be happy to keep Abby some time so that she can have a day to herself."

"I know she appreciated that."

"After church, I came back here and caught up on my letter writing. I received several letters from home on Saturday."

"That's good. How are things in Fayetteville?"

She placed her mug on the coffee table. "Good. Everyone misses me—even Chummy. Tucker wrote that Mama T says he's exchanged his perch on the porch swing for the comfort of my bed pillows."

"Tucker?" He rubbed the back of his neck. "You going to be writing him a lot?"

She studied Drew's face. "I don't know. Why?"

He shrugged. "Just curious."

She leaned over and kissed his cheek. "Drew, is that jealousy I see in your eyes?"

"Maybe a wee bit."

She swatted his arm. "Well, stop it. It's not becoming." She reached for a biscuit, broke off a piece, and popped it in her mouth. "I've been thinking. Let's visit Fayetteville over the holidays."

He grimaced. "That's not possible, Peaches. Holidays are busy for me. Stores run more ads to generate Christmas sales."

She lowered her head.

Drew lifted Emma's chin and looked into her eyes. "Don't fret, love. I'll figure out a way to get you home if you want to go."

Her eyes brightened. "You will?" She threw her arms around his waist and laid her head on his chest. "Oh, sweetheart, thank you, but I could never leave you alone at Christmas."

"You won't be. I'm not that big-hearted. I meant *after* Christmas." He kissed her nose and stroked her cheek with his thumb. "Christmas Day is ours alone. I've already told Joe and Helen not to count on us for dinner. I'm cooking."

Emma's jaw dropped open. "Really? You?" She clapped her hands. "Oh, I *must* stick around for this. Do you think we could get a tree too? It would be so much fun to decorate it together."

"Of course, we can. It wouldn't be Christmas without one." He pointed toward the balcony door. "We'll set it up right over there, where the glittering lights of Chicago will be its backdrop."

She bounced with excitement, splashing coffee from Drew's cup. "Oh, I'm sorry." She snatched a napkin from the tray and dabbed coffee from his pant leg. "I can hardly wait. This will be the best Christmas ever."

He placed his mug on the table. "My thoughts exactly." Clasping her wrist, he pulled her close and thought of the gift he had for her. "The first of many Christmases, Peaches." His lips moved toward hers. "The best is yet to come. You'll see."

Chapter Ten

Monday, September 18, 1939
Fayetteville, North Carolina
Tucker

Tucker pulled his green and black 1933 Chevrolet Master Coupe to a stop and shut off the engine. He hadn't been inside the yellow clapboard house on Maiden Lane since the night he'd encouraged Emma to give Noah a chance to explain Alice's letter. Pushing back the memory, he snatched his tweed cabbie hat from the passenger's seat and swallowed hard. Emma was gone. Her heart belonged to another. Slapping his cap on his head, he hopped from the car. *Time to let go.*

He unlatched the rusty gate, stepped onto the weather-beaten porch, and rang the bell. Within moments Mama T swung open the door. "Looky here. If it isn't Sergeant Baldwin. Come in, young man. Come right on in. It's good to see you."

Welcoming Mama T's tight squeeze, he slipped off his hat. "Mmm. It certainly smells good in here. What's cooking?"

"Got a couple of apple pies in the oven. A new neighbor from up north moved in across the street. Thought I'd give her a huge dose of southern hospitality." She squinted her eyes and tapped her pursed lips with her index finger. "The other pie … Hmmm … let's see. I suppose it could be cut for an unexpected visitor—if they liked apple pie, that is." She raised her eyebrows. "Got some vanilla ice cream in the icebox. Surely, you've got time for a pipin' hot slice of homemade pie with a big dollop of ice cream on top."

He laughed and tossed his hat on the sofa. "Just try to run me outta here."

"That's my man. Come on back. I'll pour you a glass of milk while we wait."

Tucker followed her through the sitting room into the large yellow kitchen at the back of the house. "Have a seat." She motioned toward the white pedestal table in the center of the room, then flung open the cabinet, pulled out a couple of glasses and plates, and placed them on the table. "I sure have missed having you youngsters around here. What brings you out this way on this nice fall day?"

"Had a bit of shopping to do over at Fleishman's. I wasn't about to head back to the base without saying hello. Things going good?"

She propped her hands on her hips and laughed. "Good as can be expected, I guess, for an almost eighty-two-year-old youngster."

He waved her off. "You're amazing. I hope I have your kind of energy at that age."

She bustled to the icebox and pulled out a bottle of milk and a carton of ice cream. "Can't stop now. Got too much to do and little time to do it in." She lifted a large spoon and a couple of forks from the drawer, then plopped the carton on the table and sat across from him. "You're the man I've wanted to see."

He shot her a questioning glance. "Me?"

"Yep. Gotta proposition for you."

He leaned back in his chair and folded his arms. "You don't say? It's been quite a while since I've been propositioned by a pretty lady."

She gave him a dismissive wave. "Always the charmer." Leaning forward, she folded her arms on the table. "I sure could use some help around here. This old house is startin' to fall in around me. Thought you might like to make a few extra bucks on the side. That is if the U.S. Army wouldn't object."

"He threw back his head. "Ha, no chance of Uncle Sam making a fuss. He's a tough taskmaster, always keen on hard work. What do you have in mind?"

"Suppose I should start with the front porch since that's what people see from the road. It could use a fresh coat of paint. Needs a few floorboards replaced and a new chain put on the swing." She chuckled. "Wouldn't want Chummy to go a tumbling or my guests to fall through a trap door."

"Repairs I can manage. I'll feel right at home. Mother always had odd jobs for me to do around our boarding house in Louisville."

"You don't say? I didn't know your family owned a boarding house."

"Yep. The Captain's Inn. My father's a tugboat captain on the Ohio River. He's gone for weeks at a time, and Mother always needs something done around the house."

Her eyes twinkled. "A man with experience. Hired!" She slapped her hand on the table. "When do you think you could start?"

"Is right now soon enough?"

Her mouth dropped open. "Mercy me. I should say so."

"Terrific. Jot down the items you need, and I'll run over to Powell's Hardware and pick up the supplies. Then we'll set a day for me to come and work."

Mama T clapped her hands. "Tucker Baldwin, you're a blessing from above." Sniffing the air, she sprang from her seat, snatched a couple of hot pads from the counter, and yanked open the oven door. "Whew. Perfect." She laughed. "Let's put a little meat on those bones of yours, sonny. Gotta keep you strong if you're gonna be workin' around here."

She served Tucker a large piece of steaming hot pie, then cut a piece for herself and returned to her seat. "Tell me now. Have you heard anything from Emma? It's about time someone hears."

He scooped a hefty spoonful of ice cream onto his pie and dug in. "Actually, I got a letter from her yesterday." He chased down a large bite with a swallow of milk and wiped his mouth with his napkin. "She mentioned she'd written you too. Maybe you'll get yours today."

She grinned. "I hope you're right. I sure miss that young lady."

"That makes two of us. Emma sounds happy. Likes her job at Berghoff's and says the city is amazing."

She lowered her head. "I don't know whether to laugh or cry about that news. I hate to be selfish, but there's been a small part of me hoping she wouldn't take to big city life."

He nodded. "I understand. I'm not proud of it, but that's been my thinking too. I've had to remind myself that love always wants what's best for the other person, and our happiness should never be dependent on their misfortune." He placed his napkin on the table. "Thank you. That hit the spot, but this day is getting away from us. I suppose I should get on over to Powell's and pick up your supplies."

Dropping her fork on her plate, Mama T jumped from her chair. "Oh, yes, I'll make that list right now, and you can be on your way."

Tucker pushed back from the table and crossed his legs. He thanked God for this home away from home—a place where he always felt safe and far away from the distant rumblings of war on the horizon.

Tucker lifted several boards to his shoulder, laid them against the house, then walked back to the trunk for the rest of the supplies. Setting them beside the door, he rang the bell and surveyed the ceiling. He might have to call in the troops for this assignment. Opening the screen, he knocked on the sun-bleached door, then pressed his ear to it. With images of what could be flashing through his mind, he knocked louder, then pushed open the door and shouted. "We're all set, sweet lady."

His words were met only by a soft meow. Stepping into the foyer, he peered into the sitting room. Chummy sat on the floor beside Mama T's sprawled body, mail scattered at her head. Rushing to her side, Tucker placed his thumb on her wrist and groaned.

Chapter Eleven

Tuesday, September 26, 1939
Chicago, Illinois
Emma

Emma pulled the mail from her box in the Union Park Hotel apartments and shuffled through a stack of sales flyers and bills. Her spirit sank. She'd hoped to return home to news from Fayetteville.

Pushing through her disappointment, she chatted with the new elevator attendant, then opened the door to her cozy apartment. She'd never take her view of Chicago's skyline for granted. Whether daytime or night, it was enchanting.

Sighing, she tossed the mail on the counter, watched it slide across the Formica, and heard it hit the floor in the living room. As she gathered it from the carpet, she turned over one of the envelopes and chuckled. "Tucker Baldwin, where were you hiding? You've slid into my life once again, haven't you?" Placing his letter on the coffee table, she walked into the kitchen and lit the burner under the kettle.

Emma slipped into her flannel pajamas and chenille robe, filled her Navy Pier mug with tea, and dropped onto the sofa. Tucking Mama T's afghan snugly around her legs, she laid her head on the armrest and sighed. *Finally.* She loved working at Berghoff's, but at times her customers seemed impossible. This had been one of those days. She took a sip of the warm chamomile tea and pulled Tucker's letter from the envelope. A whiff of aftershave tickled her nose. Smiling, she pictured her friend's face and nestled into the cushions.

Tuesday, September 19, 1939

Hi Em,

I hope this letter finds you doing well and continuing to enjoy your new surroundings. How's Drew? I know he's taking good care of you.

This has been a tough week, but God has blessed us in the midst of it. Yesterday, He was gracious enough to place me where I was needed. I'd picked up a few things at Fleishman's before dropping by Mama T's. It delighted her to serve me a large slice—well, maybe it was a *hu*ge slice of homemade apple pie fresh from the oven. Oh, and I mustn't forget the ice cream. What a treat. She then asked if I would help her with some repair work around the house. It certainly does need it, and I'm happy to help. I made a trip to the hardware store for supplies, but I couldn't get her to the door when I returned.

Emma sat up, her heart racing.

Whenever I stepped inside, I found her sprawled on the floor, unconscious. Of course, I feared the worst and was relieved to find a faint pulse. The hospital kept her overnight. Although she's bruised and has a cut on her forehead, she's recovering nicely and should be fine. The neighbors have pitched in and are keeping a close watch on her.

Mama T said that when she came in from the mailbox, she tripped over Chummy and hit her head on the corner of the coffee table. Again, I'm thankful God had me in the right place at the right time. I shudder to think of how long she would have lain on the floor had I not been there to help her and call the ambulance. My medic training paid off. God is good.

Letting out a long breath, Emma placed the letter in her lap and thanked God for sparing Mama T. She prayed for her complete recovery, then finished her tea and returned to Tucker's letter.

What are your plans for the holidays? I sure hope it includes a trip home. We all miss you terribly, and Mama T would love to have you under her roof again. Chummy too. Of course, you'll probably have to fight him for your pillows.

Things here at the base are ramping up. The news from Europe is dire, and our future role in this horrific war is so uncertain. Morale is still good, and most of the fellas are ready to do whatever it takes to protect our nation and the world from this mad dictator.

I'm sure you've heard of Germany's U-boat attack on the Royal Navy in the Atlantic this past Sunday evening. The torpedoing of the HMS Courageous killed 518 of our allies and has heightened our alert here at Bragg. We live in perilous times, and I understand more and more the words found in Matthew. *"Take therefore no thought for the morrow ... Sufficient unto the day is the evil thereof."*

Outside of the crucifixion of Christ, this world has never seen the likes of such wickedness. I take comfort in knowing the One who died for me now lives and will never leave us or forsake us. Whatever comes, Em, know I'll be okay ... and so will you. Don't ever doubt it.

A friend loves at all times, and this is one of those times.

Tucker

Emma stared at the Chicago skyline as she folded and

returned the letter to its envelope. Tucker's world was vastly different from hers. Perhaps it was a false sense of security, but she felt safe among Chicago's towering buildings. It was as if the skyscrapers formed a barrier protecting her from the forces beyond.

She tucked the letter into the large Bible on the coffee table and returned to the kitchen. Placing her cup in the sink, she vowed to hold onto her Pollyanna spirit and her God—the keeper of all of her tomorrows.

The next evening

Drew hung his hat and overcoat on the hall tree, pulled Emma close, and kissed her. "How was your day off?"

"Divine." Looping her arm through his, she led him to the small drop leaf table in front of the balcony's glass doors and poured a cup of coffee from the carafe. "Sit here while I pull your plate from the oven."

Tilting his head, he rubbed the back of his neck. "So what was divine about today?"

"Hang on. I'll tell you in a minute."

When she returned, she placed a plate of meatloaf, green beans, and oven-roasted potatoes in front of him, then poured hot water over a teabag in her mug. Taking the seat opposite him, she peered into his eyes and grinned.

"What?"

"Are you ready?

"Sure. Tell it."

"I started my book."

He buttered his bread. "Oh, you have. So what are you reading?"

"No, Drew. I said I started *my* book?"

His eyes grew large as he lifted his fork piled high, then

hesitated. "*Your* book? Truth?"

She nodded. "Yes, I'm telling you the truth. I can't believe it myself. I actually put pen to paper." She pulled a black and white marbled composition book from the sideboard, held it in front of him, and thumbed through several pages.

He scooped a forkful of meatloaf into his mouth, then reached for it.

"Nope," she said, yanking it to her chest. "This is for my eyes only." She laid it on the table and ran her hand across the slick surface of the cover. "Besides, you might get grease on it." She glanced up. "I'm certain romance novels aren't your genre, anyway."

He shrugged. "I've got nothing against romance." He winked. "In fact, I rather enjoy it."

She lowered her eyes as heat rose in her cheeks. "I'm not far enough into my story to let anyone read the first ramblings of my heart. A less than stellar review would crush my creativity." She thumbed through the pages. "I'm not convinced these words will ever see the light of day, anyway, but for now, I'm following my heart."

He wiped his mouth with his napkin. "I'm proud of you, Peaches. I know you can do it. And whenever you're ready, you should let me give it to Joe. Helen loves to read. Her opinion would be valuable, and I imagine she'd know someone who could edit it for you. She and Joe have a lot of connections in this city."

"Thanks. I'll keep that in mind, but I'm a long way from needing an editor." She returned the book to the sideboard. "How was your day?"

"It doesn't rise to the level of *divine*, but I do have a bit of good news."

"Really?" She placed her elbows on the table and raised her mug to her lips. "Please. Tell me more."

Laying his napkin on the table, he pushed back in his chair and pulled a small envelope from his shirt pocket.

"I was wondering about that. I noticed it peeking out of your pocket."

He held it in front of her, yanking it back as she reached for it. "Oops. Are your hands clean?"

She grimaced and plopped her cup on the table, splashing the tablecloth. "Stop it, Drew. What is it?"

"Not so fast, lassie." He tapped the envelope on the palm of his hand and stared through the glass doors. "Nice night tonight, isn't it?"

"Dr-ew!"

Throwing back his head, he laughed and handed her the envelope.

She grabbed the knife from beside his plate, slit the top of the envelope, and peeked in. Furrowing her brow, she looked up. "Tickets? Did you get us season tickets to the Cubs' games?"

He shrugged. "Maybe."

She slid a small folder from the envelope and opened it. Her eyes, filling with tears, shot to Drew's. "Are you serious? Train tickets?"

He nodded.

She jumped from her chair and landed in his lap, planting multiple kisses on his lips. "Oh, Drew. How can I ever thank you? Mama T will be so happy." Barely taking a breath, she babbled on. "I haven't had time to tell you. She fell, but she's okay, and this will lift her spirits. I can't wait to write her, and Penny, and Tucker, and—"

He placed his finger on her lips and chuckled. "Whoa. Do you think you could show a wee bit more enthusiasm?"

She wrapped her arms around his neck and stared into his clear blue eyes. "December 27th will be perfect. We'll spend Christmas Day together. I have a surprise in store for you as well." She laid her head on his chest and melted in his embrace. She hadn't been this excited about the holidays since she was a little girl.

Chapter Twelve

Wednesday, July 4, 2012
Hope Mills, North Carolina
Caroline

Claire led Kate and me down the narrow hallway of the modest home to Tucker's bedroom. "Mr. B, you have company."

The frail man opened his eyes and squinted. "I do?"

"Yes, they're pretty visitors too." She motioned for us to sit in chairs at the foot of the hospital bed. "The ladies never leave you alone, do they?

"Ha. I guess not. Raise me up, will you, Claire? And pass me my glasses, please."

Slipping them on, he peered at us. "Now, whaddya know. It's Emma's girls. So nice to see you again."

I stood and walked to his bedside. "What's nicer is us seeing you, Tucker. You gave us a real scare the other week. Kate and I are happy you're better." I handed him a bud vase containing a single red rose. "We brought something to cheer you up." I unpinned an envelope from the red, white, and blue striped ribbon.

Reaching for it, he chuckled. "They say I'm better, but I'm not sure they've told my body yet." He slipped the card from the small envelope and read the sentiment aloud. "Get well soon, friend. Friends love at all times, Caroline and Kate." He raised his cloudy dark eyes to mine, then cut them towards Kate. With tears welling, his voice cracked. "How thoughtful. Thank you. It's such an honor to have Emma's daughters as my new friends."

I set the vase on the bedside table and returned to my seat.

Kate placed her purse on the floor and sat back in her chair. "I think mother had a little something to do with bringing us together, don't you?"

"You're probably right." He chuckled. "Turns out, I almost paid your mother a visit. When I think about it, that wouldn't have been so bad." He laid his hand on his chest. "They tell me my ole ticker stopped for a bit."

"But God knew we needed you down here." Kate wagged her finger in time with her words. "Besides, you can't cut out on us in the middle of a good story. How rude would that be?"

He grinned. "That wouldn't have been gentlemanly at all, would it?"

I chimed in. "We don't want to tire you out, but we'd love for you to share more of your story while we're here."

"Of course, I'd be happy to. I never tire of talking about my early years—especially the special ladies in my life." He laughed. "Thoughts of those days take my mind off this old worn-out body for a few moments." He smoothed his thinning white hair and laid his head back on his pillow. "Where were we, anyway?"

Kate said, "You were telling us of your letters from Mother when she was in Chicago and how you'd hoped she'd come home for Christmas."

"Oh, yes. We all missed Emma and secretly hoped she'd give up on big-city life. Turns out she loved it, and the most those of us left behind could hope for was a holiday visit."

"Did she come?"

"Oh, she got home all right, but not the way we expected."

Saturday, November 25, 1939
Chicago, Illinois
Emma

Drew grasped Emma's hand as she stepped down into the hull of the *Wendella,* then followed her. She introduced him to Paul Porter, who ushered them through a crowd gathering in the stern and past the captain's wheelhouse to the front of the sixty-five-foot-long wooden vessel. Four rows of cushioned benches packed with excited passengers filled the boat's bow. A petite young lady jumped from the front row and motioned for them to join her. Paul kissed her on the cheek, then placed his arm around her waist and proudly announced, "Emma and Drew, I'd like for you to meet my fiancée, Camille."

The attractive auburn-haired girl, with a smattering of freckles across her nose, extended her hand. "It's nice to meet you both." She sat and patted the place beside her, "Emma, sit here by me. Paul has told me so much about you and the Rainbow Restaurant. I know we'll have lots in common—stories galore, I'm sure." She pulled her gloves from her pocket and slipped them on. "How was your Thanksgiving?"

"Quiet, but nice. Drew and I ate at Berghoff's. They had quite a spread."

Taking his place beside Emma, Drew draped his Leica camera around his neck, then slipped the case with his new lenses underneath the bench along with his tripod. Emma looked into his eyes and smiled. "You're excited, aren't you, honey?"

He winked. "Oh, maybe a wee bit." As his eyes scanned Lake Michigan, he took a deep breath. "It feels good to be on the water again, and we've lucked out with today's unseasonably warm weather. The light should be perfect. Hopefully, I'll come away with some terrific golden-hour shots of Chicago's skyline." He adjusted the scarf at his neck and zipped his jacket. "I feel a painting about to erupt from my bones."

Emma looped her arm through his. "I'm so happy I bumped into Paul. It never hurts to know someone who knows someone. Since you do so many nice things for me, it did my heart good to arrange this for you."

He rubbed the back of her hand. "It couldn't be nicer."

"I'm glad you're pleased. I was afraid this voyage would be

too small potatoes for the son of a Scottish sea captain, but for me—a girl who's only been in a rowboat on my Aunt Nell's lily-pad pond—it's amazing."

Drew pulled her close and whispered in her ear. "*You* are amazing. Peaches, with you by my side, nothing is small potatoes. Thank you so much."

"Oh—I have one more surprise."

"Another?"

"Yes. Captain Borgstrom's invited us to join him inside the wheelhouse later this evening. He's serving hot chocolate and shortbread cookies."

Drew's eyes widened. "You don't say? How about that. I look forward to meeting him and seeing this powerhouse up close." He pulled a folded blanket from a stack on the end of the bench and spread it over their laps. "Better button your coat. Once we pull out and the sun drops, it will get cold."

She laid her head on his shoulder. "Oh, but why do you think I brought you?"

He kissed her hair and laughed. "Smart lass, you are. I'll take this assignment any day."

As the *Wendella* eased away from the dock onto Lake Michigan, Emma buttoned her fur-collared coat and pulled on gloves matching her teal-colored toboggan. While Paul and Drew talked Chicago Cubs, Emma chatted with Camille.

Once offshore, Emma sat mesmerized. As Chicago's towering architecture glimmered in the setting sun, the tour guide directed their attention to buildings of interest. Drew pointed. "Look, Em. There's the Tribune Tower. Even from this vantage point, it's imposing, isn't it?"

"This whole city is magnificent. I still can't get over the fact I'm here—that this is my life, my city. I may never want to leave this place."

Drew pulled her closer. "Careful. Don't get too attached, wee lass. Assignments come and go, but each one is a new adventure. There's lots more for us to see across this great land. This is simply the beginning."

She kissed him on the cheek. "I know you're right. Wherever I am, as long as I'm with you, I'll be happy."

Drew bent down, pulled his photography gear from beneath the seat, and passed the camera case to Emma. "Let's set up over by the railing. The sun's about in position. It won't take long for it to drop behind the buildings, and I want to be ready."

While Drew raced to capture the fleeting rays and shifting shadows of the setting sun, Emma sat on the arm of a nearby bench, ready to pass him the next lens. She was more than willing to be his helpmate and to view life through the lens of togetherness—forever.

Drew, barely able to contain his excitement, nodded his appreciation to Carl as he and Emma passed through the doors of the Union Park Hotel apartments. "Tonight's sunset was spectacular. I can hardly wait to get my film developed. I'll be pounding on the door of the drugstore first thing Monday morning."

"I bet you will. The evening *was* marvelous. The shimmering Christmas lights made the city appear magical. I'm sure you've got some amazing images to work from. Joe will be one happy man when you hand him your cityscapes."

"I will be too. I'm itching to get the first canvas on the easel. My showing in the gallery sounds promising."

As they stopped in the foyer to pick up their mail, Emma faced Drew. "I know you have a lot to do between now and Christmas, but do you think we could get our tree soon. Tonight's tour put me in the mood to decorate."

He cupped her chin in his palm and kissed her. "Of course, we can. We'll go one evening next week and pick it out."

Emma wrapped her arms around his waist and returned his

kiss. "I'm so excited. Thank you."

Stepping onto the elevator, they greeted Tessa, the young new attendant. "Second floor? Right, Mr. Brown?"

"It is, dear. Looks like you're getting the hang of this job."

"I'm doing my best to connect my passengers with their floors, but some people are more memorable than others. You and Miss Walsh are pretty hard to forget. You two give me hope for finding my own true love one day."

"You'll meet him." Drew pulled Emma close. "It took me thirty-one years to find this jewel, but good things come to those who wait. Don't get in a hurry. Let it happen."

She leveled the elevator and slid open the brass gate. "I'll keep that in mind."

Drew kissed Emma lightly on the lips. "I'll see you sometime tomorrow. You headed to church in the morning?"

"Yes, Abby will be looking for me. Wanna go?"

"Not this time. I plan to finish my current project this weekend, so I can paint for Joe later in the week. I'll go with you soon, though, I promise."

"O-kay." She gave him a questioning gaze and grinned. "I'll be sure to pray for you."

He stepped off the elevator, looked back, and blew her a kiss. "Please do. I need it."

As the doors closed, Emma dropped back against the wall and shuffled through her mail. Her heart leaped—news from home. *Tucker was always faithful to write.*

Tessa brought the car to a stop on the sixth floor and pulled open the brass gate. "I'm off tomorrow, but I'll see you Monday."

"Excellent." Emma stepped into the hall. "Enjoy your day of rest. You're doing a great job."

Once inside her apartment, she hung her coat on the hall tree and kicked off her shoes. Dropping onto the couch, she pulled Tucker's letter from the stack, fell back against the cushions, and tore open the envelope.

Sunday, November 19, 1939

Hi Emma,

I have little time to write today, so this will be short. I hate to be the bearer of bad news again, but you need to know. Mama T was admitted to Highsmith this morning. She's stable now, but they say her heart is failing. I know Drew bought you a train ticket for the Wednesday after Christmas, but do you think there's any way you could come sooner? Although Mama T may rebound, I'm not comfortable with you waiting. She asked for you earlier this morning, and I had to remind her you were in Chicago. She's not thinking clearly. I tried to reach you today, but I imagine you were at church. Call me collect whenever you get this. If Mama T gets worse this week, I'll try again. Until then, we'll pray for the best.

A friend loves at all times, and this is one of those times.

Tucker

Chapter Thirteen

Monday, November 27, 1939
Emma

Elise came through the back door of The Annex's kitchen. "Hi, Emma. Were you able to get your tickets changed?"

"Drew's working on it for me today." She slid the last of an order onto her tray. "I don't know what I would have done without him. He's been so understanding and helpful."

"Wonderful." She hung her coat on the hook in the pantry, then walked over and hugged her friend. "Thanks for calling me last night. I know you're worried about Mama T. Hopefully, when you get to Fayetteville, you'll find her doing better than you expected."

"I pray you're right. I spoke with Tucker last night. He says she gets stronger every day, but the doctors won't release her until they're sure she has twenty-four-hour care at home. Tucker's talking with her friends, Mrs. Priddy and Mrs. Brumble. Perhaps they'll help out for a while."

Elise put her apron over her head and tied it behind her. "Abigail and I missed you at church yesterday."

"I missed being there, but I had quite a bit to get caught up on before I leave this week."

"Abby saved you a seat. Even though I told her you weren't coming, she wouldn't allow anyone to sit beside her. She sat her baby doll in your place and kept telling people, "No, that's my Emwa's seat.""

"Aww. She's a doll baby herself." She placed the last item on her tray. "I missed my Sunday hug."

"Well, here it is." She threw her arms around Emma again and laughed. "Abby told me to give you a hug from her and to tell you she's 'pwaying' for you."

"How could God not listen to her sweet voice? Hug her back and tell her I love her and am sure God will take care of me. Tell her I'll see her soon."

"I will." She reached for Emma's tray. "If you want to leave a few minutes early, I'll take this out to the table for you."

"Thank you. I believe I will call it a day. Drew wants me to stop in when I get back to the apartments. Hopefully, he'll have good news for me about my trip home."

She motioned. "Hurry off then. I've got it, missy." She lifted the tray above her head and disappeared into the dining room.

Untying her apron, Emma sighed. "I know you do, sweet friend. I know you do."

"Hi, Peaches. Come in."

Drew wrapped Emma in his arms as she entered his second-floor apartment. Kissing her, he then brushed her nose with his. "Brr. Cold nose."

She rolled her eyes, grinned, and slipped off her coat and hat. "Better than a cold heart."

He took a step back, bumping his chest several times with his fist. "Whoa. That hurts."

She giggled and batted the air with her gloves. "The temperature is really plummeting. WGN says we may see a few flurries tonight and tomorrow."

"So I hear." He hung her coat in the entryway closet, pulled her close, and pressed his forehead against hers. "Good cuddling weather. I've missed you today."

"I've missed you too." She kissed him, then tilted her head upward and sniffed the air. "Mmm. Popcorn."

He laughed. "Yeah. And you thought I couldn't cook.

Should taste good on a cold wintery night, don't you think?"

She followed him into the kitchen. "Popcorn is always good."

"Grab a couple of Cokes from the icebox, will you?" he said as he pulled a large bowl down from the cabinet. "How was your day?"

"Hectic. Besides work, my mind is cluttered with all the things I need to do before I leave." She set the bottles on the counter, pulled an opener from the drawer, and popped the tops. Taking a gulp of the frosty soda, she plopped onto a chrome Z-barstool in the corner and leaned back against the wall. "This tastes good. How about your day? Did you finish your project?"

"Almost. I worked on it early this morning, before I left for the train station."

Her eyes widened as she straightened and slid from the stool. "Were you able to get my tickets changed?"

"Sure did."

Her voice slid up an octave as she blurted, "So when—when do I leave?"

Motioning with his head toward the living room, he grabbed several napkins from a basket on the counter and picked up the bowl of popcorn. "Come in here, and I'll show you."

She followed close on his heels. "Drew, that's a huge bowl of popcorn. What on earth were you thinking? We'll never eat—" She halted, then rushed to the corner of the room. "What? Oh, honey. When? When did you ever find time to do this?" Her eyes traveled up the trunk of a tall cedar in the corner, draped with colored lights. "I don't know what to say." Her eyes shot to his. "It's beautiful. And what a lovely tree-topper."

He looked at the large metal circle with three interwoven points and hesitated before speaking. "It's a Celtic Knot. A gift passed down to my mum from our relatives in Ireland—a symbol of family. The three points represent mind, heart, and soul, or the Trinity—Father, Son, and Holy Spirit. The interwoven points suggest eternity. Mum gave it to me the day I left Dundee for

Canada. She wanted me to never forget my heritage and our family's love."

"How sweet. Your mother seems like a precious lady. I want to meet her." She spun on her heels and ran to Drew. "Maybe someday we can visit them." Wrapping her arms around his waist, she laid her head on his chest. "And hopefully, someday, we'll have a family of our own to love." She kissed him. "You are too good to me, Drew Brown."

He rubbed her back. "Impossible. Not knowing if you'd make it back for Christmas, I wanted to be sure we celebrated together."

She lifted her head and gazed into his eyes. "I can't bear the thought of us being separated this Christmas. Please go with me?"

He kissed her hair. "That's not possible, sweetheart. I'm sorry."

"Tucker says, Mama T's improving, so maybe, I'll be back by then. When do I leave, anyway?"

"Friday—ten o'clock."

She dropped her forehead to his chest.

"Don't fret. I'll fix dinner for us on Thursday." He lifted her chin. "We'll celebrate before you go. How does that sound?"

Her eyes brightened. "Perfect. Then, if I get back before Christmas, we'll have a quiet day to simply enjoy being together."

"If you get off in time tomorrow, drop by, and we'll finish decorating the tree."

"I'll make time." She stroked his cheek. "Your mama raised you right. You think of everything. I'm happiest when I'm with you."

He tapped her nose and pointed to the bowl of popcorn on the table. "Now, now. Enough of this. We've got work to do."

"Drew, there's no way we can eat all that."

"He picked up a large spool of thread. "Eat? We're not eating it. We're stringing it." Laughing, he popped several kernels into his mouth and winked. "Most of it, anyway."

Chapter Fourteen

Thursday, November 30, 1939
Drew

Drew tucked the large rectangular package behind the tree and imagined Emma's excitement upon tearing into the paper. Mama T's illness had pushed him to finish early, but after several late nights, the results had been worth it. Hopefully, Emma would be pleased.

He walked into the kitchen, opened the oven, and breathed in the aroma of the heavenly feast. Two Cornish game hens stuffed with wild rice and mushrooms sizzled in the roasting pan. He kissed his fingertips and flicked them into the air. "Perfection." Turning off the heat, he closed the door and peeked into two pots on the stovetop. One was filled with bubbling glazed yams and the other creamy snow peas. A sly grin spread across his face. Maybe he hadn't lost his touch.

A soft tap on the door interrupted his thoughts. He lowered the flames beneath the pots, then he walked into the entryway. "Who is it?"

"Now, who would you be expecting, smarty britches?"

He flung open the door and placed his hands on his hips. "Yep, that would be her."

Chuckling, Emma blew past him, then whipped around. "My, oh my, look at you in your cute little apron."

Untying it, he pulled it off and smirked.

She spun around and peeked into the kitchen. "It smells amazing in here. Are you sure you didn't miss your calling?"

He shook his head. "No one's ever accused me of being

Betty Crocker." Pulling her toward him, he said. "Gotta get me a little lassie to take over in the kitchen. Know where I can find one?"

She dropped her purse and shopping bag to the floor, flung her arms around his neck, and planted a lingering kiss on his lips. "Maybe. What do *you* think?"

He pulled back and tapped his pursed lips with his index finger. "Hmm. I may need a bit of time to consider. Maybe even a do-over."

Emma swatted him, slipped off her coat, and hung it in the closet. "Anything I can do to help you?" She followed him into the kitchen.

"Nope. Everything's ready. Have a seat at the table, and I'll dish it up."

"Wow, isn't this a switch? I'm not accustomed to being waited on." She picked up her bags and walked into the living room. "You'd better watch out. I could get used to this royal treatment, you know."

While Emma pulled a present from her shopping bag and put it under the tree, Drew entered, placed two filled plates on the table, and lit the candles.

"Would that package be for me?"

She stood, then tipped her nose in the air. "Maybe."

He chuckled. "Have a seat. I'll get the tea." He returned from the kitchen, filled their glasses, then flipped off the lights and pulled open the drapes.

Emma placed her elbows on the table and rested her chin in her hands. "Wow! Tree lights, candlelight, and the Chicago night skyline, what could be better? I'll never tire of this view." She sighed. "I'm going to miss it."

Drew took his place across from her and tapped his fork on the table. "No, no. We have no time for that."

"I know. You're absolutely right." She squared her shoulders, placed the linen napkin in her lap, and sliced into the crispy hen. "I will not allow myself to upset this beautiful evening you've planned."

Emma draped the damp dishtowel over the oven door handle and kissed Drew's cheek. "Thank you, honey. The meal was delicious." She leaned against the sink. "I don't want to hurt your feelings, but your popcorn pales in comparison."

He chuckled. "I'm glad to hear it and happy tonight's dinner was edible. It's been a while since I've cooked." He walked over to a small drop leaf table in the corner and uncovered a cake plate. "Oh, but the best is yet to be—caramel shortbread with chocolate icing. The Browns never have a Christmas without this on the table."

"Oh, how yummy. You've certainly outdone yourself tonight."

"Shall we cut into it now or open our gifts first?"

Emma held her stomach. "I cast my vote for later. I'm stuffed."

"Later it will be then," he said, replacing the cover. "Give me a second to turn on the percolator, and we'll open our gifts while our dinner settles."

Drew returned and sat beside Emma on the couch. "Did you get all your packing done today?"

"I did. I was glad I took the day off. I would have been up all night if I hadn't."

"Is your sister meeting you at the station on Saturday?"

"She'd planned to, but Fleishman's is open late, and she has to cover for a salesgirl who had an emergency in her family. Tucker will meet me."

He rolled his eyes. "Of course. Good ole Tucker. Quite a fella, that one."

She huffed. "Yes, he is. He's a dear friend and kind to Mama T. I'm not sure how she'd get along without him at this point."

Drew leaned over, kissed her cheek, and then stood. "Let's get back to us—you. There may be something under the tree with your name on it. Have you been a good girl this year?"

"You know so, but I'd rather you open your present first. I love the anticipation as much as I do opening my gifts. I'll go last."

"You sure?"

She nodded.

He pointed to the package she'd placed under the tree. "Mine, right?"

She rolled her eyes and laughed. "I don't know. Maybe you'd better check the tag."

He picked up the gift. "It's heavy for such a small package." He returned to the couch and grinned. "And too pretty to open."

"I know. I fell in love with that paper. Marshall Fields had all of their Christmas wrap on sale last weekend. I couldn't resist."

He shook his head and chuckled. "So, would you prefer I not tear into it? Maybe save it till next year?"

She rolled her eyes. "Go ahead, silly. Rip into it. I have a whole roll of it upstairs."

As Drew slowly peeled off the paper, he read the lettering on the box. "Leica E55 macro close-up lens. Wow! How did you know I wanted this?"

She looked up at the ceiling. "A little birdie told me."

He bit his lip and nodded. "Yeah ... and I bet his name is Joe." He leaned over and kissed her. "You shouldn't have done this. It was much too expensive."

"But I wanted to. Nothing is too good for you, Drew."

He finished tearing off the paper, opened the box, and studied the lens nestled in the satin lining. "Wow. What a beauty. I can't wait to use it." He thumbed through the manual. "This will give me something to do while you're away." He kissed her again. "Now, it's your turn." He walked over and pulled his package from behind the tree.

Emma's eyes grew large. "That's for me?"

He handed it to her and smirked. "Want to check the tag?"

She stood, set the package on the floor, and ripped the paper down one side, revealing the back of a canvas. She looked up at Drew standing against the wall with a broad grin on his face.

"Go ahead. Finish the job."

Emma slowly pulled the paper from the 20 x 30 painting and gasped. "Oh, honey." Lifting it from the floor, she held it at arm's length. "I love it." She walked across the room, propped it against the wall, and backed away. "You captured the beauty of our first day together in Chicago perfectly. It's all flooding back to me."

He walked behind her, put his arms around her waist, and kissed her cheek. "I'm happy you like it. The picture I snapped of you at Navy Pier is one of my favorites. You had such a sense of wonder and excitement on your face. I never want us to forget our first day together in Chicago."

She turned around and looked into his eyes. "How could I ever forget that day or any of the days I've spent with you, for that matter. I'm the luckiest girl in the world. Thank you for choosing me." She placed her hands on his cheeks and kissed him.

Drew breathed in the lavender scent of her skin and returned her kiss before leading her to the couch. "I had another present for you, but when your plans to leave for Fayetteville changed, I couldn't get it here in time." He brushed her hair away from her face. "Be assured, I'll have it waiting for you when you return."

"Oh, honey, this beautiful portrait is *more* than enough. Don't worry about not having another gift for me." She lifted his arm, wrapped it around her shoulders, and scooted next to his side. "*This* is my gift. *You* are my gift. And by your side is where I want to stay. I have mixed emotions about leaving tomorrow. I want and need to be with Mama T, but I can't bear the thought of leaving you." She sat up and turned his face toward hers. "Promise me you'll be here waiting when I return. Promise me, Drew."

The apprehension in her eyes pierced his heart. Pulling her close, he kissed her. "Emma, of course, I promise. You know I'll be here. Tell me when your train is due, and I'll be at the station an hour early." He rested his chin on top of her head and sighed. His plans for their first Christmas together were shattered, and so was his heart.

Chapter Fifteen

Saturday, December 2, 1939
Fayetteville, North Carolina
Emma

Emma gripped Tucker's forearms and stared into his dark eyes. "Tell me. Is Mama T okay?"

His expression grew solemn. "She's some better today." Lifting her suitcase from the platform, he placed his hand around her waist and guided her toward the baggage car. "Come on. I know you're exhausted. Let's grab the rest of your things and talk over dinner. You hungry?"

"Famished. There was no food served onboard this evening."

He helped her into the car, tossed her bags in the trunk, and positioned himself behind the wheel. "Where to?"

"Surely you know. The Rainbow, silly." She smoothed the wrinkles in her skirt with her fingers. "Do you suppose Penny's working this evening? I'd love to surprise her."

As he shoved the gearshift into reverse, popped the clutch, and stepped on the gas, gravel sprayed from beneath the tires. "Welp, there's one way to find out."

Eddie Cantor, crooning "The Only Thing I Want for Christmas," spilled from the Wurlitzer as Tucker and Emma slid into a booth near the kitchen. He pulled two menus from behind the small potted poinsettia and slid one across the table. Emma surveyed the room. A waitress cleared the table near the door while two couples at a window booth finished their desserts.

The doors to the kitchen flew open. A tall, slender auburn-haired waitress carrying a pot of steaming hot coffee blew past them and approached the couples. Topping off their cups, she stood and chatted.

"Psst." Emma bumped Tucker's leg with her foot and whispered. "When Penny turns around, call her over here." She flipped open the menu and held it in front of her face.

Tucker stifled a laugh and waited for Penny to finish her conversation. When she turned to clear the next table, he motioned. "Hey, Penny. What does it take to get some service around here?"

Startled, she turned. "Tucker Baldwin." Smiling broadly, she walked across the room and pulled an order pad from her pocket. "I'm sorry. I didn't know anyone else was here."

He stood and hugged her. "It's great to see you."

"It's nice seeing you too. Where have you been keeping yourself? I've missed you." She slipped her pen from behind her ear, glanced at Emma, then shifted her eyes back to Tucker. "Now I know." She grinned. "What can I get for the two of you?"

Emma slapped her menu onto the table and laughed. "I'll take my usual."

Penny squealed. "Emma. Emma Rose Walsh! I can hardly believe my eyes." She placed the coffee pot on a table nearby, bent over, and squeezed her friend. "You look amazing. What are you doing in town? I didn't expect to see you for another couple of weeks."

"Tucker called to tell me about Mama T, so I decided to come early."

Penny's eyes dimmed. "I know. I hated to hear she was ill. She's such a precious woman. Breaks my heart." She nodded as customers in the next booth got up to leave. "I'm happy to see you, though. We sure do miss you around here. Cee keeps hoping you'll get tired of paying big-city rent and come home where you belong. How's Drew?"

"He's good. Staying really busy trying to finish a large commission before leaving for St. Louis next week."

Penny stepped back and put her hands on her hips. "Okay, Let's see it."

Emma furrowed her brow. "See what?"

"The ring."

She lifted her left hand. "Still wearing my birthstone. I haven't said 'yes' yet. Drew would get married tomorrow, but I'm all for taking it slow."

"Proud of you. We'll have to plan a day to catch up." She glanced at her watch. "Now, let's get your orders in before he shuts down the grill."

Emma smiled as Penny ducked into the kitchen. Wrapping her hands around the warm mug, she settled back in her seat and lifted her eyes to Tucker's. "Thank you for calling to tell me about Mama T. You have no idea how relieved I was when I got off the train this evening, and you told me she was better. I can't imagine this life without her."

"Thankfully, she's improving, but she's not out of the woods yet." He added cream and stirred his coffee until it became a rich caramel color. "Congestive heart disease is wicked. But, I must say, things do look brighter."

"Did you go by her house today?"

"Yes, I dropped in on her before I picked you up at the station. She was propped up in bed, and Mrs. Priddy was helping her with her supper."

"That makes me happy. I wondered who would be there to help, given that her sister isn't well. Mrs. Priddy is perfect. They've become good friends since they both assist with the church's bereavement ministry. And with Mrs. Brumble's help, I'm sure she'll have the best of care. How was her appetite tonight? Did she eat anything?"

"Not a lot, but she did drink a little broth through a straw and ate a bit of applesauce."

She nodded. "At least, it's a start. I wonder if she'll feel up to my visit tomorrow. I wouldn't want to do anything to set her back."

"The only thing that will set her back is if you fail to show up. Every time I visit, she asks me what day you're coming."

"What a sweetheart. I've missed her so much."

Penny brought their meals and topped off their coffee.

Emma slathered her fried egg sandwich with mayonnaise. "Tell me how you're doing, Tucker? Anyone new in your life?"

"If you mean, am I courting anyone ... I'm not. On the heels of investing several years into a relationship with my girl back home, I'm not ready to start over."

"I understand. I love Drew with all my heart, but I must admit I still grieve Noah's death. He's never far from my thoughts."

Tucker took a large bite of his burger. "Things are going well with the two of you, then?"

"They are. I love Chicago and my small apartment. It's several floors above Drew's, so it's easy to see one another when our schedules mesh. It does get lonely when he's gone, though. Next week, he leaves for St. Louis. He'll draw for the *Post-Dispatch* and won't be back for a couple of weeks. This was a good time for me to come home. Drew would like to get married so he can take me with him, but marriage isn't something I take lightly. It's too early to make a forever commitment."

Tucker dipped his last French fry in ketchup and popped it into his mouth. "I'm glad to hear that. I worry about you, Em, and pray you don't make a rash decision—one you'll regret down the road."

"Now, Tuck. Me? Whatever would give you that idea?"

"Should I list them?" He bit his bottom lip. "Hmm ... for starters, following a man to Chicago that you've only known a few months seems a little rash to me."

She rolled her eyes. "Now, you sound like my sister." She checked her watch. "Speaking of her, we should go. I'm sure her eyes are glued to the clock."

Tucker pushed back his plate while Emma sipped the last of her coffee. Wiping lipstick from the rim of her mug with her napkin, she placed it on the table. "It's been a long trip. I can't wait to drop into my feather bed tonight and rise to Lily's homemade biscuits in the morning."

"Yeah. Sounds like my digs with Uncle Sam, minus the rave reviews for the biscuits, of course."

Tucker picked up the bill and fell in behind Emma as they walked to the register. While Penny checked them out, Emma noted *The Fayetteville Observer* on the counter. Soviet War Planes Bomb Helsinki. She looked up at Tucker. Her heart plunged.

Chapter Sixteen

Friday, July 13, 2012
Asheboro, North Carolina
Caroline

I leaned forward in my chair beside the couch in Kate's small but picture-perfect living room and tapped her on the knee. "Kate. Do you hear me?" Though my mouth was moving, I knew my words no longer registered with my sister. The pained expression on her face told me she hadn't pushed past my previous statement. Who could blame her? I didn't want to utter the words myself, much less swallow them. Who would have thought one brief call from a stranger could knock one's world off its axis— my world—and now Kate's?

Kate sprang from her place on the couch and stormed across the room. Peering out the storm door, she choked out her words. "This is a joke, right? Tell me, it's a cruel joke." She twirled around, her arms wrapped tightly around her waist as if to comfort herself. "And you invited this maniac into my home? Seriously? You know nothing about this person."

"I'm sorry, Kate. I didn't know what else to do. Stephen is presiding over a sales meeting at the house this morning, and believe me, this is not a discussion we want to have in a public place. I tried to reach you several times on the drive over here. By the way, your voice mail is full. I couldn't get through."

Kate walked to a chair in front of the window, plopped down, then looked at the large clock on the wall. "And she's going to be here when?"

"Eleven-thirty."

"Why today?"

"She's passing through from Virginia on her way to her cousin's place on the coast. Actually, I felt sorry for her. She was quite shaken. Said she was taking a few days off of work to research her suspicions."

"Why didn't she research her ridiculous supposition before she dropped a bomb on our little piece of the world?"

"She said she had something to show us. She hopes we can shed some light on the possibility of its truth."

"What's this woman's name?"

"Maggie, something. Abrams, I think."

"How old is she?"

I shrugged. "Mature. Our ages, maybe? I don't know. I'm not in the habit of asking people their age."

"Hmm, how did she arrive at this absurd notion?"

"To tell you the truth, I didn't ask that either. She was convinced that she had something we needed to see. I couldn't tell her no."

Kate looked down at her faded housecoat and raised her fuzzy-slippered feet from the floor. "I hadn't planned on entertaining houseguests today." Bolting from her chair, she scuffed out of the room and down the hall.

I picked up a *Southern Living* magazine from the coffee table and blindly thumbed through it. Pages that would typically catch my eye were blurred by thoughts I couldn't rein in. I checked the clock. Five minutes more. I prayed she'd be on time and that this meeting would be quick and painless, and whatever Maggie had to show us would be easily explained or debunked. I simply wasn't ready for more drama.

Kate called from the bedroom.

"What?"

"She's here. She's pulling up in front of the house. Answer the door if she gets there before I do."

I tossed the magazine back on the table, fluffed my hair, and walked to the window. Through the sheers, I could see a lady step from a black SUV.

"Kate, are you about ready? She's coming up the walk."

She whipped around the corner. "I'm here." Panting, she tucked her blouse into her jeans as she followed me to the door. I reached for the handle the moment the bell rang. Opening the storm door, I conjured a smile.

"Hello, are you Caroline?"

I nodded. "Yes."

She extended her hand. "Maggie Abrams."

I stood frozen. Cutting my eyes to Kate, I watched as the blood drained from her face. There was no mistaking the resemblance. This stranger, with clear blue eyes and a pleasant voice, looked more like my sister than I did. Deep within my gut, I knew this woman who'd shown up on Kate's doorstep was about to turn our lives upside down.

"Come in. Come in." I held the door while Kate greeted her and motioned toward a chair at the window.

As we dropped to the couch, Kate said, "How was your trip down?"

"Good." Sitting on the edge of the chair, she fidgeted with the large coral-colored pocketbook in her lap. "Uneventful. I like it that way."

"Yes." *Uneventful would be good about now.* Rubbing the fur throw draped over the couch arm, I continued, "Overcast days make for excellent driving."

She nodded. "I look forward to revisiting Beaufort. I haven't been in years." She scanned the room.

"My husband and I went in May. It's one of our favorite spots on the Carolina coast. There are some beautiful historic homes along the waterfront."

"I know. Lovely." Her eyes followed a Fed-Ex truck as it rumbled past the house.

"You should rent a golf cart. It's a wonderful way to explore the island."

"That does sound like fun." Spotting a row of photographs

on the bookshelf across the room, she pointed. "May I?"

Kate shrugged. "Be my guest."

Maggie placed her pocketbook on the floor and approached the shelves.

I stared at Kate as she muttered between clenched teeth. "Maybe she'd like a house tour. A little lunch, perhaps."

I smacked her hand. Fighting back a wave of nausea, I cleared my throat. "You said you had something to show us?"

She spun around and walked back to her chair. "I do." Pulling a clasped envelope from her pocketbook, she passed it to me and returned to her chair.

Opening it, I lifted the flap and inched out a worn black and white photograph. Kate and I gasped simultaneously.

"Do you know him?"

There was no holding back. Tears flooded my eyes and then streamed down my cheeks. Kate wept too. I couldn't utter a coherent sound. Then, looking up at this stranger, I waved the picture in front of me and choked out my words. "This—this is our daddy."

"I thought so. Look at the back."

Flipping it over, I read the scrawled handwriting aloud. *"Maggie's dad."*

"What?" Kate fell back against the sofa.

I followed suit. "Who wrote this, and where did you get it?"

"My brother sent it to me from Chicago. The handwriting is our mother's."

"Chicago?" Kate and I exchanged looks.

"Yes. That's where we grew up. Our mother has dementia and has lived with my brother's family for several years. A few months ago, as he searched for papers we needed to admit her to a nursing home, he ran across this picture."

"I think we know how you felt."

"It's been a lot for both of us to take in. We've always believed we had the same father. Our mother fled Germany when my brother was a year old. She told us our father was one of the thousands of Jews taken captive by the Nazis in Berlin during Kristallnacht. He never returned home. She was afraid, and our father's cousin managed to get my family to the states. Now I know I wasn't with them. I was born a couple of years after my mother settled in Chicago. Some documents my brother found said she came to America in 1939 with one child—a son. I wasn't born until 1941. There is no father named on my birth certificate."

Kate scooted to the edge of the couch and said. "And so now you want to claim ours?"

I grabbed her hand. "Please, Kate. Settle down. That will get us nowhere."

She wiped her cheeks with the back of her hand. "I'm sorry. It's so ..."

"Devastating. Believe me, I know. I hated to interrupt your lives this way, but I didn't know what else to do."

"We'll do whatever we can to help you get to the bottom of this. It's hard to believe you could be our half-sister, but your resemblance to Kate is uncanny, and our father did live in Chicago during those years."

She let out a deep sigh. "Oh, I'm so relieved. I was worried sick about how you would take the news. I haven't wanted this to be true either, but I had to follow my leads."

"How did you find us?"

She laughed. "How else? Social media."

Kate and I looked at one another and said, "Facebook?"

"Yes. A friend of mine saw an old picture Caroline posted of your dad on Father's Day. She thought he resembled the man in the picture my brother had found."

"Who's your friend?"

"Marcie Westbrook."

I shook my head and slid the photograph back into the envelope. "I don't know her. She must be a friend of a friend."

"Anyway, after a bit of online research, I called you."

I stood to return the envelope.

"No, that's yours to keep. It's a copy." She rose from her chair. "I won't bother you any longer. I know you both need time to digest this information, and I should get back on the road. My cousin expects me at her house by dinner. I'll call you next week." She moved toward the door and extended her hand.

She looked like she could use a hug, so I hugged her instead. "Sunday or Monday will be fine. Thank you." I paused. "I guess."

"Again, I'm sorry. I didn't want to upset your lives, but I felt I had no choice. At seventy-one, I need to know who I am."

"Of course. Don't worry about it."

Kate and I followed her down the steps and onto the sidewalk. "We'll work through this together. I suppose there are worse things in life than discovering we have another sister to love." I smiled. "Besides, you seem like a nice lady."

Kate and I watched her drive away, then cut our eyes toward one another and, without a word, entered the house.

What? What just happened? What were Kate and I to do now?

Chapter Seventeen

Sunday, December 3, 1939
Fayetteville, North Carolina
Emma

Emma stepped onto the porch of 405 Maiden Lane and took a seat on the swing beside Chummy. "Look at you, big boy," she said as the large yellow tomcat yawned and stretched before leaping into her lap. "Some things never change. I'm happy to see you're still watching out for this place." He nudged her hand with his cold nose. "I've missed our long chats here. Have you missed me?"

Smoothing his long silky coat, she glanced up at the cracked and peeling paint on the ceiling of the wide porch, noted the rusty light fixture, and shook her head. "Looks like Tucker has his work cut out for him." Chummy purred as she rubbed his head. "It's good to be home again, sweet friend, even if it's only for a few days."

As laughter came from inside the large yellow federal-style house, she breathed a sigh of relief. Mama T must be having a good day. Kissing Chummy on top of his head, she held him close and gave the swing a forceful shove with her feet. The cold air, which captured her long brown tresses, caused Chummy's fur to stand on end. Feeling the vibration of his loud purrs, she welcomed the warmth of his body against her fingertips.

The swing's back-and-forth motion pushed her thoughts to Noah's last evening with her in this very spot—the eve of his return to Jonesville. Their love had been brand new, and the vision for their lives brighter than the stars on a clear winter night—before the downpour, that is. The cloudburst that evening had been more prophetic than she knew but one she did remember fearing. If she could have seen into their future, perhaps she would have written Noah more often. Not been so aloof and prideful, or gullible and mistaken concerning his feelings for Alice.

Emma dropped her feet to the floor and brought the swing to a steep halt before letting it fly again. She must move on, forgive herself for her past mistakes, and apply what she'd learned to her present relationships.

Caught by a stiff breeze, the screen door slammed against the house. Bea jumped as she stepped out onto the porch. "I thought I heard someone talking. Why are you sitting out here, child? You're going to catch a death of cold." With a broad sweep of her arm, she motioned Emma toward the door. "Come on inside where it's warm. Flo's been in a tizzy waiting on you."

"I'm sorry. I didn't mean to upset her. I figured she knew me and my propensity for distraction and daydreaming." She lifted Chummy from her lap and placed him on the cushion beside her. "I was inhaling this life-giving North Carolina air and doing a bit of reminiscing.

She rolled her eyes. "Heavens. Get in here, child. You can reminisce later."

As they entered the sitting room, she motioned toward the sofa. "Make yourself at home. I'll let her know you're here."

Emma breathed in the familiar pine scent of the crackling fireplace and welcomed its warmth. *Home—home again. Was she?* Walking across the room, she ran her fingers over the multitude of books in the cases along the wall until she came to Thomas Wolfe's *"Look Homeward, Angel."* Still there. The first book she'd read from Mama T's library—the one she was reading when Noah pulled in front of the house that day. She *was* home again—and it felt good. She jumped as Bea entered the room, a crooked index finger poised at her pursed lips.

"Looks like Flo's dozed off. Let's let her sleep while we

catch up." Picking up a wicker sewing basket from Mama T's easy chair, she took a seat. "I've been passin' the time making a dresser scarf for our church bazaar next week. Christmas will be here before we know it." She tucked her hoop and colorful skeins of embroidery threads into the basket and set it on the floor. "Would you like a cup of hot cocoa? I made a large pot of it this morning."

"No, thank you." She settled into the cushions and glanced around the room. "Maybe later. I'm still full from breakfast. Lily had quite a spread this morning."

"I'm sure she did. I've sat with my feet under her table more than a few times. She reminds me of your mama when it comes to the kitchen."

"She does. I seem to have missed out on that gift," she said, shrugging. "Thank you for taking care of Mama T. It was good to hear her laughter a while ago. She must be feeling better."

"She is. And growing stronger every day. A friend dropped by early this morning. Florence enjoyed her visit, but it wore her plum out."

Emma slipped off her coat and laid it on the sofa beside her. "I can't tell you how relieved I was when Tucker told me you were here to tend to her."

She waved her hand in the air. "Don't mention it. Taking care of Flo is a pleasure. She's seen me through mighty tough times over the years, and I'm gonna do the same for her. Our generation's gotta stick together, ya know. Not many of us left."

"Maybe not, but I'm trusting you'll both be around for a long time to come."

"We're working on it." She chuckled and settled back in her chair. "So, Miss City Slicker, tell me how you're getting along."

"Other than worrying about Mama T, I'm fine. And I love Chicago." While filling Bea in on her recent adventures, the sudden sound of Mama T's weak and raspy voice jolted her.

"Who's that in there talking about my demise? Is that you, Emma Rose?"

Bea leaped from her chair, and Emma followed close on her heels.

"You know, the news of my demise has been greatly exaggerated, don't you?"

Emma walked to the bed and kissed Mama T's forehead. "That I do. And thank goodness, Mark Twain had it right." She smoothed the hair of her friend, who was as white as the sheets she laid on. "I told Bea that you were too stubborn to let a little matter of the heart stand in your way of livin' and givin'."

She clasped Emma's hands. "It's good to see you, baby doll." Looking at Bea, she said, "How about fixing my pillows so I can sit up and get a better look at this beauty. Gotta see if Drew's feeding her enough."

Bea fluffed and positioned several pillows at her friend's back while Emma took a seat on the edge of the bed.

"You gave me a real scare, sweet lady. We'll have no more of that. Next time you want me to come for a visit, say so. No more feigning sickness, you hear?"

"Believe me, I'd like nothing more. Aggravating Bea for a while longer is my plan, and there is one thing I know—I won't be leaving this earth one minute before the good Lord's ready to take me home. It seems He's got a bit more work to do on that mansion of mine." She threw her head back and laughed. "My precious Albert probably told Him I was gonna need a few more bookshelves."

"I'm guessing you're right, but I thought for sure you'd leave your library to me."

Mama T chuckled. "Take whatever you want, baby doll. Doubt I'll be rereading the likes of those books. But be warned." She flashed a broad smile and motioned heavenward. "Eliminating the need for shelves on high could hasten my departure."

Amused, she shook her head. "I love your sense of humor and am so glad to find you in such a chipper mood. I've been worried sick about you."

"You needn't concern yourself with me, child. You've got your whole life to consider." She pointed toward Bea. "Besides, I'm in excellent hands. This taskmaster will see that I do everything I'm told." She patted the bed. "Now that's enough about me. Scoot further over here before you find yourself on the floor and tell me all about Drew and your new life in Chicago."

She lifted Emma's ring finger and moaned. "I'm not seein' a band there yet. What's that man waiting on, anyway? He's gonna let the best thing that ever happened to him pass him by if he doesn't catch on soon."

Emma shook her head. "No, no. It's not Drew. He's all in. It's me. I'm the one being cautious."

"You? The girl who hopped a train and left at a moment's notice? What's gotten into this impetuous child of mine?" She raised her trembling hand in the air. "If you're having second thoughts, I haven't rented out your room yet."

Emma clasped Mama T's hand and rubbed it. "It might be good if you do. I have no plans to come back here to live. I love Drew, but something in my spirit tells me the time isn't right for marriage. I can't quite put my finger on it, but then again, I know I don't have to understand God's leading. I simply need to follow."

"My, my, I'm proud of you, baby doll. How you've grown." She reached up and tapped Emma's nose. "I'm sure you'll make the right decision when the time comes."

"I hope so. I want my marriage to be as enduring as yours and Mr. Turner's was."

As Emma chattered about her life with Drew, Mama T's eyelids grew heavy. She'd interject an occasional comment, and her eyes would close again. Emma glanced at her watch and patted Mama T's hand. "I should run. I don't want to wear you out. Besides, I promised Penny I'd have lunch with her before her shift today." She kissed her on the cheek and tucked the covers around her. "I'll visit again tomorrow. You keep getting stronger now, you hear?"

Mama T nodded, blew her a kiss, and whispered. "See you later."

Bea ushered Emma into the hallway and gave her a parting hug. "Thanks for coming. Your presence has done wonders for Flo's morale. I've not seen her this upbeat since you left."

"My spirits are lifted too. I've missed her so much. Thanks again for being here. And tell Mrs. Brumble—Opal, the same. I don't know what Mama T would do without the two of you."

She pushed open the screen door, then turned around and walked into the sitting room. Approaching the wall of books, she slipped Wolfe's novel from the shelf and looked at Bea.

She nodded her approval.

Clutching the book to her chest, Emma grinned and stepped onto the porch. "I'll call you tomorrow."

"Wonderful. It should be an even better day."

Emma wrapped her coat around her and tied the sash. "I'm counting on it."

Chapter Eighteen

Chummy skittered into the foyer as Bea held open the screen door. Emma stumbled in behind him, carrying a brown paper sack. Bea reached out to steady her. "Sorry, child. It seems Chummy's forgotten his manners."

"Indeed he has, but he's always been pretty self-absorbed." Laughing, she hugged Bea. "And how are you and Mama T getting along today?"

"It's been a good day. She had a nice long nap this morning. Ate a good lunch and has kept her eye on the window ever since. She'll be happy to see you."

Tucker followed, carrying a small spruce tree in a copper bucket. He bent at the knees for Bea to give him a peck on the cheek.

"Well, bless my soul. What on earth have you got there, son?"

"Just call me Santa Claus." He chuckled. "Uncle Sam wouldn't let me grow the beard, though." He motioned with his head toward Emma. "Miss Walsh here has had me bustling around town all morning. You wouldn't happen to have a cup of hot chocolate for a tired recruit, would you?"

"Oh, I imagine there's a little left in the bottom of the pot. How about you, Emma?"

"Sounds perfect. We're chilled to the bone." Slipping off her coat, she hung it on the hall tree. "May we go back and see Mama T?"

She swatted her hand. "Of course, you can. You're home now, child. Do as you please. I'll be there as soon as I ladle up the cocoa."

Emma walked down the hall and peeked into the small floral-papered bedroom. Chummy had wasted no time burrowing into the covers and curling up by Mama T's side. Looking up from her book, she smiled and clapped it shut. "Aha. There you are. I've waited all afternoon for you."

Emma walked to her bedside and kissed her on the forehead. "I know. I'm sorry. We'd planned to be here sooner but got tied up in town."

Mama T glanced up at Tucker and laughed. "So I see. You have an armload for sure, son. What are you children up to?"

He nodded toward Emma. "Ask the boss. I'm simply following orders. Good thing Uncle Sam taught me how to do that."

Emma shook her head and took Mama T's hand. "Knowing how much you love Christmas, I couldn't stand the thought of there not being any Christmas decorations in your house. When I mentioned it to Tucker on the way over here, he said he could fix that." She squeezed her hand and looked around the room. "So, here we are. Where do you want your tree?" She held up the brown bag. "We've come to decorate."

Mama T clapped her hands together several times, then drew them to her chest. "Oh, how wonderful. You really shouldn't have gone to all the trouble, but your efforts won't be wasted on me. I can't think of anything more splendid." She pointed to an oak steamer trunk in front of the window. "Move those things over onto the chest of drawers. That trunk will be the perfect place. With it there, I can enjoy it at night while lying on my side, and people will see it from the street."

Tucker positioned the tree on the trunk while Emma pulled a box of small ornaments from the sack, then held up a strand of colored lights. "These should brighten up your world."

"How wonderful." Mama T laughed. "Y'all look like a

couple of little Christmas elves shuffling around over there. Oh, how I wish I could get up and help you."

"No-no. Sit back and cheer us on. Every worthwhile task needs a good supervisor." Emma helped Tucker clip the lights to the branches. "We'll have this shining in no time."

Bea entered the room, carrying a tray with four cups of hot cocoa and a plate of sugar cookies. "Oh my, look at this. It's beginning to look a lot like Christmas in here, Flo." She set the tray on the dresser. "Aren't you the cat's meow. Gettin' all catered to like this." She leaned up against the dresser and crossed her arms. "Now, don't you go gettin' too used to all this pampering. If you want this treatment day in and day out, you'll have to talk Emma into moving back upstairs."

Mama T swatted the air. "Oh, hush, Bea. Let an old lady have her day."

Bea handed her a cup of hot cocoa and a napkin. "I'm thrilled for you, sweet friend. You deserve it. It's good to see you smiling again."

Emma hung the last ornament on the tree and peered into the sack. "Tucker, would you mind running back out to the car? I left the most important thing on the front seat."

He saluted while exiting the room. "Got it, Sarge."

Bea handed Emma a cup of cocoa, glanced at Mama T, and winked. "That's one fine young man, don't you think, Florence?"

"Never doubted it for a moment." She peered over her glasses at Emma. "I hear he's available too."

Emma waved them off and took a seat in a chair beside the dresser. "Stop it, you two. Tucker and I have both had experience with long-distance relationships. They don't work. Besides, why would we want to mess up a dear friendship?"

Shortly, Tucker entered the room and handed Emma a box. "Is this what you're looking for?"

"It is. Thank you." She placed her cup on the dresser and approached the tree. "Tucker, get ready to do the honors."

Opening the box, she pulled out a beautiful, white-feathered angel with a hand-painted porcelain face. She showed it to Mama T, then returned to the tree and placed it on top while Tucker plugged in the lights. A chorus of gleeful cheers rang through the room. Emma stepped back and admired their handiwork, then looked at her precious friend. As colored lights reflected and danced in her glasses, Mama T led out singing, "We Wish You a Merry Christmas." Bringing the chorus to a close with a long crescendo and a broad sweep of her hand, she threw her head back and laughed.

"Thank you, children. Thank you so much. You have no idea how much you've blessed my heart this evening." She motioned. "Bea, pass the cookies, and please everyone, sit down. I have a surprise of my own. Especially for you, Emma Rose."

Her eyes widened. "Me?"

"Yes. I've waited all day, and now you two have provided the perfect backdrop for my story. Only God can orchestrate a moment like this one." She placed her cup on the nightstand, fluffed her pillows, and pushed herself up in the bed.

"Bea and I chatted today and came to the same conclusion— this house needed a spot of Christmas." She pointed toward the dresser. "Pass me that box, please."

Bea lifted a brown box from the dresser, set it on the bed beside Flo, and returned to her chair.

Reaching in, Mama T lifted out a small stable and put it on the bedspread beside her. Chummy stretched, circled around, then dropped onto the other pillow. "This nativity set belonged to my granny. Now that I'm feeling better, I wanted to put it out. But before we do, I have a sweet story to tell you."

Emma crossed her legs and smiled at Tucker. Then, settling back in her chair, she took a sip of the warm cocoa.

Tucker leaned forward, resting his elbows on his knees.

"When I was little, my granny lived with us. Every Christmas, she'd pull out the manger scene and tell all her grandchildren—and there *was* a passel of us—the story of the very first Christmas. I can see her now, carefully settin' out each piece. I thought the baby Jesus was the prettiest little thing I'd ever seen."

Mama T pulled each porcelain figurine from the box, carefully unwrapped it, and placed it on the stable floor. "I remember one year after Christmas, while Granny was puttin' the nativity away, I slipped the baby Jesus in my pocket." Her eyes glistened as she picked up the small figure. "You see, I wanted to keep Him for myself. I should've known I couldn't get away with it cause my granny had eyes in the back of her head."

Emma laughed. "I know how that is."

"Yep. She whipped around and gave me one of those looks. You know what they're like too, don't you, Emma?"

"Yes, ma'am, I do."

"I put Jesus back real quick. Granny told me the manger wouldn't be complete without him. Not too many years later, my granny got real sick. I remember sitting on the floor in the hall outside her room and hearin' the doctor say to my papa, 'It won't be long now.' A short time later, Papa opened the door and motioned for me to come in. He told me Granny had something she wanted to say to me.

"When I walked to her bed, I looked up at her. She looked like an angel lying there on those white sheets. She had that familiar sparkle in her eyes and a big smile on her face. She told me to come a little closer cause she couldn't talk so loud. I scooted up as close to the bed as I could, and she leaned over and said, 'Sugar Dumplin', I'm gonna be going home soon.' I didn't understand that at all, 'cause I thought she *was* home. She followed it with, 'I'm going to go and live with Jesus.' Now that really confused me. I didn't know where Jesus lived. I was hopin' he lived close by because I didn't want to be without my granny.

"I turned to run out of the room, 'cause I didn't want to hear it, but she called and said, 'Not so fast, Sugar Dumplin', I've got something for you.' You better believe that got my attention. When I turned around, she held out her hand then opened it. There was the baby Jesus from the manger. Raising her hand a little higher, she said, 'Come here. Take Him. He's yours.' You don't have to steal Him, Florence. He's a gift. Your life won't be complete without Him.'

"I snatched him up and clutched him to my chest. I didn't want her to see me cryin', so I turned to leave, but before I could get out of the room, I heard, 'Wait now, Sugar Dumplin', there's one more thing.' I turned. 'You can't be keepin' him for yourself. You see, when you have Jesus in your heart, you've got to share him. He came to save everyone. How are people going to know if you keep him for yourself?'

"Ever since that day, that's what I've tried to do. Share Jesus." She gestured. "Emma, come over here."

Emma placed her cup on the dresser and walked to the bed. Mama T held out her hand and opened it up. "Go ahead. Take Him, baby doll. He's yours."

Emma blinked back tears as she stared at the tiny baby Jesus lying in Mama T's hand. As she took the porcelain figurine, Mama T said, "Now, remember. You can't be keepin' Him for yourself. You've got to share Him."

Emma stood motionless. Then, clutching the baby Jesus to her chest, she bent over and hugged Mama T. "What a beautiful story. Thank you. Thank you so much. I will never forget this day and will cherish my Jesus forever."

Mama T looked at Tucker. "How about putting this nativity under the tree for me, son."

He hopped up. "Yes, ma'am. I'd be more than happy to."

Once he'd carefully placed the pieces in the stable beneath the tree, Emma walked over and laid the baby Jesus in front of Mary and Joseph.

Mama T said, "But Emma, he's yours."

She walked over to Mama T and hugged her. "I know, but for now, he belongs right there. Didn't you say the manger wouldn't be complete without him?"

"You're right. I did, baby doll." Mama T kissed the back of Emma's hand. "Thank you for sharing him."

Chapter Nineteen

Exiting the main dining room of the Hotel Jefferson, Drew checked his watch. Too early to retire and enough time to check out the Max Safron Gallery on the mezzanine above. His agent, Joe Roth, had spoken with Mr. Safron and had scheduled a time next week to meet and discuss Drew's work. Joe had high hopes several of Drew's paintings would be hung in the gallery. The city's wealthiest clientele and guests from countries worldwide frequented the prestigious venue. The gallery had gained the reputation of representing well-known artists as well as up-and-comers to the field.

Passing through the Tudor Revival-style lobby, he admired the magnificent tree in the center of the room. Guests seated on upholstered rose-wood couches enjoyed the mellow chords of Christmas that sprang from the ivory keys of the piano at the foot of the grand stairway. As he approached a small group of people gathering around the young pianist, he nodded, then did a double-take. The profile of a lady in a red-satin dress reminded him of Emma. Her uninhibited, high-pitched laughter made him miss her all the more. Fully aware of her lingering gaze, he ascended the stairs of the twelve-story, 400-room hotel. Inhaling the pine-scent of live greenery draping the wrought-iron balusters, he admired the massive marble columns supporting the sculpted ceiling.

A small bell jingled as he passed through the glass door of

the gallery. A mature lady with perfectly coiffed hair stepped from the back and offered her assistance. He declined, assuring her he was simply browsing. Her overseeing presence reinforced the gratitude he had for Joe's representation. He'd be much too intimidated to approach a man of Mr. Safron's caliber. If only he could believe in himself as much as Joe did. Perusing paintings by American, French, and British artists exhibited along the walls, he fell into his all-to-familiar comparison trap. He doubted his work would ever rise to the zenith of the collection of paintings represented here.

He walked the room's perimeter, then shuffled through numerous matted works displayed in large bins in the center of the room. Feeling his confidence plunge, he thanked the lady who now stood behind the counter and bid her a good evening.

"Please come again, sir. New paintings arrive weekly."

"Thank you. I hope to be back soon."

As the door shut behind him, he walked toward the mezzanine's west end, which housed the elevators. Trying to evict the flood of demoralizing thoughts rolling through his mind, he pushed the UP button and leaned against the opposite wall. His eyes followed the sweep of the floor hand as the elevator rumbled down the shaft. Accompanied by a chime, the car stopped, and the attendant pulled open the brass gate for passengers to exit. Pressed to move forward by those behind her, the lady in the red dress—the one he'd seen earlier in the lobby, exited and smiled. He returned her subtle greeting and stepped onto the elevator. "Tenth floor," he said, pulling a bit of change from his pocket. He was more than ready to call it a day.

Drew placed the small box and his room key on the nightstand and pulled his burgundy sweater vest over his head. Then, loosening his tie, he kicked off his shoes, propped the pillows against the headboard, and dropped onto the bed. Leaning back, he inhaled the faint lavender scent of the pale pink envelope. *Oh, how I miss this woman.*

Tearing into the flap, he unfolded the lengthy letter and sighed. *This couldn't come at a better time.* Emma's letters always lifted his spirit.

Tuesday, December 5, 1939

My darling Drew,

How are you? I hope your work in St. Louis is going well. I know you said to call anytime, but to say all I'd need to would take far too long and cost you more than I'd want you to pay. Besides, writing has always been cathartic for me. It helps me sort through my emotions, and tonight I have a lot of sorting to do. I wish I could say or do something to make this less painful, but unfortunately, nothing will change our current reality. I have devastating news. It's hard for me to write these words, much less speak them. Mama T passed away in her sleep last night. Bea found her this morning lying on her side. We are all stunned.

I wish you were here. I know I'm not alone, but I feel like I am. How will I ever push through this pain?

Mama T was doing so well, and yesterday was a wonderful day. Tucker and I took her a small tree for her room. We decorated it, and she was so happy. We laughed and sang, and Mama T told us a remarkable story from her childhood. Oh, Drew, she only got to enjoy her tree for one night.

As we were leaving, she made me promise to come back today. She said she had something important to discuss with me. Now I'll never know what it was. I'm grateful she left us on such a happy note, but my heart feels as if it will explode. Right now, I'm crying so hard, I can barely see my words. I hope you'll be able to read them.

I thought I would be home by Christmas, but now I see there's no chance of that happening. Mama T's sister is too ill to help with anything, and I could never leave Bea here alone to deal with it all. I hope you'll understand. I can hardly bear the thoughts of you being alone on Christmas. Please see if you can spend the day with Joe and Helen. As for me, I can't even think about Christmas this year. I just want to sleep through it.

Please call me when you get this letter. Maybe by then, I'll be able to speak coherently. Opal will be here first thing in the morning to help with paperwork and funeral plans. First Baptist has offered to provide meals for us. After all of the years Mama T helped with the bereavement ministry there, she would be grateful to know that we are now the recipients of her labor of love.

I'm so sorry to have to send you this news. Hopefully, it won't distract you too much from your work since your days in St. Louis will be almost over when you receive this.

Know I love you and wish I was back in your arms.
Emma

Dropping back his head on the pillows, Drew rubbed his forehead and moaned. The news of Mama T's death was horrible, and his heart broke for Emma. If only he was there to console her. Their separation, along with the news that Emma would not be home for Christmas, simply intensified his pain.

He sat up, swung his legs over the edge of the bed, and stared at the box on the nightstand. Squeezing his eyes shut, he shook his head and dropped his face in his hands. How long? How long would it be before Emma came home?

He picked up the box and flipped it open. A one-carat, round solitaire diamond sparkled in the subdued light of the bed lamp.

The steady tick of the clock on the nightstand competed with the rapid beat of his heart. Both served as reminders of past, present, and future moments lived without Emma.

Clapping shut the lid on the box, he dropped it into the nightstand and slammed the drawer. So much for sleep. After putting on his shoes, he pulled a sport coat from the closet, dropped the room key in his pocket, and exited the door.

He took the stairs. *Twenty flights down—fast, and a glass of red wine should help.*

Drew collapsed onto the small upholstered bench in the niche off the lobby. Panting, he pulled a linen handkerchief from his pocket and wiped beads of sweat from his brow. It had been some time since he'd put his physical prowess to the test. Looked like fewer hours behind the easel and more on the tennis courts would be needed.

Rising from the bench, he stuffed his handkerchief in his pocket and combed his hair with his fingers. Then, straightening his sport coat, he squared his shoulders and entered the lobby. The earlier festivities had ceased. Only a few couples lingered in front of the large fireplace as the hands of the clock above it neared eleven-thirty.

Drew walked to the lounge and took a seat in a corner booth, distancing himself from the few customers. Judy Garland's "Have Yourself a Merry Little Christmas" spilled softly from the speaker above his head. He could mark that one off his wish list. It appeared the die had been cast for the degree of his holiday cheer.

He ordered a glass of wine from the waiter and reached for a copy of *The St. Louis Post-Dispatch* left in the adjacent booth. Headlines continued to boast of the ever-expanding war overseas. Further down on the page, news of a collision off the coast of Scotland caught his eye.

During the morning of 12 December, the Royal Navy's HMS Barham collided with the HMS Duchess in heavy fog off the Mull of Kintyre. The destroyer capsized after her depth charges exploded. One hundred thirty-six crew members were killed, including her commanding officer, Lieutenant Commander Robert C. M. White, trapped in his sea cabin when the sliding door jammed.

He sighed. *Is there good news anywhere today?* Opening the newspaper, he searched the index and turned to the daily crossword puzzle. He folded the paper twice, ran his thumb over the fold, and slipped a ballpoint pen from his pocket. He sipped his wine. Perhaps, mastering today's puzzle would be within his grasp, and then—maybe not.

He plugged several words into the appropriate spaces, then stared at the far wall as if an answer would appear.

"Thirty-seven across is *prediction.*"

He flinched and glanced up at the attractive lady in a mustard yellow boat-neck sweater and pleated skirt. A grin crept across his lips. "It is, is it? How do you know?"

"That one stumped me earlier." She slid into the booth across from him. "Do you mind?"

"Do I mind if you tell me the answers, or do I mind if you sit across the table from me?"

"Both."

He glanced at the puzzle. "Thirty-seven across … *An action that may happen or will happen.*" He filled in the blocks—P-R-E-D-I-C-T-I-O-N. "It looks like you're right. Perfect fit."

"Imagine that. Have I earned my seat?"

He laughed. "Be my guest."

She laid her small purse on the table. "Now that we've got that taken care of …" She extended her hand. "Hi, my name is Elizabeth Murray. My friends call me Liz."

He took her hand. "Andrew Brown, my friends … and perhaps a few enemies, call me Drew." He motioned toward the lobby. "I believe our paths crossed earlier this evening."

Her dark eyes sparkled in the soft glow of the wall sconce at their table. "You're right. They did."

"So you're here with friends?"

She nodded. "A group of us from work came to the city for the Christmas performance at the Fox Theatre."

"How was it?"

"To sum it up in one word—fabulous. The Fabulous Fox Tellerettes were nothing short of spectacular. Have you seen the show? You should take it in while you're in the city."

He shook his head. "Not enough time."

"That's a shame. Where are you from?"

"Originally? Or where do I live now?"

"Both."

"Scotland, but I've lived in Canada and the US for several years now. I've drawn ads for the *Chicago Tribune* for the past few months and am about to complete my two-week assignment with the *Post-Dispatch*. I'll head back to the Windy City this weekend."

"Now that's interesting. You're an artist, and we both live in the same city." She grinned. "Must be fate."

He cocked his head. "You don't say?"

"Yes. I was born in Evanston but live in Chicago now. I've managed the jewelry department at Marshall Fields since '34."

"Wish I'd known you sooner. I just picked up a ring for my lady at Bern Jewelers over on Jeweler's Row. Maybe you could have gotten me a sweet deal."

Her countenance faded. "Would that ring be as in … engagement?"

"I sure hope so. If I can get Emma home long enough to give it to her."

She stood. "I'm sorry. I should've known a nice-looking gentleman like you would be spoken for."

He rose. "No need to apologize. Under different circumstances, things might have worked out." He tapped his pen on the table. "I suppose this means I'll have to finish the puzzle by myself."

She nodded and smiled. "You can do it. I've got faith in you." She held out her hand. "It was nice talking to you. I wish you and your fiancée the best."

He took her hand. "All my best to you too. You seem like a nice lady. Thanks for lifting my spirits."

"My pleasure." She smiled and stepped away, then turned and dug in her purse. Placing a card on the table, she said, "If you ever need more jewelry for your girl, I'd love to help you."

He glanced at the card and slipped it into his breast pocket. "Deal."

She stepped away from the table, then turned again. "Prediction ... I *will* be hearing from you."

Drew sat dazed as she walked to the entrance and disappeared into the lobby. Picking up his pen, he read thirty-eight across ... *A predetermined course of events.*

Slowly, he filled in the squares.

D-E-S-T-I-N-Y. Destiny.

Chapter Twenty

Plunking my coffee mug on the table, I huffed. "Stephen, are you listening to me?"

He peeked around his morning paper. "Of course, I am. I always listen to you, Caroline."

I rolled my eyes and reached for a slice of toast.

"Why on earth would you think otherwise?" He laid the newspaper on the breakfast table.

"Let's see ..." I tapped my index finger on my pursed lips. "I haven't the foggiest notion." Folding my arms, I let out a long sigh. "Do you have plans for today?"

"Hmm, it sounds like, if I don't, I should. I'd better think of something quick."

I rolled up a section of the paper and swatted him.

He laughed. "What is it you have in mind, dear?"

"Well, Kate and I ..."

He lifted his hand, "Whoa. Stop right there. I just thought of something I promised my boss I'd do."

I furrowed my brow. "You did not."

"You're right," he chuckled. I'm kidding. But I must admit I get nervous whenever you and Kate start scheming. What's rolling around in that head of yours now?"

"Kate and I hoped you'd help us do a little surveillance."

"Uh-oh. I don't like the sounds of this. What or who would I be surveilling?"

"Maggie."

"Your sister?"

"Hush. I'm not going so far as to say that. I still can't wrap my mind around all of this." Placing my hands on the back of my neck, I rolled my head from side to side and exhaled. "If she is our half-sister, I wonder if there's more to the story? Does she want something? Money, or for heaven's sake, maybe a body organ?"

He lifted his hand. "Don't run ahead. A pretty quick solution would be for the three of you to take DNA tests. Why don't you start there? Maggie either has your DNA, or she doesn't. Case closed." His eyes twinkled. "And no further surveillance needed."

I smirked. "Kate and I have discussed that, and it does make the most sense. I'll get in touch with Maggie. Maybe when she comes by here on her way home from the beach, we could go to the lab for tests."

"There you go. Am I off the hook now?" He picked up the paper.

"For the moment. But don't stray too far."

"Why's that?"

"There's a new addition to your to-do list." Returning to his paper, he mumbled from behind it. "That's what I was afraid of."

Tuesday, July 24, 2012
Caroline

My eyes locked on those of Kate, my only sibling, who sat opposite me in my living room. She clutched a 9" x 12" white envelope to her chest while I gripped a matching one. Maggie, visible to us through face-time technology, sat one-hundred-thirty-two miles away in Wytheville, Virginia, holding the third envelope. It had been ten long days since we'd been to the lab for DNA testing with Maggie. These matching sleeves contained our siblingship DNA results and the answer to the question that had haunted us for almost two weeks.

Was Maggie our biological half-sister? If so, that reality would usher in an ocean of questions, many of which we'd never have answers for. The contents of the envelopes in our hands had the potential to wreak havoc with our lives and emotions. Not only might Kate and I find we have a half-sister, but we could also learn the father we adored, the daddy in whom our sun rose and set, had not been forthright with his family. Were we ready to know the truth? Once known, there would be no stuffing it back in Pandora's box, pretending it wasn't so.

Before our meeting, Kate and I prayed that God would give us the grace to accept the test results regardless of what they revealed. Now, with Maggie's face isolated on the laptop on the coffee table between us, her perceived resemblance to Kate was troubling. Kate either couldn't see it or refused to acknowledge it, but to me, it was apparent. Today, I would be more surprised to learn we weren't related than if we were. The silence was palpable, and I was sure the pounding of my heart could be heard across the miles. No one knew what to say as we proceeded to delay the inevitable.

Maggie broke the silence. "Caroline and Kate, I realize you didn't ask for this unbelievable scenario. It was thrust upon you as it was me. If the DNA percentages show we are likely half-sisters, I will respect whatever you both decide concerning future contact and involvement with me."

"Thank you," we chimed in unison.

"I'm sorry to put you through this, but I must have an answer for my own peace of mind. If the percentages show we aren't half-siblings, I'll have to decide for myself where to go from here. At seventy-one years old, it's hard for me to wrap my mind around the fact that I really don't know who I am. Hopefully, you understand."

"Of course, we do." I glanced at Kate. "I know I speak for us both when I say we would want to know too, even as we want to know now. Are we ready to open these envelopes?"

Kate and Maggie nodded.

I slid the letter opener under the flap and passed the opener to Kate. As the three of us slid out several pages of results, silence filled the room. I skimmed the pages containing several graphs and percentages.

"Ladies, let's cut through the details and go straight to the bottom line. We can study the rest of it later." Scanning through the pages, my eyes stopped midway through the third page, and I looked up. "The summary is about three-quarters of the way down on page three. Look there."

"Based on our analysis and the biostatistical evaluation of the hypotheses, it is highly likely that A and B share the same father. There is a 98.8 % probability that A and B are half-siblings. There is a 1.2 % probability that A and B are unrelated."

Stunned, I nervously flipped through the pages.

Kate fell against the back of the chair and shouted. "No. That can't be. There is no way our daddy would have deceived us." She stood, snatched her purse from the floor, and glared at me. "I'm done. I refuse to accept this ludicrous verdict, Caroline. If you want to believe this woman is your sister, forget about me. I don't buy this now and never will." She fumed past me, letting the storm door slam behind her.

I looked at Maggie, tears streaming down my face. She sat with her head in her hands. The pounding of my heart had slowed to an indiscernible beat. I felt as if life had been sucked from me, and without Kate, it had.

Had mother been aware of this? Had she chosen to keep it from us, or had she also been a victim of our daddy's deceit?

Chapter Twenty-One

Friday, December 8, 1939
Emma

Emma sat at the white pedestal table in the center of Mama T's kitchen and watched Bea unconsciously stir her coffee. An oppressive stillness seized the room—a hush she was hesitant to intrude on, lest there would be no words or balm to arrest the surge of grief it might awaken. Cradling her cup in her hands, she leaned back in her chair. "Pastor Gardner's words today were sweet, weren't they?"

Bea looked up, her usual in-command spirit, subdued and broken. "They were. But how could they be anything less than sweet when talking about Florence?" She laid her spoon in her saucer, picked up her cup, and sipped the warm brew.

Emma nodded. "So true."

The weighty silence returned.

Bea shifted in her chair and cast a vacant stare across the room. "You know, for as long as I've known Flo, I've never heard one soul utter a harsh word about her." Setting her cup in the saucer, she rubbed her forehead. "I can't fathom not hearing her sweet voice again."

Emma ran her finger over a small chip on the edge of the English rose-patterned saucer. "Me either." Returning her cup to the shallow dish, she walked to the sink and lifted the matching patterned sugar bowl from the window sill. She paused to watch a cardinal hop from branch to branch on the hydrangea bush beneath the window, then carried the bowl to the table. "Have you ever seen this?"

"Of course. It's been on the sill for as long as I can remember."

She took her seat. "But have you ever looked inside?"

"No. I've sworn off sugar." She chuckled and placed her hand on her plump belly. "In my coffee, that is."

"Mama T used this bowl for something much sweeter than sugar." Emma set the bowl on the table, pulled out a curled sepia-toned snapshot, and handed it to Bea. "Look at this. It's Mama T and her husband, Albert, on their wedding day—July 18, 1873. She doesn't look a day over thirteen, does she?"

She studied the picture. "No, she certainly doesn't."

"She told me she was sixteen plus one day. Her father had said she couldn't get married one day before she was sixteen, so they waited till one day later to tie the knot."

Bea laughed and shook her head. "That sounds like something Flo would do."

Emma held up her index finger. "That's not all. Look at this." She pulled a silver locket from the bowl and passed it to Bea.

Opening it, she studied the pictures of Flo and Albert inside, then flipped over the small silver heart and read the inscription, "*Now and Forever, Love Al.* How sweet. I wonder why she didn't wear this."

Emma giggled. "She said once she gained weight, it was too tight around her neck, and they didn't have enough money to buy a new chain. The years passed, and once Albert died, she wanted to keep it like it was the day he gave it to her."

Bea offered it back to Emma.

She held up her hand. "No. See if it fits you."

She shook her head and laid it on the table in front of Emma. "Oh, I couldn't do that."

She slid it toward Bea. "Please, try it on. Mama T told me I could have it if anything happened to her. You've been a good friend and took excellent care of her in her final days. It's yours."

She fingered the necklace in front of her. "Really? Are you sure?"

"Couldn't be more. Mama T thought the world of you."

Bea clasped the silver chain around her neck, straightened the heart with her fingers, and squared her shoulders. "What do you think?"

"I think it's perfect. It's where it belongs."

Tears welled in her eyes. "Thank you, Emma. This is so kind." She patted the locket. "I'll always cherish this."

She smiled. "Mama T would be very pleased to know you have it."

Bea stood, gathered several dishes from the table, and walked to the sink. "Have you decided if you'll stay tonight?"

"Yes, I told Lily I'd be here for a few days. I want to help you with all that needs to be done."

"Wonderful. I'd like that. It gets pretty lonely here at night. As you know, the third bedroom is storage now, so would you be comfortable sleeping in Flo's room? I'll help you change the sheets."

"I don't mind at all. And don't worry about helping with the linens. I'll change them. You've done enough."

"Let me get them for you," she said, exiting the room.

Emma placed her dishes in the sink and wiped off the plastic tablecloth. It was hard to believe her conversations with Mama T at this table were over. Regardless of how crazy things got beyond the doors of Maiden Lane, watching Mama T putter about in her kitchen always assured her the world was on its axis. Now, life was skewed.

Bea returned to the kitchen. "I laid fresh sheets and towels on the bed."

"Perfect." Yawning, she pulled her hair up off of her neck and let it fall back over her shoulders. "If it's okay with you, I'm going to call it a day. You should too. It's been a long, hard week for everyone."

"I'll go in a bit. I'm going to work on my embroidery for a while. It's almost Christmas. Besides, it helps me relax." She motioned her on. "You run along, though."

Emma kissed her on the cheek and walked toward the door.

"Oh, Emma, before I forget ..." Bea brushed past her. "Follow me." She walked into the sitting room to Flo's secretary and pulled down the writing surface. Slipping an envelope from one of the wooden mail slots, she handed it to Emma. "Florence had me promise that if anything happened to her, I would give you this."

Emma pressed her hand to her chest, eyes widening. "Really?"

Bea nodded and flapped the envelope in front of her.

Slowly she reached for it. Noting her name scrawled in Mama T's shaky handwriting, she lifted her eyes to Bea's. "I'm stunned. I don't know what to say. Do you know what this is about?"

"I can guess, but no, I don't know for sure."

She leaned over and hugged her friend—Mama T's precious caregiver. "Sleep well. I'll see you in the morning."

"You too, child."

Clasping the envelope over her heart, Emma walked into the bedroom, leaned against the door, and scanned the room. Memories of her last day with Mama T flooded her thoughts. When she kissed her goodbye on Monday, she never imagined that it would be the last time they would speak.

She walked to the front window and plugged in the tree lights, then took a seat in the upholstered rocker by the bed. She jolted as Chummy leaped into her lap. "Where'd you come from, sweet boy? You miss her too, don't you?" As he curled up on her legs, her eyes brimmed with tears, blurring the tree's colored lights. Laying her head back on the chair, she stared at the angel on top, then dropped her gaze to the nativity beneath it.

'Now, remember, Emma Rose. You can't be keepin' Him for yourself. You have to share Him.'

She brushed away her tears and whispered. "I will, Mama T. I promise."

Glancing at the envelope in her hands, she let out a long sigh. Life had taken an overwhelming turn. To hold further words in her hands from her precious friend was as if she'd been sent a gift from heaven. She flipped on the floor lamp, then straightened in her seat and slipped Mama T's letter from the envelope.

My Dearest Emma,
    If you're reading this, I am gone. People will say I am dead but don't believe it. At that moment, I will be more alive than I am now while writing this. I will be walking streets of gold and dancing once again with my precious Albert in the presence of King Jesus. Don't weep for me, baby doll. I lived my life and was blessed. Now it's time for you to live yours.

Emma pulled a tissue from the box on the nightstand and sobbed. As much as her heart hurt, she would never wish Mama T back. She was reaping the rewards of a life well-lived, a life in service to her Savior.

    One of the greatest blessings of my life was our brief time together. I knew from the moment you walked through my front door that we were kindred spirits. I'm so grateful you found me, and I had the privilege of knowing you. You are like the daughter I never had and well worth the wait. You breathed life into my home when I needed it most and brought a joy I'd missed since Albert was alive. Thank you for being you and for loving me as you did.
    What I'm about to share with you, I wanted to discuss with you in person, but God has seen fit for it to work out differently. Who am I to question his decisions? I regret I didn't have the opportunity to tell you goodbye or share once more how much I love you. But, I believe you know that.
    I pray that you and Drew are doing well and that you will have a happy and blessed life. I hope what I'm about to say will not complicate your lives but give you a head start. It's so hard nowadays, especially during

these depressed times, to afford a home and establish a family. Emma Rose, I am gifting you my house. It will be up to you to make it a home. Perhaps, you'll choose to sell it and use the money for another place somewhere. Whatever you decide, you have my blessing.

Emma laid the letter in her lap and looked skyward. "What? You're giving me your house?" Falling back against the chair, she tried to comprehend the fact that she was now a homeowner. "Oh, Mama T, what have you done? I'm appreciative but am now confused as to how to handle this. So much needs to be done here, and my home is in Chicago with Drew."

You and Bea can decide what to do with the furniture and remaining contents. I have nothing of real value, but perhaps my little will be much to a few.

Of course, this place needs quite a bit of work, but Tucker can do most anything around here, so I'm putting in a good word for him. He can be trusted to do what he says.

I hope you're okay with this, baby doll. I've put my plans to gift the house to you in my will, which is in my lockbox. Bea has the key and has the same lawyer as I do, so she will help you through the legal process.

That's all I have to say, except that I love you, sweet child, and will be waiting on you. I'll meet you at the Gate. Be there!

See you later,
Mama T

Emma rested her head on the chair and stared at the paint peeling from the bead-board ceiling. She sighed, returned Mama T's letter to the envelope, and placed it on top of the Bible on the nightstand.

Rising, she walked to the tree and fingered one of the shiny ornaments. Then lifting the baby Jesus from the manger, she stared into his small porcelain face. *"This is all more than I can comprehend, Lord. It's bigger than me but not bigger than you. Please, show me where to go from here—and Lord, please give me the words to tell Drew."*

Chapter Twenty-Two

Friday, December 22, 1939
Emma

"Have you heard from Drew lately?"

Emma handed Penny a few dresses from Mama T's closet and turned to get more. "Not since his phone call last Friday. He's swamped with work during the week. I'm sure I'll hear from him this weekend." She passed her several more dresses.

Penny folded them and placed them in the cardboard box for Tucker to take to The Salvation Army. "How does he feel about you staying in Fayetteville a while longer?"

"He's certainly not happy about it, but he understands." She pulled two coats from the closet and laid them on the bed. "We'd hoped I'd be back in Chicago by Christmas. Now I have no idea when I'll return."

"What did he say when you told him you'd inherited the house?"

"I didn't tell him."

Penny stopped what she was doing, her eyes widening. "What? You didn't tell him?"

"I wanted to, but I couldn't drum up the courage. I've not sorted through all of this myself. I'm waiting till I have more clarity and for the right timing." She pulled clothes from the dresser and laid them on the bed. "You can go through these next." She held up a sweater and dropped it back in the pile. "The holidays aren't the best time to bring it up anyway. It's hard enough being separated, and Drew has so much on him at work. I don't want to add to his stress. I'll tell him after Christmas."

Chummy jumped on the bed and curled up on Flo's coats. Emma smoothed his silky hair. "Don't get too comfortable there, big boy. That spot will be short-lived. If you don't watch it, you'll end up in a box too and be on your way out of here." He rolled over and mewed.

Emma grabbed another box from the corner, placed it beside the closet door, and began to fill it with hat boxes and shoes. Standing on her tiptoes, she slid a bag from the back of the shelf and peeked in. "Oh my, what's this?"

Penny looked up as her friend pulled a box wrapped in Christmas paper from The Capitol shopping bag. "Interesting. Does it have a label?"

Flipping it over, Emma's breath hitched in her throat.

"And?"

"It says ..." Her voice cracked. "To Emma. Merry Christmas." Lowering herself to the edge of the bed, she dropped her face in her hands and wept.

Penny sat beside her and pulled her close. "I'm sorry, honey. I know this hurts. When Anna died, I thought I would too. God will see you through like he did when you learned Noah had been killed." She brushed Emma's hair from her face.

She straightened. "I know you're right. I was blessed to have Mama T in my life. Loving deeply comes at a great cost, but our brief time together was worth the price." She grabbed a tissue from the box on the nightstand, picked up the gift, and placed it under the tree beside the nativity. "I won't open it until Christmas. I believe God has something special in store."

Sunday, December 24, 1939

Emma looked up from her book as Bea poked her head around the bedroom door. "I'm going home now. Are you still okay with staying here by yourself in the evenings?"

"Yes, I've done fine. I'm glad you're back in your routine. You sacrificed a lot to stay with Mama T."

"Not really. I wouldn't have had it any other way." She pulled her knit hat over her ears and slipped on her gloves. "You know you're welcome to stay with me anytime."

"I know ... and I appreciate your invitation. I'll come if I need to. Tomorrow, I'll spend the afternoon with Lily. She's planning a nice dinner, so I'll be fine."

"Okay." She blew Emma a kiss. "You have a Merry Christmas. I'll see you later this week. We'll work on cleaning out that third bedroom."

"Perfect. Merry Christmas to you too."

Emma watched through the window as Bea unlatched the gate and stepped onto the sidewalk. She marveled at the change Jesus had made in her life in the face of such grief. Emma prayed Bea's daughter would one day find it in her heart to forgive her mother. The accidental drowning of her son while in Bea's care had been heart-wrenching, but her inability to forgive had added to their pain and loss. *Unforgiveness is a thief—stealing precious years from the living, years that can never be retrieved.*

Turning off the reading lamp beside her chair, she sat in the glow of the Christmas lights and listened to Chummy's soft purring. She missed Drew. Although he'd tried to sound upbeat, she'd heard the underlying sadness in his voice on the phone that morning. She wished she could join him at Joe and Helen's tomorrow for Christmas dinner. Helen would cook all of Drew's favorites. She'd always catered to him and at times referred to him as her baby brother. At least, she knew he wouldn't be alone.

Emma lifted Chummy and placed him on the floor. He stretched out his long body and groomed himself. Stepping over him, she pulled back the bed covers, slipped off her robe, and laid it on the foot of the bed. Chummy immediately jumped on it and settled down for the night.

Slipping between the sheets, Emma pulled the covers up around her neck. She closed her eyes and listened to the cold north wind whistling around the corner of the house. The weather forecast held the possibility of a white Christmas, a rare occurrence for the North Carolina Sandhills.

Christmas Day 1939
Emma

Chummy skittered across the room and slid into the door frame. He turned with his rice-filled felt mouse in tow, then tossed it into the air to begin the chase again. The gift Emma had picked up at the church Christmas bazaar for Mama T's beloved cat appeared to be a huge hit. She giggled, then wadded the wrapping paper into a ball and tossed it into the wastebasket.

Rising from her chair, she reached under the tree for the box addressed to her from Mama T. Clutching it to her chest, she returned to the rocker and took a deep breath. "Merry Christmas, sweet lady. I can only imagine what today's celebration in glory is like. How blessed you are to celebrate the birthday of The King in His very presence."

She looked heavenward and grinned. "Thank you for my gift. You really shouldn't have, but I'm glad you did. I wish I could hand deliver one to you. Hopefully, you'll feel my love and somehow know you're in my thoughts this Christmas morning."

She lifted the gift from her lap and ripped the paper from one end. "Hmm . . . shoes, maybe?" She finished tearing the wrap from the box and let the paper fall to the floor. Chummy immediately pounced and flopped on top of it. After removing the tissue, she pulled a pair of pale-pink furry bedroom slippers from inside. Kicking off her old shoes, she slipped them on her feet and lifted them from the floor. Holding her legs straight out, she said, "Look, Chummy, I have a gift too. Aren't they lovely?"

Seeing an envelope at the bottom of the box, she pulled it out and opened it. Tucked inside the Christmas card was an embroidered handkerchief. Above a small cluster of pastel-colored flowers, Mama T had stitched the words—*See you later*. Emma sighed. Did her precious friend somehow sense she wouldn't be around for Christmas? She pressed the handkerchief to her face and inhaled its sweet, powdery fragrance. "Yes. I'll, indeed, 'see you later.' I miss you so much. Thank you for this beautiful gift."

Resting her head on the chair, she closed her eyes and thought of the swift turn her life had taken. She'd followed her heart to the man she loved, and now events outside of her control had altered her course. Her road back to Chicago grew longer by the day. Before returning to her beloved Drew, there was a lot she needed to do to get the house ready to sell. Would he wait for her? Had his words—

Startled by a rap on the door, her eyes flew open. She looked at the clock on the nightstand—10:43 a.m. Laying the box and card on the bed, she pulled her sweater tighter around her body and scuffed across the room. "Chummy Choo, it appears we have a Christmas visitor." The large yellow cat bounced at her heels. "Do you suppose it's Santa Claus?"

Making her way through the sitting room, she sensed the visitor's impatience as their staccato rap grew louder and more forceful. Fumbling with the key in the stubborn lock, she huffed. *One more thing for Tucker's to-do list.* When it finally clicked, she yanked the door open. As her eyes met those of the man on the porch, she screamed.

"What are you doing here?"

Unhooking the screen, she threw it open and jumped into Drew's arms. "I can't believe it. How did you make this happen?"

He laughed as he twirled her around. "I'm not in the habit of making promises I don't keep." Lowering her to the ground, he pressed his lips to hers, then leaned back and said, "I told you Christmas Day would be ours alone, and I'm making good on my word." He pulled her toward him and kissed her again.

Opening her eyes, she brushed off his shoulder. "Look at

you. You brought Chicago's snow." She glanced out at the fluffy white flakes beginning to stick to the ground. "Chummy and I were so caught up in our Christmas celebration, I hadn't even noticed the snow." She grabbed his hand. "Come in. Come inside where it's warm."

Pulling him into the foyer, she bounced and clapped her hands. "I can't believe you're standing in front of me." She threw her arms around his waist and looked into his eyes. "Thank you. Thank you so much for coming. My heart ached this morning. I didn't know how I was going to make it through the day." She stepped back and motioned. "Please, take off your coat and stay a while."

"Oh, I plan to." As he took off his fedora and hung it on the hall tree, flakes of snow fell onto the worn entry rug.

Emma took his coat, hung it beside his hat, and led him into the sitting room—now toasty and warm from the early morning fire she'd built. "Would you like something hot to drink?"

"Maybe later." He pulled her onto the sofa. "Your warmth is all I need."

Emma fluffed her hair and pulled her sweater around her everyday housedress. "Oh, look at me. I look a fright. Chummy and I were so absorbed in our gifts, I completely lost track of time."

Drew stared into her eyes and kissed her nose. "You are more gorgeous than I remember." Leaning back onto the sofa, he drew her to his side.

"I can't believe you didn't tell me you were coming." She swatted him. "And there I was all worried about you. How did you work this out? Where are you staying?"

"At the Prince Charles. I made my reservations and worked into the wee hours of the mornings to finish my ads. I knew there would be plenty of time to make up for all my hours of lost sleep on the long train ride here."

She leaned up and kissed him. "This is the best Christmas present ever. Thank you. With all that's happened, I needed this today." She looked at the grandfather clock in the corner. "I can't wait to call Lily and tell her to set another place at the table. She'll be thrilled to see you."

"It will be nice to see her again too." He grinned. "I can't wait to sink my teeth into one of her delicious buttermilk biscuits. She's quite a cook."

"I know." She chuckled. "I must have her show me a thing or two about the fine art of cooking." She sat up and leaned against the couch arm. "How are Joe and Helen?"

"They're good. They send their love and said to tell you they miss you."

"And I miss them. Has Joe lined up any shows for you yet?"

He straightened his shoulders and brushed his sport coat's lapel. "How does a one-man show at the Max Safron Gallery in the Hotel Jefferson sound?"

Emma's eyes widened. "Oh, honey, that's fabulous. I'm so proud of you. I knew you could do it."

"The curator wants to feature my paintings late this spring." He shook his head. "I have a lot of work to do and will need to get on it when I get back to Chicago. I'll start with some of the photos I took that night on the *Wendella*."

"Yes. You should have some wonderful painting material there." She stood. "If we're going to Lily's, I need to change clothes." She turned to walk away. "Make yourself—"

He grabbed her hand. "Whoa. Wait. Sit here a minute longer."

She furrowed her brow as she lowered herself to the couch. "What is it?"

He laughed. "Don't look so worried. It's all good. At least, I think it is." He placed his hand in his pants pocket. "I haven't given you what I traveled all this way to bring." He pulled out a wrapped gift and held it in front of her.

"Oh, Drew." She covered her face with her hands. "I feel horrible. I don't have anything for you."

He shook his head. "Now, you know that's not why we give

gifts. *You* are my gift. Spending time with you is enough." He held the present closer to her face. "Are you going to open this or not?"

She giggled. "Try and stop me." She tore into the wrapping. "What are you up to, Drew Brown?" She noted a gold-foil emblem on top of the small white box and read aloud, "Bern Jewelers, St. Louis, Missouri." She looked up, her eyes growing large. "What is this?"

He waved her on. "Open it and find out."

She removed the lid and turned the box over. Her breath caught in her throat as a black velvet case fell into her hand. "It's not what I think it is, is it?"

He shrugged, his eyes twinkling. "What am I—a mind-reader?"

She slowly opened the hinged lid. Gasping, she snapped it shut.

Drew laughed.

She locked eyes with his. "Oh, Drew, you didn't."

"What? You don't like it?"

She slowly reopened the lid, revealing a one-carat solitaire diamond. "Like it? It's the most beautiful ring I've ever seen."

"Does that mean you'll marry me?"

She paused, her smile fading.

"What? What's that look about?"

She scooted over, threw her arms around his waist, and laid her head on his chest. "Drew, I have something I need to tell you."

Pulling away, he took hold of her shoulders and gently sat her up. "That doesn't sound good. What do you mean, you have something to tell me? What something?"

She dropped her eyes to the ring, and a tear rolled down her cheek. She'd known this moment would come, but she hadn't planned on it being today.

Chapter Twenty-Three

"Thanks for coming with me today. I would've had a hard time explaining your absence to Tucker."

"I'm glad I came too. I'm sorry I blew up like I did on Saturday. I know none of this is your fault, but I couldn't—and still can't, accept the possibility that Maggie could be our half-sister." Kate placed her drink in the cup holder in the console of my car and shifted in her seat to face me. "Caroline, do you really believe Daddy would deceive us?"

"Everything in me wants to believe not, but how do we dispute the DNA test? And I know you don't like to hear it, but Maggie does look like you. Surely you see it?"

"I do. I see her resemblance to you too."

Shrugging, I pulled the car into Tucker's driveway. "I don't understand any of this and am at a loss for a rational answer." I cut the engine. "We'll continue this conversation later. For now, let's go in and see how our sweet friend is doing."

Claire met us at the door and led us back to the den. Tucker sat in his chair, the morning paper a few inches from his face. As we entered the room, he peered over his glasses and greeted us with his warm smile.

"Wow. Look at you, Tucker." I leaned over and hugged him.

Kate followed suit. "You look so much better than you did when we were here a couple of weeks ago."

He folded the newspaper and laid it on the TV tray beside

him. "I don't know about lookin' better, but I sure feel better." Slipping his glasses from his nose, he motioned toward the sofa, then dropped them on top of the paper. "Have a seat. Y'all care for something to drink?"

"No, thank you. We grabbed a bite on the way here."

Claire excused herself and walked around the kitchen counter that separated the two rooms. "Holler, Mr. B., if you need anything. I'll be in here cleaning out the fridge. We'll need the space for tomorrow's groceries."

He picked up a calendar from the side table. "I thought tomorrow was our day to visit Emma?"

"No, we planned to do that on Friday, remember?"

I looked at Kate.

She nodded in response to my unspoken question, an ability our close relationship had refined through the years.

"Kate and I plan to run by the cemetery today. Would you like to ride out there with us?"

His clouded brown eyes widened. "That's a mighty tempting offer. Claire took me for a doctor's appointment Monday, so I haven't had a chance to go this week."

"Perfect then."

He shook his head. "Thanks, but I'd slow you spring chickens down too much. Claire will take me Friday."

Kate piped in. "We're in no hurry, and besides, we'd love to have a handsome escort."

His eyes gleamed as he tilted his head. "Ya don't say?" He raised his voice. "Claire, whaddya think? You reckon I could ride out to the cemetery with these pretty ladies today?"

"If you feel up to it, I think that would be nice. It's warm, but the air is clear. I believe you'd enjoy the change of pace."

He scooted to the edge of his chair, then paused and looked toward the kitchen. "How about my rose? Have you got it?"

"Yes, sir. It's right here in the fridge."

His eyes twinkled. "Ladies, it looks like we have a date." Grabbing his cane, he stood, then lifted the small oxygen tank from its holder and looped its strap over his head. "As soon as I change my shoes, I'll be ready to roll."

Claire brought out a rose wrapped in a wet paper towel and handed it to Kate. "Thank you for offering to take him with you. He's thrilled. I've not seen him walk with that lilt in his step for some time."

"We'll take good care of him."

"I know you will. Just be sure to steady him on his way to the plot. The ground out there is pretty uneven. If he gets tired, have him rest on the bench."

"We will. Perhaps this will give you time to do a few extra things around here. Don't you leave for vacation next week?"

"No, not until Saturday, the eighteenth."

"Will Tucker's daughter and grandson come from Charleston to stay with him?"

"Yes. They'll be here the Wednesday before I leave and stay for a couple of weeks. I hope you get to meet them. They ooze Tucker's southern charm."

"Did I hear someone call my name?" Tucker entered the room with slicked-back hair and a pair of Asics slip-on sneakers on his feet. "You ladies ready to go?"

I dangled my car keys in the air. "We are, and Kate's got your rose."

"Perfect." He lifted his Fort Bragg cap from the library table in the hall and plopped it on his head. Then tapping his cane on the hardwood floor, he moved toward the door. "Let's go, ladies. Your mother is a-waitin'."

I brushed pine needles from the top of Mother's headstone, then picked up the glass bud vase, removed the dead rose, and poured water into it. Tucker inched closer to the polished granite marker, then paused and whispered something before patting it. When he turned and faced me, I held out the vase and took out the wilted flower within it. Grinning, he dropped in the fresh red rose. "Number forty-five."

Kate and I shook our heads.

"You're something else," I said. "What a special friend you were to our mother and now to us. Thank you. You're one big-hearted guy."

Kate looked up at the tall, longleaf pines and into the azure sky. "We couldn't ask for a prettier day." She reached for Tucker's arm. "Would you like to sit on the bench and rest a bit?"

He nodded. "That would be nice. This breeze feels good. Unusual for an eastern North Carolina August."

He sat on the bench, scanned the cemetery, and pointed with his cane. "One of my army buddies is laid to rest a few plots over." He lowered his head. "I sure do miss him. He was one fine fella."

"Did Mother know him too?"

"She did. One Christmas, neither of us could go home for the holidays, so we decided to have Christmas dinner at the Rainbow instead of in the mess hall. Before we went, we dropped by Emma's house so I could give her a Christmas present."

Christmas Day 1939
Emma

Emma smoothed her skirt and tossed her hair over her shoulders as she rushed to the door.

"Ho. Ho. Ho. Merry Christmas, Em!"

Her smile erupted into laughter. "What a pleasant surprise." She pushed open the screen door. "Don't stand there grinning like two Cheshire cats. Come in out of the snow." She flicked the white ball on Tucker's red velvet hat as he entered the foyer. "I didn't know Santa served in the US Army. What are you two doing here all decked out?"

"Cee is serving the troops Christmas dinner at the Rainbow today. Our ticket in is our dress uniforms."

"That's wonderful. I'm glad you're going. Penny said he was prepared for a large turnout. Cee may be small in stature, but he has a huge heart for our Bragg soldiers."

Tucker motioned toward his friend. "Emma, this is Hank— Hank Morrison from Dalton, Georgia."

She extended her hand. "It's nice to meet you. Any friend of Tucker's has to be a fine man. Come on into the sitting room. How about something warm to drink?"

"No thanks," Tucker said, following her. "We have to save every inch of room for turkey and—"

Drew rose from the sofa.

"Honey, look who's here." Emma motioned. "You've met Tucker, and this is his friend, Hank."

Drew smiled, shook their hands, and wished them a merry Christmas. Then cutting his eyes toward Emma, he took a seat in a chair beside the fireplace. Tucker and Hank sat on the sofa while Emma seated herself in Mama T's chair.

Several moments of uncomfortable eye-dodging passed before Tucker stood and broke the silence. Stepping across the room, he handed Emma a large wrapped package. "Merry Christmas, Em."

Her eyes lit up as she stood and hugged him. "Thank you so much. You didn't need to do this."

"'Need to' wasn't a factor."

She sat in her chair and bounced the gift in her lap. "Goodness, it's heavy," she said, glancing at Drew.

Averting his eyes, he leaned forward in his chair, placed his elbows on his knees, and folded his hands.

Emma slipped her fingers under the folds of the red, green, and gold-swirled Christmas paper and slowly tore it away from the box. She looked up at Tucker.

He grinned.

"I can't imagine." Ripping it further, she exposed the

words—Philco Model 84 Cathedral Radio. Her voice went up an octave as her eyes shot to Tucker's. "A radio?"

He looked at Hank and laughed.

She tore the remainder of the paper from the box and squealed. "Thank you. Mama T's has been broken for months."

"I knew that. When Hank found this one on sale over at The Capitol, I knew I had to get it for you. It's a dual Christmas and house-warming gift. We can't have you living here alone in silence."

Drew's head shot up, his eyes bolting to Emma's.

Swallowing hard, she rubbed the slick surface of the box. "I'm at a loss for words. I love music and know I'll enjoy this."

Drew cleared his throat and straightened in his chair. "Honey, why don't you show the fellas the gift I brought you this morning."

"Oh, yes, of course." She set the radio on the floor and walked to the sofa. Extending her left hand, she flashed a broad smile. "Have you ever seen a ring this beautiful?"

Tucker and Hank's eye's bulged as they shook their heads.

Drew dropped back in his chair, locked eyes with Tucker, and smiled.

Chapter Twenty-Four

Later that evening

Emma unlocked the door and flipped on the light. Stomping the snow off her shoes on the doormat, she hung her coat and hat on the hall tree. Drew followed.

"Would you mind building a fire while I put these leftovers in the icebox and get us something hot to drink?"

He blew into his palms and rubbed his hands together. "I'd be happy to, and anything hot sounds swell."

Emma stacked enough food containers in the icebox from Lily's table to feed herself for most of the week. She took a couple of mugs from the cupboard, lit the burner under the pot of cocoa, and shouted to Drew. "Bea made a batch of Christmas sugar cookies. Would you like a couple?"

"I wish, but no thanks. Lily's spread filled me up. I don't know where I'd put them."

Minutes later, she ladled steaming cocoa into the mugs and dropped two marshmallows in each one. Carrying them into the sitting room, she handed a cup to Drew and curled up beside him on the sofa. "Thanks for the fire. It feels wonderful. I'm chilled to the bone."

She sipped her cocoa, then stretched out her arm to watch the firelight dance in the facets of her ring. "Look, honey, isn't it beautiful?"

He leaned over and kissed her cheek. "*You* are what's beautiful." Setting his mug on the table, he placed hers beside his and took her in his arms. "Merry Christmas, darling."

"Merry Christmas." She tilted her face upward and received

his kiss. The warmth of his embrace and the familiar scent of Old Spice was the therapy she needed after the crushing events of the last few weeks. "Thank you for coming. I never dreamed you'd show up at my door this morning. Your visit has certainly lifted my spirits."

"Mine too," he said, stroking her cheek with his thumb. "We needed to be together this Christmas."

"I agree. I've missed you so much. It's been hard living in this house without Mama T. I long to hear her call me doll baby and see her walk through the door." She sat up and faced him, her eyes brimming with tears. "And thank you for understanding my need to stay here longer to handle the affairs of the house. I know it was a disappointment."

"It was, but the way I see it, you really have no choice. You've got to do what you've got to do." He reached for his mug, leaned back, and placed his feet on the coffee table. "I admit, Tucker's comment when he gave you the radio this morning jarred me. I wondered if you'd made long-term plans you hadn't told me about. Have you? Is there more to the story, Emma?"

She stood and warmed her hands at the fireplace. "Drew, the truth is, I don't know what the truth is. I don't know what short-term or long-term means." She twirled around, her eyes meeting his. "I've never owned a house before, and so much needs to be done here. I'm overwhelmed."

"Tomorrow, I'll help you all I can, but on Wednesday, I'll have to catch the early train out."

She returned to the couch and took hold of his hand. "I wish you could stay longer."

"Me too, but after being in St. Louis for two weeks, I have a lot to get caught up on at the *Tribune*. Between that and preparing for my spring show, I have all I can do." He tapped her on the nose and grinned. "It will keep me out of trouble."

She shook her head. "It better."

"By my show date, this will all be a memory, and you'll be back in the Windy City where you belong."

She lowered her head. "I hope you're right."

"Everyone at the Berghoff hopes I'm right too." Chuckling, he lifted her chin. "Spring is a season of fresh starts. After a successful show, our future together will blossom. You'll see."

Her eyes widened as a smile spread across her face. "Drew, let's set our wedding date."

Placing his feet on the floor, he gulped the last of his cocoa and plopped his cup on the coffee table. "Let's do it. I'm ready."

Emma walked across the room to the secretary, took out Mama T's day planner, then returned to the sofa, flipping through the pages. "What are your thoughts? Any time better than another for you with your work?"

"The early summer months are slow." He looked at the calendar. "June sounds like a good month for a wedding. Chicago is beautiful then."

"June—being a June bride sounds magical." She looked up from the planner. "I don't want anything showy, though. Just us … and a few friends." She ran her finger over the calendar. "How about Sunday, the fifth? Will that work for you?"

"If we must wait that long, it's as good a day as any." He took the planner from her hands and placed it on the table, then pulled her close and kissed her.

The next day

Emma stood at the kitchen counter sorting through stacks of dishes, examining each piece for cracks and chips."

"Emma, I've been thinking." Drew looked up from the piles of papers and pushed his chair away from the table."

Furrowing her brow, she turned to face him. "Uh-oh. I don't like the way you said that. Sounds a bit dubious."

He stood and walked toward her. Taking an English rose saucer from her hand, he placed it on the counter and looped his arms around her waist. "I tossed and turned most of the night." Tightening his embrace, he looked deep into her eyes. "I've decided I don't want to get married—"

She broke from his embrace, heat rising in her cheeks. "You don't want to get married?"

He reached for her. "Whoa. Whoa, Emma Rose. Hear me out."

"I've heard all I need to. No explanation you have can change what you said." She spun on her heels and walked to the window. Hugging her waist, she pushed back tears. "How can you come all the way here to give me a ring and change your mind overnight? I guess I don't know you at all, Drew Brown."

She felt the warmth of his body against her back as he slipped his arms around her waist.

"Shh. Darling, it's not what you think."

She whirled around and pushed him away. "Sounds pretty matter of fact to me." She tugged at the ring on her finger.

Drew grabbed her hands and pressed them between his. "Stop. I should have phrased it differently."

"Ha." She ripped her hands from his grip. "How many ways can you say. 'I don't want to marry you?'" She dropped into a chair at the table and covered her face with her hands.

"*That*—is not what I said." He knelt in front of her. "Emma, what I tried to say was, "I don't want to get married *in June*. I want to get married *today*. I want to marry you before I leave tomorrow."

Easing her face from her hands, she strained to focus on Drew through her tears. "You what?"

"I said, I want to marry you ... *today*."

"Today? As in *now*?"

He brushed the tears from her cheeks and nodded. "Yes. This time you heard me right. Today is exactly what I'm saying."

She leaned forward and collapsed against his chest. "Oh, Drew. I'm so sorry. I should have let you finish instead of jumping to the wrong conclusion. I feel like such a fool. With all that's happened lately, I suppose I'm always expecting the worst."

He lifted her chin and kissed her nose. "It's okay. I don't need an apology. I need an answer." His eyes twinkled. "What do you think? It's a good idea, right?"

A smile spread across her face. "There is nothing I'd love more—"

Jumping up, he lifted her from the chair and whirled her around. "All right then, throw on something pretty, and let's go."

"Drew, stop. Now you're doing it."

He lowered her to the floor. "Doing what?"

"Jumping to a conclusion before I finish my sentence."

A puzzled look replaced his broad smile. "I'm sorry. What more did you want to say?"

She stroked his face. "I would love nothing more than to marry you today, but I can't."

He pulled her closer. "Of course, you can."

"Drew, I can't. I want our day to be special. I want to feel free. Not loaded down with all these peripheral worries. Anticipating our wedding day, making plans with Penny, and dreaming about our life together is what will get me through the tough days away from you." She peered into his eyes. "You do understand, don't you?"

He took her hand from his face, kissed it, and nodded. "I do. But it's hard. I don't want to leave you again. Even for one night. I hoped we could spend my last night here as husband and wife."

"I love you for that, but for me, it would make our separation harder. I think it would work for you too."

He sighed, then kissed her on the nose. "You're probably right. June will be here before we know it. I'll have to lose myself in my painting." He returned to his place at the table and picked up his pen.

Emma walked to the counter. As she placed the cracked English rose saucer in the discard stack, a tear slid down her cheek.

Chapter Twenty-Five

Monday, August 6, 2012
Asheboro, North Carolina
Caroline

Singing, I carried the carrot cake to the dining room table, placed it in front of Kate, and flashed a big smile. "Guess who made it."

Her eyes bulged. "I'm afraid to … and thanks for the warning."

I swatted the air and laughed. "Hush. It's good. I know. I licked the spoon."

She winced.

"You're gonna love it." I leaned in, speaking with a sing-song voice. "Happy Birthday to my *older* sister."

Kate smirked. "If I didn't know you'd put hours into making this cake, I'd be tempted to splat you with it."

"You wouldn't dare." I laughed and waved her off. "Hurry up and make your wish before the blaze covers the cake with wax."

Closing her eyes, she blew them out with one long breath.

I clapped. "Ah. Not bad for someone your age."

She helped me remove the candles from the cake, licking a couple in the process. "You certainly didn't get your kindness from our parents. Are you sure you're my sister?" She hesitated and grinned. "Maggie favors me more than you do, ya know?"

I slowly lifted my eyes to hers. "Whoa, Sis. That hurts." But I am glad you can laugh about it now. You've come a long way."

"I can laugh, or I can cry, and I've done my share of the

latter. I refuse to shed any more tears over this, just as I refuse to believe it."

I lifted a large square package from the sideboard and passed it. "Here. Let's lighten up this party. Open your gift while I cut the cake."

Reaching for it, her eyes widened. "Oh my, this is a bit large for jewelry."

I placed a thick slice of cake on a plate and set it in front of Kate. "Jewelry is the last thing you need. I wracked my brain for something I've never given you before, something you've never received, and something you'll never guess."

"That's scary." She furrowed her brow and lifted the package up and down. "It's lightweight. Gotta be clothing."

Grinning, I shook my head. "I guarantee you won't guess this one."

She ripped the paper from the box. "Okay. I'll take your word for it and won't waste time trying." Lifting the lid, she pulled back the tissue and took out a floral Vera Bradley tote bag. "This is beautiful," she said, then shot me a puzzled look. "You've given me totes before, though."

I waved her on. "I know. You're not through. Look inside."

She unzipped the satchel and peered in. Placing her hand in the center pocket, she slipped out a white envelope. "Hmm. This *is* interesting." Opening it, she pulled out a ticket. "American Airlines?" She slipped her reading glasses from her hair and onto her nose. Her voice went up an octave. "Greensboro to Chicago?"

"That's right." I placed a slice of cake on my plate and sat down. "We're bound for the Windy City."

"Friday, August 17th? Are you serious?"

"I am," I said, forking a large bite of cake in my mouth. "Mmm, scrumptious, if I do say so myself. My compliments to the chef."

Kate chuckled. "You're not only kind, you're modest too."

"We can't deny our genes." She raised her voice. "*Or* whose sister I am. Looks like you're stuck with me for a few more years."

"I hope lots more." She stopped eating and looked up. "I love you, Sis, and thank you for the gift. What are your plans?"

"I figured we'd fly to Chicago and do a bit of research. If it's okay with you, I'd like to invite Maggie to meet us there. Maybe her brother will show us around and shed more light on his mother's early days in America."

Kate raked the cake crumbs with her fork and said nothing.

Shoveling another bite in my mouth, I waited for her to break the weighty silence.

She returned the ticket to the envelope, tapped it on the table, then moved her eyes to the window. "Wow. This is so hard. I don't want to know, but at the same time realize if I don't know, I'll never have peace."

She slapped her hand on the table and looked at me. "Okay. Let's do it. Chicago sounds like a great place to visit." Returning the shoulder bag to the box, she said, "This calls for a shopping trip. I've heard the Windy City is sweltering in the summer. I'll need some cool clothes."

She pulled the plate toward her, placed a forkful of cake in her mouth, and moaned. "Yum, Caroline. On second thought, perhaps you *are* my sister."

Friday, August 17, 2012
Chicago, Illinois

The wheels of the American Airlines Boeing 737 touched down at O'Hare International Airport at 4:43 CST—seven minutes early. Kate and I followed a family of four up the ramp leading to gate G18. The weary-looking mother juggled her tote bags while tugging on the arm of a less-than-in-a-hurry small boy. He flew a toy airplane over his head. His little sister, sporting mouse ears, peered at us over her daddy's shoulder. I waved. She grinned, then quickly buried her face in his neck.

The terminal bustled with hordes of end-of-the-summer

vacationers. I scoured the area for Maggie while Kate struggled with a wheel on her luggage.

"I knew I should have invested in a new suitcase before coming on this trip. I'm going to wear myself out dragging this dinosaur around."

"It'll be okay," I said, craning my neck. "If it gives you much trouble, you can buy a new one before we go home."

"Caroline, over here."

I turned to see Maggie waving her hands over her head. Beside her stood a tall gentleman with a grey beard. "Kate, hurry up. There they are."

Maggie rushed toward us, greeted us both with a quick hug, then turned and motioned for her brother to catch up. "Seth, this is Caroline Myers and her sister, Kate Gordon."

Seth Kauffman extended his hand. "Ladies, welcome to the Windy City, despite the fact we'd appreciate one small puff of wind from the North Shore about now. August can be blistering, and today, it's living up to its reputation."

He reached for my bag. "Here, let me help you with that."

"Thanks. I'm fine, but I know Kate would welcome your help. The wheel on her carry-on is giving her a fit."

Turning, he lifted the case from the floor and walked toward baggage claim. Maggie took my tote as we followed. "How was your flight?"

"Perfect. It was a beautiful day to fly in. The view of the city with the sun sparkling on Lake Michigan was gorgeous. Neither of us has been to Chicago, so we're excited."

We retrieved our luggage then hopped a shuttle to the parking lot before the four of us grabbed a bite to eat at Uno's Pizzeria. Afterward, Seth drove us around the quaint northern suburb of Glencoe, which had been their home for over fifty years.

By the time we reached our hotel, Kate and I were ready to call it a day. Pulling the curtains on the balcony doors, I said, "What did you think of Maggie's brother, Kate?"

She shoved her empty suitcase into the closet. "He's very

nice, but our dinner conversation was a bit awkward, don't you think?"

"It was. Talking around the real reason we're all together was hard, but not taking time to know more about them would have been rude."

"I agree. They've gone out of their way to make us feel welcome. Driving to the airport from Glencoe on a Friday evening can't be an easy commute. Hopefully, we'll all relax, and things will be less strained as the weekend goes on."

The next day

As Seth held the door for us at Dinkel's Bakery on North Lincoln Avenue, Maggie nodded at one of the young men behind the counter. The mingled aromas of hot-out-of-the-oven pastries and freshly brewed coffee smacked of heaven. Various tempting breakfast sandwiches, stollen, scones, and their world-famous donuts, tantalized our appetites. My stomach rumbled.

We ordered and waited for several businessmen to clear a corner booth, then swooped in to claim it and inhale our meals. The conversation we'd waited for opened up as we let our breakfast settle and enjoyed our second cups of coffee.

Maggie pointed to the teenager she'd greeted earlier. "He's the owner's grandchild. Our cousin Joseph began working here in his father's bakery as a teenager and now several generations later, it's still family-operated."

Seth popped the last bite of a chocolate cream-filled donut in his mouth, then wiped his fingers with his napkin. "I was too young to remember the first time I walked into this bakery, but as we grew, our mother would bring Maggie and me here several times a month. I worked here in high school—when it wasn't basketball season, that is. We owe our cousin a lot. After my father was captured by the Jews during Kristallnacht, Joseph was the one who saw that we arrived here safely from Germany."

"Is your cousin still alive?"

"Yes. He's almost ninety-six, and needless to say, our favorite cousin. He's been like a father to us. Still relatively independent and lives with his daughter in Skokie."

Maggie piped in. "If we have time, I'd love for you to meet him. He's a wealth of information, and his fortitude is truly amazing."

Maggie and Seth were perfect hosts. Following breakfast, we walked the length of Navy Pier, did a bit of souvenir shopping along the way, and rode the famous carousel. We then viewed the city from the top of the Tribune Tower, where Daddy used to work.

Later, we peeked into mother's world apart from her Southern roots by enjoying a late lunch at Berghoff's Annex cafe.

Before returning to our hotel in Glencoe, we stopped at the health and rehab facility where Seth and Maggie's mother, Ann-Marie Kauffman, lived. Maggie shared that her mother's days in skilled care were drawing to a close, and she would soon need the shelter of the Alzheimer's Unit. They'd arranged for us to visit with her in the facility's atrium. Kate and I stepped outside to admire the grounds while they went to her room to get her. We walked the manicured garden then sat on a bench beside the Koi pond, enjoying the sound of the water cascading over the rocks.

When we returned to the atrium, Seth rolled his mother into the room. Maggie walked beside her, holding her hand. As Seth introduced us, Mrs. Kauffman smiled, her eyes darting from Kate's face to mine as if trying to recall who we were.

Maggie took a seat beside the couch where Kate and I sat and whispered that her mother appeared to be having a good day. "More alert than usual."

Mrs. Kauffman chatted about the weather, the lovely garden, and her caregivers. Seth eventually pulled out a photo album he'd brought, hoping to spur her memory and initiate a conversation that would give us the answers we sought.

He addressed his mother. "Maggie and I ran across this album the other week and hoped you'd help us with the names of some of our relatives."

Her sweet smile diminished as she glared at him. "Humph. It's been a while since any of them have been to visit me, but I'll see what I can do."

He pushed her closer to the couch and laid the album in her lap.

Brushing her gnarled fingers over the pebbled surface of the black leather album, she looked up at Seth. "This is so pretty. Where'd you find it?"

"In the attic along with a few old newspapers and mementos."

"That's nice. Is it yours?"

"No, it's yours."

"It is? Where did you find it, Son?"

"Upstairs in the attic, Mom."

She nodded. "Really? I don't think I've ever seen this before. Does it belong to you?"

Seth looked at us and shrugged. "No, Mom." He slid a chair beside his mother and opened the album. "Let's look inside. Maybe there will be someone you recognize." The first photo in the album was a picture of Mrs. Kauffman and her husband while in Bavaria. She was seated on a bench, holding Seth in her arms.

She let out an admiring sigh. "Oh, look here." She brushed her fingers over the shiny surface of the photo. "What a beautiful family. Who are they, Seth?"

"We hoped you would tell us. You don't know?"

She lifted the album closer to her face, squinted her eyes, and studied the picture. Shaking her head, she said, "No, can't say that I do. If I know them, they certainly haven't been by to see me in a while. I wonder how old that sweet little baby is now?"

"No telling," Seth said. "Let's look at a few others. We'll come back to this one. Perhaps, you'll remember who they are later."

Mrs. Kaufman thumbed through several pages, with no hints of recognition, before Seth turned to the photograph that Maggie had brought to North Carolina the day we met her.

Their mother dropped back in her chair and stared at the picture of our dad. She sat quietly for a few moments with no outward signs of recognition, and then a tear rolled down her cheek.

Maggie glanced at us, her eyes widening. "Mother, who is that? Do you know him?"

She nodded. "Oh, yes, I know him." She brushed at her cheek. "I could never forget this dear soul."

Maggie and Seth's eyes stayed glued to their mother. She sat silent.

"Mom," Seth said. "Who is it?"

She looked at her son, then across the room at Maggie. "I don't think you children ever met him. Clem Berghoff introduced us. That's—" Her voice broke. "That's—my dear friend—" She hesitated. "Malcolm."

My eyes darted to Kate's, then bounced between Maggie and Seth.

"Are you sure, Mother?" Maggie said.

She nodded.

"What's his last name?"

She sat silent, then stared out toward the garden and shook her head. "I don't know. I only remember calling him Malcolm."

Maggie slid to the edge of her seat and rested her elbows on her knees. "Are you sure Malcolm is his name?"

She nodded again.

"It's not Drew?"

"Drew? Who's Drew?

"The man in the picture. Could his name be Drew?"

She shook her head. "Why would it be Drew? His name is Malcolm. I'm not losing my mind, you know." Her lips trembled as tears slid down her cheeks. "I'm sure it's my precious Malcolm."

My mouth fell open as my heart threatened to escape the walls of my chest. Kate's eyes shot to mine. Her face was ashen. *Had our father lied to Maggie and Seth's mother, just as he had to ours?*

Chapter Twenty-Six

Thursday, December 28, 1939
Emma

Emma tossed several items into a box for The Salvation Army. "Bea, thank you for helping me clean out this bedroom." She pulled back the dingy lace curtains and peeked out the front window. "This is such a cozy room. It has a nice view of the magnolia tree and Mama T's flower garden. If I were going to keep this house, I know what I'd do with this room."

Bea placed a handful of knick-knacks in a box. "What's that?"

"I'd put a desk beneath this window." She pointed toward the corner. "And I'd set that amber-glass hurricane lamp on it and turn this area into a sweet writing space."

Bea turned with an armful of ledgers, her eyes widening. "I didn't know you liked to write. My mama loved to write. She tried to encourage me, but I couldn't be still long enough. I had to be outside seeing what I could get into." She stacked the ledgers in a box of things to keep, then placed her hands on the back of her hips and groaned as she straightened up. "What are you writing?"

"A novel—a New York Times bestseller."

She laughed. "That's the spirit. I love your confidence. Dream big. Dream beyond tomorrow, young lady. We can do whatever God puts in our hearts to do."

"Bea, do you mind if I ask you something personal?"

Shrugging, she eased into a chair to sort through some old

clothes. "Ask it, and I'll let you know."

"Do you ever hear from your daughter?"

She hesitated. "No. Ever since Richie drowned in the Cape Fear while fishing with me, she's shut me out. She and her husband later moved to Ohio. They sent me a note telling me of the move but didn't give me their address." She pinned a few stray strands of hair into her bun. "Not sure why they bothered. I keep praying and trusting God to work it out. We can't make people want us in their lives."

"I'm sorry. I find you delightful. Your daughter doesn't know what she's missing out on."

Bea smiled. "Thank you. You're a blessing. I'm going to miss you when you leave for Chicago."

"It will be hard for both of us. I'll miss you too."

"Was Drew upset when you told him you had to stay a while longer?"

"He was disappointed, but he handled it well. He has a spring show to prepare for, so he'll stay busy." She chuckled. "And he won't have me to distract him."

Emma dropped several more items in the box, then jolted at a knock on the front door. After running down the stairs, she peered through the curtains and opened it. "Look at you. What have you got?"

Opal Brumble pushed past her with a large tray in her hands. "I thought y'all might be ready for a break about now. How does fresh chicken salad sound? Made it this morning." She disappeared into the kitchen, then hollered. "Call Bea, and we'll eat."

Amused, Emma shook her head and grinned. "I will. We'd love that."

The next day

Tucker pointed to a stack of boxes in the corner. "Are these ready to go?"

"They are," Emma said, placing a yellow-flowered vase in the box in front of her. "And I'll have this one packed by the time you get back."

He took several cartons to his car, then returned and dropped in the chair across from Emma. "How do you feel? Still overwhelmed with everything?"

"I am, but with every box that leaves this house, the load gets a little lighter. Thanks for helping. I'd never finish without you." She examined a porcelain figurine and added it to the box. "You certainly impressed Mama T with your skills. She only had good things to say about you. Said you were a Jack-of-all-trades, and there was nothing on the face of God's green earth you couldn't do."

He raised his eyebrows. "She did, did she? I owe it all to my upbringing. My parents own a boarding house in Louisville—the Captain's Inn. My dad's a tugboat captain on the Ohio River and is gone for long periods of time. When I was little, Mom always had a long to-do list taped to the pie safe whenever he came off the river." Laughing, his eyes twinkled at the memory. "If he wanted pie, he knew he'd better chalk off a chore. Whenever he was home, I wanted to be with him every minute. I'd follow him around the house and pass him the tools he needed. When I turned ten, he bought me a tool belt of my own and eventually showed me how to do most everything."

"You were a good student." Her voice softened as she remembered her youth. "My father died when I was thirteen. He'd had a stroke and was an invalid for most of my growing-up years. I missed out on all those daddy-daughter days."

She heaved a sigh, closed the flaps, and slapped the top of the box. "Okay, muscle man, here's one more load for you to carry. Think you can handle it?"

"Watch me." He hoisted it from the floor and walked toward the stairs.

"I'm calling it a day," she said, brushing the hair from her eyes. "Come back in after you take that to the car, and I'll treat you to a glass of ice-cold tea."

"Got pie?"

"No. Sorry. Only tea."

"Aw, shucks." He laughed as the screen slammed behind him.

Emma closed the bedroom door and dropped back against it. Sighing, she looked heavenward. *I'm trying, sweet friend. I'm trying.*

Back inside, Tucker walked into the kitchen. "All set. One more load outta here." He extended his arm and flapped a piece of paper in her face. "This was on the floor in front of the couch. It caught my eye as I came through. Thought it might be something important."

She passed him a glass of tea, then wiped her hands on the dishtowel and carried the paper to the table.

Throwing his leg over the back of the chair across from her, he dropped into the seat.

She unfolded the paper and studied it. "This must've fallen from Mama T's day-planner when Drew was here Christmas night. I'd taken it from her desk so we could decide on our wedding date."

He dropped his eyes and swirled the tea in his glass. "So … did you?"

"Yes. Sunday, June 5th. Isn't that exciting?"

"Can hardly stand it," he muttered as she chattered on.

Dewy-eyed, she looked toward the ceiling and sighed. "Just think …"

"I'd rather not." He gulped his tea.

"Me—a June bride." She pressed the note to her chest, then lowered it to her lap and read Mama T's scrawled handwriting. "Call Miss Parker after Christmas. Dial 3940."

"Hmm, interesting. Perhaps, I should give this woman a call and let her know Mama T has passed."

"Probably a good idea." He downed the last swallow of tea and plopped his glass on the table.

Emma walked to the phone on the wall beside the icebox and dialed the number. It rang several times before a lady answered.

"Hello. Is this Miss Parker?"

"It is."

"My name is Emma Walsh. I'm calling for Florence Turner."

"Wonderful. I've been expecting her call."

"I'm sorry to have to tell you this, but Florence passed away a few weeks before Christmas."

Silence prefaced her words. "This breaks my heart. I looked forward to getting to know her. She seemed like such a sweet lady. Are you a relative?"

"No, but I leased a room from her before I moved to Chicago. She became like a second mother to me. I was astonished to learn she'd willed me her house."

"And a lovely house it is."

"I don't know why Mama T was to call you, but is there something I can help you with?"

"I'd spoken with her about renting a room, and she told me she hoped to have one ready after Christmas. Will the room still be available?"

"I'm sorry. Probably not. Once the painting and repairs are finished, my plan is to sell the house."

She sighed. "I'm sorry to hear this. It seemed like the perfect place for me to write."

"You're a writer?"

"I am—my debut novel releases at the end of next year. My manuscript is due soon, and I'm desperate for solitude. Right now, I stay with my brother and his family, but it's not the best arrangement for creativity. Would you consider renting the room for a while? At least until I can find something else?"

Emma glanced at Tucker. "I don't know. I hadn't considered renting. If you give me a day or two to think about it, I'll get back to you."

"That would be perfect. I appreciate you considering it and

hope you have a nice day."

"You too." Emma placed the handset in the cradle and watched the cardinal that had returned to the bush. As it leaped from branch to branch, scouring for bugs, her unsettled spirit searched too. She let out a long breath and returned to the table.

Tucker stretched out his legs and placed his hands on the back of his head. "Sounds like you've got a major decision to make."

She rubbed her forehead. "I do." Crossing her arms on the table in front of her, she leaned forward, hoping for some keen insight. "What do you think? Would it be smart for me to rent a room?"

He shrugged. "It's hard to say. Maybe. In this depressed economy, it will probably be hard to find a buyer. Renting might be the way to go." He scratched his head. "If this lady is ready to rent, and it sounds like she is, I think I'd let her. You could put the extra money into house repairs, then put it on the market and see what happens. A buyer may like the fact that there's a renter and a built-in source of income."

She settled back in her chair. "You may be right. I need to pray about this ... and talk to Drew, of course. How long do you think it will take to get the house in good enough shape to sell?"

He looked up at the paint peeling from the ceiling. "Since I can only work on my days off, it will take a while. A few months at the minimum."

"Do you think you could have it ready by spring?"

He tilted his head from side to side as he figured. "If I can hogtie Hank into helping me, maybe."

She picked up Tucker's empty glass from the table and placed it with hers in the sink. "If I do rent, I can't think of anything more exciting than having an author in the house. Perhaps her muse would rub off on me."

Wednesday, January 3, 1940

Emma leaned against the dresser and crossed her legs at the ankles. Celeste Parker was younger than she'd imagined. Thirtyish, maybe? Her throaty telephone voice had led her to envision a more mature woman.

"I love it. A fresh coat of paint certainly makes a difference, doesn't it?" Celeste stood in the middle of Emma's old bedroom and flashed a broad smile, her dark eyes shining. "When can I move in?"

"Hank comes tomorrow to put the final coat of paint on the woodwork. How does Monday sound? We should have the room put back together by then."

She pushed her round tortoise-shell glasses up on her pert nose and giggled. "Perfect." She reached in her large fabric shoulder bag, pulled out a white envelope, and handed it to Emma. "Here's half of January's rent. I'll have the balance on Monday."

"Thank you. I hope you'll be happy here. I know I was." As they walked into the hall, Celeste descended the stairs in front of her. "Wait." Emma waved her back. "There's something I want to show you." She led her past the bathroom and opened the door to the third bedroom. "It's still a work-in-progress but should make a lovely workspace. You're welcome to use it when it's finished."

Celeste's eyes widened. "Are you serious? This is a dream come true." She walked to the desk beneath the window and ran her hand over the tiger-oak surface. "How lovely." She spun around. "I knew from the moment I walked into this house that it was a special place. Thank you for your generosity. I would love to type 'The End' to my story in here."

Emma motioned. "There's a small bookcase downstairs that I plan to put on this wall." She turned and pointed across the room. "And a small day bed will go there with a pressed-back lady's rocker beside it."

"What more could one ask for?" She glanced at the oversized watch on her wrist. "I should be going. I have lots to do before next week, and so do you." She extended her hand. "Thank you for letting me move in."

Emma closed the door and followed her down the stairs. "I look forward to having you. It's been lonely here without Mama T." She opened the front door and followed Celeste onto the porch. Chummy jumped from the swing, huddled beside the door, and mewed. "Chummy Choo, meet our new houseguest."

Celeste squatted and smoothed his silky coat as he brushed up against her and purred. "Don't worry, big boy. You're welcome in my room any time." She stood and stepped down onto the sidewalk. "Thank you again for opening your home to me. If there's ever anything I can help you with around here, let me know."

Emma smiled. "Thank you. I appreciate the offer." She watched her pass through the gate and then turn to latch it. "Celeste."

She shifted her purse on her shoulder and looked up. "Yes."

"There is something I'd love for you to do for me."

"Of course."

"Whenever you have time, will you read the first few chapters of my book and tell me what you think?"

Her eyes bulged as her mouth dropped open. "You're an author too?"

Emma shrugged. "I don't know. That's what I hoped you could tell me."

"How exciting. I'd love to look at it." She threw up her hand and all but skipped toward the corner.

Chapter Twenty-Seven

Sunday, April 7, 1940
Chicago, Illinois
Drew

Drew stepped back from his easel. Tilting his head first to the right and then to the left, he grimaced and let out an audible groan. Every stroke of his brush took him further away from the image he held in his mind's eye. With his show opening less than three weeks away, the pressure mounted. Everyone would soon know he was an imposter—someone who would join the ranks of "starving" artists and the countless wannabes who'd sought the limelight and lost. He'd keep company with those who sketched on the sidewalk and hoped to sell enough work for a cup of coffee and their next meal.

He supposed he wasn't as talented as he'd led himself to believe, and now Emma—his greatest admirer and encourager—wouldn't be at the show to support him. He wished he'd never committed to Mr. Safron. If not following through with his commitment would only affect him, he'd find a reason to cancel, but he couldn't disappoint Joe. His loyal agent had worked too hard to acquire this opportunity of a lifetime. Letting him down and, more than that, betraying his best friend was not in his tartan-plaid Scottish blood.

He pulled the canvas from his easel and propped it against the wall at the end of a long row of misfires. Their number multiplied daily. After placing a clean canvas on the easel, he thumbed through a pile of photographs, then tossed them across the room. As they hit the wall and fell to the floor, Drew dropped into the threadbare sun-bleached chair by the window. Resting his eyes on Emma's letter on the side table, he picked it up, revealing the book's title beneath it—*How to Paint Your Best Every Time.*

"Humph," he muttered.

He slipped Emma's letter from its envelope—a letter he'd read no less than a dozen times as if rereading it would somehow change its contents. Propping his feet on a soiled ottoman splotched with paint, he read.

My darling Drew,

I hope you can step away from your easel long enough to read this letter. I pray daily that every stroke will be your finest. I hope this news doesn't interrupt the flow of your progress. It's not a letter I've looked forward to writing.

Unless something drastically changes, I don't see how I can attend your show at the Safron Gallery. It crushes me to write these words. We'd both hoped by now, I would be back in Chicago for good. The housing market has dried up, as have many other things this depression has brought our way. With no sale in sight, I must attend to house affairs and hang on to my renter. Her rent enables me to invest the little Mama T left into the final repairs on the house. Without Tucker's help, I would have run out of money long before now.

Know that I will be with you in spirit and will continue to pray for your success. No one in attendance will be able to turn a blind eye to your exceptional talent. The picture you painted of me at Navy Pier hangs on the wall at the foot of my bed. When I look at it, I lose myself in the memories of that day and continue to dream beyond tomorrow. I know our time will come. Please don't give up on me. I can't wait to be your wife. Write me when you get a moment. I love receiving your letters—especially the ones with paint smudges and the faint smell of turpentine. Each one assures me that you cared enough to stop and write regardless of how busy you were. How lucky I am to be yours.

    I'll love you forever,

    Emma

Drew placed his feet on the floor and tossed the letter on the table. At this rate, he wondered if Emma would even make it back for a June wedding? Leaning forward, he dropped his head in his hands and sighed. He needed some fresh air. Perhaps the combination of turpentine and linseed oil had muddled his thoughts.

He walked to the bedroom, slipped his wallet and room key into his pants pocket, and stepped into the hall. "Hey, hold up!" he yelled as the elevator doors slid shut. Wincing, he fell against the wall. As he watched the sweeping hand of the floor indicator count down the floors and then hit bottom, his spirits hit bottom too.

Friday, April 26, 1940
St. Louis, Missouri

Drew sipped his wine, then checked his watch and leaned back in the booth of the Hotel Jefferson lounge. He tugged on his tie, then wiped his sweaty palms with his handkerchief and stuffed it back in his pocket. In less than an hour, he'd make his appearance at the opening of his show in the Max Safron Gallery upstairs. He'd managed to produce enough paintings for a good presentation but feared they weren't his best work, or worse yet, maybe they were.

Ella Campbell, the gallery curator, seemed pleased enough, but at this late date, would she really tell him if she wasn't? Joe was presently upstairs taking care of the last-minute business. Drew was thankful all he had to do was show up and smile. Hopefully, there would be at least one patron tonight to smile at.

He picked up the St. Louis Post-Dispatch and scanned the headlines. The Nazi invasion of Norway on April 9th had dominated the month's news. Norway was taken by surprise, and the allied forces who'd moved in to help had fallen back. While reading, his ears perked up when a lady seated at a nearby table mentioned his name.

"I want to be there when the doors open. I haven't been able to get Andrew Brown's skyline painting out of my mind since I saw it on Wednesday." She laid her hand on the man's arm. "Honey, what would you think about taking his beautiful piece back home with us? It would look stunning over the library table in your study."

The man seemed more interested in his dessert than in the prospects of purchasing artwork. "If you want it, Doris, we'll get it. As well as being a nice remembrance of our time here, it should make a good investment. Mr. Brown's work shows promise." He shook his head. "Incredible talent for one so young."

Leaning over, she kissed his cheek. "Thank you. I'm thrilled you like it too." She shook his arm. "Hurry now, honey. Finish your dessert. I'm afraid that painting will sell before we get there."

The lady's words were precisely what he needed to hear. When the couple left, he rose from his booth encouraged. If no one else attended, at least maybe he'd sold one painting. At this point, he'd settle for anything.

As the couple from Vancouver walked toward the counter with the painting of Chicago's skyline at sunset, Joe handed Drew a cup of punch and patted him on the back. "Way to go, young man. Didn't I tell you that you had nothing to worry about? One day you'll learn to believe in yourself." He glanced at the clock above the door. "The night is still young, and you've already made a nice sale. You're going to do fine, just fine. Your name will be on everyone's lips tomorrow—here and in Vancouver. Next time you show, your numbers will double. And whenever we get through this national depression, your career will skyrocket. I feel it in my bones."

Drew breathed a sigh of relief and brushed the freshly vacuumed carpet with the toe of his spit-shined shoe. "Thanks for pushing me out of my comfort zone. Maybe one day, these events will get easier."

"They will. You'll see." He stepped away to speak to a young couple about a piece they'd stood admiring for a while.

Drew grinned. *A wheeler-dealer, that man.* He downed his punch, set the cup on a side table, and walked over to straighten a painting on the wall. Stepping back, he double-checked its position.

"That one's a real beauty, isn't it?"

Turning in the direction of the cheerful voice, his eyes widened as the stately woman approached him, smiling. "It's my favorite, actually." She stepped up to examine it closer, then whirled around, her dark eyes meeting his.

Drew stood silent.

"What's the matter." She offered her hand. "You do remember me, don't you?"

"Of course, I do, Miss Murray." Shaking her hand, he cleared his throat and smiled, trying to ignore the warmth rising from beneath his collar.

She wagged her index finger. "Tsk. Tsk. It's Liz. We're on a first-name basis, remember?" She glanced around the room at the swarm of admirers. "Or has your newfound fame gone to your head?"

He reached over and gave her a quick hug. "Of course, we are, Liz. Your appearance took me by surprise, that's all."

She lifted her chin and flipped her hair over her shoulder. "I do hope you approve."

"What's not to," he blurted without thinking. "Thank you so much for coming."

"I wouldn't miss this for the world. Actually, I was in the city earlier this week and strolled through the gallery." She pointed to the painting in front of them. "I returned to purchase this one. I hope it's still available?"

His heart raced at the thought of two sales in one night. "It is. I'm flattered you like it." He motioned toward the desk. "Mrs. Campbell will be more than happy to take care of that for you." He took the painting off the wall and walked her to the desk. "Thank you so much. I hope you enjoy it." Smiling, he laid the picture on the counter. "You've made this starving artist's day. I can eat for another week now." Admiring his artwork, she batted the air with her hand. "Phooey. I know that's an understatement." She chuckled. "You haven't noticed, but I've been here for a while now. You were busy making a sale when I came in, so I browsed. The buzz in this room is electric. I've heard so many nice comments. You're going to come out of this smelling like a rose."

She turned and motioned toward the registration table. "And by the way, in case you're wondering, that vase of red roses is from me. I brought them when I came in earlier this week. Congratulations on your debut."

He stepped back, rubbing his neck. "Thank you. I noticed them earlier but haven't had a chance to walk around the room and admire all of the flowers." He threw back his head and laughed. "Funny. When I came through the door, my first thoughts were that it smelled like a mortuary in here. I hoped it wasn't an omen of imminent doom."

She waved him off. "You're too modest—no chance of that. Mark my words, tonight is the start of an amazing career for you—a star rising."

"Thanks for that vote of confidence. I've certainly been encouraged by this turnout. My agent rides me incessantly about not believing in myself."

Her eyes pierced his. "Listen to him. He sounds like a smart man. Knows a good thing when he sees it." She placed her hand on his arm. "And so do I."

He shifted his gaze and noted a couple entering the gallery. "Go on and attend to them. I'll come back over before I leave."

Shoving his hands in his pockets, he turned.

"On second thought, I won't. I'm expecting a business call and need to return to my room. How about a late dinner after the show?" She grinned. "My treat for the starving artist."

He raised his eyebrows and chuckled, then hesitated. *It would be nice to have someone to celebrate with. He'd planned to call her soon anyway.* Raising his palm, he shook his head. "Sounds swell. But the treat will be mine. You've done enough." He looked at his watch. "What time?"

"How about nine-thirty in the dining room?"

He nodded and smiled. "I'll be there."

As Liz leaned in and kissed his cheek, he embraced her. Peering over her shoulder, his eyes met those of the young lady standing in the doorway. He gasped.

She held a single red rose.

Emma.

Chapter Twenty-Eight

Sunday, August 19, 2012
Glencoe, Illinois
Caroline

Kate and I sat in the rockers on our hotel room's balcony, enjoying our second cup of coffee. It wasn't even seven-thirty, and the temperature was already in the seventies. Today's forecast for lower humidity and a light breeze would hopefully make our last day in Chicago more comfortable.

It was nice to have the morning to ourselves. After yesterday's full day of sightseeing and nonstop talking, we needed it. Our sweet visit with Maggie and Seth's precious mother, Ann-Marie Kauffman, was enjoyable but confusing at best. It was apparent she wasn't going to be the one to give us answers we could depend on. We had suspected that from the start, but one never knows about dementia. Perhaps this afternoon's visit with Maggie's cousin Joseph would shed a ray of light on our situation.

Kate set her mug on the railing and picked up the book she'd started reading on the plane. Pressing her bare feet against the iron balusters, she pushed the rocker. "So far, it looks like our trip to Chicago has been a dead end. We may walk away from here knowing no more than we knew when we came."

I sipped my coffee and nodded. "You might be right, but at least we've had the opportunity to experience some of our parents' world, meet Seth, and get to know Maggie better. It sounds as if their childhood was a good one, despite the horrible loss of Ann-Marie's husband. If it hadn't been for their cousin, they probably wouldn't be alive to tell of it."

"I agree." She slipped the marker from her book and began reading.

We sat quietly for a while, enjoying the early morning breeze. Then, moving to the edge of my chair, I looked at Kate. "I've been thinking."

"That's dangerous," she muttered, never glancing up from her book.

"I'd like to go to Berghoff's again tonight for dinner. I find it interesting that Mrs. Kauffman said Clem Berghoff introduced 'Malcolm' to her. Since Mother was a waitress at The Annex during that time, her story lines up with the possibility that this Malcolm *is* our father." I circled the rim of my mug with my index finger. "Maybe Daddy told her his name was Malcolm. What do you think?"

She slipped her sunglasses from her hair to her nose and laid her head back on the chair. "I don't know what to make of it all. You could be right. I believe we know the truth, though, not only based on circumstantial evidence but also on what our hearts tell us. Denying that Maggie is our half-sister doesn't mesh with any of the information we have so far."

"I know, but I wish we knew more of the story behind Dad and Ann-Marie's meeting. If Joseph can't tell us, maybe someone at Berghoff's can."

She shook her head and frowned. "I don't know, Caroline. Clem Berghoff is dead and gone. Who would be alive that knows anything?

I dropped back in my chair and rocked. "No one, but I still want to go."

Kate gave her rocker a hard push. "I can't believe we're sitting over eight hundred miles away from our home, seventy-some years later discussing this. We were simply minding our own business, and then boom, our world was flipped upside down in a heartbeat. I like Maggie. She's certainly someone I could accept as our sister. It's the gut-wrenching disillusionment with Daddy that's so hard to reconcile. In the pit of my being, I can't help but believe there's a huge piece of this puzzle missing."

"I know. I think that too, and then wonder if it's wishful thinking." I rose from the rocker and leaned against the railing. "Let's talk to Maggie and Seth this afternoon about eating at Berghoff's. We've nothing to lose and everything to gain." I grinned and patted my stomach. "Maybe in more ways than one. If we hit another roadblock, at least the Wienerschnitzel and German Chocolate cake will be excellent consolation prizes." Laughing, I slid open the doors and entered the room.

"You've got that right, Sis. And don't forget their amazing apple strudel. Deciding what to order may be the hardest part of this trip yet."

Later that afternoon

Joseph Dinkel lived in a quaint one-story row house on Babb Avenue, a short walk from the heart of Skokie. Leah, his daughter, greeted the four of us at the front door and led us back to the den. Mr. Dinkel sat in his chair, engrossed in an old black and white Dragnet episode. It played decibels louder than we were accustomed to.

"Papa." She raised her voice. "Papa." Walking to the table beside his chair, she picked up the remote and lowered the volume.

He jerked his head toward her. "Hey. What are you doing?"

"You can catch the show again later today, Papa. Right now, you have company." She clicked off the television.

He leaned into the chair arm and craned his neck. "Company? I do?"

Maggie walked over and hugged him. "You do, indeed."

His eyes widened. "My, oh, my, Magpie. Where have you

been keeping yourself?"

She stepped in front of him, took his hand, and seated herself on the ottoman. "I live in Virginia now, remember? I've been there for several years. So you've missed me?"

"You know I have." His brow furrowed as his eyes set intensely on hers. "You don't like it there, do you?"

She smiled and nodded. "I do."

"Dagnabit," he said, twisting his mouth and snapping his fingers. "I hoped you'd move back."

"No. My plans are to stay." She motioned to us. "Joseph, Seth's here with two of our new friends from North Carolina."

Seth patted his cousin on the back, embraced him, and then introduced us.

"So you're from North Carolina, huh? I traveled there once. Back when I was young and spry. It's a pretty place to be from."

"We think so. Both the mountains and the sea are only a few hours away from our homes. We have the best of both worlds."

"So what brings you to the Windy City?"

Maggie patted him on the knee. "They're researching their family tree. There's a chance we're related. We hoped you would be able to answer some of our questions."

He shrugged and tapped his temple with his crooked index finger. "I don't know about that. This old brain doesn't function as good as it once did. But, I'll do what I can."

Leah invited Kate and me to sit on the couch across from Joseph. Maggie moved to the chair beside him while Seth brought in two chairs from the dining room for himself and Leah.

"My goodness. This room hasn't seen this much company since my brother and his family came from New York a couple of years ago." He looked at Leah and fanned himself with his hand. "Will you pump up the air a bit, honey? It's warm in here today." He shifted his attention and scanned our faces. "I like this. Beats Dragnet any time."

We laughed.

As Maggie and Joseph reminisced about her old

neighborhood and friends in Chicago, I squirmed and checked my watch. I thought she'd never get around to the reason we'd come.

She motioned toward Kate and me. "Joseph, my friends and I hoped you could tell us more about Mother's life after she came to America. We've heard stories of her early years here—of how she helped you in the bakery and of taking in ironing so she could stay with us kids, but we've heard nothing about her social life.

"You know I've learned I didn't come with her and Seth from Germany but was born here in Chicago. Mother doesn't realize I know that, and I don't want to upset her. She's easily agitated, so we're cautious about what we say to her. We hoped you would be able to shed more light on my situation." She paused. "Cousin Joseph, do you know who my father is?"

His expression changed as he dropped his head and picked at a piece of lint on his trousers. He shook his head. "No. I'm sorry, Magpie, I don't. Your mother never courted anyone that we knew of. Oh, she was a looker, and through the years, there were quite a few young men who'd come into the bakery and want to take her out. Her life revolved around Seth at the time, so she'd always put them off. At least that's what we thought. When she got pregnant with you, it was a shock to everyone. The wife and I tried to talk with her about it, but every time we did, it would upset her, so we backed off. After all, she was a grown woman and didn't owe us any explanations. We hoped one day she'd open up and tell us, but she never did. Embarrassed by it all, she pushed through the best way she knew how. I don't know if she ever saw the fella again after she found out she was pregnant."

Maggie reached into her purse, pulled out a photograph, and handed it to her cousin. "Yesterday, we visited Mother at the facility and showed her this picture. Have you ever seen this man? On the back, Mother had written, 'Maggie's dad.'"

"You don't say." He raised the photo closer to his face, squinted his eyes, and pursed his lips. "Hmm, he does look familiar, but I can't recall his name."

Kate and I traded glances. I moved to the edge of the couch and leaned forward. "Was his name Drew?"

He looked at me, cut his eyes to the window, and hesitated. "Doesn't ring a bell."

"How about Malcolm?"

He shook his head. "No, that doesn't sound right either?" Smoothing his thinning silver hair, he looked at Maggie. "I'm sorry, Magpie. That was a lot of years ago. I wish I could help you, but my memory escapes me."

"That's okay. We understand." She reached for the photograph.

He held it out, then pulled it back. "Wait. I do remember. This man had a brogue. Yes. A slight brogue. I used to like to hear him talk. He was from Ireland or Scotland, I believe." He tilted back his head and drummed his fingers on the arm of his chair. "What was his name?"

Maggie waited a few moments, hoping the man's identity would click in with him. "That's all right. Don't worry about it. You've enlightened us more than you know."

Kate looked at me with a downcast expression and shook her head. Mr. Dinkel's words were not at all what we'd hoped to hear. Room for any doubt concerning our father's involvement with Ann-Marie was rapidly eroding. Still, I held out hope our trip to Berghoff's would reveal something different and uncover the missing piece we hoped was there.

Obviously, you don't go to The Berghoff on a Sunday night without a dinner reservation. The line to the over 100-year-old, family-owned restaurant serving traditional German fare snaked its way out the door, underneath a two-story-tall orange-neon restaurant sign and along the Adams Street sidewalk. By the time the hostess called our name, my stomach had ceased to rumble.

I'm sure it thought I was in fasting mode.

We followed the waitress through a wooden revolving door leading to the maître d' stand. From there, we walked across brown and cream-colored tile floors to a table at the back of the sizeable oak-paneled room. Our table was topped with a white linen cloth, brown napkins, and a lovely red rose in a crystal vase.

While waiting to be served, Kate and I admired the brass chandeliers hanging from the twenty-foot ceiling and viewed several Old Chicago photographs lining the walls.

Our meals were well worth the wait, and I wasn't the least bit guilt-ridden when I ordered the dark chocolate cake with coconut filling, topped with chocolate sauce and toasted almonds.

Kate enjoyed the salted caramel cheesecake, smothered in caramel sauce and whipped cream. As an older sister, she sets a terrible example for me.

When the young waiter brought our checks, I thanked him for his excellent service and chatted with him for a while. His eyes lit up when I told him that in 1939 our mother had worked downstairs in The Annex. He clung to my every word and asked more questions than I asked of him.

I apologized for keeping him from his other guests. He assured me we were his last customers of the evening and told me he wanted to show us something.

We followed him into a back hall to a stairwell lined with early photographs left by Clement Berghoff. As we walked down the steps, our waiter stopped at each picture, telling us what he knew about it. As he pointed to a photo of Mr. Berghoff with his wait staff, I looked for Mother, but she wasn't among those pictured.

When we reached the landing, another photo of Mr. Berghoff and several men caught my eye. I examined it further, then grabbed Kate's arm. "You've got to see this."

"What?"

I stepped aside. "Look at this picture."

After studying it, her eyes shot to mine. "It's Daddy. I'd know that smile anywhere." She hugged her waist. "This sends chills down my spine."

I nodded. "Mine too."

Viewing it again, her hand flew to her mouth.

"What's wrong?"

She stepped back, her face ashen. "Take a closer look."

"What is it?"

"Here." She tapped her well-manicured, hot-pink fingernail in a staccato-like fashion on the glass. "Look right here. On the opposite end of the row. It's our missing piece."

I fumbled in my shoulder bag for my glasses, slipped them on, and stepped closer. My heart pounded. Looking at Kate, I said, "I'm stunned. Why didn't we think of this?" I embraced her. "We've done it, Kate. We've solved this crazy mystery."

Turning, I called Maggie, who stood at the bottom of the stairs talking with Seth and the waiter. As she walked up to the landing, I said, "You're not going to believe this, but Kate and I have found your answer—the missing piece to this puzzle."

Her eyes widened. "You have? Are you sure?"

"One hundred percent sure." I pulled her closer to the picture. Take a look? Do you see anything unusual?"

She leaned in. "Oh my goodness, that's your dad—the man Mother says is my father as well."

"Yes, but that's not all. Look at the other end of the row."

She studied the picture again. "This is crazy?" Her eyes met mine. "I don't understand."

"I know you don't. Kate and I will explain in the car. Can we go back to Joseph's house tonight? Will he be up this late?"

She glanced at her watch. "Yes. It's only eight-thirty. He doesn't usually go to bed before ten." She took out her cell phone. "I'll call and let him know we're on our way."

Kate and I followed Maggie and Seth up the stairs. With this new information, we hoped Mr. Dinkel could answer our few remaining questions.

Chapter Twenty-Nine

A short time later
Caroline

Kate and I settled on the couch we'd occupied a few hours earlier. Mr. Dinkel sat across from us in plaid pajamas and a navy terry cloth robe. A book lay open in his lap. His daughter, Leah, sat in the chair by his side.

Adjusting the pillow at my back, I apologized for visiting so late. "Kate and I have to catch an early flight in the morning, and we knew tonight would be our last opportunity to talk to you."

"It's quite all right. I hardly ever go to bed before ten." He turned toward Maggie. "From the excitement in your voice on the phone, it sounds like you came away from Berghoff's with a lot more than a full stomach. What's going on with you? You're all grinning like Cheshire cats."

"We had a wonderful meal and the nicest young waiter, who shared much of Berghoff's history with us. He showed us pictures from the restaurant's early days. Many were taken during the time Caroline and Kate's mother worked there."

"Yes," Kate said. "We'd hoped to find Mother in one of them, but she wasn't pictured. Probably because she worked at The Annex for such a short time."

Joseph placed his book on the table at his side. "That's a shame."

Maggie looked at us and smiled. "Oh, but we found something better."

He straightened in his chair, his eyes widening. "Better?"

STARR AYERS | 177

"Yes. Earlier today, I asked you about my father."

He nodded.

"Our trip to Berghoff's answered a lot of questions for us."

Taking my cell phone from my purse, I walked over to Mr. Dinkel. "I have something I want you to see. Tonight, I snapped a picture of one of the photographs hanging in the stairwell." I handed him my phone and pointed as I spoke. "This is Mr. Berghoff and a few of his regular customers in the late thirties. The man on the right is my father."

"Yes, that's the man in the photo you showed me earlier today."

"Now, look at the other end of the row." I seated myself on the ottoman in front of his chair.

He picked up his glasses from the side table, pulled the phone closer to his face, and squinted. "Will you look at that—bookends. I'd forgotten about those fellows."

"Does the name Mac ring a bell with you?"

He laid his head back on the chair, then nodded. "It does. I should have thought of him earlier. He was from somewhere up in Canada."

"Did you ever meet him?"

"I did. One summer, he came to Chicago to visit his brother. Was your Dad's name Andrew?"

"Yes. Drew for short."

"Ah ... Mac and Drew. I only knew him as Andrew." He threw back his head and laughed. "One morning, your dad, Drew, came in and placed his regular order—coffee with cream and a chocolate éclair. He paid and took his usual seat in the corner booth in the back of the shop. A few minutes later, I heard his Scottish brogue again— 'Joseph, my man.' When I turned around, he placed the identical order.

"Another éclair? You mean you've already eaten the last one?

"He looked perplexed. 'Eaten? I can't eat the éclair until you give it to me?'

"You don't remember ordering coffee and an éclair a few minutes ago and paying for it?

"He dipped his chin, looked over his glasses, and frowned. 'Are you okay, Joseph? I'm sorry, my friend, but you're mistaken. I just walked in. I haven't ordered anything.'

"I struggled with how to handle this with Andrew, but I remembered my papa saying, 'the customer is always right,' so I nodded and prepared the same order. My heart hurt because I felt there was something terribly wrong with my friend.

"When I turned back around, I was astonished. Andrew and Mac stood on the other side of the counter with their arms draped over each other's shoulders. They were almost bent over double, laughing. I could have slugged them."

Kate and I cracked up. "That sounds like something our dad would do. Those two were as identical as they come. We never got to meet our Uncle Mac, but Daddy would tell us hilarious stories of their pranks."

Taking my phone from Mr. Dinkel, I walked back to the couch. "On the way over here tonight, I googled DNA and twins. I'd never thought about identical twins sharing the same DNA code, but they do. Maggie's father could be our Uncle Mac, and according to what her mother said about the man in the picture's name being Malcolm, I believe he is."

Joseph looked at Maggie. "Wow, Magpie. What do you think?"

"It makes perfect sense to me." She turned toward Kate and me. "Seth and I are going to the center tomorrow to sign some paperwork. If Mother is having a good day, we'll try and find out more about Malcolm."

"That would be wonderful. I hope you can. Please text one of us if you learn anything new."

"I certainly will." She looked at her watch. "Seth, we should leave so Joseph can go to bed. Caroline and Kate have an early morning flight too."

Kate spoke up. "Thank you all for your hospitality and for

chauffeuring us around Chicago."

"Yes. We've had a wonderful trip. The only thing that could make it better would be if your mother affirmed our findings tomorrow. I trust she will."

The next day
Monday, August 20, 2012

I loaded our luggage into the back of my car, climbed into the driver's seat, and exited Piedmont International airport's parking deck. "It feels good to be back under Carolina blue skies, doesn't it, Kate?"

She laid her head against the seat and let out a long breath. "Yes, God's country for sure."

"Our time in Chicago couldn't have been nicer. Maggie and Seth were great hosts, but there's truly no place like home.

"I agree. When my head hits the pillow tonight, I'm certainly not going to miss the city's honking horns and siren twerps." Kate rummaged in her purse and pulled out her phone. "And speaking of Maggie, I forgot to take my phone off airplane mode when we landed. Maybe by now, we have a text from her."

I sailed down the Interstate 40 ramp and edged my way into rush hour traffic. "I sure hope so. I'm anxious to hear how their visit went with Ann-Marie." Several notification chimes rang from Kate's phone.

"There it is. Maggie's text came through." Tapping it open, she shifted in her seat and looked over at me. "I'm almost afraid to read it."

"I know how you feel."

She took a deep breath and read aloud.

Hi, Caroline and Kate,

Hopefully, you had a smooth flight home and have your land legs back. Seth and I had an excellent visit with Mother this morning. She was the most lucid I've seen her in quite some time. With low humidity and a light breeze, the weather was perfect, so we wheeled her out to the Koi pond. She enjoyed it and was in a talkative mood. I felt I had a window of opportunity, so I took it. I told her about going to Berghoff's for dinner and showed her Mac's picture on my phone. She called him Malcolm again.

I didn't want to upset her but came right out and asked if he was my father. For a few moments, she simply stared at me. My insides quaked. Her eyes soon welled with tears, and she wanted to know how I knew. I told her Seth had found Mac's picture among some of her papers. She sobbed and apologized for keeping the truth from me. I told her I understood and that she had been a good mother. It was then I saw the tension leave her body, and the flood gates opened.

Mother and Mac corresponded with one another often, and he visited her in Chicago several times. When she discovered she was pregnant, they planned to wed, but within a month, Mac was gone. Since he was your uncle, you've probably heard stories of what an excellent tennis player he was and of how he had a heart attack on the court. He was dead before the ambulance arrived.

I felt terrible for Mother—first the horrific killing of her husband by the Nazis and then losing a second chance at love. Life seems so unfair—actually, it is. It wasn't fair for Jesus to pay our debt on the cross either, but because of his love for us, he did.

Seth and I loved having you. Call me when you get settled in. There is more about our visit I can tell you.

Just Cuz!
Maggie

Kate laid her phone in her lap and sighed. "Case closed, Caroline. Ann-Marie Kaufmann has confirmed Maggie is our cousin."

"She has, indeed ... and that Daddy is the kind and gentle soul we always knew him to be."

Chapter Thirty

"Pardon me," Drew said, bolting past Liz and almost bumping into a young couple entering the Max Safron Gallery. "Emma. Wait! Please, wait."

Sprinting across the mezzanine, he bent down, swooped up the long-stemmed red rose, and shouted, "Peaches, please, stop. It's not what you think."

Emma hit the elevator's down button. When she turned and saw Drew running toward her, she slipped through the exit door leading to the stairs.

As Drew entered the alcove, the elevator chimed, and the doors slid open. Dashing into the car, he instructed the attendant and fell against the wall, panting. They reached the first floor just as Emma came through the stairwell entrance. Drew bolted in front of her. She moved from side to side, but with one long step each way, he blocked her. Taking her by the shoulders, he pulled her toward him. "Please, let me explain."

She beat his chest with her fists and hollered. "Let me go, Drew Brown. You don't deserve my love." She tried to squirm from his embrace, but he held her firmly until she collapsed against his chest, sobbing.

He could feel her heart pounding and stroked her hair. "Emma, please let me explain. It's not at all what you think."

Her body shook as she whimpered in his arms.

Lifting her chin, he kissed her tears and whispered, "Come

sit over here and let me explain." He led her to a bench beside the elevator door, wrapped his arms around her shoulders, and pulled her close. Smoothing her hair, he kissed the top of her head, then lifted her face toward his. "Peaches, listen to me. The lady's name is Liz. I bumped into her once before in St. Louis when I worked at the Post-Dispatch. She came tonight to buy one of my paintings. I don't know why she kissed me, but she did. I didn't invite it." He pulled back. "Please, believe me when I say there is nothing between us. Yes, she asked me to dinner, and I told her I'd meet her. I guess I shouldn't have, but I thought it would be nice to have someone to celebrate the evening with, and—"

Emma bristled and tried to break away.

He held her tighter. "Wait. Let me finish. I wanted to surprise you with this later, but it looks like further explanation is needed now."

She furrowed her brow as her glassy eyes pierced his.

"Liz manages the jewelry department at Marshall Fields in Chicago. I thought over dinner tonight, I'd talk to her about buying your wedding band."

"Really?"

He nodded.

She inhaled deeply, dropped her forehead on his chest, and shook her head. "Oh, Drew, I'm sorry. I've done it again." She lifted her eyes. "I've allowed the poison of my past heartbreak to infect our relationship." She shook her head. "I'm trying. Really, I am. I'm sorry I doubted you."

He kissed her lips, then pulled her close and rested his chin on top of her head. "Thank you, but no apology needed. I know it looked suspicious." Leaning back, he held up the red rose and smiled. "I believe you dropped this, madam."

She took it and laughed. "Oh my, I suppose I did. How clumsy of me."

Taking her hand, he stood. "Now *you* have some explaining to do?"

She looked puzzled. "Me?"

"Yes, you. What on earth are you doing here?" Glancing at his watch, he stepped in front of the elevator door and pushed the call button. "You can tell me over dinner. Right now, I need to get back to the show. Joe's probably standing on his head about now."

He watched the sweep of the floor indicator as the elevator rumbled down the shaft. Settling, its bell chimed, and the elevator attendant pulled open the brass gate. Liz Murray stood alone in the car.

Drew's eyes darted to Emma, then returned to Liz.

She smiled and stepped out, her eyes meeting Drew's. "Here's the star of the show. I wondered where you'd run off to. I thought I'd grab a bite to eat in the lounge. Would you and your lady friend care to join me?"

"Thank you, but we can't. I need to get upstairs before my agent decides he no longer wants to represent me."

"Oh, I don't think that's going to happen. The last time I saw him, he had a big smile on his face. The room is bustling."

Drew's eyes widened.

"I predict a sellout. I saw several people leave with paintings under their arms." She looked at Emma. "Hold on to this one, sweetie. He's something special, and I'm sure you are too." She shook their hands and turned to walk away. "Enjoy your evening, and celebrate your success."

Drew and Emma's eyes met. She shrugged and smiled.

"Going up, sir?"

Drew grabbed Emma's hand and stepped into the elevator. "Sorry to keep you waiting, sir. Yes, we are. Going up indeed."

Later that evening

Drew looked at the contract in his hand. "I'm stunned. Liz was right. I never dreamed of a sellout show, much less an offer to be represented indefinitely by such a prestigious gallery."

"This girl's not surprised. I know I'm partial, but you, Drew Brown, are amazing. You evidently have no concept of how gifted you are. You've got to stop comparing yourself to other artists. That's certain death. You have your own style, and as evidenced tonight, it's one people love."

She lifted her glass of soda water with a slice of lemon and tapped it against his. "Congratulations, Mr. Andrew Brown. You're on your way. Your career has just begun, and I can hardly wait to see where it takes you—*us,* I mean. I plan to be by your side every step of the way."

Drew folded the contract and tucked it into the inside pocket of his sport coat. "You'd better be. I'm afraid to let you out of my sight ever again." He passed her the basket of warm bread. "Which brings me to my question—what on earth are you doing here?"

She bit into the roll, then picked up her knife and slathered it with butter. "The appointment I'd had on the calendar for weeks with my real estate agent and lawyer fell through. My agent had to reschedule due to an emergency, so Tucker and Celeste insisted I come. Celeste has rented from me long enough now that I know the house is in good hands, and Tucker handles the contractors better than I do."

Drew fiddled with his fork. "I know he's been a huge help to you, and I'm appreciative, but I must admit your close friendship with him makes me nervous."

She reached for his hand. "Drew, you don't have to worry. You know he's like a brother to me."

"Do I?" He swirled the water in his glass. "But are you like a sister to him? That's the question. I'm not sure you are. I think he bears watching."

Emma frowned, then looked up at the waiter who'd brought a tall, slender vase to the booth. "Would you like this for your flower, miss?"

She smiled. "Yes, thank you. That's very thoughtful." As he

walked away, she dropped the rose in the vase and laughed. "Interesting how the rose I brought for you has now become mine."

"Let's say it's *ours*. We'll share everything soon. Very soon, I hope."

"Me too. I still pray we can keep our June wedding date."

"It can't get here soon enough as far as I'm concerned." He sat back in his seat. "Let's talk about you. How's your book coming. Has Celeste read your first chapters yet?"

"She has. She read them this week and gave me some excellent suggestions." Her face lit up. "She thinks my story has great potential and said whenever I complete my first draft, she'll introduce me to her editor."

"Get busy then, young lady. Not everyone gets the nod from a soon-to-be-published author. Don't let this opportunity pass you by. Believe in yourself." He winked. "What was it Bea told you?"

She paused, her eyes brimming with tears. "Dream beyond tomorrow."

He nodded. "Do it then, soon-to-be-author, Emma Rose Walsh, or better yet, Emma Rose Walsh Brown. Your readers await."

The next day
Saturday, April 27, 1940
Drew

Drew descended the bus's steps onto Washington Avenue in St. Louis and reached for Emma's hand. "Watch your step, Miss Walsh."

She lifted the hem of her polka-dot shirtwaist dress and bounced onto the sidewalk. Throwing her white sweater around her shoulders, she quickly moved to one side, allowing a lady pushing a baby buggy to pass by. "Where are you taking me, Mr. Brown?"

He grinned and pointed up the block to Loew's Theatre. "What does the marquee say?"

She threw her hand over her mouth, then turned toward Drew, her eyes bulging. "Are you serious? Gone with the Wind? You're taking me to see Gone with the Wind?"

He nodded. "You do want to see it, don't you?"

"Do I want to see it? I've dreamed of seeing this movie ever since it hit the silver screen in December. Who knows how long it will be before it comes to Fayetteville's theaters."

He leaned over and kissed her lips. "Today's your big day."

She squealed. "Goodness. Wait till I tell Penny. And at the Loew's no less."

Grabbing her hand, he weaved his way through the Saturday afternoon shoppers. Emma lagged behind as she craned her neck, trying to take in the big-city window displays featuring colorful spring fashions.

Stepping up to the black marble ticket booth, Drew paid seventy-five cents each for their tickets and ushered her into the white marble, rotunda-shaped lobby flanked by two fountains.

Emma's mouth dropped open as she surveyed the room and gazed overhead. The polished-brass railings of the theatre's balcony glowed, while most of the ceiling was covered with gold leaf. A crystal chandelier illuminated the white marble grand staircase leading to the upper lobby.

Drew led Emma upstairs toward the auditorium. The second-floor lobby was abuzz with excited patrons. Some waited patiently on plush sofas and chairs, while others stopped to have snapshots made in front of large movie posters of Rhett Butler and Scarlett O'Hara.

"Isn't Clark Gable the dreamiest man you've ever seen?" swooned a young lady to her friend as she pretended to kiss Clark on the cheek, raising her high-heeled foot behind her.

"Let's just say I wouldn't play hard to get if he chased me."

Amused, Drew chuckled as they passed. "How about you, Emma? Is Mr. Gable the dreamiest man you've ever seen?"

She tapped her pursed lips with her index finger and rolled her eyes. "Hmm. He's not bad." She nestled closer to Drew's side and kissed him on the cheek. "But I prefer the man on my arm."

He clucked his tongue and winked. "And I'll take you over Vivien Leigh any day."

"Good answer, Mr. Brown," she said, tilting her head and laughing.

The usher checked their tickets, then led them to their seats in the center section. On the side of the stage, a man at a Wurlitzer pipe organ kept tempo with his whole body as "Dream a Little Dream of Me" spilled from his fingertips. As the house lights lowered, the red velvet curtains parted, exposing a giant screen, and the MovieTone newsreel started to roll.

On the world front . . .

On Tuesday, April 2, Adolf Hitler signed the order for the German invasion of Denmark and Norway. One week later, German warships entered major Norwegian ports, from Narvik to Oslo, deploying thousands of German troops and occupying Norway. At the same time, German forces occupied Copenhagen and surrounding cities. Inferior in numbers and equipment, King Christian X convinced his army they could not fight off a German invasion. In less than six hours, Denmark's military forces were forced to surrender to Germany. On Thursday, April 11, a British flotilla approached Narvik. Surprising a German force at the harbor entrance, the British sank two German destroyers and heavily damaged several others. The British ships were then confronted by three more German destroyers. Two British destroyers were lost in the ensuing battle, and a third was heavily damaged by a torpedo. The British ships left the battlefield, damaging another German destroyer as they went. The German vessels, now short on ammunition and fuel, did not pursue the British. Both the German and British naval commanders were killed in the battle. A second attack on April 13 was a British success.

On Thursday, April 25, President Roosevelt recognized the war between Germany and Norway and reaffirmed America's neutrality in the conflict. Norwegian submarines were added to the list of ships forbidden to enter American territorial waters.

Scooting closer, Emma took hold of Drew's arm and whispered. "This war makes me nervous. Does it you?"

"Yes. I'm especially concerned about my family in Scotland. My younger brother David is with the Mediterranean Fleet in the Royal Navy. Mum and Dad worry about him constantly. Air raids and blackouts aren't uncommon in Dundee. So far, they've had minimal structural damage, but the emotional toll it's taking on the people is horrible."

As the opening credits rolled, she laid her head on his shoulder. "I worry about Tucker too and the military families at Bragg. Every night, I pray for their safety and that this horrible war will come to an end before America gets pulled in."

Chapter Thirty-One

Later that evening
Emma

Emma tugged on Drew's arm and pointed behind her as they walked down Washington Avenue.

"Honey, this is our corner. You passed our stop."

With long strides and eyes fixed straight ahead, he continued across Sixth Avenue. "We did?" He stepped up on the curb and turned. "What do you know. I do believe you're right, lassie." He leaned over and kissed her on the forehead. "You've always been a huge distraction." Shrugging, he grabbed her hand and continued on. "Too late to turn back now."

Emma skipped to keep up with him. "Drew, where are you going? We'll miss our bus."

He wrapped his arm around her shoulders. "Come on. You haven't been gone that long, have you? City buses run all night, remember?"

"But—"

"Stop fretting. Have I ever steered you wrong?"

"Well—"

He pulled her closer. "Relax. I know what I'm doing."

As they approached a well-lit department store window, Emma slipped from beneath his arm to admire the trendy spring fashions. "Look." She sighed. "How I've missed the thrill of big-city shopping and these incredible displays." She turned to face Drew. The lights from the window made his clear blue eyes dance. "I'm so excited. What else have you got up your sleeve? First, Rhett and Scarlett, then the world's best pizza, and now strolling beneath the city's nightlights with you by my side. Could this day get any better?"

He squeezed her hand and winked. "Hold on to your bonnet, my love. It's about to."

Pulling her through the bustling crowd, he opened the door of Stix, Baer, and Fuller's Washington Avenue entrance. After several ladies toting shopping bags passed through, he flashed a broad smile at Emma, bent at the waist, and swooped his hand toward the door. "Lassies first."

Tilting her head, she batted her lashes and blew him a kiss, then stepped into the expansive room with massive Italian marble columns. She stood frozen, then cast a wide-eyed stare at Drew.

"What do you think?" he said, pulling her away from the stream of shoppers.

"I'm stunned." She inhaled the fusion of fragrances from the perfume counter—the likes of jasmine, rose, vanilla, and sandalwood wafted through the air. "I've never been in a store this huge."

"It's a sight to see all right, whether one likes to shop or not. Personally, I prefer hole-in-the-wall art stores that smell of turpentine and linseed oil, but I'll follow you anywhere." He led her across the highly polished floor and down one aisle. "Come with me. I have something special in mind."

He passed the cosmetics counter, handbags, millinery, gloves, and leather goods, before pausing at the watches and gold and silver bracelets. Then, stopping at a counter filled with rings, he stooped down and peered inside.

"May I help you, sir?"

Emma studied the middle-aged woman with fair skin and bright red lips. Clothed in a navy A-line dress with a pleated bodice and puffed sleeves, she fingered a single strand of pearls at her neck.

He stood. "Yes, you certainly can. I'm looking for wedding bands."

Emma's heart skipped a beat.

"Certainly," the clerk said, smiling. "Follow me to the other end." She pulled a key from a drawer beneath the register and unlocked the display. "We have a nice selection. Let me know if you see anything you'd like this lovely young miss to try on."

Drew placed his arm around Emma and pulled her close. "What do you think, doll? Does anything here catch your eye?"

Trying to appear reserved while her insides sprang cartwheels, she leaned over the counter and looked down at the rings. "Honey, what's not to like? Any woman would be thrilled with one of these."

He tapped on the glass and looked up at the saleslady. "I'd like to see the thin yellow-gold band with the small diamonds."

"Of course. You have excellent taste. That ring came in yesterday's shipment from Italy." She slid open the case, pulled out the band, and wiped it with a cloth before placing it in Drew's palm.

He squinted his eyes, tilted it back and forth, then held it up to the light. "It's a beauty, isn't it, Peaches? Let me see your ring finger."

She extended her arm and steadied her hand at the wrist with her other, hoping neither the clerk nor Drew would notice her trembling. Drew slipped the ring on her finger. "Ah. How'd I do?" He chuckled. "And it fits ... like Cinderella's glass slipper."

The clerk smiled at Emma. "Lovely. It sits flush against your engagement ring. How does it feel? Do you like it?"

Emma admired the ring and choked back tears. "It's too beautiful for words." Leaning into Drew, she whispered, "But this is way too expensive. We should go with something more simple, don't you think?" She slipped the band off her finger and handed it to him.

He tapped her nose. "The cost is not for you to fret about. You're worth far more." Motioning to the clerk, he stepped away and spoke with her in low tones.

Emma walked across the aisle to the sportswear department while Drew completed the purchase. As she thumbed through a rack of blouses, he approached her, flapping the small paper bag in the air.

"All set. Now all I need is a bride." He slipped the bag in his sport coat pocket, wrapped his arms around her waist, and placed his forehead against hers. "Know where I might find one?"

Giggling, she felt her face flush as his arms tightened. "Honey, people are staring. Are you taking auditions in the middle of the sportswear department?"

"Yes, and you're the first …" As Drew pressed his mouth to hers, she melted in his embrace. "And the last," he said, tracing her lips with his finger. "The position is yours if you want it."

"You'll get no resistance from me, Mr. Brown."

He straightened. "All right then, this calls for a celebratory toast before you head South tomorrow, and I know just the place. Come on, it's time to walk the aisle." Laughing, he offered her his arm. "How about a milkshake to celebrate?"

Her eyes danced as she wove her arm through his. "Drew, you never cease to amaze me. I would absolutely love a milkshake—chocolate, of course." Her index finger punched the air, keeping time with her words. "But only if you promise one smothered with whipped cream, a drizzle of chocolate, and a cherry on top."

"You've got it, doll." Dodging tunnel-vision shoppers, he weaved his way down the aisle toward a colossal octagonal-shaped soda fountain that occupied the center of the room.

Emma's mouth fell open as her eyes traveled up the twenty-foot-tall mirrored column topped with a bronze statue of the goddess Plenty. A circle of dancing cupids surrounded by dolphins spouted water into tiny glass bells at her feet.

Drew spun the top of a stool at the counter. "Care to take a seat?" He took her hand, helped her onto the gold-colored, vinyl-cushioned stool, then took the one beside her. "Pretty amazing concept, huh? There are one hundred stools around this fountain. Genius."

"I'll say. I wish you had your camera with you. We'll have to come back. Cee and the Rainbow girls will never believe this."

Once Drew placed their orders, Emma turned and faced him, her eyes brimming with tears.

"What's the matter, Peaches?"

"I don't want to leave tomorrow."

"I don't want you to either." He pulled a napkin from the container and blotted a tear from her cheek. "But we'll be together soon. Less than two months, and you'll be a June bride."

She grabbed his hand and clung to it. "But what if the house doesn't sell?"

"Shh." He placed his finger on her lips. "We're not going to even speak of such a thing. A lot can happen in a few weeks, and I believe it will."

She shook her head. "I wish I had your confidence. I pray you're right."

"I am."

The waitress set their shakes before them, and Emma leaned forward. "Yummy." She pursed her lips over the straw.

Drew swatted her arm. "Uh, uh."

"What?" she said, jolting and furrowing her brow.

"Haven't you forgotten something?"

She threw her hands out and shrugged.

"Our toast?" He picked up his shake.

"Oh, I'm sorry. It looked so good, I couldn't resist." Picking up her glass, she tapped it against his. "To us."

"Yes, to us." His eyes met hers. "I love you, Emma Rose Walsh. May we never forget what is worth remembering or remember what is best forgotten. Here's to dreaming beyond tomorrow. May all of our tomorrows be as magnificent as today."

Interlocking their arms, they sipped from one another's straw.

Chapter Thirty-Two

Tucker beamed as he introduced us to his daughter, Trish, and his grandson from Charleston.

"Ryan was recently promoted to Head Professional at The Ocean Course on Kiawah Island. Been playin' golf since he was knee-high to a grasshopper."

The broad-shouldered young man sitting beside his grandfather lowered his head, his dark hair falling across his brow.

"I hope he'll take his eyes off the ball long enough to find a wife. Would be nice to see him settled down and happy before he gets to be an old man."

Ryan shook his head and laughed. "Pop, you think I'm not happy? Who knows, I may be happier than most men at forty-one. No ties. Uncomplicated. Things have changed a bit since you were a young pup, you know."

Tucker reached over and patted him on the knee. "You're right, son. They have. If I was your age and had the world by the tail, I'd be a pretty happy camper too. When the time is right, God will open those big brown eyes of yours to some pretty young lady. Until then, you keep on enjoying your life."

I looked at Trish and smiled. "Nothing like a proud grandpa."

She cast me a knowing look. "Ryan was daddy's first grandchild, so he holds a place of honor in his pop's heart."

"I understand. My daughter, Jenna, was my mother's first. Too bad she lives out of state, I could fix him up."

Ryan squirmed in his seat and laughed it off while Kate jumped in to rescue him.

"We've looked forward to meeting you both. Tucker mentions you every time we visit, and it looks like everything he's said is true. All good."

Trish smiled and rose from her chair. "Daddy, this has been a nice break, but Ryan and I need to get back to our yard work before the sun gets too hot. We'll check in on you later." She looked at Kate and me. "If you'd like a bottle of water or a cold drink, Claire stocked the refrigerator before she left. Please, help yourself."

Tucker laid his head back on his chair as they left the room. "Sure has been nice havin' those two around. I'm glad you made it back from Chicago in time to meet them." He adjusted his recliner to an upright position and rocked. "How was your trip?"

"It couldn't have gone better." Kate and I shared the highlights of our time in Chicago.

"I'm glad things went well for you. Your mother loved the city. She and Drew were to be married the June after Mama T died, but they had to postpone their wedding.

"Following Drew's show at the Max Safron Gallery, his career in the States soared, and he was on the road most of the time. Emma was one unhappy girl. Marriage and traveling with Drew were out of the question until she could dig out from under the obligations of homeownership. I hated it for her, but it's no secret now—I loved your mother. Although it hurt me to see her pining, I was happy she'd be in Fayetteville a while longer. Turned out, it was longer than either of us expected—a lot longer. At one point, Emma thought she had a buyer for her house, but there were lots of delays, and eventually, the deal fell through. After a year of disappointments, she was pretty distraught.

"Emma dealt with her loneliness by filling every waking moment. Celeste encouraged her to keep writing, but staying ahead of the bills made it necessary for her to return to work at the Rainbow. I helped with the house all I could while keeping my commitment to Uncle Sam and my finger on the pulse of the war in Europe.

"Then, in late November, Drew received devastating news from home."

Sunday, December 7, 1941
Fayetteville, North Carolina
Emma

Emma hummed along as "Joy to the World" poured from the Philco cathedral radio on the dresser. She placed the white-feathered angel on top of the small spruce tree at the window and plugged in the colored lights. Stepping back, she admired its austere beauty and remembered her last visit with Mama T.

She'd come with Tucker to put a small Christmas tree in this very room, only it was for Mama T's enjoyment, not her own. Mama T had especially loved the angel. Who knew it would be her last night on earth and that she would soon be ushered into the very presence of God and His heavenly angels. *One never knows. Life here is brief, and events are so uncertain.*

Emma sat on the bed beside Chummy and rubbed his back. "What do you think, Chum?"

Sprawled across her pillow, he opened one eye, stretched, rolled onto his back, and squeaked out a faint meow.

"That good, huh? I can tell you're excited. Hopefully, Drew will be a little more enthusiastic."

It was a few days shy of three weeks since Drew had left Chicago for his dad's funeral in Scotland. Although it wasn't the best time to travel to Europe, he knew he needed to be with his mum and sister. His dad's unexpected passing would be tough on his mum since Mac had died a short time before, and his brother, David, was out at sea,

"I'll be glad when this year's over, Chum. Nineteen forty-two has to hold better tomorrows for us."

She looked at the calendar hanging on the wall. Four more days, and she'd feel Drew's arms around her, taste the sweetness of his kiss, and they'd plan for their tomorrows. His brief stopover in Fayetteville before returning to Chicago was his Christmas gift to her. There was nothing she desired more. Their time apart had been longer than they'd ever imagined, but Joe felt keeping Drew and his work on the road and in the public eye was necessary for his career.

Glancing across the room at her reflection in the mirror, she frowned. Had she changed much? It certainly felt like she'd aged ten years. She brushed her index fingers over the dark circles under her eyes. Her late-night writing would have to stop. She'd need a few nights of good rest before Drew's visit.

She rubbed Chummy's belly. "Okay, boy. This mess isn't going to pick itself up. I suppose I should get ..." Her words were halted by a breach in the carol playing on the radio. She listened to the hail of static before a broadcaster's voice boomed across the airwaves.

"We interrupt this program to bring you a special news bulletin. The Japanese have attacked Pearl Harbor, Hawaii, by air. President Roosevelt has just announced, the attack was made on all naval and military activity on the principal island of Oahu. His brief statement was read to reporters by Steven Early, the President's secretary.

"A Japanese attack upon Pearl Harbor would naturally mean war. Such an attack would bring a counter-attack, and hostilities of this kind would mean that the President would ask Congress for a Declaration of War."

Ripping Chummy from the pillow, Emma clutched him to her chest and rocked feverishly. The broadcaster's muffled words melted into the distance as her thoughts scrambled to absorb what she'd heard. Her chest tingled. Her heart raced, and she found it hard to take a breath. She shook her head. *No. No. This isn't so. It can't be.*

She checked the clock—2:20 p.m. A knot rose from her stomach and lodged in her throat. *Drew—Tucker—oh, Jesus—*

Chummy squirmed and clawed to free himself from Emma's death grip as she leaped from the bed. Dropping him, she rubbed the scratch on her arm and raced through the door, hollering for Celeste. Then, remembering, she came to an abrupt stop. Celeste was out. Gone for the evening.

She threw her hands to her head as the room started to spin. *Jesus, help me. I'm alone. Are You even here?*

Weaving to the front door, she unlocked it, then unhooked the screen. She inhaled the cold winter air and plunged toward the swing. Collapsing, she pushed it back as far as it would go with her feet, then lifted them and let the swing sail through the cold air. It felt good as it brushed across her hot skin. She took long, deep breaths and placed her hands over her heart. *Please. Please be still.*

She sat bleary-eyed as her familiar surroundings now seemed distant, foreign, surreal. She shook her head. *I'm dreaming. Yes, that's it. I'm dreaming.* Shaking her head again, she slapped her leg. The words of the announcer ricocheted through her head. *A Japanese attack upon Pearl Harbor would naturally mean war ... naturally mean war ... naturally mean war ...*

She dropped her feet to the floor to halt the back and forth motion of the swing. Leaning forward, she lowered her head between her knees and heaved ...

The soft lights shining from the tree in the window failed to usher in the Christmas spirit. Neither did the muffled chorus of "Silent Night" drifting from the radio inside.

The coming nights would be neither silent ... nor holy.

Chapter Thirty-Three

Friday, July 27, 1942
Fayetteville, North Carolina
Emma

Emma slipped off her apron, dropped into the corner booth at the Rainbow, and pulled Drew's well-worn letter from her purse. She'd read it more times than she could count. It had been less than eight months since President Roosevelt called the unprovoked December 7th attack on Pearl Harbor a "date which will live in infamy." That same night, Drew's plans to return to the States were squashed by a narcissistic, deranged dictator and his fascist regime.

She hadn't blamed Drew for his decision to return to Dundee. His family needed him now more than she did. At least she could still receive his letters. His mother had received her last letter from their youngest son three days before his destroyer, the *HMS Hasty*, was torpedoed by Germans in the Mediterranean Sea on June 14th. The horror that rained upon Drew's family ceased to let up. How much could one woman stand—war, the sudden death of Drew's twin brother, the loss of her beloved husband, and then the tragic loss of her youngest son—all within three years.

Penny cleared the last of her booths. "How's your head, Emma?"

"Pounding." She placed her elbows on the table and massaged her temples.

"How about a hot cup of tea? It might help."

"Sure. Thank you. I've little to lose."

Penny set Emma's tea on the table and slid into the seat across from her. "I'm sorry. I know you're hurting. Life sure throws some hard curves." She shook her head. "My heart breaks for Drew and his family. David's death must be excruciating for all of them."

She nodded. "Yes. Drew's mother is in poor health, and his sister has a young family, so he wants to help her with them as much as possible. Who knows when I'll see him again."

Sitting back in her seat, she set her gaze on Penny's. "I worry about him. Small towns in Scotland have seen their share of bombings. Dundee's electrical generator was bombed not long ago. Residents woke to streets littered with debris—chimneys, slates, stones, glass. It was a miracle there was only one person killed. What a nightmare. I can't imagine laying my head down at night, fearing the sky will fall in. But, now that I think of it, that's exactly what I do."

"I understand, Emma. It's hard not to let fear prevail. Prayer is our best weapon in times like these."

"Believe me, I'm praying."

"What does Tucker say about all that's happening overseas?"

"Not a lot. When I ask him questions, his answers are vague, and he quickly changes the subject. I know he doesn't want to worry me, but I see the anxiety in his eyes."

She turned as the bell over the door jingled, then glanced at the clock. "Well, well. Look who's here—and just under the wire, I might add."

Tucker squared his shoulders, tilted back his head, and sniffed the air. "Following my nose, that's all. Am I too late for coffee?" He slid in beside her, playfully bumping her with his hip.

Penny stood. "It's your lucky night, Sergeant. We don't close for five more minutes. I'll see what I can find in the kitchen."

"Thanks." Turning his attention to Emma, he patted her

hand. "And how are you, pretty lady?"

"Besides my head pounding, I'm okay."

"Why am I not convinced?"

She stuffed Drew's letter in her purse, then turned and leaned against the wall. "Enough about me. What are you doing in town so late?"

"Out clearing my head. Hoped I'd get to see your friendly face. Do you need a lift home?"

Leaning forward, she gripped his arm. "Once again, you're heaven sent. I'd love a ride home. As hard as my head is pounding, I'd probably get arrested for public intoxication while walking down Hay Street."

He threw back his head and laughed. "At least your sense of humor is still intact."

Penny placed Tucker's coffee on the table. "Enjoy. It's on the house," she said, untying her apron. "Y'all, have a good night. I'm clocking out. This girl's turning in early."

Tucker stood as she left, then seated himself on the opposite side of the table. "Stretch out, Em. As soon as I finish my coffee, we'll go."

When Tucker brought his 1933 Chevrolet Master Coupe to a stop, Emma straightened in the seat and looked up at the second-story window. "It looks like Celeste is writing tonight. The light is still on in the front room." She turned and faced Tucker. "Come sit on the porch and stay awhile. It's a nice night, and I'm not ready to turn in."

"Thanks for the invitation, but don't you need to get some rest? How's your head?"

"Actually, much better. The warm tea helped me relax. Come on, you said you needed to clear your head." She motioned toward the porch. "No better place than on that swing over there."

He glanced at his watch. "All right. You've twisted my arm.

I'll stay awhile. I'm not ready to call it a night, either."

Stepping onto the porch, Tucker lifted Chummy from the swing, then sat and placed him on his lap. "Howya doin', big boy? You out here waiting for the lady of the house?"

Emma opened the screen and put her purse on the foyer table. Returning to the porch, she pulled a rocker closer to the swing and sat down. Chummy bounced from Tucker's lap and up into hers. "Goodness. Did you miss me?" She rubbed his ears. Purring, he bumped her head with his, circled her lap several times, and plopped.

"Well, Chum, if you're going to desert me, I'll take up your side and mine too." Propping a pillow against the armrest, Tucker stretched out his legs, clasped his hands behind his head, and leaned back. "Boy, this sure beats the straight back chairs on the barracks stoop. The company's better too."

"I would hope so." She looked up at the ceiling. "I've always loved this old porch. Problems seem to melt away when I'm out here." She stopped rocking. "Shh. Listen. Hear that?"

He cocked his head. "Hear what?"

"The whip-poor-will. I bet you don't hear those on the barrack's stoop."

"Nope. Can't say I have." He dropped his foot to the floor and gave the swing a push.

"Their lonesome cry always reminds me of home," she said, stroking Chummy's silky coat. "Mother and I would sit on the swing for hours and listen to them call to one another. Our talks on the porch are some of the things I miss most about her."

"I understand. When I go home to Louisville, Mama and I sit on the porch and listen to the ship's fog horns on the river."

"Hmm, nice. I love to hear the sound of boats cutting through the water at night and the wake lapping against the shore. So restful."

Rocking, she listened to the rhythmical creaking of the swing and the occasional call of the whip-poor-will, while Chummy's eyes followed a small green tree frog as it hopped across the porch and disappeared into the bushes. Emma loved how her friendship with Tucker needed no words. His calm presence always made her feel safe.

"Tucker?"

"Yeah?"

"What do you hear on the base about the war?"

"Whaddaya mean?"

"Are many troops being shipped out of Bragg?"

"A few."

The cool night air brushed her warm skin as he gave the swing another push.

"Tucker?"

"Huh?"

"How about you? Will you be shipped out too?"

He hesitated, closed his eyes, and took a deep breath. "I don't know, Em."

Their weighty silence was interrupted by the lonesome cry of a whip-poor-will.

Shortly, its mate replied.

Chapter Thirty-Four

The next morning
Saturday, July 28, 1942

KABOOM!

Emma shot up in bed. Heart pounding. She threw back the covers and darted across the braided rug to the door.

"Celeste, are you okay?"

Hearing nothing, she raced into the sitting room and up the stairs. She peeked into the writing room, then crossed the hall to the bedroom and knocked. Pressing her ear against the door, she rapped louder. "Are you in there, Celeste?"

Hearing a faint cry, she rushed down the steps.

"Emma, I'm out here."

She entered the foyer and opened the door. Celeste sat on the swing drinking her coffee, Chummy sprawled at her side. Letting out a long sigh, she pushed open the screen and stepped onto the porch in her nightgown. "Celeste, you scared me."

"Why? What's wrong?" she said, furrowing her brow.

"I couldn't find you."

"Em, you know it's not unusual for me to bring my coffee out here in the mornings. What's going on with you? You look like you've seen a ghost."

She raked her fingers through her hair and dropped into a rocker. "I don't know. I think I'm losing my mind." Her eyes pierced Celeste's. "Tell me you heard that big boom a minute ago."

"Yes, I heard it. Fort Bragg is conducting field maneuvers today—training soldiers for amphibious warfare. There was a notice in yesterday's paper. We'll hear simulated artillery fire all day."

"Oh, good grief." She dropped her face in her hands and shook her head. "I was in the middle of a terrible nightmare. Drew's house in Dundee had been bombed, and I ran through the rubble calling his name. Air raid sirens blared, and then—boom."

Clapping her hands over her heart as if to keep its rapid beating from bursting through her chest, her voice caught in her throat, and tears rolled down her cheeks. "Oh—that horrible boom."

Celeste left the swing and hugged her. "Emma, I'm so sorry. I know it must've been a terrible scare, but it's going to be okay." She rubbed her back. "It was a dream. Everyone's fine."

"I hope you're right." She placed her hand on her forehead. "I've been so anxious lately. I've got to get hold of myself."

Celeste returned to the swing and pushed it with her foot. "Throw yourself into your writing. That's what I do." She brushed her hand over Chummy's soft coat. "I journal. It helps me sort through my emotions. Do you keep a prayer journal?"

"I have, but not lately. I've been mad at God and figured He wouldn't hear me."

"Oh, it's the exact opposite. Psalm 34 tells us the Lord is close to the brokenhearted, that He hears our cries, and delivers us. Talk to Him, Em. Pour out your heart. It will make a huge difference in your peace."

She nodded. "I know you're right. Thanks for reminding me."

"And while we're on the subject of writing, how's your book coming along?"

"It's not. Since Pearl Harbor, my work, this house, and volunteering with the Red Cross have taken most of my time. Whenever I do get a moment to be still, I fall asleep."

"I know you're worn out, but don't let go of your writing. It will keep you sane." She snickered. "Believe me, I know." She shook her finger toward Emma. "You've got talent. Don't waste it."

"Thanks. Words like those coming from you, a published author, mean a lot." She placed her bare feet on the rung of the rocker and laid back her head. "How about you? How's your sequel coming?"

"Slow. I've hit a snag but am writing through it."

"That's good. I can't wait to read it." She stretched her arms above her head and yawned. "I feel so much better. Thanks for talking with me." She stood and walked to the door. "Maybe there will be a letter from Drew in the box today. Would you like more coffee?"

She lifted her cup. "No thanks, this is my second one." She looked at her watch and rose from the swing. "It's time for me to start pounding the keys."

Chummy bounced to the floor and skittered through the door before the screen clapped shut. KABOOM!

Emma pulled several envelopes from the mailbox and shuffled through them. Lifting a letter from the stack, she flipped it over. Her heart leaped. Its postmark read—*Dundee, Angus, 3:45 pm, 13 July 1942.*

Her smile morphed into a frown when she saw a long white label wrapped around one end, resealing the edge that had been opened. The words inside, written for her eyes only, had first passed through the hands of a censor—*Opened by Examiner 3740.* Although read to prevent sensitive information from potentially reaching enemy eyes, she resented the intrusion. She wondered if #3740 delighted in reading the intimate details and exploits of people's lives. Did this person laugh, cry, smile, or maybe even cringe while reading the news they were paid to scan?

She shrugged, placed it on top of the stack, and clutched it to her chest. *What does it matter? She held a letter from her darling Drew. As long as they didn't snip out the mushy parts, she'd choose not to fret.*

The gate clicked shut behind her as she ran to the porch and dropped onto the swing. Laying the rest of the mail beside her, she lifted the letter to her lips, kissed it, and tore open the flap. As she unfolded the pages and a pressed rose slid into her lap, she thought her heart would burst. Lifting it to her nose, she inhaled its delicate scent.

Sunday, July 12, 1942

My Darling Emma,

It seems like a lifetime ago since I've seen you. I wish this letter held news of my return, but the truth is, I don't know when I'll be stateside again. I continue to stay in close touch with the consulate here in Dundee. Now that America's involved, hopefully, this war will break soon.

Since David's death, Mum barely lets me out of her sight. She's afraid she will lose me too. I understand her concern and hope things will improve soon, for I must return to you, my love. We are long overdue for a wedding. We were almost there. How could we have been so close and yet now be so far?

My sister Dorothy and her two boys left minutes ago after our usual Sunday tea. It's not as nice as it used to be. We can't get biscuits without points. Young Willie was asked to say the grace, so he said, 'bless this and bless us.' That wee lad keeps us in stitches. I'm glad Mum has those two rascals to distract her from her grief. Children have a way of peppering dark and heavy situations with splashes of joy, much like shimmering sunlight pierces through a Scottish mist. Wee bairns can bring smiles to faces creased with anxiety and despair. Mum has always said, A merry heart doeth good like a medicine. I think that's Scripture, isn't it? See, some things do stick.

Anyway, Peaches, I hope we have a house bursting at the seams with children and laughter. Oh, how I long to be with you in America. Soon, I hope—very soon.

I hear America is rationing now too. When I heard coffee was in short supply, I thought of you—but then, when don't I? I have a tin I wish I could send, but nothing in the food line can be sent across the big pond. If people didn't bombard stores to buy as many restricted items as possible, there wouldn't be a shortage. Dad can hardly afford to keep his pipe going. Tobacco that used to be 3 pence per ounce is now 2 shillings. It's very changed days for us here in Dundee as I suppose it is in most of the world.

This letter does carry a morsel of good news, though. Last week when I went to the market, I stopped in at Goodfellows for coffee and pastry and bumped into an old art school chum, Finn MacGill. He lives across the River Tay in St. Andrews and has invited me for a painting holiday. I plan to take the train over the first week of August to join him for a few days of plein air painting with a couple of other fellas. Of course, I'll see how Mum feels about it. I don't want to do anything more to upset her. Her wounds are too fresh.

KABOOM!

Emma cringed. She'd never get used to those explosions and couldn't imagine what it would be like for those on the battlefield. She lifted a quick prayer before returning to Drew's letter.

This fellow hasn't dabbled in paint since I left Chicago. Not sure I even know how to wield a brush anymore. Could probably use a refresher course. When I go to the market next week, I'll purchase a few canvases at the art shop and use Dad's brushes and paints. A few days behind the easel is what I need. Maybe painting again will give me a renewed sense of my old life. This cruel war has cost us all immeasurable losses.

I hope the rose arrived in one piece, or an examiner didn't toss it. I clipped it from a bush in Mum's garden. She wanted you to have it and said to tell you she can't wait to meet her future daughter-in-law. I hate that Dad won't get to meet you, but you and Mum can sit and embroider and talk about her son—your amazing husband. Bet that brought a smile to your face. Simply dreaming beyond tomorrow, my love.

Any news on the house? How about your book? I'm glad Celeste is there to encourage you. Give my regards to Tucker, Cee, and all of the Rainbow Girls. Oh, how I'd love to sit at the counter and place my usual order with Rainbow Girl #9—the prettiest lassie this side of heaven.

Please write me a long letter soon. I think of you day and night and can't wait to hold you in my arms again.

Good night, sweetheart,
Drew

She tucked the rose back into the envelope with the letter, then flinched at the toot of a horn. Tucker pulled in front of the house and waved. Then cutting the ignition, he jumped out.

His reserved expression concerned her. "What are you doing in town? I didn't expect to see you today."

With long strides, he approached the porch and cleared both steps with one leap. "Where's your sidekick?" he said, dropping into a rocker.

She giggled. "Off to find dinner, I suppose. He isn't one to miss a meal, you know."

He nodded. "Ah, that's one smart cat. A tom after my own heart." He motioned toward the letter in her hand. "Looks like maybe you heard from Drew today?"

She flapped the envelope in the air. "I did. He sends his

regards. He's terribly homesick for the States."

"... and you, of course."

Heat rose in her cheeks. "Well ... maybe a wee bit," she said, pushing the swing with her foot. "In about a week, he's going on a painting holiday with an old school friend. I'm happy to hear he's taking time for himself. His mother hasn't wanted him out of her sight."

"I can imagine. The Browns have been through a lot, as have families all across Europe."

"What brings you into town?"

"Out running errands."

She dipped her chin and glared. "Running errands, huh? Tucker, I know you better than that. What's up with you? I see it in your eyes."

He dropped his head.

"Come on. I know you've got something to say."

He stood and walked to the swing. "Scoot over."

Not taking her gaze off of his, she slid to one side. "What? You're scaring me?"

He took hold of her hand and sighed. "I'm shipping out, Em."

She froze. A wave of nausea rose from her stomach and lodged in her throat, threatening to cut off her air supply. "When?" she whispered.

"Ten days from now—August 6th."

"Where are you going?"

"Leaving out of New York City for the United Kingdom— Carrickfergus, Ireland. Then later this year, we'll move to a staging area in England."

Fear pressed into her heart.

He squeezed her hand. "I don't want you to tell anyone what I'm about to tell you, Em. Promise?"

She nodded.

"Say it."

"I promise."

He put his arm around her shoulders and pulled her close.

"The stage is being set to invade Sicily."

She leaned back and looked into his eyes.

"Sicily? I don't want you anywhere near Italy. Benito Mussolini is a madman."

"Precisely. Hitler and Mussolini have got to be stopped. Our soldiers will go in with the British to remove the fascist regime and regain control of the Mediterranean."

"But you—"

"Shh." He placed his finger over her lips. "I won't be in the first wave of the beachhead invasion. Our battalion will move in a couple of days after the infantry. Some will set up aid stations to give immediate care to the wounded. From there, others will carry them by ambulance to pick-up points, and they'll be transported to medical evacuation ships offshore. As we travel through the countryside, one medic will be assigned to each platoon. Medics always bring up the rear to care for the wounded. This will be one time that I'll be happy to finish last."

Tears flooded her eyes. "I can't believe my ears. Tucker Baldwin, you're a brave man. I'm proud of you." She wrapped her arms around his waist and laid her head on his chest. "But how can I ever let you go? You're my rock. You've always been here for me. What will I do without you?"

He lifted her chin. "You'll lean on One stronger than me, Em. You'll lean on Jesus. We'll both lean on Him. He's the One that will see us through to the other side of this horrific war."

Tears welled in his eyes. Placing his hand in his pocket, he pulled out the silver pocket cross she'd given him the day she left for Chicago. "I still carry it with me."

She smiled and fingered the silver cross at her neck. "I'll pray for you every day." She leaned in and kissed him on the cheek. "You will come home to me, won't you?"

"You know I will."

"Promise."

He nodded.

"Say it."

"I promise," he whispered, pulling her to his chest.

Chapter Thirty-Five

Tucker sat in his car in front of the Rainbow, unable to comprehend the finality of his visit. Only heaven knew when he would return to American soil—if he returned. He prayed he would, and in his heart-of-hearts believed it, but his days were in God's hands.

He pushed back the sleeve of his army-green dress uniform to expose his watch. Emma had wanted him to wait until closing, so they would have uninterrupted time together before he shipped out.

On Thursday, August 6th, his unit, the 261st Amphibious Medical Battalion, would sail from New York's Port of Embarkation for the British Isles. It would be the first leg of his journey into a war that had raged for almost three years. Following Pearl Harbor, America could no longer remain neutral.

Trying to relieve the strain, he rubbed the back of his neck and rolled his head. His emotions were as unpredictable as the war—all over the map. He never knew what would erupt from the core of his being. At times, he couldn't wait to see the U.S., and its Allied forces, France, Great Britain, and Russia, bring the Axis of Evil, Germany, Italy, and Japan to its knees. At other times, he could do nothing but fall on his own. It was then that an unexplainable peace would flood the depths of his soul.

Today had been a good day. Perhaps because he knew he would see Emma. She called him her rock, not realizing how much he fed off of *her* strength and encouragement. Her stalwart and compassionate support always lifted his spirits. He would miss his soulmate. She and his family were his incentives to answer his call and hold onto the hope of his return. With gritty determination, he would do everything within his power to make that happen.

A soldier he recognized from Company C exited the restaurant with a petite brunette by his side. Tucker smiled and held up his hand as they passed. His comrade waved in return, but the young lady's gaze toward the man on her arm remained unbroken. *If only Emma would look at him that way.*

The neon OPEN sign in the Rainbow's window clicked off as someone pulled the shade on the door. Placing his cap on his head, he stepped from the car and stuffed his keys in his pocket. As he hopped onto the curb, *The Fayetteville Observer* box beside the door threatened to steal his peace. Visible in the subtle light of the street lamp, the newspaper's headline touted— *Germany's Successful Advance Toward Stalingrad Continues.*

Reading it made his blood boil. *Don't press your luck, Adolf, ole boy. You ain't seen nothin' yet. You're about to meet your superior. Your men are no match for our troops.* Shaking his head as if to expel any seed of doubt from his mind, he knocked on the door. This night belonged to Emma. From the moment she opened the door, his heart rested in its rightful place. Even following a long workday, she was radiant.

"Look at you, Sergeant Baldwin. Don't you look handsome?"

He stepped inside and took off his cap. "I clean up pretty good when I try." He leaned over, kissed her on the forehead, then took her hand and twirled her around. "Can't hold a candle to Rainbow Girl #9. You shine without trying."

"You're too kind," she said, giggling. I credit my glow to a hot kitchen, but thank you." She motioned and led him to a table in the center of the room. A homemade red, white, and blue banner hung over it—*Go get 'em, Tucker! You're our hero.*

We're rootin' for you.

Penny stood at one end of the table and Fran at the other. As the ladies applauded, Cee burst through the kitchen door carrying a seven-layer chocolate cake topped with hissing sparklers.

Emma pulled out a chair. "Take a load off your feet, soldier." Tucker dropped into the seat, his face growing warmer by the second.

Cee placed the blazing cake in front of him, then patted him on the back. "Thanks for all you're doing, young man. Don't stay away too long. This crowd doesn't like waiting."

He guffawed. "I'll try my best to not inconvenience y'all too much."

Penny picked up a large knife and pulled a plate from the stack on the table. "How big of a slice do you want, Sergeant?"

"You mean this piece isn't mine?"

Emma put her hands on her hips and huffed. "Didn't your momma teach you to share? We'll cut it at least five ways, sir."

He lowered his chin and muttered, "Okay. If I gotta."

Penny plunked down a large piece of cake with a scoop of ice cream in front of him. "You gotta."

"Okay. I never did like to eat alone anyway." He picked up his fork and shoveled a large bite into his mouth. "Have a seat and join me, folks. Cake's on the house."

Once they'd eaten their fill, Emma tapped her fork on the side of her glass. "Attention, everyone." She reached for a package beside her chair and placed it in front of Tucker. "Gift time."

His eyes widened as he wiped his mouth with his napkin. "Wow. Do I have to share this too?"

Emma grinned. "Nope, It's yours and yours alone. It's from all of us."

"O-kay," he said, rubbing his hands together, then tearing away the red, white, and blue flag-patterned paper. He opened the box and took out a white cardboard folder with a photo inside. "Will you look at that—the whole crew." A lump rose in his throat as his eyes scanned the sentiments on the opposite flap. "This is wonderful," he said, his voice cracking. "Cee, how'd you manage to get everyone to show up at once?"

"Oh, they'll do anything for a raise."

Tucker laughed. "Ah, so you paid them off, huh." He looked around the table. "Thank you, everyone. This will go everywhere with me. Your prayers and this photograph are the best gifts you could give me. I'm going to miss all of you."

Each person hugged him, speaking words of encouragement and thanks. Looking over at Emma, he winked. As tears welled in her eyes, he fought back his own. This evening was going to be harder than he'd expected.

Thursday, August 6, 1942

As New York City's skyline sparkled in the morning sun, Tucker stood on the top deck of the *Wakefield*, formerly the luxurious ocean liner *S.S. Manhattan*. Before the outbreak of WWII, the 24,000-ton vessel had transported the upper-crust of society to Europe. At over twenty knots, the ship had been the world's fastest passenger ship. Today, though far from one of the elite, Tucker sailed for Europe too, but not for a glamorous European holiday.

The *Wakefield*, now painted battleship gray, was part of the largest troop convoy ever assembled. A dozen transports escorted by twelve warships carried troops and thousands of mail bags filled with letters for those in the European Theater of Operations—letters from home. Tucker would soon come to know how life-giving mail call was to those serving overseas.

From his current vantage point, the 305-foot tall Statue of Liberty in New York's harbor appeared to be less than an inch high. America's soil was the only land he'd ever walked on. Its freedoms, all he had ever known—liberties acquired at an inconceivable cost, the blood of those who fought before him. Now, he was one of seven thousand aboard, entrusted with the colossal mission of defending the "land of the free and the home of the brave."

Unable to tear his eyes from the outline of the city, he watched as it appeared to dip below the horizon. He was less than thirty minutes off-shore and homesick already. The expression in Emma's eyes as they said their goodbyes haunted him. Despite trying to remain strong, she couldn't hide the angst that hovered beneath the surface of her heart—not from him, anyway. He knew her too well.

He shook his head in frustration. What was the matter with him? Why hadn't he told Emma he wished she was his? Yes, he knew what it was like to have a sweetheart torn from his arms, and yes, he'd sworn he'd never inflict that heartache on another man, but playing the nice guy had simply ushered in grief. He'd chosen to be a man of honor at the expense of honesty. Now he considered himself neither honest nor honorable. They said nice guys finish last, but it wasn't the nice guys that lost out—it was fools—dupes like him. He considered himself the biggest of them all.

"A penny for your thoughts, my man."

Tucker turned to see Hank lighting up a Lucky Strike.

"Ever been on a ship before?" He dropped the pack of cigarettes and matches into his shirt pocket.

"Not one this large, but I've had plenty of ringside seats. My dad's a tugboat captain on the Ohio River, and at times I'd accompany him on short jaunts. I love being out on the water. How about you? Have you ever been on a ship this large?

"Nope. Always wanted to, though. I guess it shows ya, we need to be careful what we pray for. From here on out, I'm going to be more specific—*real* specific."

He took several long draws on his cigarette, tossed it overboard, then slapped Tucker on the back. "It's time to head below and check out our new digs, compliments of Uncle Sam.

What's your bunk location? As for me, I landed in the nose-bleed section—Deck 4, Aisle 3, B30-5—top bunk. They're stacked five-high, ya know."

"Terrific," he said with zero enthusiasm. Reaching into his shirt pocket, he pulled out his assignment card. "You're in luck. I'm right below you, friend—B30-4."

"I hope you brought your earplugs."

Tucker rolled his eyes. "I wasn't inducted into the Army yesterday, Sarge." He picked up his government-issued denim blue duffel bag and hoisted it to his shoulder. "Let's go. This morning's chow line is gonna stretch from here to Timbuktu."

Hank slung his bag onto his back, and with long strides, walked toward the steps. "I'm ten paces ahead of you. I'd hate for us to be the last ones in line for our first gourmet meal at sea."

"Lead on, pal. I've grown accustomed to finishing last."

Chapter Thirty-Six

Drew leaned his paintings against the bedroom wall in the home of his friend, Finn MacGill. Finn lived alone with his Sheltie, Fifer, in a quaint two-bedroom cottage on Nelson Street. Following a meal of fish and chips at a local pub in the heart of St. Andrew's shopping district, they'd walked back to his quiet residential neighborhood.

Stepping away, he assessed his week's work. Beside the canvas of St. Andrew's castle sat a panoramic seascape, then next to it, the scene he'd painted that morning on the rugged coastline of Fife. Finn had taken him along with two other friends to the top of a hill overlooking the small fishing harbor of Crail. Its tiny colorful houses provided the perfect backdrop for a myriad of boats, reflecting in the brilliant blue water.

He sighed. *Not bad, ole chap. Maybe you haven't lost it.*

Raking his fingers through his hair, he sat on the bed and kicked off his shoes. It had been a good day. He was born to paint, and his time away from the easel had been detrimental to his soul. As he stretched out on the bed and leaned against the headboard, a wave of peace washed over him. While painting, he'd had plenty of time to think and sensed God's presence with him in a way he never had before. Following the events of the last few months, Emma's words about his need for the Lord had penetrated his heart. Tonight, he would lie down with a newfound sense of purpose and hope—something this war had stolen from him. He shook his head. "No more."

A rap on the door jolted him from his thoughts.

"Care to join me in the garden for a smoke, my man?"

He leaped from the bed and opened the door. "I'd love it." He picked up his pipe and grabbed his tobacco pouch from the bedside table.

"Better bring your jacket too. It's a wee bit nippy out there."

Snatching it from the chair, he slipped on his bedroom shoes and followed Finn through the kitchen. Fifer led the way, tail wagging.

As they stepped out onto a patio surrounded by flowering bushes, he placed his pipe between his teeth and slipped on his wool blazer. "Nice night," he said, dropping onto a metal glider.

Finn took a seat across from him while Fifer rested his head on his beloved master's feet.

Lighting his pipe, Drew blew a puff of cherry-scented smoke into the air and gazed into the starry sky. "We can see most of the constellations tonight."

Finn nodded as he tamped the tobacco in the bowl of his pipe, circled the match over its surface, and puffed.

"You have a nice place here. Thanks for inviting me. Being with the fellows and dabbing paint on canvas again was exactly what I needed."

"My pleasure. I'm bummed you have to leave tomorrow." He reached down and rubbed Fifer's head. "We get a little lonesome sometimes, don't we, fella?" Fifer licked Finn's hand. "It's been nice catching up with you. I was sorry to hear about David." His tousled blond curls fell across his high forehead as he shook his head. "He was a fine man whose life was cut way too short."

"Yep. I sure do miss him. One never knows."

"I guess you're itching to get back to Emma. She's a real beauty." He lifted his chin and slowly blew smoke into the air. "So you're planning to tie the knot, are you?"

"You'd better believe it. As soon as I can hop the next plane home, I'm outta here."

"Might be a while."

Drew grunted. "I know. I'm afraid you're right, but I'm praying not."

They sat in silence, listening to the raspy song of katydids and the thoughtful melancholy ring of blackbirds. A light breeze lifted a swirling puff of smoke into the cool night air.

Finn spoke up. "I've been thinking.

"That could be dangerous," Drew teased.

"Hear me out. If you're going to be around for a while, you might want to apply for the Recording Scotland Collection. My work was approved, and as fine an artist as you are, I have no doubt yours would be accepted too."

He leaned forward, resting his elbows on his knees. "You don't say. Never heard of it. You forget I've been away a while, chum."

"The program serves a dual purpose. It preserves Scotland's history and puts our country's artists back to work. The collection was established this year by a British businessman from America, Edward Harkness. His funds are overseen by The Pilgrim Trust to create a permanent, visual record of Scotland—places our soldiers are fighting to protect."

Drew's eyes widened as his interest piqued. "Wow. I'd love to be part of something like that."

"I figured you would."

"So, what types of scenes do you paint?"

"Anything and everything from castles, churches, and crosses to stone cottages, barns, and chickens. People can be part of the landscape, but they aren't the focus. The committee will accept a few oils and pencil sketches, but watercolors are encouraged since they're distinctly British and a cultural tradition."

Drew straightened and slapped his knee. "I love it."

"Now, bear in mind, you won't get rich. You'll be paid somewhere between 5 and 20 pounds per painting." He tilted his head and shrugged. "But times are what they are, so we take what we can get, right, my man? Anything's better than nothing."

Drew nodded, "Indeed." Settling back in his chair, his words waned. As they sat silent, his thoughts, accompanied by the melodious sounds of nature and the rhythmical squeak of the glider, turned to Emma. He curled his lips around the stem of his pipe, inhaled, then blew out rings of sweet-smelling smoke.

Life was good.

KABOOM!

Chapter Thirty-Seven

Saturday, August 8, 1942
Fayetteville, North Carolina
Emma

"I don't have anything else for you, big boy. You're on your own till suppertime." Meowing, Chummy paced back and forth, rubbing against Emma's legs. After drying and stacking her lunch dishes in the cabinets, she stooped and scratched the affectionate cat behind the ears. "You're so rotten, but I'm determined to take good care of you. Males have become a rare breed around this town. Europe has our finest—namely Drew and Tucker."

Lifting him, she buried her face in his fur. The soft buzzing sound of his purring always soothed her. "Run along now," she said, returning him to the floor. "I have work to do, and you have a nap to take."

"Afternoon, Em."

She turned. Celeste stood in the doorway. "Hi. You headed out?"

"I am." A broad smile lit up her face as she held up a black binder. "Ta-da! Taking the first draft of my second book to my editor."

She clapped. "How wonderful. I can't imagine how freeing that must be."

"Yes. It gives me a bit of breathing space before I plow through my editor's suggested changes. 'Seeing red' has a different connotation for authors. An abundance of red pencil marks strikes fear in our hearts."

Emma smoothed out Mama T's embroidered tablecloth and pushed the chair she'd sat in at breakfast under the table. "I suppose it does."

Celeste hugged the binder to her chest and leaned against the doorframe. "Speaking of such … how is *your* book coming? Any progress?"

She shook her head as twinges of guilt chastised her.

"Em-muh," she said, drawing out the last syllable of her name. "Books don't write themselves, you know."

"How well I do." She lowered her eyes and followed the outline of an embroidered flower with her finger. "My mind has been too cluttered lately."

Celeste laid her binder on the oak Hoosier cabinet beside the door, stepped into the kitchen, and pulled a chair from the table. "Have a seat," she said, pulling out another for herself.

Fighting back tears, Emma plopped into the chair and lowered her head.

"I'm sorry. I can't conceive of what it's like for the two most important men in your life to leave at the same time."

"I try to be strong, but my mind won't cooperate." She looked up at Celeste, blinking back tears. "Remember the dream I shared with you?"

She nodded.

"I've had it more than once. Quite a few times, actually." She reached for a napkin in the center of the table and blotted her eyes. "Not the same scenario, but a similar setting." Hesitating, she wound the napkin around her finger. "And a loud explosion is *always* what wakes me."

"Heart pounding, I'm sure."

"As if it will burst through my chest."

Celeste reached over and laid her hand on Emma's. "I pray for him, as well as Tucker, and that an end will soon come to this horrible war. I'm grateful God has kept us all safe and that you wake up to realize it was all a dreadful nightmare."

"I know prayer is my answer. I've got to trust God. Living

in fear has worn me out. I go to bed later and later every night because I'm afraid I'll dream it again. On mornings I don't have to work, I can sleep in, but those are few and far between. The repetition has taken its toll on me. Yesterday at work, I kept dropping things. When a tray of food I carried crashed to the floor, Cee told me to come home and rest for the weekend. I'm thankful to have a boss who cares."

"Love that man. God broke the mold when He made that one." She paused. "Are you journaling?"

"I am, and it does help clear my head. Hopefully, my mind will settle down as time passes."

Celeste looked at her watch and stood. "I've got to run, but I'll be happy to talk with you more when I get back."

"Thanks. I'll be fine." She rose and slid her chair under the table.

Celeste picked up her binder and turned. "I'll be gone most of the evening. That means my typewriter is free. Why don't you go upstairs and get to work on your book?"

Emma shook her head and shrugged. "I don't know. Maybe."

"Okay, that leaves me only one recourse." She spun on her heels and walked toward the foyer.

Emma followed. "What's that?"

"Prayer." Her voice faded as the screen clapped behind her. "I'll sic the Hound of heaven on you."

Emma watched as her friend walked down the street. She was grateful for Celeste's presence in her life. She missed her precious Mama T, whose words had always lifted her spirits. Turning, she moved past the stairs, then stopped. Her eyes traveled upward. Maybe she should heed Celeste's advice. Perhaps writing was the antidote she needed to pull herself out of this pit.

Giggling, she walked through the parlor and into her room. *I hear a dog barking. Celeste must be praying.*

Emma rolled two pieces of onion skin paper into the carriage of Celeste's typewriter. Scooting the chair closer to the desk, she straightened her torso, poised her fingers over the keys, and …

After waiting several minutes for the muse to hit her, she muttered. "Great. Writer's block, and I haven't even typed the first word." She wiggled her fingers. "Shouldn't a smidge of Celeste's writing ability rise from the keys, invade my thoughts, and flow through my fingertips?"

Sighing, she picked up the black and white marbled composition book containing her handwritten first chapters. *I should read through this first.* She slapped the book shut. *Or start over.*

She moved the typewriter carriage to the center of the page, backspaced ten times, poised her fingers over the keys, and typed—*Dream Beyond Tomorrow* by Emma Rose Walsh. Then, hitting the carriage return lever three times, she pounded out— Chapter One.

Hours later, she put the period on her first chapter, stretched her arms over her head, and yawned. She was drained. She could only hope that the more she wrote, the easier it would become. At her current pace, she wasn't sure which would culminate first—the war or her story.

Pulling the final page of her chapter from the typewriter, she clipped it with the others, thumbed through them, and dropped back in her chair. A brand-new beginning was exactly what she'd needed—perhaps in more ways than one. She was proud of herself. Celeste would be too.

She glanced at her watch. Chummy would be sprawled on the floor beside his food bowl by now, tail twitching, dreaming of Puss'n Boots. The finicky feline often turned up his nose at leftovers, but she was had no doubt he'd scarf them down the moment she turned her head.

She slipped the typed pages of her story into her composition book, flipped off the desk lamp, and walked downstairs. Stepping onto the porch, she inhaled the cool breeze that refreshed the day's mugginess. She'd eat out here at the café table. As she turned to enter the house, several clear resonant rings of a bicycle bell broke the silence.

"Afternoon, Miss Walsh," Billy said, whizzing past.

The evening paper struck her walk as she waved. "Thanks, Billy. Tell your mother hello."

"I will. Have a nice night," he shouted as he pedaled down the street, tossing papers into neighboring yards.

She stepped onto the walk and picked up *The Fayetteville Observer,* then returned to the porch. Unrolling the paper, bold headlines caught her eye—"Bombs Rain on St. Andrews." Her heart pummeled her chest as she gasped and dropped onto the swing. Had her haunting dreams become a reality?

High explosive bombs dropped on the Scottish East Coast town of St. Andrews on Thursday night, August 6th. A lone enemy raider caused considerable damage to a wide swath of residential property. A house on Nelson Street receiving a direct hit was lifted from its foundation and piled onto an adjoining house. It was also demolished. Throughout the area, twelve people were killed and a number seriously injured, while others remain missing. Rescue Squads and local volunteers were on the scene digging through the rubble. Several of the missing were visitors from the neighboring towns of Glasco and Dundee.

Her eyes darted across the last line—again—and again. *Several of the missing were visitors from the neighboring towns of Glasco and Dundee. Several of the missing were visitors from the neighboring towns of ... Glasco and ... Dundee. Several of the missing ... Dundee*

"No, Lord. Please. No—*not Drew!*"

Emma stared at the clock, collapsed into the chair beneath the wall phone, and counted forward five hours—10:20 p.m. Dundee time. Gasping for air, she pressed the receiver to her ear, dialed, and then lowered her head to her knees. *Breathe, Emma. Long. Deep.* Blood rushed to her head as she listened to a woman converse with the long-distance operator.

"Miss Walsh, I have Dorothy MacIver on the line."

"Thank you." Heart racing, she straightened in her seat. "Hello, Dorothy."

"Good evening, Emma."

"I'm sorry to call so late, but I just read about the bombing. Is Drew with you?"

Her voice quivered. "No, I'm sorry, he isn't."

"Was he in St. Andrews Thursday?"

"He—" She paused to collect herself. "I'm afraid he was."

"Please, tell me you've heard from him."

"I wish I could, but no one has been able to get through. All the lines are down."

She erupted into tears.

"I'm sorry. I wish I had a better report for you, Emma."

A queasiness rose from her stomach as she tried to gather herself. "How is your Mother?"

"Mum's not doing well at all. The doctor has her sedated. She's resting now."

Emma waited as Dorothy said something in response to a child's voice.

"I'm sorry. Willie wanted me to help him get the lid off of the jam jar."

"And how are you, Dorothy?"

"I'm okay. Holding it together for the sake of my mum and praying we'll get news of Drew's whereabouts soon."

"I'm terribly sorry. Your family has had to endure so much

lately." She stood and looked out the window. "Please let me know when you hear something?"

"I certainly will. Please pray for us. This war had already taken a huge toll on our nerves, and now this has happened. Some days, it's all we can do to put one foot in front of the other."

"I can only imagine." She wiped her tears with her sleeve. "Please know, I'll storm the gates of heaven night and day until we hear."

"Thank you. I'll let you know whenever we hear something. Hopefully, it will be soon."

"Thanks, and God bless you. Please give your family my love and prayers."

"I will."

Emma listened as the line went dead, then dropped the receiver into the cradle and slumped back into the chair. Chummy jumped into her lap and mewed. Burying her face in his fur, she wailed.

Chapter Thirty-Eight

Thursday, August 6, 1942
St. Andrews, Scotland
Drew

Sirens screamed, piercing the cold night air. As Drew ran down Nelson Street, the headlights of stalled vehicles lit his way. Plumes of dust and smoke spiraled above the slate rooftops of the middle-class neighborhood, several of its homes now reduced to piles of rubble. Blood pulsed through his temples as his feet pounded the debris-filled cobblestone streets, drowning out the cries of disoriented people in the night.

Finn, leading the way, shouted back. "Drew, are you still with me?"

"I am," he said, gasping for air as dust permeated his airways and the taste of dirt coated his mouth. "Don't worry about me. Just get to the corner." Running, he passed dazed survivors covered with gray ash, consoling residents numb with shock while others cried hysterically. He couldn't believe this was the same street he and Finn had walked down a few hours earlier.

They neared the corner at Nelson and Bridge Street, where several men responded to cries surrounding a demolished home. Attempting to reach those trapped beneath the rubble, they formed a chain, then passed stones and large pieces of slate down the line.

As Finn and Drew approached, a woman, her face blackened with soot, pointed to a spot in the rubble and wailed. "My baby! My baby! I hear him crying." Grabbing Drew's shoulders, she shook him and glared through horror-stricken eyes. "Please. Please, sir, save my little boy."

Bending over, Finn and Drew pulled away debris, hoisted large rocks from the rubble, and started a second chain. Two rescue squad vehicles pulled to a stop behind them. As the doors flew open and medics jumped from the trucks, Drew straightened and waved his hands above his head. "Over here. We need your help over here."

Finn grimaced as he and several others pulled back a large slab of concrete and strained to hold onto it. "Drew, there's the baby. Pull him out. Hurry. Get him before we lose our grip."

Stepping through the rubble, Drew fell to his knees, reached into the opening, and lifted out the panicky toddler caked with white powder. "I've got him," he said, rising and cradling the child to his chest.

As the men let go of the concrete slab, a searing pain shot through Drew's left foot and up his leg. Trying desperately to maintain his hold on the child, he screamed. "My foot! It's caught."

Finn's eyes filled with terror. He and others scrambled to lift the slab while a medic grabbed the baby from Drew's arms. Grasping his leg, Drew wiggled his foot free and crumpled to the ground writhing in agony.

Medical technicians stooped, draped his arms over their shoulders, then stood and placed him onto a stretcher. Their every step across the debris-covered ground sent intense pain through his body. As they prepared to slide him into the ambulance, the mother of the child he'd saved approached the stretcher and took his hand in hers.

"Sir, I'm so sorry you're hurt. I can't thank you enough for saving my baby boy's life. Know I'll be praying for you."

Drew nodded. "Please do. I'm sure I'll be fine, and I trust your child will be too."

Medics helped the young mother into the ambulance transporting her baby to the hospital, while Finn climbed in the one carrying his friend. Taking a seat, he raked his fingers through his hair repeatedly and shook his head.

"Drew, I'm sorry. I feel so responsible for this."

"It wasn't your fault, chum. We were all doing what we could to save the child. He's alive, and that's all that matters."

Red lights flashed, sirens screamed, and Drew prayed as both ambulances raced toward the Dundee Royal Infirmary.

The next day

Lifting his head from his pillow, Drew squinted and cupped his hand over his eyes to shield them from the glare. Muffled voices echoed throughout the walls of the pristine white room lined with beds. As blood pulsed in his temples, he dropped back on his pillow and moaned. *Where was he?* Shifting his body to relieve the dull ache in his back, a burning pain shot up his leg. He hollered.

"Mr. Brown, is there something I can do for you?"

He groaned. "I don't know, is there?" He tried to bring the face of the lady who had come to his bedside into focus. "I certainly hope so? Where am I anyway?"

"You're at Dundee Royal Infirmary. You were injured in last night's bombing in St. Andrews."

He raised his arm and dropped it across his forehead. "Oh, yes. I had hoped that was a nightmare, but by the pain in my foot, I suppose it wasn't."

"You are one lucky man, Mr. Brown."

"From what little I remember, I believe I'm more than lucky. I'm blessed by God to even be alive today."

"I agree. When you were brought in last night, Dr. McClarty performed surgery on your foot. He'll be in soon to answer your questions. However, I can tell you your operation was successful, and the doctors expect you to make a full recovery."

He felt the tension leave his body. "Whew. That's good news." He squinted at the clock on the wall. "What time is it?"

"Four-twenty in the afternoon."

"What? I've slept the day away?"

"Almost, but rest is what you need above everything else right now."

Amused, he chuckled. "And pain relief."

She looked at her clipboard and nodded. "You'll be happy to know the doctor has prescribed something for you."

She left his bedside, returned with the pain medication, and injected it into his hip. "There's someone in the waiting area who would like to see you. Do you feel like company?"

"I'd love some. It will help me get my mind off of myself. Which reminds me, has my family been contacted?"

"We've tried several times. There are so many people calling loved ones, all of the circuits are busy. We'll continue to try until we reach them."

"Thank you. I know my mother is distraught and won't rest until she hears."

She lifted the sheet at the end of his bed to check on the position of his foot. "Things look good. You should feel the effects of the injection shortly." She took a small bell from the bedside stand. "Ring this if you need anything else." Placing it back on the table, she turned away. "I'll send your visitor right in."

He closed his eyes, then snapped them open at the sound of his name. A young woman's stood beside his bed. "Hello, I'm Bess Fleming. I'm certain you don't recognize me. I look nothing like I did last night—thank goodness."

He winced as he pushed himself up in the bed. "Last night?" He pointed. "Oh, are you …?"

She nodded. "Yes, I'm the mother of the little boy you pulled from the rubble."

He motioned toward a straight-back chair. "Please, have a seat."

She moved it closer to his bed and sat. "I wanted to stop by before we left today and thank you for all you did for us."

He shook his head. "Thank you. You're kind, but I did what anyone would have done under the circumstances."

"Maybe, but *you* are the *anyone*, and I'm deeply grateful. Because of you and the other men there last night, my little boy is alive and doing well today."

He exhaled. "Oh, that's great news. I've been praying for him" He extended his hand. "I'm Drew, by the way, and I'm happy I could be there for you and your son ..."

"Ian."

He nodded. "Sweet little Ian. So he's going home?"

"Not exactly. Our home isn't livable. We will stay with my parents here in Dundee until we can get back on our feet."

"Excellent."

Her eyes brightened. "You seem to be doing well. I hear you had surgery last night."

He laughed. "So, I've been told. I don't know any of the details, but I know what's important—they expect me to make a full recovery."

She smiled. "I'm pleased to hear that. Do you live in St. Andrews?"

"No, Dundee—Broughty Ferry, actually. I was visiting with an old school chum when the bomb dropped."

"Ah, good ole Broughty Ferry, the home of Winkie, the blue chequered pigeon."

He chuckled. "Yes. Winkie's been the talk of the town since she saved the crew of the downed RAF bomber in February. She put us on the map. Flying 120 miles from the North Sea to her loft in Broughty Ferry was incredible. Because of her, the four crew members were located within fifteen minutes of her return." He shook his head. "Such an amazing story. Winkie is quite a hero."

Her dark eyes glistened. "As are you." Standing, she offered her hand. "I must get back to Ian. Hopefully, the office has finished his paperwork, and we can go home."

"I appreciate you stopping by. You've certainly been a welcome addition to my afternoon."

"Hopefully, you'll also be on your way home soon."

"I'm counting on it."

As she left the room, his eyes followed her. He'd noticed she wasn't wearing a ring.

Chapter Thirty-Nine

Sunday, August 9, 1942
Fayetteville, North Carolina
Emma

"Celeste. Celeste." Emma raced up the stairs and banged on the bedroom door.

Yanking it open, Celeste stood with a horrified expression. "What? What's happened?"

Panting, Emma clapped her hand to her chest, barged past her, and flopped onto the bed. Celeste sat beside her. "I'm sorry. I didn't mean to scare you, but I've heard from Dundee." With one long breath, she blurted. "Dorothy called and said Drew is in Dundee Royal Infirmary, has undergone surgery for several fractures in his foot, and will be fine." Grabbing Celeste's shoulders, she shook her. "Isn't that the most wonderful news ever?"

"It is. What a relief. I'm so happy for you."

Jumping from the bed, she walked to the window. "My goodness, I feel like my heart is going to explode. Drew was injured while pulling a small child from the rubble." She grimaced as she remembered Dorothy's words. "A large slab of concrete dropped onto his foot. Oh, how I wish I was there to tell Drew how proud I am of him." She twirled around, grabbed Celeste's hand, and pulled her out the door. "Come on. This calls for a celebration."

Tearing down the steps with Celeste in tow, she ran into the kitchen and yanked a chair out from under the table. "There. Sit down. I'm pouring both of us a glass of milk and serving up two large slabs of the triple-layer chocolate cake I made from Mama T's recipe."

Celeste leaned back in her chair and laughed. "Sounds wonderful. You do that. I'll sit here and enjoy watching."

Emma waved her off, fixed their plates, then plopped Celeste's in front of her. "On second thought, come on." She whipped around and walked into the sitting room. "Let's eat at the table on the porch. I'm about to burn up."

"I can see why." Grinning, she shook her head and followed her outside.

Emma wiped the sweat from her brow and dropped into the wrought-iron chair. "Whew! It's a lot nicer out here."

Chummy sat at her feet and mewed.

She shielded her cake with her hand. "Nope. Not this, Chummy Choo. I share my cake with no man, woman, child, or beast." Leaning over, she peered into his large green eyes. "And you, big boy, fall into the last *cat*-tegory."

After seating herself across from Emma, Celeste took a large bite of cake and rolled her eyes. "Mmm, yum. You're getting to be quite a cook. Drew will be pleased."

"I hope so. He has a real sweet tooth." She placed a large bite of cake in her mouth and stared into the distance. "I haven't heard from Tucker since his ship left New York. I hope he's okay."

"My goodness, Em. I'm sure he's fine. He's only been gone four days."

She furrowed her brow and pursed her lips. "You mean Tucker just left this past Thursday?" She shook her head. "That seems impossible. With all that's happened with Drew, it feels like a lifetime ago."

Celeste nodded. "It does, doesn't it? I'm sure no letters will be mailed until his ship reaches Ireland, so be patient. He'll write. And I've heard the new V-mail system has cut delivery time from Europe down from six weeks to twelve days." Her eyes brightened as she sipped her milk. "How about you? Are you writing? And I don't mean letters."

"I am. I wrote another chapter last night. I noticed your light was off in your room. I hope my typing didn't disturb you."

"Didn't hear a thing," she said, shaking her head. How's the story coming?"

"Slow—but it *is* coming. Parts of it are set in Scotland, so I'm killing two birds with one stone. I'm developing my plot and learning about my precious Drew's homeland at the same time. I can't wait to visit one day. It must be a beautiful place."

"Do you think when you two marry, you'll move there?"

"I doubt it. There are many more opportunities for Drew's artwork here in the States. Besides, he says it rains a lot in Scotland, and he prefers living in America."

"Hello, ladies. It's a beautiful evening, isn't it?"

Emma turned to see Bea and Opal coming up the walk. "This is a nice surprise. What brings the two of you here?"

Bea's forehead glistened with beads of sweat. "Out getting our exercise and walking off Opal's peach pie."

Emma laughed. "Care for a little company? I feel sure Celeste and I outdid you with our cake." She motioned. "Pull up a couple of rockers."

Opal plopped down and fanned herself with her hand. "Whew! It feels good to take the load off my feet. Bea's load isn't as heavy as mine. I'll either have to fatten her up or find a new walking partner."

Bea placed her hands on her hips. "Oh, so that's why you invited me for pie?"

"Something like that," she said, rocking as hard as she could.

Celeste grinned. "I'm going to have to remember to write you both into my novel. You two are hilarious."

Bea rocked forward, then stopped and stared into Emma's eyes. "I've got good news."

"You do? Tell us." Emma scooted to the edge of her seat and shifted her eyes toward Celeste. "We could use more good news around this house, couldn't we?"

"That's for sure."

"I've heard from my daughter."

Emma's mouth fell open as she slapped her knees. "You don't mean it?"

Bea and Opal, smiling from ear to ear, nodded in unison.

"So what prompted that?"

"God. All God." Bea leaned back in her chair and gazed into the trees. "I knew He'd come through in our situation. He always does."

Celeste turned her chair to face them. "Hurry. Tell us."

"My daughter called me this morning, crying. I could barely understand her. Several weeks ago, she received a call from an FBI agent about skeletal remains found on the bank of the Cape Fear River. They thought the bones might be my grandson's. My daughter waited for the results of the pathology report before calling me. After pathologists examined the bones and teeth, they determined they were from a child about Richie's age."

Emma leaned in. "Were they Richie's?"

She nodded.

"But how can they be sure?"

"They asked if he'd ever broken his left arm, and he had." She shook her head and grinned. "That little scamp fell from an apple tree when he was four and broke it in two places."

Emma rose from her chair and hugged Bea. "This is such a blessing. I'm so happy you now have closure."

"Oh, and it gets better."

"Better?" Emma's eyes widened as she returned to her seat.

"Indeed. My daughter will be in Fayetteville next week and wants to see me." Tears streamed down her cheeks. "I'm so happy. She said she misses me and wants to try and move forward with our relationship." Pulling a handkerchief from her pocket, she wiped her eyes. "God has answered my prayers. He's not only healed my deepest hurts, He's healing hers."

Emma leaned back in her chair. "God is good. This morning in church, Pastor Gardner quoted Charles Haddon Spurgeon. He said, *'Prayer pulls the rope below, and the great bell rings above in the ears of God.'* The bell tolled loudly for Richie. God heard, and He moved."

Bea nodded, then rested her head on the chair and rocked. "He did. He certainly did. God is always faithful." She shook her head. "Ever so faithful."

Chapter Forty

Monday, August 17, 1942
Carrickfergus, Northern Ireland
Tucker

Rain pummeled the arched corrugated-iron roof of the Nissen hut at Sunnylands Camp. Tucker slipped off his jacket, shook it, and hung it up to dry on a hook beside his bed. Then, unzipping his duffle bag, he pulled out the last of his clothing and placed them in the footlocker at the end of his cot. "Feels like home, right, Hank?"

"Yep," he said, leveling three spirited jabs at his pillow. Stretching out, he placed his hands behind his head and crossed his ankles. "Would never know the difference."

Tucker laughed, reached into the bottom of his bag, and pulled out the photograph of his friends at the Rainbow. He dropped onto his cot, studied the picture, and reread each sentiment before resting his eyes on Emma. *No greater girl around. Drew was one lucky man.*

He glanced over at Hank. For him, sleep came quickly, but for those within earshot, not so much. Lifting the spiral tablet and pen from the small bedside table, he flipped on the gooseneck lamp and leaned back against his pillow.

Top of the evening to you, dear Emma,
    After ten days at sea, our ship has landed on God's green earth—The Emerald Isle. So far, no sightings of leprechauns or pots of gold, but I intend to keep my eyes open—especially for the latter. Our accommodations don't rival the Ritz, but at least my bed won't pitch

through the night. And as long as the snoring of twenty-four GI's doesn't ricochet off the walls of this tin can we're sleeping in, maybe I'll get a good night's rest. I'll need it. Guess who has KP his first morning ashore? How's that for the luck of the Irish?

Overall, our troops were given a hero's welcome. The Irish are filled with gratitude. Our presence has given Great Britain a renewed sense of courage and hope, proving President Roosevelt is committed to defeating Hitler and securing peace in Europe. Although it's never occurred to them that they could lose the war, they've also wondered if they could ever win it. Our combined slogan is *"Finish Hitler in 1942,"* and you know, I'm all for that. The faster Hitler and his evil regime are defeated, the sooner my return to the States.

How are things going with you? Got that book written yet? I sure can't wait to read it and tell everyone I know that I'm the friend of a New York Times best-selling author.

I suppose I should close. It's lights out around here at nine. I'll write again as soon as I can.

Please write me often. I'm already homesick. Oh, to be on your front porch swing, listening to the cries of the whip-poor-wills. Give my love to all.

A friend loves at all times, and this is one of those times.

Tucker

The next morning

"Hey, Sarge, serve that up a little faster. Gotta keep this line movin'. You're not in the laid-back South anymore, ya know."

"How well I do." Tucker's blood neared its boiling point.

Better knock it off, buddy. Twisting his mouth sideways, he murmured to the soldier serving beside him, "If you want to know who a man really is, give him a bit of power. This guy's true colors are on full-fledged display this morning."

Private Leo Lewis nodded. "Couldn't agree more."

Tucker slapped a spoonful of hash browns onto the next soldier's plate. "Where are you from, Private?"

"Billings, Montana. You?"

"Louisville, but my heart belongs in North Carolina. Hope to settle down there someday."

"Ah, pretty state. Gotta girl?"

"Nah. The one I want is spoken for. How about you?"

He flashed a toothy grin and puffed out his chest. "Prettiest girl in Billings. We're going to tie the knot as soon as I get home."

"It shouldn't be long now. Our troops will have Hitler and his vile cronies on the run in no time."

"I hope you're right, sir."

Tucker swallowed hard and scooped up another spoonful of potatoes. *Me too.*

"So is the girl you've got your eye on married?"

"Nope. Engaged."

"What?" He straightened and squared his shoulders. "Only engaged?"

Nodding, Tucker dumped the last hash browns from his serving pan into a steaming hot tray from the kitchen.

"Good grief, man. That means you've still got a fighting chance."

He chuckled and shook his head. "I don't think so. She's pretty taken with this fellow, and he has more to offer her than I do."

Leo's eyes widened as he threw his hands in the air. "What? So you retreat? You just give up? Where's your grit, soldier? Maybe she waited for you to make a move and got tired of waiting."

He shrugged. "You may be right. Maybe she did. Couldn't say that I'd blame her."

"Haven't you heard that war takes you to unexpected places, but it's love that brings you home? You do want to get home, don't you, Sarge?" He placed several strips of bacon on the plate of the next soldier. "Now's not the time to be shy." He flailed his arms, waving his tongs. "Step up. Tell her how you feel. It's act now or live with regret."

Tucker scooped a serving from the pan and placed it on the plate held out in front of him.

"Thank you, sir."

Looking up, he stared into eyes that mirrored Emma's. "You're welcome." His gaze followed the petite soldier's shapely figure as she walked across the room and took her seat next to a fellow in his platoon.

He bit his lip and nodded. *Tonight. Yeah. I'll write Emma again tonight.*

Tuesday, August 18, 1942

My Dear Emma,

I hope this letter finds you happy. I'm good but homesick. There's little to do around here in the evenings but smoke cigs or stogies and play cards or checkers. Since I'm not a big fan of any of those, I'd rather spend my time writing you.

It's been a tough day—physically as well as emotionally. I was up before Reveille for KP duty, then went straight to field training, where I received my assignment. I'll serve in the ambulance corps with Hank. Thank God. It helps to know who's beside you in the fox hole. We'll evacuate the wounded from battlefield aid stations to small field hospitals for triage. Those less critical who can make longer ambulance rides, we'll carry to evacuation hospitals farther away from the frontlines.

Don't worry about me, Em—just pray. As perilous as it sounds, I'm not afraid. I love my assignment—doing what I can to restore life in the middle of a killing field. I count it a privilege to wear America's uniform and serve my country. I pray I do it well. My comfort comes from knowing I'm on the winning team and that the Lord is in the foxhole with me.

In light of this, I've done a lot of thinking and know I must share my whole heart with you. Until now, I've shied away from doing so for fear of jeopardizing our friendship, but I can no longer keep my true feelings to myself.

Today, as I prepared for battle, I realized I've failed to fight for the most important person in my world. I've failed to fight for you—for us—for the life we could have together.

Emma, I love you!

There, I've said it.

No more living with regret.

I'm sorry if this puts you in an awkward position, for you say you love Drew, and I know he loves you. But I can no longer pretend your relationship with him is okay with me. It's not. I've tried to be happy for you but realize I will never find happiness outside of the truth. I'd lay down my life for you, Emma Rose Walsh, and I love you enough to risk it all.

I don't know how I expect you to respond to this other than being true to yourself. If you proceed with your plans to marry Drew, I'll understand and be content knowing I've given it my all.

As for now, I must say good night and sign off. It's lights out here in Ireland.

A friend loves at all times, and this is one of those times.

Tucker

Chapter Forty-One

Fayetteville, North Carolina
Friday, October 22, 1942
Emma

Seating herself at the wrought-iron table on the porch, Emma buttoned her sweater and breathed in the crisp fall air. She wasn't about to stay cooped up inside on a day as spectacular as this one. The golden leaves of the trees in the side yard rustled in the light breeze and sparkled in the late afternoon sun. It was Indian Summer. Mama had always called it summer's last hurrah, and that it was.

Though beautiful, fall had never been her favorite season. She supposed it was because the promise of winter nipped at its heels, and this year, she dreaded it more than ever. Bears certainly had the right idea. Sleeping through the cold, dreary winter days ahead seemed like the perfect solution.

Leaning back, she chuckled as she reread Tucker's last letter. He had a way with words, and as a budding author herself, she always enjoyed a story told well.

Emma opened the stationery she'd found at The Capitol's end-of-summer sale and uncapped her pen. Although the yellow and white daisy paper wasn't the most appropriate for harvest time, daisies were happy flowers, and she could use a dose of happiness. She knew Tucker could too—probably more so than her.

Hi Tucker,

I hope this letter finds you doing well. Have you

seen any leprechauns yet? I can hardly believe another month has come and gone, and this war still rages on. Although I've only received a few letters from you since you left, I continue to write because I know you need mail more than I do. By the way, I'm out of V-mail stationery, so I hope you like my happy daisy paper and that it brings a smile to your face.

Fayetteville's streets are eerily quiet since most of Fort Bragg's soldiers have been deployed. Please know your sacrifice is not taken for granted here on the home front. Prayers go up daily for you—and not mine alone. Cee and the Rainbow Girls send their love and prayers, as do many of my customers. Not a day goes by that someone doesn't ask about you.

It's hard not knowing where and how you are, but not nearly as difficult, I'm sure, as being in the thick of battle. I know you'll write when you can. We all look forward to receiving news from the frontlines.

I've yet to have a serious bite on the house, but with the increase in jobs and the freeze on new home construction, previously owned or rented houses are in demand. At this point, I'm not in a hurry to sell. Until Drew returns from Scotland, I don't know where I'd go if it did. Right now, I'm grateful to have a roof over my head and food on the table.

I continue to volunteer at the Red Cross and work on my book. Celeste has been a wonderful mentor, and her editor said she'll edit my manuscript when I finish. Writing has kept me sane during these months of missing you and Drew.

Today is absolutely gorgeous, but this season is way too short. I dread the holidays with you and Drew gone. I'm ready to put this year to bed and usher in 1943. There's got to be good news on the horizon.

Drew says his foot is healing nicely. He still has a

limp but is walking without a cane. We are grateful the injury was to his foot and not his hands. The work he submitted to the Recording Scotland Collection was accepted, and he will soon get around well enough to accompany Finn on painting field trips.

I must close and get ready for work. I have the evening shift all weekend. Stay safe and hurry home.

Lovingly,
Emma … and Chummy too.

She placed her letter in the envelope, gathered her things, and walked to the door.

"Emma, wait. Don't go in yet." Celeste rushed up the walk. "You've got to sit back down. I have great news."

"What is it? You're beaming." She laid her things on the table and hugged her. "Have a seat. I can't wait to hear."

Placing a large Manila envelope on the table, Celeste sat across from Emma and grinned.

"What's that?"

"One guess—only one."

Amused, she squinted, twisting her mouth. "Hmm…one, huh?"

Celeste held up her index finger and nodded.

"Can I hold it?"

Her eyes traveled to the ceiling as she drummed her fingers on the envelope. "Okay."

Emma picked it up and weighed it with her hands. "It's a little heavy." She paused and gazed into Celeste's eyes. "I've got it," she said, flashing a big smile. "It's a book contract."

Celeste shook her head.

"No?" She looked puzzled. "It's not a contract?"

"Nope."

"Uh. What is it then?"

"You really want to know?"

She slapped her hand on the table. "Celeste, will you stop playing games and tell me what's in that envelope."

"It's not a contract …" Her eyes widened, and her voice rose a couple of octaves. "It's … *three* contracts."

Emma squealed.

Leaping from the table and throwing their arms around each other, they jumped up and down.

Emma spun Celeste around. "Congratulations! I knew they'd love your second manuscript."

She nodded, grinning from ear to ear. "And they've signed me for two more. Can you believe it?"

"I'm not at all surprised." Emma stopped to catch her breath. You're an excellent writer. I'm so happy for you."

She blushed. "Thank you." Lowering her eyes, she returned to her chair and brushed the envelope with her fingers. "I'm always surprised when someone likes my work. To get a three-book contract is beyond my wildest dreams. If this can happen to me, Emma, it can happen to you, and I'm going to do all I can to see that it does."

"How nice of you. You've been a huge inspiration to me. If it wasn't for your encouragement, I'd still simply be dreaming about writing."

Celeste patted the table and pointed to the chair. "Emma, sit. I have more news."

Her eyes grew large. "More?" Furrowing her brow, she eased into the chair. "This sounds serious. I'm almost afraid to ask."

"It is serious, but I'm certain you'll be pleased with this news. As a matter of fact, you may like it better than the first."

"Oh, I doubt it. Three contracts will be hard to top." She waved her hand and leaned back in her chair. "But go ahead, I'm ready. What's the news?"

"On the way home from meeting with my publisher, I stopped by the bank and signed for a loan."

She leaned forward with a puzzled look. "Are you paying to

have your book published?"

"Oh, no." She reached into her purse, pulled out a check, and passed it to Emma.

Her eyes widened as she flapped the check in the air. "What's this? A year's rent?"

She shook her head. "Nope. It's a down payment—a down payment on your house."

Emma looked perplexed. "What?"

"Emma, I'd like to buy this house."

She covered her face with her hands. Then folded them under her chin and locked eyes with Celeste. "Are you serious? You want to buy this house?"

"Dead serious. This place is home to me. With my advance and a guaranteed income, I can afford a permanent writing space." She pointed toward the ceiling. "And I can't think of a better space than in that room right up there."

"Oh, my goodness. I can't believe my ears. You are really going to buy this house?" Tears streamed down her cheeks.

She nodded and smiled. "If you'll let me."

"Let you? This is beyond my wildest dreams. God is so good and faithful. There isn't anyone I'd rather have own this house than you." She walked over to Celeste and hugged her. "Thank you. Thank you. I can hardly wait to tell Drew." She returned to her seat, shaking her head. "Is this really happening? My house has sold, and *you* are the owner."

"I thought you'd be rather happy—and there's more."

"Still more?"

"Yes. I want you to stay here with me until you and Drew marry. You can remain in your bedroom. For now, I like being upstairs across from the writing room."

Emma drew her hands to her chest and shook her head. "I'm stunned. In my book, *Dream Beyond Tomorrow*, I've written Ephesians 3:20 in the preface. *'Now unto him that is able to do exceeding abundantly above all that we ask or think, according to the power that worketh in us.'* That's exactly what has happened today. I can't even begin to comprehend God's goodness to us both. Thank you again. I can tell it's going to take a while for all of this to sink in."

"I know. I feel the same way. We should celebrate."

"I agree." She looked at her watch then leaped from her chair. "But I can't. I almost forgot. I'm to be at work in thirty minutes. I'm sorry. Our celebration will have to wait."

"Of course." She motioned. "Go ahead. Hurry up and get dressed."

Emma hugged Celeste and hurried to the door. Opening it, she turned. "I wish everyone was as happy as I am right now. The only thing that could make this day better would be to hear that my precious Drew, and Tucker, were on their way home."

She entered the foyer. "Please, Lord, please. Let it be soon."

Chapter Forty-Two

Friday, August 24, 2012
Hope Mills, North Carolina
Caroline

I tapped Kate's arm as Tucker shared about his letter to our mother, then sat wide-eyed with both hands pressed against my chest. At times, I thought my throbbing heart would break for this precious man sitting across from us.

"So you *did* tell Mother how you felt about her?"

He brushed a tear from his cheek and nodded. "Poured my heart out."

"What happened?"

Kate slid to the edge of the couch. "Yes. What did Mother say?"

"Nothing."

As our mouths fell open, my eyes darted to Kate, then back to Tucker. "What?" We spoke in unison, our voices swelling. "What do you mean—nothing?"

"I allowed a couple of weeks for my letter to reach her, then a couple more for me to get one from her. It was the longest month of my life. When her letter finally arrived, it was mid-September. You'd better believe after the mail call, I made a beeline for our barracks. You could have heard a pin drop in that tin hut as fellas read their mail from home. Those who hadn't received mail napped or played darts or horseshoes outside. Anything to get their minds off of their disappointment."

I squirmed. "Breaks my heart to hear about it."

"Emma mentioned receiving my first letter but said nothing

about my second, so I waited to receive another one from her before I said anything. Again, she never mentioned my assignment, much less my confession of love for her, so obviously, my letter never made it home. I was sick."

"What did you do?"

He stared out the window. "I tried to write it again and almost wore a hole in the paper with my eraser. The words wouldn't come. I decided to wait and write the next day, but orders for our battalion came in overnight. We were up and out to a staging area in Birkenhead, England, at the crack of dawn. Lovely place. Wish I could have been there under different circumstances.

"The children loved us, and we loved them. They were bright spots in a sea of khaki fatigues. We'd carry gum in our pockets to pass out to them, and before long, whenever they'd see us on the streets, they'd say, 'Got any gum, chum?'" He laughed. "Amazing how something as simple as a stick of gum brought so much joy and laughter—not only for them but for us." Shaking his head, he turned to face us again. "I have nice memories of my days in England, but our stay there was short.

"In January of '43, our 261st Amphibious Medical Battalion sailed for North Africa—Arzew, Algeria. Soldiers in our unit rotated between operating 100-bed clearing stations, dispensing medicine, providing dental care, evacuating the wounded, and being schooled in battlefield etiquette."

I giggled at his tongue-in-cheek storytelling.

"As for Hank and me, most of our days were spent in the cockpit of an ambulance. We'd transport patients that came into the La Senia Airport from the Tunisian front to the port of Oran for embarkation.

"Whenever we'd change locations, it took a while for the mail to catch up with us. By the time it did, we were on our way again. Your mother's letters were a breath of fresh air. I wrote when I could but had little time to reply and never enough time to say what I wanted to.

"Next, we were on our way to Gela, Sicily, as part of Operation Husky. We arrived on July 11th in support of Major General George S. Patton's Seventh United States Army. Coming in two days behind the initial invasion worked in our favor. Things had quieted down by then. Hank and I continued transporting wounded troops for sea evacuation, this time to Tunis and Bizerte. I was glad they kept us together. We made a great team. I knew he had my back, and I for sure had his.

"About six weeks from the time the Italian Armistice was signed on September 3rd, our battalion sailed for Italy to set up an aid station near Caserta. It was here my Italian holiday took a dramatic turn."

Saturday, October 23, 1943
Somewhere near Naples
Tucker

After the ship pitched all night like a toy boat in the angry Mediterranean Sea, Tucker opened his eyes to a misty gray morning. Groaning, he splashed water on his face and put on combat fatigues. Today was no dress rehearsal. This—*this* was war—the real thing.

Slinging his gear onto his back, he breathed a prayer and joined his platoon on deck. One by one, the men climbed down the cargo net to the landing craft below. As he anchored his feet in the net's ropes, he scrambled over the rail behind Hank and eased his way down. Nearing the bottom, he let go with one hand and turned to jump, right as the landing craft swung away from the ship.

"Doggone it!" he said, dangling in mid-air.

He winced as the rope tore his skin, then waited for the churning sea to return the craft to the ship's side. It slammed back and forth. Timing would be everything.

Now.

Dropping toward the steel floor, Tucker twisted his body so

that his gear would break his fall. Then, struggling to get a foothold in the rolling vessel, he crawled to the jeep emblazoned with a large red cross on its hood and climbed into the passenger seat.

Trying not to laugh, Hank gripped the wheel and looked straight ahead. "Come on up, partner."

He smirked. "I believe I will, wise guy."

"You ready for an adventure?"

He took off his helmet and wiped the sweat from his brow. "There's more? I thought I just had it."

Adrenaline coursed through his veins as Lieutenant Huckaby waved the okay sign to the pilot of the LCPR. As the vessel increased speed, it crashed into the waves and bucked like a bronco. Cold sea spray swept over the heads of the thirty-eight men from Tucker's platoon. Huddled against the sides, some whooped, a few cried, while others crossed themselves, but Tucker knew—*all were praying.*

After what seemed like a rollercoaster ride that would never end, the craft's motor dwindled from a roar to a purr. Anxious men tightened their packs, gathered ammo boxes, and snapped loaded clips into their M1 rifles.

"Good luck, soldiers," bellowed a voice from the speaker overhead. "Remember who you're fighting for and make them proud. The sooner we whip these heartless bullies, the sooner we'll all go home."

Tucker's eyes met those of Private Leo Lewis sitting on the opposite side of the craft. Leo nodded and threw up an okay sign.

The churning Mediterranean was no match for the land craft's skilled pilot. His perfect landing brought them a few yards from the sandy beach. As the ramp crashed to the ground, thirty-eight proud troops from the 261st Medical Battalion, pumped and ready to go home, charged ashore just South of Naples. Hank rolled the jeep out behind them, towing a trailer filled with medical supplies protected by a tarp.

As Tucker's unit joined other troops on the quiet beach, they ducked behind brush-covered sand dunes and stayed low to the ground. They had paratroopers from the 82nd Airborne Division and America's allies to thank for a job well done. Little resistance from the Germans meant they were on the run. *Good call. They'd chase them clear to the far side of hell before they'd let them dominate Italy and the world stage.*

The infantry led out as a string of foot soldiers and vehicles followed white tape that marked a safe route through minefields dotted with tank traps and foxholes. Hitting the main road leading to the city of Caserta, Tucker struggled to comprehend what he saw as their column zigzagged its way through havoc wreaked by the Germans. As plumes of smoke carried by ocean breezes hung low to the ground, they passed wrecked vehicles and dead Italians who'd stood in defense of their homeland. Crashed planes, burned tanks, and bombed-out buildings still belching smoke littered the once picturesque and peaceful countryside.

As they passed mile upon mile of wreckage, Tucker and Hank's disbelief turned to a matter-of-fact acceptance of the gruesome landscape surrounding them. Then—just short of being lulled into complacency—a barrage of machine-gun fire pummeled their convoy. While the infantry upfront opened fire on the unseen enemy, troops scattered in all directions to find shelter in the rolling terrain.

Tucker and Hank pulled out their pistols, the one firearm a medic was allowed to carry, and hunkered down in the sand behind the jeep. Hank fumed. "So much for the Geneva Convention and not shooting at those wearing the red cross."

"What do you expect from a tyrant who doesn't play by the rules? Heck, he's never even owned a rulebook."

As shells whizzed past and exploded around them, a desperate cry rose from a hill to their right. "Medic! Medic!"

Tucker and Hank stayed low to the ground, ran to the wounded soldier, and knelt by his side.

Writhing in pain, Private Leo Lewis pleaded as blood spurted from his chest. "Help me. Please, help me."

"That's what we're here to do, pal. Your job is to hold on."

He ripped open the soldier's coat and inner garments and poured sulfa powder into the deep wound. Then, as Hank packed it with gauze and applied pressure with his full body weight, Tucker administered morphine, prayed, and tried to keep Leo calm.

"I'm not going to make it, Doc!"

"What? So you just give up? Call it quits? Where's your grit, soldier? Of course, you're going to make it."

His pained expression eased into a slight smile. "I guess I deserved that." Then, gasping, he pointed to his breast coat pocket. "Get it. The letter."

Tucker slid his hand into Leo's pocket and pulled out an envelope addressed to Miss Irene Taylor in Billings, Montana.

As his breathing became more shallow, he struggled to keep his eyes open. "See that my girl gets it, will you, Tuck?"

He fought back tears as a lump formed in his throat. "You know I will, pal."

"And tell her … tell her … I said …."

His head fell to one side.

"I love—"

His breathing stopped, and his eyes rolled back in his head.

Hank quit applying pressure to his chest, searched for a pulse, then reached up and closed the fallen soldier's eyes.

Tucker rolled back on his heels and sat frozen. Staring at Leo's lifeless face, he choked back emotions. *"So this is what you're gonna do, huh? You're going to call it quits? You've got a wedding to …."*

He lowered his chin as his voice cracked, slipped the envelope into his coat pocket, and rose from his knees. A burst of machine-gun fire reminded him the war was still on, but before he could react, shells screamed overhead and peppered the soil at his feet.

He flinched. Searing pain cut through his skin. Grabbing his shoulder, his vision blurred, and he struggled to breathe. As the ground swirled about him, his arms flailed. Falling forward, he—

No, no, no, this isn't happening. Emma …

Chapter Forty-Three

Wednesday, March 15, 1944
St Andrews, Scotland
Drew

As the sun lowered in the western sky, Drew pulled his wool scarf tight around his neck, then blew into his hands and rubbed them together. Keeping his eyes fixed on St Monans Auld Kirk, he picked up his brush and laid a second wash of Cerulean Blue across the sheet of rag paper. St Monans's sturdy stone church sat on a hill within twenty meters of the high cliffs of the North Sea, closer than any other parish in Scotland. From almost any direction, the ocean's deep sapphire-blue water served as a breathtaking backdrop for the historic church.

"How's it shaping up, my man?" Finn ambled up behind him with his sheltie on his heels.

Drew stepped back from his work. "You tell me. The sky wasn't intense enough, but by George, I think I might have fixed it."

Finn looked at the painting, shifted his eyes to the sky, and then back to the watercolor. He slapped him on the back. "Yes, I think you've got it. It's stunning. I'd say this one is certain to make the collection."

He laughed and sat down in the chair beside his easel. "I'm glad you're certain. With this blustery wind, I've struggled to lay my washes in fast enough. If this piece doesn't make the cut, I'll send it to Joe in the States. He's done a great job of maintaining interest in my work despite this horrible war. He's even sold several nice-sized paintings. How has your day gone?"

"I've battled the wind too." Stretching out on the ground,

Finn crossed his ankles and leaned back on his elbows. Fifer rested his head on his master's knee. "I'm pleased with the end result, though. You can see it when we get home. I'd like your opinion. You about ready to call it a day?"

He nodded. "I am. I need to put my foot up. It's begun to ache."

"I'd say you've done well to stay out here this long. It's nice to have you back. I've missed your company."

"I've missed being out here with you, as well. It was nice at Mum's, but her doting got hard to bear. I understand her concern, but I've been independent far too long to be waited on hand and foot. I can only take so much of it."

"Tell her if she wants someone to dote on, I'll let her dote on me." He chuckled. "At least from my house, you can scuttle across the bridge and be home in thirty minutes. It's a good compromise."

"Indeed. Close enough but not too far." Drew gathered his supplies and put them in his paint box. "I appreciate the open-ended invitation to stay with you."

"As I've said before, it gets rather lonely puttering around the house by ourselves." He gave Fifer's head a brisk rub. "Doesn't it, fella?"

Fifer cut his brown eyes up at Finn and whimpered.

"Interesting you should say that. I know someone you need to meet."

Finn tipped his head and raised his eyebrows. "You do, do you?"

"In a sense, you've already met her, but you probably wouldn't recognize her."

Finn sat cross-legged on the grassy carpet and brushed his hand over the soft turf. "Her?" He rolled his eyes. "Say what's on your mind, chum."

"Her name's Bess Fleming. She's the mother of Ian, the little boy we pulled from the rubble in August."

"You mean you've kept in touch with her?"

"Not exactly. She stopped by the room to see me before she

left the hospital with Ian. I noticed she didn't have a ring on."

"Drew, shame on you. You mean you still check?"

"I looked for you, my man, not myself. Anyway, I talked with the nurse, a school friend of hers. She said Bess's husband was a bomber pilot with the Royal Air Force when his plane was shot down during the Clydebank Blitz in '41. She was pregnant with their son."

He shook his head. "Such a shame. I don't remember much about her. You think she's my type?"

"I don't know what your type is, but the nurse gave me her phone number. I've saved it for you." Pulling his wallet from his pocket, he took out a slip of paper and handed it to him. "Give her a call sometime. I think you'll be pleasantly surprised. She said she would stay with her parents until she could get back on her feet and find a place of her own."

Finn sat silent, rubbing Fifer's coat, then slipped the paper in his pocket. "This is something my buddy and I will have to talk over. I'm not sure how he'd take to a woman in the house, much less a child. It's always been the two of us, and he's grown rather accustomed to being front and center."

"Sure. Take your time. Just a thought." Drew laughed. "Besides, I'm not ready to move out yet. Hopefully, this war will be over soon, and I can go home to Emma." He stood and took his painting from the easel.

"Grab your chair and your paint box." Finn jumped up to fold the easel. "I'll carry this. I've already put my things in the car."

Fifer leaped into the back seat as Drew settled in front and stretched out his leg. "It's been a good day," he said as Finn slipped behind the wheel. "I needed this to clear my head. Too much heavy stuff happening lately. Thanks for bringing me over."

"I was glad to. I know you'd do the same for me." Turning right onto Station Road, they drove several miles along the rugged coastline before turning inland toward St. Andrews. "I haven't heard you say lately. Anything new on Tucker?"

Drew groaned and shook his head. "Not that I know of. Emma's last letter said they were still searching for him. I'm sure if she hears anything different, she'll give me a ring."

"But didn't you tell me they'd found his platoon on the side of the road leading to Caserta?"

He nodded. "Yes. All dead. Tucker's body wasn't among them unless it was one of the unidentified ones."

"I'm sorry. How's Emma handling it?"

"Not well. It's been over four months now, and the more time that passes, the more anxious she becomes. I wish I could be there with her. Unfortunately, life throws us cruel twists and turns. So far, she's managed to hold on to her faith, but I sensed more despondency in her last letter. She and Tucker were really close. I think if he could have had things his way, she'd be his girl, not mine."

"If she's as pretty as her pictures, can't say that I'd blame him. She's a beautiful woman." He turned onto Nelson Street. "I hope she hears something soon. I think not knowing is worse than knowing. At least when you have the facts, you can take steps toward acceptance and closure."

"I agree."

After Finn pulled the car into the driveway of his small house, Drew followed Fifer into the cozy living room. He placed his painting on the mantle, then stretched out on the sofa and studied it, while Fifer flopped on a pillow beside his master's easy chair.

"You two look useless." Finn shut the door and latched it. "It feels good in here. That wind was chilly today.

"It certainly was. 'Chilly for June,' my dad used to say regardless of the month."

Finn propped his painting on the mantle beside Drew's, then sorted through the mail he'd pulled from the box beside the door. "Wish I'd get something besides—" His eyes widened. "Aha. Look here, my man. You'll be happy about this one." He tossed a daisy patterned envelope into Drew's lap."

Picking it up, Drew held it to his nose and inhaled the

lavender scent. "Smells better than daisies, that's for sure. A word from my baby is what I need." After tearing off the end resealed by the censor, he tapped the envelope in the palm of his hand and slid out the letter.

"I'll leave you and Fife to yourselves while I forage around in the kitchen and see if there is anything here for us to eat tonight. If not, we should stroll down to the pub and get one of their St. Paddy's Day specials—corn beef and cabbage or finnan haddie." Finn walked into the kitchen, then peeked back around the doorframe. "On second thought, maybe I won't check. My mouth is watering already."

Drew laughed, rested his head against the cushion, and unfolded Emma's letter.

February 29, 1944
My Darling Drew,

I hope this finds you feeling much better and that you've gotten in some painting days with Finn by now.

Celeste and I are doing okay. She stays busy writing and has made nice progress on her third book. When she's not at the typewriter, she enjoys her new role as 'home owner' and looks forward to sprucing up the yard this spring. She'll do things I wanted to do but didn't invest in since I had plans to sell the house.

As for me, I stay busy at the Rainbow, and with the blood bank taking more and more of my time, my writing has fallen by the wayside. Sometimes, I try to write late at night, but since I learned of Tucker's disappearance, it's hard to stay focused. I often have nightmares of his death or of him wounded and wandering around in the countryside somewhere. The not-knowing is horrible.

Today has been a tough day. I hated not to show up for work, but I called Cee to tell him I couldn't make it. He was very understanding. I'm so thankful for him.

Yesterday, I heard from Tucker's mother in Louisville. His family received a telegram from President Roosevelt's Secretary of War, Henry L. Stimson, expressing his deep regret concerning Tucker's disappearance. The letter stated that the United States Military had officially designated him as Missing in Action.

Hearing it was like scraping the scab off of a fresh wound, although I don't suppose it changes anything. Whether officially designated or not, missing is still missing, and our pain is excruciating. Of course, we continue to pray that somehow, someway, Tucker will surprise us all and show up somewhere. My heart breaks for his mother. As bad as I hurt, I know her pain and loss run much deeper.

How is your mum? She knows the heartbreak of war and has been through more than I have. Tell her I continue to pray for you all, and I can't wait to meet her.

Oh, how I miss you and wish you were here. I need to feel your arms around me again. Only then will I be convinced that you're okay—that you're not a figment of my imagination—a fabricated character scrawled across the pages of my book. If I could sit at the typewriter and pound out our happy ending, I'd do it today. Now. This minute. Instead, I can't shake the ominous feeling that bad news looms on the horizon. I try to give my fears to God, but as soon as hope peeks above the murky surface, something else happens. Drew, I'm afraid. I want you home.

Write me often and dream with me beyond our tomorrows. I pray our time will come soon, and your next letter will read—*Darling, I'm coming home.*

How blessed I am to be yours, and I can't wait to be your wife.

I'll love you forever,

Emma

Chapter Forty-Four

Friday, August 24, 2012
Hope Mills, North Carolina
Caroline

Kate and I sat mesmerized as Tucker recounted his harrowing story. It was difficult to picture this frail man who struggled for every breath as a tan and fit young soldier in the hills of Italy. The sacrifice he'd made was incomprehensible, but the purple heart medal that hung on the wall beside the fireplace was proof he was one of life's true heroes. We could tell reliving his experience was difficult for him but sensed this was a journey his soul needed to take.

He took a sip of his water, cleared his throat, and shared the events of seventy years prior in extraordinary detail.

"It was October 23rd, and we were somewhere near Caserta. Lying on my stomach, I tried not to flinch as rounds of machine-gun fire peppered the earth around me. I expected to be pummeled any second. Once the shelling stopped, I waited to open my eyes for fear of the carnage I'd see. Although the pain in my left shoulder felt like a hot poker sizzling in my flesh, I sensed I was one of the lucky ones.

"I laid still, listened, then reached for a large clod of dirt and tossed it into the air. Expecting a barrage of gunfire, I held my breath, but silence followed—a *long* silence.

"Feeling safe, I struggled to my feet and surveyed the landscape. My shock escalated to anger, then plummeted to grief all within seconds. I wanted to run but knew my feet wouldn't carry me. I fell to my knees and wept over my fallen comrades.

It was then I realized I wasn't *one* of the lucky ones, I was *the* lucky one—the sole survivor from my platoon. But walking among the dead felt anything but lucky.

"I sat on the ground to treat my wound and took a blood-caked medical kit from my breast coat pocket. Tucked inside the small, metal case was my silver cross—the one your mother gave me. It was a staggering reminder that every breath I took was due to the hand of a Sovereign God who had determined He wasn't through with me yet.

"Wincing, I did my best to remove bullet fragments from my shoulder and clean and pack the wound. By the time I slipped on my shirt and jacket and put my arm in a sling, I was exhausted. I moved to Hank's lifeless body and prayed. I prayed for his family, thanked God for my protection, and begged Him for further guidance."

Tucker's voice cracked.

"I needed to move on. The sun had dropped, and so had the temperature. Hoping to find a warm place to lie down for the night, I slung my backpack over my good shoulder and followed the road. It was hard to leave my buddies, but I had no choice. I resisted the urge to look back. I'd never felt so alone."

Lowering his head to his chest, he wept.

Kate and I waited without speaking, wiping away tears of our own.

Grabbing a tissue from the TV tray beside his chair, Tucker blew his nose, then continued with his story.

Saturday, October 23, 1943
Somewhere near Caserta

Having walked for miles, Tucker gulped water from his canteen, then slipped into a large pasture where two horses grazed. He hoped their presence indicated life on the other side of trees that bordered the field. As he walked toward them, 88mm rocket fire sent him diving to his belly, slamming his injured shoulder into the hard clod-covered soil. Once several minutes had passed, he realized the mortars exploding in the distance were not aimed at him.

Pressing one hand to the ground, he heaved his tired, stiff body to an upright position and brushed off his knees. *Old habits die hard.* He almost broke into laughter as visions of his mama flashed through his mind—her furrowed brow, obvious disapproval of his mud-caked britches after playing Army with the neighbor boys. At that moment, he would have given anything to have been confronted with her hands-on-hips stance. Instead, the indignant stares of horses greeted him

They raised their heads, sniffed the air, and snorted. The larger one dipped his head low to the ground and ambled toward him. The other followed. They nudged his hands, obviously hoping for a carrot or a handful of oats.

As he stroked their noses, his heart broke at the appearance of their ribbed bellies, implying they could have used a good meal. "Sorry, fellas, I wish I had something for you. It looks like pickings have been pretty slim for all of us these days." He patted their necks. "It's time I move on. You got a family around here?"

He slipped through the barbed wire fence and walked into the thicket. Midway in, a deep, raspy cough broke the still evening air. He froze, wavering between relief at the sound of life and fear as to whose life it was. Pulling out his pistol, he moved as stealthily as he could with his mud-crusted, size-ten boots and stiffened at every snap of a twig.

Coming to the edge of the clearing, he ducked behind the gnarled trunk of a massive olive tree. Its bizarre shape reminded him of the trees in the enchanted forest his mother would read about from the pages of Grimm's Fairy Tales. His surroundings felt like it, too—only this forest was far from enchanting.

Peeking through a low branch, he watched a short, pudgy

farmer fork hay into a small shed from a wagon hooked to a horse. At each toss, a small, mixed-breed dog would scuttle back and forth, leap into the air, and snap at the falling hay.

Life here felt insulated—detached from the horror that had taken place a short distance down the road. Shifting his weight, he startled himself as the loud snap of a tree limb sent the small dog into a tirade. Tucker pressed his back against the tree as the raucous dog charged toward the thicket, stopping short of the underbrush. Yapping, he zipped back and forth along the edge of the trees.

"*Enzo, silenzioso!*" The dog got quiet as his master shuffled toward the trees and shouted, "*Uscire! Uscire!*"

Though not versed in Italian, Tucker sensed it meant to come out. He hesitated, but knowing there was no way around it, he put his pistol away, took a deep breath, and stepped into the opening, his one good arm in the air. He flinched and held his breath, eyes widening as the farmer charged at him with the pitchfork, stopping short of his stomach.

"*Chi sei? Chi sei?*"

Exhaling and not understanding the question, he shrugged, then pointed to the Red Cross on his helmet. "*Medico, Medico— Americano, Amico.*"

The older, curly-haired man patted his dog and eased his pitchfork away from Tucker's stomach. Then holding it to his side like a staff, he stepped forward and offered his hand, a slight smile curling his lips. "*Amico. Mi chiamo Paolo.*"

Smiling, Tucker shook his hand and nodded. "*Mi chiamo Tucker.*" Afterward, he stepped away, pulled a dirty handkerchief from his pocket, and wiped beads of sweat from his brow.

Paolo motioned and led him along the wagon-rutted dirt drive toward a modest stucco farmhouse with a red-tiled roof. Tucker followed him through a barn attached to the house, then entered a side door that opened into a simple kitchen. Paolo pointed to a chair at a table pushed up against the wall. "*Siediti,*" he said, striking a match and lighting a candle before walking across the room and pulling black fabric down over the windows.

Tucker laid his backpack on the floor and leaned back in the chair. It felt good to sit down. His shoulder throbbed.

Paolo placed a glass of water on the table in front of Tucker, then opened a wooden box on the counter. He lifted out a loaf of brown bread and a large knife. *"Pane?"*

He nodded. Grateful for anything as hunger gnawed at his stomach.

When Paolo had cut a thick slice, he put it on a plate along with a slab of cheese and set it in front of Tucker. Filling a glass of water for himself, he poured part of it into Enzo's bowl then sat in the chair across from his guest.

Sitting under Paolo's watchful eye as he ate made Tucker uncomfortable. Whenever he'd glance up, Paolo would flash a broad smile, his teeth yellow and worn. He smiled back, finished his bread, and pushed away from the table. Nodding, he spoke one of the few Italian words he knew. *"Grazie."*

"Prego," Paolo said with a look of satisfaction. Picking up the candle, he motioned for him to come.

Tucker lifted his pack from the floor and followed him down a narrow hallway. Paolo stopped to point out the water closet, then opened the door to a small, austere room at the end of the hall.

Tucker sighed. Though sparsely furnished, it felt like a slice of heaven to him.

Paolo placed the candle on a small table beside an iron bed with a lumpy mattress. Its faded hand-sewn quilt was the one spot of color in the room. The funny little man shuffled to a crude chest of drawers. Above it hung a wooden cross and a picture of the Virgin Mary. He took a long flannel nightshirt and a pair of wool socks from one of the drawers and laid them on the seat of a ladder-back chair, then smiled. *"Dormi Bene."* Then before Tucker could thank him, he disappeared into the hallway.

Dropping onto the bed, Tucker watched as the candle's flickering flame danced across the wall. Though grateful, he struggled with his circumstances. *Why was he here while his comrades lay dead beside the road?*

He lowered his head and wept.

Kate and I were shocked to hear what Tucker had experienced and the anguish our mother must have endured during the months of not knowing his whereabouts. Although Tucker's breathing became more labored as he relayed his story, he refused to save it for another day and continued on.

"Who would have thought, when I stumbled upon Paolo, that my stay would have been as long as it was. Only God knows what would have happened to me had it not been for the fat little man in the stucco house in Italy. On his small farm, this man of humble means insulated me from the dangers of war. *Mio amico,* Paolo, nursed me back to health, cleaning and dressing my wound daily. Although the enemy's bullet remained lodged in my shoulder, and I had limited use of my arm, the deepest wound was right here." He pointed to his head.

"There were nights when my own cries would wake me as shells exploded in my head, and shouts of 'Medic! Medic!' taunted me. Although I carried the tools of healing in my bag, they were never enough to mend dismembered bodies or instill hope in the desperate eyes of my helpless comrades." His voice trailed as he shook his head. "They were never, never enough.

"When the night terrors would come, I'd lie trembling in my bed and hear Paolo in the adjacent room praying—crying out for mercy on my soul and for God's peace to wash over me. Before long, I'd drift off to sleep and rest until the rooster crowed and ushered in the break of another day.

"Paolo had no phone or transportation besides a tired old horse and a rickety wagon. Because of treacherous winter weather and Germans still lingering in the area, we waited until Spring to better our chances of getting safely to the U.S. Army Station Hospital in Caserta. Once there, I was finally able to get word to those in the States that I was alive.

"In late March, at the hospital entrance, Paolo and I said our goodbyes. He kissed me on both cheeks, then climbed into the wagon to make the long trip home alone. Hollering, *'Vertigini,'* he snapped the reins, and his old workhorse, Vito, lumbered away.

"I worried about my friend and watched until the wagon disappeared over the hill. At one point, it looked as if he pulled out a handkerchief and wiped his eyes. Because of the language barrier, I never heard from Paolo again. Although I received a purple heart for my service in Italy, the true hero lived on a small farm near Caserta with his dog named Enzo.

"Two months after my shoulder surgery, weeks of physical therapy, a considerable amount of talk therapy, drugs, and hypnosis, the United States Army declared me well enough to return to Fort Bragg.

"I was going home."

Chapter Forty-Five

Thursday, May 18, 1944
Fayetteville, North Carolina
Emma

Shouting, Emma bolted from the writing room, her feet shuffling so fast she almost plummeted down the stairs. "Celeste! Tucker's here. He's home. He's home. Can you believe it?"

She shoved open the screen door, then bounced on her toes as Tucker stepped from the car in his dress uniform. He looked more mature than she'd remembered, but in a good sense. She supposed war would do that to a person. Squealing, she leaped from the porch, broke into a run, and threw her arms around his neck. "Is that you, Tucker Baldwin? Is it really, really you?" she said, peering into his dark eyes.

He brushed back her hair and leaned in, then hesitated. *"Ciao, Bella,"* he said, kissing one cheek and then the other. Squeezing her, he chuckled. "I haven't changed that much, have I?"

Locking into his gaze, she grabbed both of his hands and walked backward, leading him to the porch. "You better not have. I loved you the way you were." Lifting Chummy from the swing, she dangled him in front of Tucker's face. "Look, big fella. Look who's back in town. Our soldier boy is home."

Chummy squirmed.

Taking the large yellow cat from her grasp, Tucker cradled him and rubbed his belly. "My, my, old Chum, aren't you happy to see me? It looks like you've put on a few pounds. Have you been eating my share too?"

"Tucker, come over here and sit." Emma patted the swing. "You must sit here right now and tell me all about the war. I am so proud of you."

He lowered Chummy to the floor and sat leaning against the swing's arm to face her. "Hmm. All of it, huh?" He raised his brows. "How much time have you got?"

She waved him off. "You know what I mean, smart aleck." Reaching over, she brushed long yellow cat hairs from his coat. "You look mighty handsome in your uniform."

He squared his shoulders and puffed out his chest. "You think so? Wearing my dress greens again feels wonderful. Two years walking the earth in khaki fatigues gets a bit boring."

"I can't begin to tell you how worried I've been. When I heard you were in the hospital in Caserta, I was so happy." She slapped her hand to her mouth as her breath caught in her throat. "I'm sorry. That was a horrible thing to say. I meant … although I hated to hear you were hurt, at least I knew you were alive. How's your shoulder? Does it hurt much?"

Tucker chuckled. His eyes grew larger with her every sentence. "Em, take a breath before you hyperventilate."

Feeling as if her heart would explode, she grabbed his hands and shook them. "I should, shouldn't I? But I can't help it. It's hard for me to believe you're sitting in front of me. On my porch. In my swing. I want to hear about everything. Is Italy as beautiful as they say?"

He nodded. "It is, but there's tremendous devastation there. Much of Italy's beautiful buildings and history are lost forever. It's heartbreaking. Italy is not the place you want to be right now.

"Once our plane landed on the tarmac, and my feet touched American soil, I knelt and kissed the ground. America has never looked so beautiful. She is truly the land of the free and the home of the brave." His lips pressed into a tight, flat line as he paused to collect himself. "Thousands of brave soldiers will never come home." His voice cracked. "Upright, anyway."

She took his hand in hers. "I can't imagine all you've been

through. But you're home now—with us—back where you belong. I pray this war will be over soon, and all of our troops will come home."

"He nodded as she spoke, then cleared his throat. "How's the new homeowner? Is she here?"

"She's good. She's upstairs. I think she wants to give us time to ourselves."

"Nice. We need it. There wasn't a day I didn't think about you." He reached into his pocket and pulled out his silver cross. "I still have it, Em." He smiled. "I see you're wearing yours too."

She fingered the small silver cross at her neck. "I haven't taken it off in almost two years. It's reminded me to pray for you—not that I needed a reminder, but wearing it made me feel more connected to you."

"I know what you mean. This cross stayed in my medical kit on the inside of my coat." He dropped it into his breast pocket and patted it. "It sat right over my heart. I believe it kept me alive. At least, the God of the cross did. It would be impossible for me to tell you all He brought me through. Believe me, I felt His presence and never more than when I was injured and living with Paolo. Paolo was Jesus with skin on. I've never met anyone like him and don't expect to again. This world needs more Paolos. Even though our conversation was limited, we understood each other." He lowered his head and shook it. "I helped around the farm as much as I could with a bum shoulder, but I wish I could have helped him more. I hope he's all right."

She lifted his chin. The pain in his eyes was unmistakable. "Tucker, I know you helped him more than you realize. Your presence in Italy helped free the Italians from an evil dictator. Because of your sacrifice, Paolo is free today. Don't ever minimize your time there."

He lifted her hand to his lips and kissed it. "Thanks. I've not thought of it that way." He let out a long breath and straightened. "Speaking of injuries, how's Drew? Getting around better by now, I hope."

"Yes. He's back doing what he loves—wandering around the countryside, painting with Finn."

Celeste opened the screen door and stepped onto the porch. "Is there room out here for one more?"

Emma turned and smiled. "Always. Come and join us."

She hugged Tucker and welcomed him home, then took a seat in one of the rocking chairs.

Easing the swing back and forth with his foot, Tucker said, "How do you like being a homeowner?"

"Love it. This is a comfortable house. Plenty of space and a perfect place to write. There are still improvements I want to make but can't afford them all at once." She slipped him a curious glance. "Would you like your old job back? I could use a handyman around here." She cut her eyes toward Emma. "You come highly recommended."

He nudged Emma with his elbow. "It's nice to know I have one satisfied customer. I guess it pays to be good friends with the one giving the reviews." He laughed. "Sure. I'll be happy to help. Let me know what you need and when you want me, and we'll work something out."

"Terrific. I hope to have things in tip-top shape by the time this war ends because when it does, I predict I'll be hosting a wedding."

Tucker snapped his head toward Emma. "Is she talking about you?"

She nodded.

"You're not getting married in Chicago?"

She shook her head. "No. Drew and I talked about it and agreed there would be no better way to start our lives together than in Mama T's yard surrounded by all of our friends."

Tucker's face brightened as he leaned over and hugged her. "Thank you. Letting you go won't be easy, but to watch you leave and not be able to share in your special day would be gut-wrenching."

She cupped his face in her hands. "There's no way I could

leave and not share this important day with you and all of our friends."

His eyes crinkled at the corners. "It sounds perfect. Tell Drew I'm grateful." He checked his watch. "I don't mean to change the subject, but how's your book coming?"

She sighed. "Oh, my goodness. I finished it a couple of weeks ago. It felt good to finally type 'The End.' My manuscript is with Celeste's editor now." The thought of it made her heart race. "I'm nervous." She patted her chest. "I'm afraid I'll see a lot of red when it comes back to me."

Celeste laughed. "You should have seen my first draft, Em. It's okay if there are a lot of edits. I grew by leaps and bounds during the process, and you will too." She looked at Tucker. "My editor tells me she thinks Emma's writing has great potential."

He nodded. "I'm not surprised. I've known it all along. We'll be holding her book in our hands one day soon." He rubbed Emma's shoulder. "You'll see. Mark my words." He rechecked his watch and stood. "I need to get back to the base, but I don't want to leave without telling you I'm going to Montana this Monday."

Questioning him with her eyes, she rose from the swing. "You're leaving? Again?"

He clasped her hands in his. "Don't worry. It'll be a quick trip." He stepped from the porch and led her toward the car. "Before my friend took his last breath on the battlefield, he pointed to a letter in his pocket addressed to his girlfriend. He had me promise I'd see that she got it." He paused at the car to face her. "The army is flying me out. It's a tough assignment, but I consider it a privilege to grant his last request."

Choking back tears, she kissed him on the cheek. "It is. I will pray for you."

His fingers slipped from hers.

"Oh, and Tucker ..."

He turned.

"When you come home, I want to talk to you."

He checked his watch. "I still have a few minutes."

She shook her head. "No. We'll need more time."

He cast a questioning glance and nodded. "Sure thing. I'll call."

Blowing him a kiss, she closed the gate and waved as he pulled onto the street. *Lord, when he returns, give me the right words to say and him the right response.*

Chapter Forty-Six

Tuesday, May 8, 1945
St. Andrews, Scotland
Drew

Fifer lifted his head from his pillow and whined as Drew carried his coffee into the living room and settled into the chair.

"Sorry, boy, I didn't mean to wake you. I know you and Finn like to sleep in."

The Sheltie yawned, then burrowed his nose in his pillow and closed his eyes.

Drew wrapped his hands around the warm mug, put his feet on the ottoman, and studied his painting of St. Andrews Cathedral on the mantel. Tilting his head, he grimaced. *Nope. Not there yet, but straightening the parapet on top of the tower should do it.*

A lover of Scottish history, he was intrigued by the story surrounding the medieval tower. Legend suggested it was haunted—the home of the White Lady. Allegedly, the spirit of a woman who died of a broken heart could often be seen roaming the passageways of the tower in a long white dress.

Drew was grateful for the opportunity to play a role in preserving Scotland's history and considered all he'd learned about his homeland a fascinating bonus to his work. If he and Emma hadn't needed the money, he'd be tempted to pay the committee for allowing him to be part of such a worthwhile endeavor.

He set his cup on the side table and stepped outside for the newspaper. Inhaling the cool morning air, he searched the yard and shook his head. *Late again.*

"Here it is, Mr. Brown," Stuart hollered, ringing his bicycle bell and tossing him the paper.

"Splendid catch, sir." Bumping down the cobblestone street, he yelled back. "We have good news this morning."

Drew chuckled to himself. "I hope so. We could all use some." He returned to his chair, sipped his hot coffee, and unrolled the *St. Andrews Citizen.*

> *GERMANY SURRENDERS*
> *Nazis Yield to Allied Powers at Eisenhower's Headquarters*
> *Reims, France, May 7 (A.P.) — Germany surrendered unconditionally to the Western Allies and Russia at 2:41 A.M. French time today, 8:41 P.M. Eastern war time Sunday. The surrender has brought the war in Europe to a formal end after five years, eight months, and six days ...*

Drew shot out of his chair and pounded on Finn's bedroom door before barging inside. Fifer barked at his heels.

"Wake up, chum. You've got to see this."

Finn jolted up in bed, wild-eyed and arms flailing. "What? What is it?"

"Look at this." He held the newspaper in front of Finn's bewildered gaze and jabbed it repeatedly with his index finger. "Look at this. Germany has surrendered. The war in Europe is over." He slapped his friend several times on the back. "Hahaha. Over. Do you hear that, pal? The war here is over."

Throwing back the covers, Finn hopped out of bed. "Now that's something worth opening my eyes for. I thought this day would never come."

"It's incredible, isn't it?" Drew read aloud the rest of the article while Finn threw on his clothes. "I wonder what this means for air travel." He followed Finn into the kitchen. "You think I'll be able to fly back to the States soon?"

Finn flipped on the radio. "Maybe not right away, but I would think before too long." He poured himself a cup of coffee, refilled Drew's, and seated himself at the table as the newscasters relayed the details of the historic signing in France.

Drew leaned against the counter and crossed his legs at the ankles. "I can't believe after almost four years, I will see Emma soon." He walked to the table and sat across from Finn. "By the way, how are things going with you and Bess?"

"Couldn't be better. I'd say you're a pretty good matchmaker. Another example of how God can take a horrible situation and use it for good. The icing on the cake was when I met her son, Ian. He sticks to me like glue when I'm around."

"Excellent. Now I won't feel as bad going off and leaving you." He downed the last of his coffee and plopped his mug on the table. "Who knows? Maybe there are two weddings on the horizon."

Finn smiled, leaned back in his chair, and winked. "Maybe so, my man. Maybe so."

Tuesday, September 25, 1945
Dundee, Scotland

Drew walked along the stone walls of Broughty Castle on the banks of the River Tay in Broughty Ferry. The 15th-century castle, built to defend Dundee's vital sea route from English invaders, had maintained its sentinel throughout the centuries. It had borne its share of action, including the impassioned battle cries of Drew and his boyhood chums skirmishing within its bulwarks.

The wind of a storm brewing in the North Sea blew inland, its unforgiving squall threatening to deter the determined flight of gulls crying overhead. As waves crashed against the rocks below, Drew tucked his scarf into his jacket and seated himself on the wall, inhaling the moist salt air. Glancing up at the central tower which housed the defense post, he mourned the loss of Scotland's bravest, especially David. Always the warrior, his brother had fought his final battle and paid the ultimate price.

He would miss this seaport city. Although he'd gained and lost much here, it was no longer his home. Home was with Emma. They'd been apart far too long, and for the first time in almost four years, their life together loomed on the horizon. He could see it, and he wasn't about to let it slip from view.

Uncapping his pen, he pulled a sheet of paper from a small portfolio and fought against the wind to keep it within his grasp. He'd never lost a battle along these walls, and he wasn't about to start now. He'd pen his final letter from Scotland to Emma.

Hi Peaches,

Today, I returned to one of my favorite places in all of Scotland, Broughty Castle. I've spent many an afternoon here as a wee lad, sitting along this wall with my brothers. Me with my binoculars, hoping to be the first to spot our father's freighter, the SS Altona, as it sailed into port from some far-off land.

As Dad would pilot the 672-ton vessel into the mouth of the River Tay, the three of us would stand straight as arrows and wave small flags of Scotland. We'd beat the wind with the white saltire against azure blue and yell, "Home is the sailor. Daddy is home."

Thomas Wolfe had it right. I've found you can't go home again. Although I'll always hold memories of Dundee close to my heart, my heart is no longer here. It abides in my dreams beyond tomorrow, my life with you, and the memories we'll make together.

I must make this short. A storm is blowing in, and I can already smell the rain.

I told you I'd drop you a line with the details of my return whenever I had something concrete. I'm happy to say, I heard today that American Export Airlines will begin transatlantic passenger service to the UK from New York in October. I wanted to be on the first plane out, but it appears everyone else did too. I will leave from Hurn Airport near Bournemouth, England, at 1:20 a.m. on Thursday, October 12th. Our flight will make several stops before arriving in New York at 11:30 a.m. your time. From there, I'll travel to Chicago to handle business with Joe and Helen, then as soon as we can pack his car, the three of us will be on our way to North Carolina.

I can hardly believe the day we've waited for is almost here. I long to hold you in my arms, and with every shred of my being, every drop of my tartan-plaid blood, I'll try to make you happy.

You make the wedding plans, Peaches. Tell me when, where, and what I need to do, and I'll show up. Until then …

I'll see you in my dreams,
Drew

Chapter Forty-Seven

Saturday, October 20, 1945
Fayetteville, North Carolina
Emma

Emma lifted her arms as Opal helped her slip the ivory, satin and lace gown over her head. As the shimmering fabric floated across her face and settled around her body's soft curves, a delicate lavender scent filled her nostrils. Smoothing the dress with her hands, she stepped in front of the beveled, oval floor mirror and stared at the young woman gazing back at her.

Bea fanned the air in front of her face, then clapped her hand over her mouth. "Oh, child, if you aren't an angel on earth, there's never been one."

Stooping in front of Emma, Penny tied the satin sash at the dress's wrapped waist and pressed the large loops with her fingers. With a nod of approval, she stood and stepped back. "Wait till Prince Charming sees you. He could search the world over and never find a more beautiful bride."

Giggling, Emma held her hands out from her sides and twirled one way and then another. The soft folds of the filmy dress swirled about her ankles. "I do feel like a princess."

"Maybe that's because you look like one," Opal said, beaming.

Emma turned and squeezed her. "Thank you for this lovely dress. I never dreamed I would have anything as fine as this to wear on my wedding day. I'm glad you happened to walk into that little London dress shop years ago."

Opal brushed tears from her cheeks and smiled. "It looks

more lovely than I remember. God knew the day I found this dress who would wear it, and He doesn't make mistakes. I couldn't be more pleased it's you."

"Hold on. Let's not forget these." Stepping behind Emma, Bea clasped a single strand of Mama T's pearls around her neck. She looked over Emma's shoulder at her reflection in the mirror and clicked her tongue. "Yes, I'd say, those were exactly what that lovely lace bodice needed."

Emma ran her fingers over the exquisite pearls. "I wish Mama T was here to see me today."

"Oh, I have a notion she's smilin' down on you, baby girl."

"I agree." Penny took the chapel-length ivory veil from the closet and hung it on the edge of the window frame. "We'll leave this here till later." She checked the clock on the dresser. "You still have thirty minutes before you need to finish dressing."

She took Emma's hands in hers. "Is there anything else you need? If not, the three of us will give you time to yourself."

"I'm fine." She hugged Penny, her maid-of-honor, who looked dazzling in her blush pink tea-length dress, then squeezed Bea and Opal. "Thank you for all you've done. I couldn't make it through this day without the three of you."

Turning to leave the room, Penny tapped her watch. "Don't worry. I won't forget you. I'll be back shortly to help you with your veil."

Emma nodded and watched as the door closed behind her friends and on this season of their lives together. A lump rose in her throat. *How she would miss them. They had been her lifeline while Drew and Tucker were gone. Although she looked forward to traveling with Drew—*

She fanned her face with her hand as she stifled her tears and turned toward the sound of muffled laughter. Pulling back the sheer lace curtains, she peeked into the side yard, where her sister, Lily, and Celeste were putting the finishing touches on the serving table. She tapped on the glass and blew them a kiss.

Soon, the table would be laden with a wide assortment of

pot-luck dishes made by the best cooks in Cumberland County. No one would leave hungry—the ladies of the First Baptist food committee would see to that. Several large pans of banana pudding were already prepared and stacked in the icebox, and Fran had promised to bring a large bowl of her celebrated wait-your-turn potato salad. She only hoped she wouldn't be too jittery to feast on the spread. Right now, the butterflies in her stomach were in full flight with no signs of lighting anytime soon.

A soft rap on the door startled her.

"Come in."

Bea stepped into the room. "I hate to bother you, but you have a letter."

Emma took the ivory envelope from her hand. Recognizing Tucker's handwriting, she raised her eyebrows. As the door clicked shut behind Bea, she eased herself into the chair by the window, slid her fingernail beneath the flap, and slid out the letter.

My Dearest Emma,

Wow. Your long-awaited day is here. I can't imagine what's going through your head right now. I can hardly filter my own thoughts. Thank you for allowing me to share my heart several months ago. I suppose face-to-face was how God wanted it to be since my letter from England never arrived. Who knows, maybe one day it will show up in your mailbox. At least, there won't be any surprises, and I won't live with regret.

I confess that when I returned to the car after our conversation, I dropped my head on the steering wheel and wept. I would never have guessed things would have turned out like this for us, but I—

Penny's soft Tennessee drawl filtered through the door. "Emma, it's almost time. May I come in and help you with your veil?"

"Give me a minute." She skimmed the rest of the letter, slid it back into the envelope, and laid it on the windowsill. Standing, she smoothed out her dress and brushed away her tears. "Come on in."

Penny walked over to Emma, clasped her shoulders, and looked into her eyes. "Are you okay, honey?"

She nodded.

"You sure?"

"Lots of mixed emotions, that's all." She slipped her feet into her ivory-satin peep-toe pumps. "Is my groom here yet?"

"Yes. He arrived about ten minutes ago, and I might add, looks very handsome—nervous, but quite dapper. He's talking with Pastor Gardner now."

Lifting the veil from the window frame, Penny stood with her back to the mirror and motioned for Emma. With a flick of her wrists, she sent the sheer silk tulle billowing over Emma's head. As it floated over her shoulders and drifted to the floor, Penny lowered the delicate seed-pearl halo onto her head. "This veil is heavenly." Positioning it, she pried open several bobby pins with her teeth and fastened them in Emma's hair. "There now. How does that feel?"

Emma tossed her head back and forth. "Good."

Penny fluffed Emma's long dark tresses and smoothed the veil trimmed with Venice lace. "You really do look like an angel now." She stepped to one side so Emma could see her reflection in the mirror.

Shaking her head, she sighed. "I'm excited. Having planned this day for so long, I can't believe I'm about to walk toward the man of my dreams."

"Knock, knock." Bea burst through the door with Opal.

Emma beamed, held her arms out to her sides, and spun on her toes. "What do you think?"

"You're the prettiest thing this side of heaven." Bea walked over and hugged her. "Opal and I are here to take inventory."

"Inventory?" Emma said, furrowing her brow.

"Child, don't you know a bride can't walk down the aisle

unless she has four things?" She ran her short chubby finger over Emma's pearls— "something old." Lifted the hem of her dress— "something new, your shoes. Something borrowed, this exquisite dress, and something blue, your ..."

Worry infused Emma's eyes as she covered her mouth with her hand. "I don't have anything blue."

Bea pulled a flat square box from the pocket of her navy dress, handed it to her, and smiled. "Now you do."

Slipping off the lid, Emma pulled back the tissue. Inside lay a powder-blue handkerchief embroidered with a white initial B. Choking back her tears, she fell into Bea's warm, bear-like hug. "How thoughtful and lovely. Thank you, I will cherish this always."

Opal moved closer. "We'd better hurry. I hear the cello playing." She held out a bouquet of shell pink and white camellias. "My bushes showed out this year."

Emma arched her brows. "I'd say they did." She tucked the handkerchief inside her bodice, then took the bouquet and hugged Opal. Lifting the flowers to her nose, she breathed in their sweet vanilla-like fragrance. "Mmm. These are gorgeous. Thank you."

Opal turned to Penny and handed her a similar but smaller bouquet, then clapped several times. "Okay, ladies. Hurry on out." She swatted her hands at them. "We've got a wedding to attend. Shoo. Shoo."

Bea and Opal dipped into the kitchen while Penny walked Emma toward the foyer. "Go on in. He's waiting on you." She hugged her and kissed her cheek. "I'll see you at the altar."

The chords of a cello playing "Stardust" filtered through the house as Emma took a deep breath and walked toward the foyer. With heels tapping on the wood floor and folds of satin swishing about her ankles, she entered the room. Tucker stood at the screen door, hands behind his back, looking into the yard. When she entered, he turned. As her eyes met his, she stood still.

"Wowee! You are a vision."

Blushing, she walked over and hugged him, then smoothed

out the burgundy silk pocket square in his grey herringbone suit. "You look rather dashing yourself."

He bent at the waist. "Thank you, madam. I suppose I clean up pretty good. At least, I'm not wearing khaki or army green." He took her hands. "How are you?"

"Besides feeling like my knees are about to buckle, I'm good."

He laughed. "Don't worry, I'll be right beside you and won't let you hit the ground too hard."

She swatted his arm. "Swell. Am I supposed to feel better now?"

He took something from his trouser pocket and held it with a tight fist. "Close your eyes and hold out your hand."

Tilting her head, she weighed his request. "What are you up to?"

"Go ahead. Follow my instructions, and you'll see."

She second-guessed his intent but closed her eyes and eased open her hand.

A small object dropped into her palm. "Now open them."

She inspected the silver coin, similar to a dime. "What is this?"

"It's a British sixpence—six cents. I brought it from England. It's British tradition for it to be placed inside the bride's shoe as a symbol of good fortune and prosperity."

She brought her hand to her chest and looked up at him. "I love that."

He stooped down and held out his hand. "Give it to me." He tucked it in her shoe, then stood and kissed her forehead. "There now. You'll never be broke."

As the cello's soft, mellow chords escalated into the jubilant strains of "The Wedding March," Emma's eyes bulged.

Tucker chuckled. "Are you ready?"

Swallowing hard, she nodded.

Clasping her hand, he opened the screen and led her onto the porch. Then straightening his shoulders, he extended his elbow and winked. "May I have the pleasure, ma'am?"

Escorting her down the front steps, Tucker followed the slate path he'd recently laid for Celeste. Emma looked up at the tall, handsome man on her arm and thanked God for sparing his life and for bringing him safely home. The night Tucker declared his love for her would be forever rooted in her heart and soul. It was heart-wrenching for him not to hear the same expression of love from her, but he'd said, "In my spirit, I knew your heart belonged to another. I also knew if I didn't express my true feelings for you, I would never be able to let go and move on."

They both realized it was not in God's plan for them to marry, but their rare and exceptional bond was a God-given gift that would never be revoked, broken, or replaced. She was grateful that God, in His grace, had someone waiting in the wings for Tucker. He deserved someone whose whole heart would belong to him.

As the music reached a crescendo, they stepped into the garden, and their friends rose to their feet. Tucker's dark eyes merged with hers as he squeezed her hand and whispered, "Friends love at all times ... and *this* is one of those times."

Gazing down the grassy aisle scattered with camellia petals, her eyes flooded with tears. She had to remind herself to breathe. Then placing one foot in front of the other, she stepped wholeheartedly into the future she'd dreamed of.

Drew

With each deep satisfying breath, warmth spread throughout Drew's chest. The most remarkable woman he'd ever known walked toward him. As their eyes melded, their gaze remained unbroken, as did their love. Emma had never looked more lovely. In a matter of moments, not days or months but moments, this incredible lady would be his. Their years of separation had not divided their hearts, and neither would the years to come. Their love, tested in the fires of adversity, had simply grown more durable, more resilient. With the Lord as their guide, there would be nothing they couldn't overcome.

Drew was grateful for the man on Emma's arm who'd respected the boundaries of her heart. Tucker's friendship had carried her through countless dark hours. For years, he'd been her loyal companion, trustworthy confidant, and valiant protector. Today, he would entrust her care into Drew's capable and willing arms.

As Emma and Tucker stood in front of the raw pine table crafted by her father years before, Pastor Gardner and Drew moved toward them. Drew, followed by Joe, his best man, took their places beside Tucker, while Penny stepped in beside Emma.

Smiling, Pastor Gardner welcomed the intimate gathering of family and friends with his deep raspy voice. "We are gathered here today in the presence of God to celebrate one of life's greatest moments, the joining of two hearts in Holy matrimony— those of Emma Rose Walsh and William Andrew Brown. Marriage was God's idea." Lifting his large open Bible from the table, he read from the second book of Genesis.

"Then the Lord God said, 'It is not good for the man to be alone; I will make a helper suitable for him. For this reason, a man shall leave his father and his mother and be joined to his wife."

Looking up, the aging pastor peered solemnly over his wire-rimmed glasses. "If there is anyone here who can show just cause why this couple cannot lawfully be joined together in matrimony, let them speak now or forever hold their peace."

He scanned the guests and waited an appropriate amount of time before motioning for them to be seated. "Who gives this woman to be married to this man?"

Tucker squared his shoulders and cleared his throat. "Her family and friends do." Leaning over, he kissed Emma's forehead, then stepped away and seated himself on the front row beside Celeste. Smiling, he pulled her close and brushed her cheek with his lips.

As Drew moved beside Emma, the look in her eyes took his breath away. He squeezed her hand and whispered. "You're beautiful."

Her soft reply cracked with emotion. "I love you."

Although Drew and Emma had spoken on the phone since his arrival in Fayetteville, they'd agreed not to see one another until today. The warmth of Emma beside him and the softness of her hand in his made it difficult for him to concentrate on Pastor Gardner's remarks. Overwhelmed by her presence, he was surprised he could repeat his wedding vows without stammering.

As he slipped the ring on her finger, he lost himself in her eyes, and Pastor Gardner's words melted into the distance.

"Having pledged your fidelity to love, honor, and cherish one another, and with the power vested in me, it is my honor in the presence of this gathering to pronounce you husband and wife. Drew, you may kiss your bride."

Startled by the mention of his name, he chuckled to himself—*finally*. Placing his hands on the sides of Emma's face, he kissed her. Then pulling away, he searched her eyes and kissed her again, slower this time but not as slow as he would have liked. The snickering and playful chatter of the guests signaled he needed to move on.

Pastor Gardner cleared his throat. "Ladies and Gentlemen, those God has joined together, let no man put asunder. It is my esteemed privilege to introduce to you Mr. and Mrs. William Andrew Brown."

Applause and well wishes greeted them as the cello erupted into a lively processional. Sweeping Emma into his arms, he lifted her from the ground, kissed her, and carried her down the aisle. He'd promised to love, honor, and cherish her until death parted them, and he meant it—but he wouldn't think about the latter now.

This was their beginning. Their life beyond so many yesterdays. As their lives spread out before them, so did the countless roads they would travel, but never alone. There would be no more goodbyes or long farewells. Emma was his to have and to hold, and from this day forward, they'd dream beyond tomorrow—as one.

Chapter Forty-Eight

Monday, September 10, 2012
Hope Mills, North Carolina
Caroline

As the funeral procession pulled onto Ramsey Street from Jernigan-Warren Funeral Home in Fayetteville, I flipped on my car's flashers and settled back in my seat for the slow eight-mile drive to the historic Hope Mills cemetery.

Kate pulled down the visor, looked at herself in the mirror, then slapped it back up. "I'm a mess," she said, fumbling in her purse.

"No, you're not, Mom. You look fine." Laura resumed her conversation with Jenna in the back seat.

Our daughters hadn't seen one another since Jenna had taken a job as the front desk manager of a resort in Pawley's Island, South Carolina. They had a lot to catch up on.

Kate pulled her compact from her purse, popped it open, and patted her face with foundation. "I felt sorry for Trish today. She's taking things really hard."

"I understand why. Her father was one-in-a-million. If losing Tucker is hard for us, I can't imagine how difficult it is for his family—and Claire. She's taken care of him for over a year now."

Kate reapplied her lipstick. "I'm thankful Trish came with Ryan to spend a couple of weeks with him last month. Isn't that just like God? Always merciful." She pressed her lips together and dropped her lipstick into her purse. "He sees the whole picture and knows what we need."

Trying to wrap my mind around everything. I shook my

head. "It's hard to believe we won't see Tucker again this side of heaven. Now I know why he was so insistent on finishing his story when we were there a couple of weeks ago."

"Do you think he sensed his days were few?"

"Probably. He's struggled for quite a while now. His absence is hard, but I'm grateful he's been released from his suffering."

She shifted in her seat to face me. "It's uncanny that Tucker died one year to the day after Mother's death, isn't it?"

I tilted my head and shrugged. "They were kindred spirits."

She slid back in her seat. "For real. I'm happy the girls could come and visit their grandmother's grave today, as well as meet Tucker's family. I'm sorry they never got to meet him."

Laura scooted up behind the front seat. "Are y'all talking about us up here?"

I glanced over at her. "Yes, and it's all good. Your mother and I said we'd wished you and Jenna could have met Tucker. You would have loved him."

Jenna slid up beside Laura. "Didn't you say Grandma used to date him?"

"They didn't really date. Although I'm sure Tucker would have liked to, he respected Mother's wishes. He knew she was in love with your grandfather and wasn't about to intrude. Tucker's fiancée had broken his heart, and he didn't want to inflict the same pain on another man." Brushing a tear from my cheek, I sighed. "I'm thankful we got to hear him tell his story before he passed."

"Me too. It was touching." Kate looked at me, eyes widening. "Caroline, did you find yourself wishing he and Mom could have gotten together? I did, and then I realized—you and I wouldn't be here if they had."

"Uh ... none of us would," Jenna blurted.

The four of us laughed. It felt good. Being together made this day more bearable.

"We're here," I said as the taillights of the car in front of me lit up. I pulled into the cemetery's dirt drive and passed between two time-worn brick columns. Following the hearse, we looped our way over the sandy soil, past weather-beaten markers. I pointed to my right. "Girls, there's your grandmother's grave. We'll come back after Tucker's ceremony."

Jenna peered over Laura's shoulder. "Oh, how pretty. I haven't been here since you planted the rose bush."

Kate tapped on the window with her manicured nails. "Look at all of the roses. The bush has really thrived in this soil." She glanced over at me. "I guess we didn't do such a bad job of planting it."

I laughed. "I suppose not. That was a fun day." I turned and looked at Laura. "You should have seen the expression on your mother's face when I asked her to step into the hole I'd dug so I could see how deep it was." I cracked up at the memory, tears rolling down my cheeks.

Kate swatted my arm and dabbed the corners of her eyes with a tissue. "Don't make me laugh. I just redid my makeup." She looked back at Jenna. "It was a fun day, and it was the day we met Tucker. Talk about divine providence."

As the hearse pulled in front of the tent, I fell in line with the cars in front of us and parked beneath the towering long-leaf pines. We sat in the car and waited while the pallbearers lined up behind the hearse, then in formation, carried Tucker's flag-draped coffin to the gravesite. Remembering, my eyes filled with tears. Like so many, he'd fought for everything our flag represents—love of God and country, liberty, justice, freedom for all. I could hear him telling Kate and me about his days in Italy—the bloodshed, his heartache, fear, and of course, Paolo—precious Paolo. Tucker had served his country well, and now we'd come to honor him.

Once the family was seated, we joined the small gathering and stood behind them. The short, sweet service was soul-stirring, but then, why wouldn't it be—we were honoring Tucker.

After the 21-gun salute and the bugler played "Taps," I stood in awe of Trish as she closed out the service by singing the heartrending words of Janet Paschal's, "Another Soldier's Coming Home."

"His back is bent and weary. His voice is tired and low. His sword is worn from battle, and his steps have gotten slow. But he used to walk on water, or it seemed that way to me. I know he moved some mountains and never left his knees. Strike up the band, assemble the choir, another soldier's coming home . . .

There wasn't a dry eye in the crowd—except for those of Trish. But for God, I don't know how she did it.

While others greeted Tucker's family after the service, we stood to the side and talked with Claire. Since we hadn't met Trish's brother and his family from San Diego, and none of them had met our girls, I wanted time to chat with them.

Claire spotted the sterling cross around Jenna's neck and looked at me. "Caroline, isn't that the cross Tucker gave your mother?"

I smiled. "It is. I thought today would be an appropriate time to follow through with Mother's wish for the necklace to be passed along to her first granddaughter."

"I agree." She nodded and hugged Jenna. "You're a beautiful young lady. I wish you could have met your grandmother's friend. My father was an extraordinary man. I will miss him." She blotted her tears.

"I wish I could have too."

Jenna fingered the cross at her neck and looked into my eyes. "Thank you, and thanks for bringing me today. Being here has made me feel more blessed than ever to have this."

We hugged. "Of course, I'm glad you came. I love you."

As Trish and her family admired the flowers around the casket, we walked over and greeted her. Claire introduced us to the rest of the family. They were delightful, but my heart was especially drawn to Ryan, who stood by his grandfather's casket, speaking in low tones. I couldn't forget Tucker's countenance the day we met Ryan in Hope Mills. He was incredibly proud of his first grandchild and teased him incessantly. Their rapport was precious, and there was no mistaking Ryan had been the apple of his grandfather's eye.

Later, Trish reached for her son's hand as he walked toward her. "You remember Caroline and Kate, don't you, Ryan?"

"Of course," he shook our hands and smiled. "Thank you for coming. Pop thought a lot of you both."

Hugging him, I expressed my condolences and introduced him to Laura and Jenna. "Jenna is my mother's first grandchild too. Actually, she doesn't live too far from you. She works in Pawley's Island."

Jenna's eyes widened as she poked me with her elbow.

Nodding, Ryan smiled and studied her face, then lowered his eyes to her necklace. "Is that your grandmother's cross?"

"It is." She slid it back and forth on the chain. "Mother gave it to me today. I love it."

Turning, he looked at his mother, slipped his hand in his pocket, then held his hand toward Jenna. "It looks like my grandpa and your grandmother never stopped thinking alike." He opened his palm. "Pop gave me this on my last visit."

My eyes met Kate's as we gasped in unison. In Ryan's palm was the silver pocket cross Mother had given to Tucker the day he gave her the necklace. On the cross was the inscription, *"A friend loveth at all times."*

And *this* … was one of those times.

A Note from the Author

Dear Readers,

Thank you for journeying with me through the pages of *Emma's Quest* and the Dream Beyond Tomorrow series. I'm confident Noah, the young soldier, who penned letters to my mother in 1938 with hopes of winning her heart, never dreamed that after eighty years, he'd win mine and yours too.

I find it nothing short of a miracle that words hidden in a trunk or lying dormant beneath the soil of the recipient's heart can spring to life generations later. Our life stories don't always end where we think. God, the Author and the Finisher of our days, may put a comma where we've placed a period. Don't box Him in. Leave room for Him to do the miraculous. His ways are higher than ours, and He *"is able to do immeasurably more than all we ask or imagine."*

The process of writing *Emma's Quest* has been more of a solitary journey than when I wrote *For the Love of Emma*. Although a less crowded path is evidence of my growth as a writer, I'm aware no book is birthed in a vacuum. A story's successful passage from the writer's heart to the reader's hands depends on those who guide its development and the readers who adopt it.

Everyone may have a story, but the author's labor bears little fruit without readers.

I send a huge thank you to all who've read one or both books in my series. If you've placed a review on Amazon, Goodreads, BookBub, or have shared on social media, I'm ever grateful. Reviews are golden. Your personal endorsements breathe life into books. There is no better gift a reader can give an author.

The Dream Beyond Tomorrow series is a work of fiction

based on facts found in letters written to my mother, her own journal entries, and from what I know of my parents' lives. If you've not yet read *Emma's Quest*, there is a spoiler in the following text, so you may want to stop reading now and not spoil your journey through.

In *Emma's Quest*, Caroline, Kate, Emma, Drew, Mac, Penny, Jenna, Laura, Joe, and Helen are factual characters. Their relationships are authentic, but most of their names were changed. The remaining characters sprang from the story's pages. I always stand amazed when that happens. I suppose it's similar to life. We never know who we'll meet along the way and how their presence will impact our lives.

The paternity circumstances surrounding Mac, Ann-Marie, Maggie, Caroline, and Kate are not factual. However, my father did have an identical twin brother who lived in Canada.

The locations within the book are real places tailored to suit the era. The World War II scenes in Ireland, Scotland, and Italy are based on recorded events and venues, but their circumstances are fiction.

As I type 'The End' to my Dream Beyond Tomorrow series, tears well in my eyes, and I find it hard to let go. I'll miss eavesdropping on Emma Rose's world and the men who vied for her affection. Perhaps one day, I'll run my fingers over the spines of countless books on the shelf, pull *For the Love of Emma* and *Emma's Quest*, and immerse myself in Emma's story once more—maybe you will too.

In the meantime, I'd love to hear from you. You may contact me via social media or through my website at *www.starrayers.org*. While there, please subscribe to my newsletter to receive future updates by leaving your email address in the subscription link.

"Now to him who is able to do immeasurably more than all we ask or imagine, according to his power that is at work

within us, to him be glory in the church and in Christ Jesus throughout all generations, for ever and ever! Amen" (Ephesians 3:20-21, NIV).

Dream Beyond Tomorrow,

Emma and Drew, one month after their marriage.

Broughty Castle in Broughty Ferry, Dundee, Scotland.
Completed in 1495, the castle sits on the banks of
the River Tay, facing the North Sea.

Discussion Questions

1. In chapter one, Tucker speaks of his love for Emma to her daughters. He states, "I learned a long time ago you can't live with regret. I guess we all ask *what if* at times, but *if onlys*— they're deal-breakers. Can't live there. Gotta learn to let go." Do you think Tucker ever let go? Is it possible to let go and still remember?

2. Against the advice of those who loved her, Emma boarded a train for Chicago to meet Drew, a man she'd only known for a few months. Do you believe in love at first sight? Do you consider Emma's actions courageous or reckless? When was the last time you made a life-altering decision in haste? If so, knowing what you know now, would you handle things differently? How?

3. In chapter five, a vendor at Navy Pier hands Emma a red rose. Later, while kissing Drew, the wind steals it from her grasp, and it drops into the water. If you've read, *For the Love of Emma,* and are familiar with Emma's relationship with Noah, discuss the possible meaning within this visual with your group.

4. In chapter six, Emma gets a birds-eye view of Chicago from the Tribune Tower and is mesmerized by her enchanting new world. Have you ever had a similar experience? Where were you? Describe your initial reaction.

5. Emma's sister had told her "happy endings" were only found in fairy tales? Have you ever felt this way? In hindsight, has your perspective changed? Is real happiness possible in the midst of chaos? If so, how?

6. In chapter eleven, World War II rumbles in the background of Emma's fairy-tale existence. The nation is on heightened alert. In Tucker's letter to Emma, he shares the source of his comfort in the storm. What was it? Do you share this same comfort in times of trouble? Explain.

7. In chapter sixteen, Maggie Abrams shows up on Kate's doorstep with potentially life-altering news. What was it? The sisters responded differently. Which sister do you relate to most? Explain.

8. In chapter eighteen, Mama T gives Emma the baby Jesus figurine from the nativity. What was her message to Emma? Do you find it easy or challenging to share Jesus with others? Do you have a unique approach to sharing Jesus that those in your group might benefit from?

9. In chapter twenty-seven, Emma shows up unexpectedly at the Max Safron Gallery. What does she witness? Have you ever jumped to conclusions that resulted in conflict only to find later that your assumption was wrong? How did you handle it, or how should we handle situations like this?

10. In chapter forty, Tucker writes Emma from Ireland and shares his true feelings for her for the first time. Have you ever been afraid to tell someone something, then finally did? Regardless of the outcome, how did speaking the truth affect you personally?

11. Emma struggled to find a buyer for her house. In chapter forty-one, who bought it? In response, Emma quotes Ephesians 3:20. Has God's answer to your prayers ever been above and beyond anything you could ask or think? Please share.

12. In chapter forty-four, after Tucker's convoy is attacked in Italy, Paolo takes him into his home and nurses him back to health. Tucker didn't need to speak Paolo's language to be comforted by his prayers when he was too troubled to pray for himself. Have you ever had someone pray for you when you were too distraught to pray? Looking back, how did it affect you? Have you been that person for someone? Share.

13. In chapter forty-seven, Tucker walks Emma down the aisle to marry Drew. How did this make you feel? If you could rewrite the end of this story, would you change it? How so?

14. At Tucker's funeral, Ryan and Jenna meet and discover they'd both received their grandparent's sterling silver crosses. What do you think happened after this encounter?

15. What stood out to you most about the book? Would you recommend it to a friend? If so, please consider sharing it on your social media sites and/or writing an Amazon, Goodreads, or BookBub review. A review is one of the greatest gifts you can give an author.

Made in the USA
Columbia, SC
22 March 2022

58009698R00173